CAPITOL CRIMES

CAPITOL CRIMES

H.L. Katz

Apprentice House
Loyola University Maryland
Baltimore, Maryland

First Edition

Printed in the United States of America

Hardcover ISBN: 978-1-62720-057-8
Paperback ISBN: 978-1-62720-047-9
E-book ISBN: 978-1-62720-048-6

Design by Kelly Quane

Published by Apprentice House

Apprentice House
Loyola University Maryland
4501 N. Charles Street
Baltimore, MD 21210
410.617.5265 • 410.617.2198 (fax)
www.apprenticehouse.com
info@apprenticehouse.com

To my wife for her love and patience and without whom this
book would not have come into existence.

To my children who have made my life worth living.

ONE

The FBI sniper peered through the scope affixed to the top of his government-issued McMillan TAC-338 sniper rifle. He pulled his jacket lapel closer to his mouth and steadied the weapon on his right shoulder. His index finger tapped the trigger, softly, every few seconds. He pressed the Talk button of the black Motorola walkie-talkie strapped to his uniform.

"Not sure I can get a clean look even if there is somebody out there, Captain," the sniper said. He never removed his eye from the scope. "Can we do anything about this crowd? This is nuts."

The crowd he was referring to began lining up as soon as word spread of the hearing which would begin within the hour. Traffic on the street was at a standstill due to a combination of pedestrian gridlock surrounding the Hart Senate Office Building and the usual D.C. morning commute. From the few who had slept on the sidewalk to the thousands who had arrived on the streets of the Capitol before the crack of dawn, each of them hoped to secure one of the precious few seats inside the hearing room. Their goal on this humid summer morning was to be present at what USA Today called "the most important twenty-four-hours since the Tea

Party at Boston Harbor." The morning editorial of the Washington Post wrote that the events in the Senate today were, "as crucial for the country as any testimony since Watergate," while the New York Times labeled the witness at the center of the firestorm, "the most controversial private sector figure in American history."

On the steps of the east entrance of the Senate Building all of the major news networks jockeyed for position while bloggers, sprinkled amongst the crowd tapped their laptop keys with real-time updates for their websites. Everyone was live from the eye of the storm. Meanwhile, a few hundred feet above the ground, FBI snipers scattered along the rooftops surveyed both Constitution Avenue and 2nd Street for any suspicious activity.

Mixed-in among the mass of people were two Middle-Eastern looking men, one dressed in faded blue jeans and a Kansas City Royals tee-shirt, the other in black Dockers and a blue Nike golf shirt. They searched the crowd in vain for the witness they were hired to silence. They soon realized, along with the rest of the gawkers in the crowd, that she was nowhere to be found.

When Callie Wheeler arrived at the Central Hearing Room through an underground walkway that connected the two Senate office buildings, she was very much aware she was national gossip fodder. Dressed in all white, including her Jimmy Choo heels, Callie was an image of tranquility at the witness table next to her attorney, Miles Goodman. A veteran jurist of more than thirty years, Goodman came straight out of central casting complete with the sandy brown hair and young features that made him look twenty years more youthful than he was. On the tablecloth in front of them were two microphones, four drinking glasses and two pitchers of water. To Callie's left, a bay of television cameras were poised to record her every move, while behind her, the room slowly began to fill. The retractable brown walls had been moved and extra chairs were set to accommodate the overwhelming press requests and public demand.

On a normal day, the hearing room hosted over 300 people but as of twenty-four hours ago, everyone involved with the United States Congress knew this would not be anything close to a normal day.

"Did you want me to tell them that you're planning on making an opening statement?" Miles Goodman whispered into Callie's ear.

"I'd rather keep the bastards guessing."

"You're the client," Goodman said. "But you know they're not gonna be happy."

"Like I give a shit. Fuck 'em."

Seated on the "U" shaped dais at the front of the room were twenty-six United States Senators, twenty-one men and five women. The Committee on Lobbying Affairs had broken down along party lines. There were thirteen democrats seated on the left and thirteen republicans on the right. Of all the committees in Congress, none could be considered less appealing than COLA, but the substantial perks kept the committee's membership packed with leaders from each party. The majority of the Senators that were present had made the rounds on early morning television, strategically placing themselves in interviews that were sure to be watched by their constituents on a day when Congress would be the focus of the national news cycle. A few of the more prominent among them were huddled together behind the platform, occasionally peeking at Callie and her attorney. Shortly after their strategy session had broken up, Chairman Lester Rice, a thirty-two year veteran of the Senate, gaveled the morning hearing to order.

"Ms. Wheeler, on behalf of this committee, I want to welcome you and thank you for appearing before us today. We understand that agreeing to testify could not have been an easy decision for you to make, but we appreciate your choosing to help our committee, especially on such short notice."

Callie, as always, looked as if she was better suited for an advertising campaign than a Senatorial proceeding. She always had. Having just turned twenty-nine years old, she knew she would only get one shot at this regardless of how messy it got. She would take full advantage of the opportunity.

Maintain eye contact, Callie reminded herself as Rice continued with his instructions.

"Ms. Wheeler, each Senator will ask you questions for a period of five minutes and it will continue that way until such time as we determine your testimony has concluded," Rice said. "Do you have any questions?"

With a calm, controlled elegance, Callie reached for the microphone in front of Goodman and moved it closer to speak.

"Mr. Chairman and members of the committee, I want to thank you for the opportunity to testify before you today. As you know, my testimony here is not without controversy. Nevertheless, I feel it is my duty to address this Body and I do so against the advice of counsel."

Callie nodded to her attorney.

The room fell eerily silent as everyone focused their attention on Callie Wheeler. She paused to purposely milk the moment. The crackle of the court reporter's stenograph was the only noise that could be heard throughout the venue.

"My experiences on Capitol Hill have taught me that things are never quite what they seem. When I think back on my almost six years in Washington, I recognize that my only desire was to help those less fortunate. Instead, I became an obscenely wealthy and powerful woman, while those I tried to help are no better off today than they were before I began."

Miles Goodman placed his hand on top of Callie's microphone

and carefully spoke in her ear.

"Callie, I've got to tell you again, that this is not a good idea. I think if you invoke your Fifth Amendment privilege, you'll be protected, and as your attorney, I strongly advise you to do so before saying another word. Please. Shut. Up."

Callie stared at Goodman's hand, which was still on the mic, before looking back at him.

"Miles, you've got to trust me...now please..."

Goodman removed his hand.

"Callie you're making a huge mistake. Be very careful," he said louder but still too low for the digital recording devices in the room to pick up. Goodman pulled back from the microphone. He shook his head. Callie smiled as she tried her best to assure him it would all work out okay.

From the left side of the dais, Senator Wilbur Lank, a seven-term Democrat from Tennessee, interrupted the proceedings.

"Mr. Chairman, I was not informed that the witness would be making any opening remarks. It is our usual protocol, is it not, for a witness to make us aware of any opening statements and provide us with those statements beforehand, along with a copy of their remarks?"

"Nor was I informed, Mr. Chairman." Charles Shulman, a four-term Democratic Senator from New Jersey, screamed. He echoed Lank's sentiments with his usual dramatic flare. Shulman was someone who could most appropriately be described as ornery on his best day and this particular day was not shaping up to be all that good. His mood reflected that.

"To be quite honest with you, it is a massive breach of committee protocol and I believe sanctions against this witness may be in order," he said.

Callie continued on in spite of the great tumult in front of her. She derived great pleasure from the obvious discomfort she was causing. "The things I have done on Capitol Hill and else-where are beyond my own description. It hurts just to think about them." Callie smoothed her shoulders, as if there were wrinkles but there were none. "I am not proud of what I've done, but I do take full responsibility for my actions."

She lifted her head and gazed intently at the lawmakers in front of her. "However, I believe I may be the only one in this room to do so."

Chairman Rice interrupted her and peered down at Callie from over his bifocals.

"Ms. Wheeler, we were led to believe you would not be mak-ing any opening remarks."

Callie looked in control and seemed to gain strength from the simmering tension in the room. She leaned in closer to the microphone. The photographers clicked away while the television cameras zoomed in on her face.

"Well, I changed my mind."

Callie confidently pushed back from the microphone and smiled, letting her last comment sink in. The chamber erupted, most of the noise coming from the Senators.

Chairman Rice gaveled the room quiet before the hearing spun out of control. Senator Mike Gorman, a Democrat from Colorado, had already served four terms in the Senate after being elected to Congress at a mere thirty years old. His perfect hair, flawless teeth and well-cut suits were his trademark. Gorman was using this hearing as well as any other occasion to bump his sag-ging poll numbers in an upcoming race no one thought would be close. His campaign was in trouble and everyone knew it.

"In light of these events, Mr. Chairman, I reiterate...I think this session needs to be held in private. As you know, I've been against this entire exercise and am on record with that opinion. However, if we are going to move ahead with this, the least we can do is clear the room and save the public the embarrassment?"

Senator Gerald Macklin, a six-term Republican from Illinois, was also unhappy. Senator Macklin had watched his years in office expand along with his waistline. He tipped the scales during his most recent physical at close to four-hundred pounds. "I would agree, Mr. Chairman," he said. "I think it is best we clear the entire chamber at this time..."

"I am not sure what good an open hearing does for the people of this great country," Senator Lank said, interrupting.

The noise in the hearing room grew louder. The onlookers in the gallery began talking amongst themselves while a number of Senators continued to interrupt.

Senator Shulman, speaking loudly into his microphone, addressed the hearing once again. "Mr. Chairman, I would like to raise an objection to the presence of this witness before our committee and I would also like the official record to reflect my opinion as to how ridiculous I feel her testimony is and will be."

Chairman Rice pounded the gavel on his podium. "Quiet, please."

Callie watched intently. Senator Shulman covered his mic and leaned in to whisper something to Chairman Rice. Before he could say a word, Callie rattled their cages one more time.

"Mr. Chairman, I would like to continue..."

The gallery once again buzzed with chatter. Chairman Rice pounded the gavel loudly. "Quiet. We cannot proceed like this. We need quiet."

Senator Shulman took advantage of the ruckus. He leaned over to whisper in the chairman's ear. "Lester, you need to postpone this. I am telling you, this bitch is hell on wheels. We need to get control of this situation and I mean right now."

Chairman Rice nodded as Shulman talked in his ear. Before he could finish, Rice was already on it. "Ms. Wheeler, would you be willing to postpone your testimony a day or two so we can sort out a few procedural details?"

Goodman quickly placed his hand on Callie's microphone. He offered her some advice drawn from his three decades of work. "Callie, listen to me. Take him up on his offer and play ball with these guys. They do not fuck around. As your attorney, I am advising you in the strongest possible terms to say 'yes'. These people will make your life a living hell. Just do as they say."

Callie let her lustrous brown hair fall over her left shoulder. She smiled and slowly moved Goodman's hand off the microphone.

"No sir, Mr. Chairman, I would not. I will testify today and no other day. If you like, feel free to subpoena me, but I am quite confident that I'm the last person Congress wants to hear from."

In the back right corner of the chamber, Mike Ferguson sat quietly. More than any other person in attendance, he knew all too well about Callie Wheeler. The seasoned litigators who sat on the committee had media pundits wondering aloud how Callie would hold up against their intense rounds of questioning. Mike Ferguson knew better and couldn't help but feel bad for the Senators sitting in front of her. As he thought about the long day they had ahead of them, the trace of a smile began to form on his face.

TWO

The anticipated arrival of the Congressional summer recess in D.C. was Callie Wheeler's favorite time of the year. Cherry blossoms had all but vanished off the trees and the humidity that plagued the population during the summer months had been dormant. Congress was four weeks away from its annual summer vacation. As the most successful lobbyist in Washington, Callie savored the relative peace and quiet their departures granted her, if only for a few days. She had hoped to use the time to get away for some well-earned R&R with her fiance', but she learned long ago: wishful thinking had no place when her boss was concerned. Under that cloud, Callie Wheeler sat in the conference room at the Law Offices of Miller & Gladstone, awaiting her turn to speak.

Miller and Gladstone had once been and was again, the top lobbying firm in Washington D.C. Better known on K Street as M&G, the firm rose to prominence during the two-term presidency of William Gordie Bannon. Derek Gladstone, the 'G' in M&G, had played college football at Stanford with the President. His close friendship with the most powerful man in the world carried influence across America and around the globe. It was no secret that Derek and his lobbying firm had intimate access to the White House. That perception not only curried favor in the halls of Congress, companies lined up at their door for the opportunity to draw close to the administration. And Derek too.

During President Bannon's eight years, the media hounded him incessantly about the appearance of impropriety that his relationship with Derek suggested. Yet to his credit, Bannon never distanced himself from his college roommate. Everyone understood the message that loyalty conveyed. More importantly, the attention M&G received as a result of the constant publicity, whether good or bad, made Miller and Gladstone the hottest lobbying firm in the country. With the 2004 election of former U.S. Senator, President Alan Conroy, the fortunes of M&G had changed overnight. Not for the better. Access to the Oval Office and Congress were not easy to come by for what the press had once called "the world's most prestigious law firm."

A new chief executive in the White House brought with him new standards of access. President Conroy made a concerted effort to distance himself from the ways of his predecessor. To make matters worse, a deliberate strategy by some in the halls of power to settle old scores, left M&G, once the ultimate insider, on the outside looking in. While business was still good, it was far from the windfall of the Bannon years.

Callie Wheeler had single-handedly changed all of that.

"Where do you stand on this, Callie?" asked Barry Miller. He was her boss and a man she thoroughly distrusted.

"I'm not even sure why we're discussing this at the moment..."

"Of course you're not, because it's not about you," Whitaker Jordan interrupted Callie. He could not help but sound pompous. Jordan, a talented lobbyist in his own right, resented everything about Callie Wheeler. His distaste for her was the worst-kept secret at the firm. A former aide to retired Senator Andrew Abeles, he had butted heads with Callie quite a few times while working on Capitol Hill. He despised her then and that sentiment had not changed since he joined the firm two years earlier.

"What is it that bothers you more, Whitaker? Me being a woman, or me being a woman with an opinion?" The other lawyers seated around the conference table sat quietly. They had seen this confrontation plenty of times before.

"Stop, you two. We're not doing this again," Barry said. "Callie, what's the problem?"

Callie glanced over at Jordan and gave him a sarcastic smile. She stood up and sashayed towards the dry-erase board. She picked up a red marker from the tray and yanked off the cap. The heavy smell from the marker made Callie recoil. As the fumes receded, Callie zeroed in on the proposals Barry had laid out on the white board in front of her.

"This...here...is a non-starter," Callie said as she drew a thick long red streak diagonally across nine lines of information. "The legislation on nuclear waste is dead; I killed it before the Memorial Day break." With the Sharpie in her hand like a sword in search of its next victim, Callie strode over to the adjacent section of the board and drew a large 'X'.

"Drilling off the southern coast is going to happen no matter what so we don't have to insert anything into the Wildlife bill..."

"Who says it's gonna happen?" Jordan asked.

"I do," Callie said as she turned around and faced Jordan and the other thirty-one attorneys in the room. "I already took care of that in the last appropriations bill and as far as that section over there," Callie said, pointing to the far end of the board as she made her way back to her seat. "It makes no sense and we should get out of it as soon as possible..."

"Do you agree with that, Barry?" Jordan asked, obviously dissatisfied with Callie's assessment. Jordan stood just above six-feet-tall and fancied himself a good looking man, which he was. His disheveled brown hair helped to give off a care-free attitude which he felt should have endeared him to all women, but especially Callie Wheeler. He was unsure if his hatred for her was mostly due to her success or her rebuffing of his constant advances when they had first met on the Hill five years before.

Barry hesitated a few moments before answering the question. "I think we need to consider what Callie said, but in the long run we have to protect our clients."

Whitaker looked over at Callie. He wanted to return her sarcastic smile, but she never saw him. She'd seen this scene before from Barry and had prepared herself for the onslaught. While she had gotten used to his games, they usually involved someone else. She sometimes thought things would have been different if Derek was still around. It was at times like these that she missed him the most.

● ● ●

Derek Gladstone was forty-one years old when he met Callie for the first time in the Lobby at M&G. Callie had spent the previous week preparing for her interview yet none of that mattered. She was immediately struck by Derek's athletic six foot-two frame as if it had been designed in a laboratory. After exchanging pleasantries, Callie followed him into a large office overlooking the city, where red and white carpeting dominated the decor. Behind a ten-thousand-dollar mahogany desk, a long eight-foot window exposed a skyline accented by the White House and Capitol Hill.

"Callie, this is my partner, Barry Miller."

"How do you do, Ms. Wheeler? Welcome to Miller & Gladstone." Barry only referred to the firm that way. He was sure it sounded more dignified than using a catchy set of initials.

"It is a pleasure to meet you, sir," Callie said.

Before he took his seat across from her, Derek motioned Callie to the corner of his office where a set of white couches were situated underneath a picture of Derek and President Bannon sharing a laugh in the Oval Office. To the left of the massive photo, another huge frame displayed a shot of Derek and the President wearing their football uniforms following Stanford's Rose Bowl upset of Ohio State twenty years earlier. Callie gently smoothed the back of her skirt as she sat down, while Barry grabbed a black executive chair from the conference table behind him and positioned himself next to Derek.

"How do you like the view?" Derek asked, with a smile.

Callie glanced around the office. "Very impressive, sir."

"Please, call me Derek."

"Yes, sir…yes, Derek."

Derek crossed his legs and leaned back in his chair. "A Bruin, huh?"

"Proudly," Callie said and smiled at his reference to her alma mater, UCLA.

"It almost cost you," he said. "But you did your penance at Georgetown. Professor Watkins told me you are his pride and joy."

Callie was a bit uncomfortable by the compliment, but remained confident, "I did okay."

"Top of your class?" Derek asked. "I'd say you did a bit better than okay."

She toyed with the sapphire ring on her middle finger. "I enjoyed my time there. But as you can see, I'm ready to move on."

Callie had been destined for big things from an early age. Born in Kingston, Pennsylvania in 1982, she competed as a three-sport athlete at Wyoming Valley West High School in the late nineties and landed on the honor roll every semester. Voted first team all-state in both basketball and softball, Callie captained her teams to two State Championships in each sport. During her sophomore year, she won the Pennsylvania Junior Miss Pageant and spent most of her free time fulfilling her duties across the state, then vowed never to do it again.

After graduation, Callie chose to attend UCLA on a full athletic scholarship, forgoing an Ivy League education for a chance to compete on softball's highest level and live somewhere warm. She pitched and played shortstop on three National Championship teams for the Bruins then capped off her athletic career with an Olympic gold medal as a member of the United States Women's Softball team at the 2004 Olympic Games in Athens. Having decided to leave college after only three years, Callie attended Georgetown Law School where she graduated first in her class. It was because of that success and hard work that she was sitting in Derek's office and interviewing for the job of her dreams.

"Human resources was very impressed with your previous interviews and that's why you are one of the two candidates we're still considering for this position. However, Barry and I feel you're the best one for the job."

Barry bobbed his head and smiled at Callie. He said nothing. She wondered for a moment what exactly Barry did at the firm. His expensive suit and Bruno Mali shoes did little to cover up his thinning black hair and uncomfortable smile. It was evident from the outset that he did not possess the same confidence that Derek did. She assumed that Barry was the managing partner while Derek excelled at the hand-grabbing and schmoozing that's required on the Hill.

"By the time most applicants get to us, they're all questioned out. The good news is, we only ask one." Derek smiled at her again. "Why do you want to work at our firm?"

Callie slipped her hair behind her left ear, exposing a silver bamboo hoop earring, which drew the attention of both men. She clasped her hands together and rested them on top of her knee, before giving her answer.

"I want to help people, nothing more, nothing less. Far too many citizens in this country are disenfranchised and feel they have no say in our political process. I want to be their voice. I want to make a difference in the lives of people who don't have access to the decision-makers."

As Callie answered his question, Derek stared at the stunning young woman who sat across from him. He was distracted by her heart-shaped face and the light brown hair that fell slightly below her shoulders. He did his best to remain professional, but her long legs kept drawing his eyes back to them.

"Callie, we think you are exactly what we're looking for," Derek said, finally lifting his eyes to meet hers.

Barry Miller all but confirmed Callie's original assessment of the partnership. "Ms. Wheeler, we've had quite a number of accomplished lawyers apply for this position, but no one has impressed our committee more than you have. We would like to offer you a job here at Miller & Gladstone. You'll start at $140,000.00 with full benefits."

"All we need to know from you is, would you like to work here?" asked Derek.

Callie had waited weeks to hear those words and took no time at all in giving her response. "When can I start?"

Derek handed her a contract. Callie spent a few minutes reading the fine print, much to the approval of the two men sitting across from her. "If you have any questions, Callie, please do not hesitate to ask," Derek said.

"We know how daunting something like this can be," Barry said, playing his part in the double team approach.

Callie signed the contract and handed it back to Barry who

placed it on the coffee table in front of her. Derek stood up and held out his hand. "We shall see you in the morning, Ms. Wheeler."

Callie was barely able to contain her excitement, having landed the job she had wanted since her sophomore year in college. She gracefully stood up from the couch and met Derek's hand. "Thank you for the opportunity."

"It is great to have you aboard."

A few moments later, Callie confidently strolled out of Derek's office. Her smile extended from ear to ear. Standing in the lobby, it struck her that she would be working a few short blocks away from the most powerful legislative body in the world. *Not bad for a small town girl*, she thought.

"How cool is this?" Callie said to no one as she stepped inside the empty elevator.

Following Callie's departure, Barry began to pace the room. Derek took a seat behind his desk. "I mean is she not perfect? Do you have any idea what she will do for this firm?" Barry said. "She will own the Capitol."

Derek smiled as he thought about the possibilities. "Smart," he said. "Ambitious, focused and not to mention she's breathtaking. She's about to cause some ridiculous damage, Barry."

Derek removed a pen and a small notebook from his jacket pocket and began to jot something down then stopped and shook his head. "What do you think Bannon's gonna say when he gets a load of her?" he asked. He laughed proudly thinking of the former president's penchant for women like Callie.

It had been almost two years since M&G was the toast of K Street and no matter what they had tried, the firm could not attain the success they once enjoyed. They watched helplessly as others moved in on what used to be their exclusive territory. The time had come to change the game and Derek could not wait to unleash Callie on the public.

• • •

Six years later, Callie did own the Capital as Barry had predicted, but that meant nothing to Whitaker Jordan.

"I agree, Barry, our clients should be our top priority on this and I vote to move forward on the entire agenda you put on the board."

"Are we all in agreement on this?" Barry asked. He surveyed the room and noticed the large number of hands that assented with the motion Jordan put forward. Across the table, Callie was visibly agitated. "Why waste the political capital on legislation that has already passed through Congress?" she asked. "Am I the only one who sees that?"

Barry wasted no time in responding. "No, you're not, but we are running a business..."

"And we used to be a legitimate one," Callie said. "Since when did we start billing new clients for work we completed for someone else?"

"I guess we aren't privy to your outstanding efforts, Callie," Jordan said, dripping with more sarcasm than usual.

Callie looked at Barry. She raised her eyebrows anticipating he would speak up on her behalf. No words were forthcoming.

"Seriously?" Callie asked looking at him in response to his ten seconds of silence.

"We'll move on these today," Barry said as if Callie was no longer in the conference room. "Whitaker, you take the lead on Alford Chemical and I'll divvy up what's left within the hour. Callie, you stay here; the rest of you are free to go."

Callie leaned back in her chair as she watched the other lawyers shuffle out. After the last attorney exited the boardroom, Barry walked slowly to a seat across from Callie, but stayed on his feet.

"Don't you ever throw me under the fuckin' bus again," Barry said, as he pointed his finger at the only other person in the conference room.

"Me, throw you under the bus? You're kidding me, right?"

"What do you call it?"

"You asked my opinion and I gave it to you," Callie said.

Barry leaned across the table and drew his face closer to Callie's. "I asked your opinion as a courtesy, not to have you piss all over me."

"Since when do we rubber-stamp shit around here?" Callie asked, glaring right back at her boss.

"Don't do it again." Barry pointed at her a second time then turned and started for the door.

Callie picked up her pen and legal pad and prepared to go. "You ever gonna pull your pit-bull off me?"

Barry slowly rotated his body back towards her. "My pit-bull?"

"You know what I'm talking about."

"Whitaker gets it done," Barry said, more to piss her off than anything else.

"That's bullshit, Barry and you know it." Callie dismissed his last comment with a wave of her hand.

"Don't do it again, Callie."

"Is that a threat?"

"Don't do it again," he said as he stepped out of the conference room, leaving Callie alone in her thoughts. She thought about Derek and just how different things had become since his departure. The void his absence created changed the fortunes of so many lives, but most notably, her own.

THREE

The sound of gunshots hitting their target were usually not distinctive in relation to other shots fired at the Maryland Small Arms Range. However, anyone who was around when Mike Ferguson showed up for target practice would swear that the shots coming from his gun just sounded different. He'd been compared to that one hitter in baseball whose swing makes the ball jump off his bat unlike anyone else's in the sport. No one knew for sure what it was about his firearm that distinguished his rounds from the rest, but when they witnessed it, there was no doubt who was doing the shooting.

Located just off interstate 95 near Andrews Air Force base, the range was home to the best shooters on the eastern seaboard and Mike Ferguson was, by far, the best of them all. Todd Goodwin, a tall lanky man with a slight limp when he walked, stood uncomfortably behind Mike, watching him unload on the target in front of him.

"You fuckin' make me sick," Goodwin said as Mike checked out his handiwork, six shots within three millimeters of each other, all near the heart.

"Stop cryin' and shoot."

Todd wandered up to the counter and adjusted his protective glasses before he squeezed off six shots that were near perfect. He pressed the button drawing the target in his direction, eager with anticipation that this time he had maybe beaten his partner. Both men looked closely at the human silhouette laid out on white paper, six bullet holes neatly placed near one another.

"Shit," Todd said. Five shots near the heart, one to the left of it. Mike stepped back up to the counter and stuck six more shots, one right next to the other, creating a large hole in the forehead of the target.

"I mean, what the fuck? Why do I let you talk me into these stupid ass bets?"

Todd pulled up and ripped six shots into the target's forehead. Four dead center, one to the right and one missing completely. He grabbed two twenty dollars bills from his wallet and handed them to Mike. "You should fuckin' name your savings account after me, you piece of shit."

"Thank you for your weekly deposit," Mike said. He kissed the twenties and stuffed them into his pants pocket. "We gotta get to Langley by ten, so quit your whining and pack up."

Todd raised his middle finger at Mike, then turned to grab the gym bag he'd brought with him. "Hey you gonna be around this weekend?"

"Yeah, Why?"

"'Cuz I wanted you to meet this girl I'm seein' kinda' tell me what ya' think."

"Should be," Mike said as he placed his Beretta into the holster strapped to the left side of his belt. "She the one from last month with the Honda Civic?"

"Naw, I'm with this girl a couple weeks. Talks a bit too much, but I got ways to keep her mouth busy."

Mike shook his head and chuckled, "You like her?"

"I think I do, but she gotta' pass the friends test, know what I mean?"

"I know what you mean."

"Yo' lookie here." Todd reached into his bag and pulled out a small key that looked like it came from an old bus station locker. "Found it under the couch last night looking for the TV remote. Remember this?"

Mike peeked at Todd and recognized the key instantly. His mind raced back to 1996. Mike, only twenty-one years old, had settled into his second field assignment since leaving 'The Farm'. He spent a few months in Egypt and Lebanon doing some routine information gathering. Mike hung out each day at some of the local hot spots and cafes and when he tired of that, he walked the streets listening for anything that might be of interest to his country. The life he carved out for himself in the Middle East became rather mundane and unassuming until he happened upon a group of Islamists who were talking a little too much out of turn. Mike made all his superiors aware that something big was going to go down in Saudi Arabia and repeatedly sent messages to his handlers that the Kohbar Towers had been under serious surveillance for several months. His warnings went ignored.

The last message he sent was dated June 24, 1996. He urged the CIA offices in Langley to alert the government of an imminent threat to the buildings housing American military personnel. Less than twenty-four hours later, nineteen Americans were dead and another 372 were injured. Mike was furious. He had reported back to the agency all the information he thought they needed to know in order for them to take the necessary precautions. In his report, Mike made a very specific mention to his handlers in Virginia about the orchestrator of the entire operation, a man they knew of, but had never seen, named Ibrahim Hakef.

The intelligence failure was massive. In the aftermath, the CIA was excoriated. Soon to be outgoing President Watkins was not happy, but chose to take no action, fearing that any mishaps would sully his legacy. The CIA had its own ideas. Director Sam Miller, who despised Watkins, ordered a covert action, but let it be known that he would deny any knowledge of the operation if plans went awry. Mike was not a part of the hit-squad that Miller sent to Canada to find those responsible and eliminate them. Ted Biggs, Mike's direct supervisor at the agency, was in his office when Mike showed up unannounced.

"Aren't you in Lebanon?" Biggs asked when he saw Mike standing in front of his desk.

"I was, sir, but what is happening here ain't right."

"What do you mean, son?"

"Sir, I told you about the towers. I did my job on this one and you know it, but now they're talking like I'm part of the problem."

Biggs took a sip of the cup of coffee that was on his desk, then licked his lips before wiping them with a Dunkin Donuts napkin that was on top of his daily planner. "Who's they?"

"Everyone...the politicians...the media..."

"They named you specifically?" Biggs asked with a giggle, trying to loosen up his tightly-wound protege'.

Mike refused to take the bait and ignored the question. "This is wrong, sir. I should be out there fixing it."

"Mike, we think you're a great asset, one of our up-and-coming stars, but this is just way too big for you."

Mike was having none of it. "Too big for me?"

Biggs picked up his coffee, but did not drink from it. "We can't afford any screw ups on this."

"With all due respect, sir, it was never me who was not up for the job. The politicians in Washington and Virginia, more concerned with covering their own asses, were the ones not up for the job."

Biggs took another sip from the cup in his hand, then placed it on his desk. "And you're telling me this because...?"

"We know who did it and I want 'em. It kills me that I knew about this and was helpless to do anything to stop it."

Biggs shook his head, "Sorry, Mike, I can't."

"Bullshit, you can't...you won't..."

"Damn right, I won't." Biggs jumped on Mike's last comment as soon as the words left his mouth.

"I knew it..."

"You know shit. I'm not sending in some greenhorn to do a job that needs a seasoned professional."

Mike slammed his fist on the desk startling Biggs, "Fuck that shit, Ted. I need to go to Canada because I got this right and y'all back here messed up big time."

Biggs stood up behind his desk and leaned over it in a feeble attempt at intimidation. He knew it wasn't going to work, but felt the need to regain some control. "Who the hell do you think you are, talking to me like that?"

"Am I wrong?"

"It don't matter who's wrong."

Mike waved his hand at Ted and turned his head away. "Man... I thought you were different."

"Fuck you, Mike." Biggs said, jumping on his words again. "I don't need some snot-nosed little shit coming in here and telling me what I can and cannot do."

"But you know I can fix this, Ted."

Biggs hesitated before he answered. As much as he agreed with Mike, he wasn't sure if he wanted to get him involved in a controversial operation this early in his career. Not to mention one that had no support from the White House. If the action was compromised, all those involved could lose their jobs or worse. Mike was far and away his favorite and Biggs believed he was also the Agency's future. More than anything else, Biggs knew that Mike was the one man who could get the job done as clean and as quick as possible.

"I know you can handle it, which is why I won't send you," Biggs said. "This is gonna be a massive cluster-fuck and you don't need to be anywhere near it."

Mike sat down on the other side of Biggs's desk, bent over and rested his face in the palms of his hands.

"I can't let something happen to you because this agency is caught in a political football game. I can't do it," Biggs said, impressed with the maturity of his 6'4 pupil.

A minute later, Mike sat up straight, leaned back in his chair and stared directly into Biggs's eyes. "Ted, I need this...I can't sleep...I can't eat...this was horse shit and you know it."

Mike stood up. He placed both palms flat on Biggs' desk. "I told you this was going down...I was not the fuck-up on this, y'all were."

"Yeah. You told me that already."

"I want this guy and I'm going to go find him whether you assign me to this or not."

"Mike, you don't have the experience for a gig like this..."

Mike straightened up. "Experience, my ass. Do you think I can do this?"

Biggs hesitated. "I think you can do anything we assign to you."

"Assign me to this, because I'm going whether you do or not."

Mike turned around without waiting for a response. He walked out of Biggs' office, closing the door behind him.

Mike ended up in Quebec where he personally hunted down and killed three of the architects of the tower bombings, but missed finding Ibrahim in his safe house by less than three minutes. The apartment Ibrahim was holed up in had one lamp, an old desk, a mattress without a box-spring and a small black and white TV in the corner. On the floor under the mattress was a key from a storage facility in Toronto. Inside 21C, the small storage closet Ibrahim had rented, were surveillance photos of not only the Khobar Towers in Saudi Arabia, but also buildings and landmarks in Russia, Israel, Great Britain, Algiers, Yemen, Buenos Aires, Pakistan and the United States. After taking stock of the contents, Mitch met up with Todd, who brought all the evidence back to Langley, along with the key he was holding in his hands.

"Yeah, I remember that key. What did they say, three minutes? If I was three minutes earlier, I could have saved the world a whole lot of pain and suffering."

Todd zipped his knapsack then pulled out a stick of trident gum from his shirt pocket, unwrapped it and stuffed it in his mouth. "If I called you five minutes earlier, we'd have had him. You can't keep blaming yourself."

"But three minutes…"

"Got to deal with what you can control, not what you can't, partner."

"I know…just pisses me off is all." Mike took his gym bag and flipped it onto his right shoulder, then motioned for Todd to follow. "Let's get outta' here."

FOUR

"It was strange," Callie said speaking into her cellphone. "He threw me under the bus in front of the entire firm, then accused me of doing the same thing to him." On the other line was Mike Ferguson, her boyfriend of almost six years.

"Hasn't he done stuff like that before?"

"Not to me, he hasn't."

Mike walked into his office at the headquarters of the CIA and set his jacket over the black chair that was situated directly across from his desk. He had first met Callie on a muggy July evening in 2005 while playing on his neighbor's co-ed softball team during a local tournament. Mike had taken off from first base and debated whether or not he should slide into second. The answer hit him square in the forehead and Mike knew it was going to hurt well before he saw her release the ball. Reacting to a hard ground ball hit to shortstop, Callie scooped it up on a hop, stepped on second then threw a laser onto first to complete the double play, but the ball never got there.

Sprawled on the infield dirt, all he heard the girl say was, "You should have slid." No apologies, no sympathy, only advice he already knew. She made sure to check up on him after the game and slipped Mike her number, "In case you want to file a lawsuit or take me out to dinner," then she turned and jogged away. He had never met anyone quite like her. Within a few days, he took Callie up on her offer for dinner, but reserved the right to file suit. By the time three months had passed, they had become a couple. Thereafter, they were known to everyone as Mike and Callie.

"I wouldn't worry too much about it," Mike said. "Barry is Barry. Just let it go." He settled into his desk chair and brought his computer to life.

"Easy for you to say, you don't work with him."

"Hey, I'm gonna be home late tonight, some sort of briefing then a meeting with Biggs afterwards."

"I've got things to do anyway. You won't be missed."

"Note to self, forget the 'I'm sorry roses' for Callie."

"You always know what to say to make a girl feel wanted."

"Think I should send the roses anyway?"

"I gotta' go, hon. Love you."

Mike heard her disconnect before he had a chance to say goodbye. He smiled as he stared at the phone, having grown accustomed to her many habits and idiosyncrasies. All these years later, she was still different than any other woman he'd ever met and the more he got to know her, the more he wanted to be with her.

Callie hung up the phone and found Barry standing at the open doorway to her office. She motioned him in and waited for Barry to walk towards her. Instead, Barry headed for the set of chairs that surrounded a small conference table to the right of her desk and sat down in the chair at the head of it. Callie stood up, followed him, then took a seat and waited for him to talk. As she watched Barry turn to the bar behind him to pour himself a drink, her thoughts drifted to Mike and the first time he bought her roses…

• • •

"Callie? You here?" Mike had said, as he gently placed the flowers he was hiding behind his back onto the antique red table in the foyer. His townhouse was pitch black with the exception of the flickering light that emanated from the two candles on the dining room table.

"Cal?"

The aroma of lamb chops and garlic bread overtook his senses. Mike closed his eyes and enjoyed the long moment of subtle pleasure that came with the recognition of a well cooked meal enveloping his home. Walking up discreetly behind him, Callie gently wrapped her arms around his body and slid his winter coat off his tall, muscular frame. She loved how his sinewy torso seemed to never end and how the touch of his hand sent chills across her entire body. She stood on her toes, seductively kissing the back of his neck, while slowly taking off his necktie. Mike waited until she removed it, then latched onto her hands, spun her around and kissed her passionately on the lips.

"Honey, I'm home."

"Mmmm...yes, you are," Callie said before she kissed him again. She held the kiss for a moment longer, pressing her body up against his and running her hands through his thick light brown hair. "I got the job..."

"You got the job?"

Callie kissed him another time. "I did. 140 to start, full benefits."

"Know what?"

"What?" Callie asked and smiled as she wrapped her arms around his neck.

"I'm thinking it's time to celebrate," Mike lifted Callie into his arms and carried her over to the couch.

"Hold on, Tarzan, I made dinner."

"Me no want dinner, Tarzan want Jane."

"I mean, I slaved over it," Callie said with feigned frustration. "When will you ever appreciate me?"

"I'm about to...over and over again."

Mike sat down on the edge of the couch and stared at his girlfriend. He could not take his eyes off of her face as his fingers brushed the hair away from her right eye. There were moments, just like this one, where Mike got so lost in Callie's beauty that he'd forget about anything else he had on his mind.

"What are you looking at?"

"You."

Callie smiled bashfully and pulled him down towards her, kissing him as she unbuttoned his shirt. Mike allowed his hands to roam Callie's body and started to caress the inside of her thigh, when a frantic knock interrupted their time alone.

"Callie...Callie..."

"No way, Cal. Tell me you called her?"

Callie's face told him all he needed to know. "Oh my god, I totally forgot. She's going to kill me."

Callie sat up and closed the top three buttons of her blouse. Once on her feet, she attempted to regain her composure even as Mike tried to pull her back onto his lap. Callie turned slightly behind and slapped his hands off of her, "Stop," she said, then headed for the door.

"Just a second." Callie straightened her skirt and paused at the mirror in the hallway. She flipped her hair a few times then ran her pinky finger across her lips twice before flipping her hair once more.

On the other side of the door stood Robyn Baxter, a thirty year old African American woman and a friend of Callie's from law school. She was still pounding and screaming Callie's name until she saw the door open just a crack then pushed her way inside, already talking, as if she had a time limit.

"Okay, I so thought you were dead...I mean why else would you not have called me to tell me how everything went? You had to be dead, right?"

"Sorry, Robyn, I got so caught up in everything..."

Robyn noticed Mike standing in front of the messy couch with his shirt open. She turned to her left and saw the two long candles on the dining room table and obviously knew she had interrupted something. Undaunted, Robyn plowed ahead. "Well, now, this explains what you were caught up in."

Robyn laughed and gave Mike a long hug then seductively ran her fingers along his bare chest. "He is so yummy. Let me know when you're done with this guy, 'cuz I'll be glad to take him off your hands."

Mike wasted no time responding to Robyn's come-on. "What about your husband?"

"Who?" Robyn nestled her head under Mike's shoulder. "Honey, when I'm in your arms Kenny doesn't even exist."

"What about your husband? What kind of question is that?" Callie asked as she slapped Mike on the arm.

Robyn released Mike, but not before she pinched his ass. "Mike, you seein' the way she treats you? I'll handle you good, honey," Robyn said then turned to Callie, folded her hands and began to tap her right foot. "You gonna make me wait all night? C'mon, girl, what happened?"

"What happened with what?"

"Stop playin'. You get the job?"

"I got the job."

"Oh my god, Callie, you got it?...you really got it?...this is so great," Robyn said then slapped Mike's ass. "Okay, I just stopped by to make sure you weren't dead. Gotta' get home to what's his name. Love you guys."

Callie and Mike walked Robyn onto the porch before Callie hugged her good-bye. "I think your man got you some roses, honey. You see them?" Robyn asked whispering in Callie's ear.

"I saw them, they're beautiful, but I think I'm going to make him sweat it out a bit."

"Damn, Cal, you're bad." Robyn said as she released her embrace and walked down the steps towards her car. She opened the door of her 2004 Toyota Camry, stood silent for a moment, then closed the door and walked back towards the porch. "You told Kacey, right?"

Callie slowly shook her head, realizing that she had dug herself in deep.

"Are you crazy?" Robin said turning and walking back to her car. "She is gonna shit…if she finds out that I know…I mean, she is totally gonna shit--"

"I get the point, Robyn."

"Y'all need to stop this sex thing and call your girl or you'll never hear the end of it." Robyn opened the Camry and slid inside. "Love you guys."

"Love you…say hi to Kenny…"

Robyn blew Callie a kiss as she pulled away.

"What about your husband? Seriously?"

Mike rubbed his stomach, totally ignoring the question. "Yum, lamb chops."

Callie playfully punched Mike on the arm and headed inside. "I'd better call Kacey."

• • •

Barry swirled his glass of Southern Comfort while he gathered his thoughts then punctured Callie's daydream when he began to speak. "Callie, I wanted to apologize for what happened before."

"Okay…"

"I shouldn't have done that to you in front of everyone and I was wrong."

Callie heard the words, but had a hard time believing they were coming out of Barry's mouth. She nodded her head in agreement and sat quietly as he continued on.

"The points you brought up at the meeting were valid and I'm sorry for blowing them off like I did."

"Are we still going to bill clients for work we did for someone else?"

"I'm going to address that issue as soon as I finish with you. I only stopped by to let you know I was sorry and I'm in your corner and always will be. Don't ever doubt that."

She already had. Callie had learned over the years that there was only one thing Barry cared about more than power and that thing was money. She was well aware that when it came to revenue, no one brought in more than she did. Barry understood that better than anyone and Callie knew it was the sole motivation why he had made his way to her office with a half-hearted mea culpa. She also knew him well enough to know that he did nothing by accident.

"Let's get together in the next few days. There's something I wanted you to work on."

"What about Whitaker?"

Barry stood up, walked towards Callie then stopped as he approached her chair. "You are all we need on this project. I'll finish with the loose ends, then we'll talk."

"Sounds good," Callie said as she watched Barry leave her office and wondered if anything he had just said to her were true.

FIVE

The Washington Post was the oldest daily in the Nation's Capital and had long been the paper of record when it came to Washington politics. The technological advancements of the twenty-first century had made newspapers an endangered species. Gone were the days of the journalist working their beat to break stories for the morning edition. With instant real-time news updates accessible on numerous websites, a paper like the Post that could not deliver the very same news item until the next morning, had to find a way to compete in the real-time arena. For most dailies, the Post included, the website had become their anytime of day salvation, but the nuts and bolts of their revenue stream was still the morning edition of the actual physical newspaper.

Kacey Mercer had recently been promoted to the congressional beat at the Post after toiling in the obscurity of the City section since being hired straight out of college. As a sophomore at Wilkes University, Kacey was awarded an internship at the Times-Leader, the oldest local paper in her hometown, Wilkes-Barre, Pennsylvania. While there, she was taught the ins and outs of journalism from her mentor who was leaving the paper to join the Washington Post staff at the end of that summer. Kacey spent the next eighteen months at the Times Leader, while she completed her senior year in college, when out of nowhere she received a call from the paper's editor, Bob Kravitz.

"Kacey Mercer?"

"This is she."

"This is Bob Kravitz from the Washington Post. I'm calling regarding a possible summer opportunity for you at our paper."

A dumbfounded Kacey could barely manage a word in response. "Yes?"

"Do you know someone named Marge Viviano?"

"I do, yes, Margie." Kacey, still in a state of shock, walked over to her bed and sat down on its edge.

"She's looking for a research assistant for the summer and we were wondering if you might be interested in applying for the internship. There is a small stipend that might help you offset some expenses, but I have to tell you upfront, it's not much."

"Umm...yes, sir, I'd be very interested in applying for it," Kacey almost squeaked. "How long is the application process going to take?"

"Well, the way I see it, about another two minutes."

Kacey was confused by his answer, "Two minutes?"

"Maybe less, if you say you'll take the job."

"You mean...?"

"Yes, if you'd like the job, it's yours."

Kacey sat in stunned silence, the phone pressed against her ear like a new appendage. Margie had been tough and demanding, a mentor, but also a great friend and confidante and, as far as she could tell, a terrific reporter.

"Kacey?"

"Yes, sir, I will take it." Kacey jumped up off her bed, her heart pounding at a rapid pace.

"Great. You start on the first of June and it will run 'til the end of August. Does that work for you?"

"Yes, sir, it does…um…may I ask you a question, please?"

"Of course."

Kacey, a huge smile on her face, paced back and forth in her bedroom too excited to sit back down. "You offering this position to me…do you mind me asking how this happened?"

"Margie's one of our best reporters and she's gone through four research assistants in three months. I asked her what kind of person she was looking for and she said a person like you."

"A person like me?"

"Actually she said you, by name, Kacey Mercer in Wilkes-Barrough, Pennsylvania."

"Wilkes-Barre, sir." Kacey made sure to pronounce the city's name slowly and clearly.

Kravitz laughed at her meticulousness. "Yes, Wilkes-Barre," he repeated with the exact same enunciation that Kacey had used. "So we'll see you on the first?"

"Yes, sir, I'll be there."

Kacey hung up the phone and let out a joyful shriek. She sat down on her bed, picked the phone back up and began to dial. Her first call was not to her parents or her sometimes on-again off-again boyfriend, Keith Springs. It was to Callie Wheeler, the best friend she had since before they both could talk.

"Cal, you will not believe what just happened to me, you won't believe it."

"Hey Kace…"

Kacey laid on her back and slid the phone under her ear. "I got a call from this guy, right, and he says he is so and so from the Washington Post…"

"What?"

"Listen, listen. He says do you know Margie? You remember

Margie, right, Cal? Remember her?"

"The lady reporter from the paper back home?"

"Yeah, her. Anyway, he says do you know Margie, right?" Kacey could no longer contain her enthusiasm and would have been talking too quickly for anyone else besides Callie, who had learned to decipher Kaceyspeak long ago. "So he says, she wants you to work for her this summer as an intern, I say who does, he says Margie, I say why me, he says Margie wants you and he says something like she wanted Kacey Mercer from Wilkes Barrough or something like that, you know how people do."

Callie laughed, "I know."

"How cool is this, Cal? Can you believe it?"

"So wait, did you take the job?"

"Are you serious?"

"You took it?"

"Of course, I took it, who wouldn't take it?"

Callie paused for a moment and did the math. "Did you say the Washington Post?"

"Yeah girl! The Washington Post. Amazing, huh?"

"Oh my god, you'll be living here? With me?"

"Well in the same city—"

Callie interrupted her. "No, you'll be living with me. My apartment. I'm already set up and everything."

"Well I don't know about where I'm gonna..."

Callie interrupted her again. "You think I'm gonna let you live somewhere else?"

"I just thought, ya' know, you're probably busy with law school and all..."

A third time. "Shut up. You are living here wi..." Callie stopped mid-sentence and suddenly broke out in uncontrollable laughter.

"What's so funny?" Kacey asked as she listened to Callie laugh.

She pulled the phone away from her ear, looked at it, then brought it back to her mouth to talk again. "What's so funny, Callie?"

"I was just thinking...did you tell Pop yet...ya' know that you'll be working at the Washington Post?"

The line went silent as Kacey began to appreciate the reality of her situation. She sat up straight and leaned back against the headboard of her bed. In a soft, barely audible, voice, Kacey whispered into the phone. "No, I haven't told him yet."

Callie dropped the phone overwhelmed by laughter. She bent over, picked it up and slowly tried to regain her composure. Having missed Kacey's original response she asked the question again, "Did you tell him yet?"

"No, not yet."

"This is too much, Kace." Kacey could hear her take a few deep breathes between her chuckles. "When do you have to be here?"

"June first."

"Great, you can stay in the second bedroom, which at the moment is filled with a bunch of boxes and stuff...I can't wait."

"You sure it's okay?"

"Stop...and no you won't pay me."

"Yes, I will."

"Forget it and no, we're not gonna talk about it later. It's settled. You're moving in with me and that's final," Callie said with a wide grin on her face. "I have to run to class, but there's a part of me that wants to stay on the line just to listen when you tell your dad...he's gonna go crazy."

"I can hear Pop already," Kacey said. "Screamin' at the top of his lungs...that communist piece of shit paper...they can't be trusted those Marxists bastards over there..."

Callie chimed in with her own imitation of Kacey's dad. "Those friggin leftists...they should burn that..."

Kacey joined her and said it with Callie at the same time "...
that shit hole to the ground." The two woman laughed at the iro-
ny of Kacey getting a great opportunity at a paper she had never
been allowed to read at home.

"Gotta' go, good luck with Pop. It's gonna be hilarious."

"A regular riot. Love you, Cal-pie."

"Love you too, Mer-maid. Call me later?"

"Yup"

That internship turned into full-time employment at the Post
after she graduated from Wilkes University Magna cum laude and
was assigned to the city section in July of 2005. Margie Viviano
continued to work at the paper, but Kacey's two favorite people at
the Post were the paper's editor, Bob Kravitz, who loved Kacey's
work ethic and persistence, and Walter Bloom, a thirty year veteran of the paper, who liked to remind Kacey that he was at his desk
working on the Israeli withdrawal from the Sinai Peninsula, the
day she was born in April of 1982. It had been almost six months
to the day that Bob promoted Kacey to her current position. She
waited until just before lunch to approach Bob about an e-mail
she'd received the night before.

"Can we talk a sec?" Kacey asked as she knocked on Bob's door
and disrupted his solitude.

"What's on your mind?"

Kacey walked towards his desk and handed him the one page
e-mail.

"What's this?" Bob said as he grabbed the page from her extended hand.

"I got it late last night. No idea who it's from or anything."

Bob read the three lines and handed the paper back to her.
"What do you think?"

Kacey fidgeted with the pen she'd been holding, winding it
through her fingers like a majorette in a marching band. "I have

no idea, that's why I'm coming to you."

Bob leaned back in his chair and thought for a moment. "Check it out and see if there's any truth to it. If it has legs, we can run the story and see what it flushes out."

Kacey's eyes widened just a bit. "You want me to do it?"

"It's your e-mail."

"What about Walter? Or Margie?"

"Not your concern."

Kacey tried to contain her smile as she turned towards the door. "You sure?"

"Don't make me second-guess myself," Bob said with his head down already moving on to the next urgent crisis on his agenda.

Kacey ran down the hallway to find Walter Bloom. Walter was sixty-three years old, a father of four, and a grandfather to nine and counting. He still had all of the hair on his head, albeit exclusively white, wore glasses that he took off constantly in order to read and had a belly that, very shortly, was going to make his belt disappear from view.

She searched for Walter in his office and the newsroom before finding him alone in the break-room munching on a Kit-Kat bar. "You sure you should be eating that?"

"No," he said as he swallowed the last piece then smiled at her. "What's up?"

Kacey reached out to hand Walter the e-mail, then pulled back and reconsidered. "Wash your hands."

"What for?"

"Chocolate."

"Who are you, Miss Manners?"

"Have it your way," Kacey said as she turned to leave.

"Wait." Walter walked to the sink and ran cold water on his fingers while Kacey stopped dead in her tracks at his command. "What ya' got?"

Kacey slipped him the e-mail and waited for his response as he read the short note.

"Where'd you get this?"

"No clue"

Walter wiped his mouth with his bare forearm. "Anything to it?"

"Bob just asked me to find out."

Walter picked up a cup from the counter and headed back toward the sink. He turned on the cold water and watched it cascade across his index finger. "Normally I'd say it's a dog except the Senator Lank thing intrigues me."

"You think there's something there?"

"Did Bob say it's your story?"

Kacey nodded her head and smiled.

Walter, satisfied with the water's temperature, filled up the cup halfway, then took a drink, but left the water running. "He say if we'd run it?"

"If there's legs…"

Walter filled the cup again. "Nothing left to do but find out… if this thing has legs though, we're talking huge story…"

"Like how huge?"

"Like front page, make the politicians piss themselves, huge."

Kacey ripped the e-mail from Walter's hands, leaned in and kissed him on the cheek. "Thanks, Walter."

"Be careful, if there is something here, there will be plenty of people trying to destroy it," Walter said. "And the best way to destroy it, will be to destroy you."

SIX

"You want to get together for lunch?" Callie lifted her hair and turned around, her usual sign for Mike to zip up her dress.

"I have a meeting with the Director at eleven in Langley, but if you want to meet me at the Dirksen Cafeteria, I think I can be there by 12:45. Before that, I have to sit and listen to Senator McCombs tell me why he thinks the CIA should be abolished," Mike softly kissed the middle of Callie's back as he slowly slid the zipper to the top of her dress.

It had been two years since Mike worked in the field. In the aftermath of another Congressional lobotomy on the intelligence community, Mike accepted an appointment by Ted Biggs to be his assistant in the CIA's new Covert Operations Center. He had grown increasingly frustrated with the red tape and government bureaucracy that hampered the work he and his colleagues were doing in the field. Mike became acutely aware that constant congressional interference was costing agents their lives and he jumped at the opportunity to change the status quo from the inside. The other reason he agreed to work at the new COC had to do with the woman he intended to marry. Life as an operative left very little time for family. Moving to Langley gave him a chance to spend more time with her at home. Though she never came straight out and said it, Callie persistently hinted around the subject of marriage. She had grown tired of Mike's procrastination and little by little became more obvious with her frustration at his feet dragging. For his part, Mike was well-versed in how she felt and had every intention of asking her, but he was having too much fun messing with her head. It wasn't until two nights ago however, that he finally got around to putting an end to her misery.

"My mom wanted to know if you were coming with me to Kingston for Labor Day," Callie had said, as she pulled a cut-off tee-shirt over her head and slipped into bed.

"Not sure I want to do that."

Mike loved her parents and they loved him, which would explain why his response to her question felt like a punch to the gut. Earlier in the day Callie had accepted her mother's invitation telling her they would both be there for the holiday weekend.

"Why do you say that?"

"I think it's kinda' weak, me going over to your parents house and not being able to sleep with you in the same room. What are we, eighteen?" Mike actually had no problem with her parents rule that only married couples could sleep together in their home. He respected them for it, but with an opportunity to wreak havoc in Callie's head, he couldn't resist.

"Wait a second. We talked about this..."

"I know we did, but I'm darn near thirty-five years old, been running ops for the CIA in eighteen different countries, been shot at a few hundred times, killed more bad guys than I care to admit and I'm not allowed to sleep with my girlfriend at her parents home because we're not married? I mean, it's the twenty-first century for god's sake."

Callie wasted no time broaching her favorite subject. "Ya'

know, if you don't like the rules, there's always a way you can...
um...play within them."

"C'mon Cal, you know how I feel about that."

"Why get married if we already have everything we want
now?" Callie said.

"Exactly."

"Then don't complain, asshole."

Mike pulled the covers back and laid down on the bed. "How
am I an asshole? They're not my rules, they're your dad's."

"And you know how he is. So if you want to sleep with me
in their house, you know how to do that. Otherwise, keep your
mouth shut and make sure your calendar is free for Labor Day."

Mike turned onto his side to face Callie. He leaned his elbow
on the bed then rested his head in his open palm. "Why you gotta'
be such a bitch about it? You know I wanna' be with you."

"I mean, you say you do..." She let her comment hang in the
air knowing it would get a rise out of him.

"'I say I do'? What the hell does that mean?"

"It means I never should have given it up to you for the last
five years. I spoiled you," Callie said then turned over on her side,
her back now facing Mike.

"Screw this." Mike got out of bed with feigned agitation,
walked across the room and got down on one knee. He reached
under her pillow and pulled out a blue box.

"What are you doing?" Callie asked. She looked at Mike, then
at her pillow, then back at Mike who opened up the blue box and
pulled out the two-carat emerald-cut diamond ring that was nestled away inside. Callie covered her mouth with her hands when
she finally realized what was happening.

"Callie Wheeler, the love of my life, will you marry me?"

Callie wiped away a tear. "You are such an asshole. I hate you."

"Is that a yes?"

Callie kissed Mike on the lips, pulled away, then kissed him again. "I would be honored to be your wife."

• • •

Mike let go of the zipper and turned her around. "You gonna call, Kacey?" It had been two days since Mike proposed and although they enjoyed sharing a secret just between them, the time had come to tell their friends and families.

Callie reached up and fidgeted with Mike's tie. She wiped off his white pinstriped Van Heusen shirt with her newly manicured nails. "I don't think I can keep it from her any longer or I'm going to explode."

Mike kissed Callie on the lips. "Gonna make some coffee. Want some?"

"Please. I won't be too long…and don't leave before I see you," Callie said as she watched Mike exit the bedroom. Out of the corner of her eye, she caught a glimpse of the diamond ring she had slipped on earlier, still getting used to seeing it on her finger. She was enamored with the way it sparkled when the light hit it in a certain spot and could not stop herself from staring at her own hand. She knew it would take some getting used to, but for the moment, enjoyed being surprised at the sight of it. She moved into the bathroom to work on her makeup, something Mike reminded her daily she did not need. She glanced at the Stanford University clock hanging on the bathroom wall, a gag gift from Derek on her one-month anniversary with the firm. Callie mentioned to him at the time that there was only one appropriate place she could think of to display it. She thought about Derek and how much she missed him as she applied eyeshadow to her right eye. They had worked side-by-side on the Hill every day during the two months before his untimely demise. She considered him her mentor and he considered her his finest pupil.

Callie knew Derek had grown frustrated with Barry and confused about what to do moving forward. He had committed to making serious changes at the firm and confided in her many times about the crumbling relationship between the two of them. It had gotten so contentious, they hadn't spoken the last few weeks of his life, instead choosing to communicate only through their secretaries. Associates at the firm had chosen sides and much to Callie's chagrin, almost all of the other attorneys and office staff had sided with Barry. Callie, however, had single-handedly changed the balance of power on K Street. Revenues for the firm skyrocketed due to renewed interest from old clients who had left and were now interested in doing business again. Word on the street was out and new prospects fell all over themselves asking to work with M&G. With the increased interest in the firm came increased business, but, instead of making peace with Derek, Barry divided the firm even further. Callie had considered leaving a few times in the aftermath of Derek's departure, but Barry enticed her with larger bonuses and pay raises until eventually she grew comfortable with her place in the office hierarchy and with Barry himself. While she didn't trust him, she knew he needed her and she used that to her advantage.

After applying her lipstick one last time, Callie shuffled down the stairs and found Mike at the kitchen table, reading the morning paper. Callie walked up behind him, pulled his head toward her and kissed him on the lips from behind. "You are one gorgeous man," Callie said then walked to the counter and poured herself a cup of coffee. "We on at Dirksen...12:45?"

"Make it 12:30 so I can tell Biggs I have to leave early without really lying to him."

"Works for me," Callie said as she sat down next to Mike, coffee in her right hand, the sports section of the morning paper in her left. "Nationals lost again...ouch," Callie said skimming the headline.

Mike folded 'section A' back a few pages and slid it towards his fiancé. "Might want to read Kacey's story," Mike said, looking at Callie who was still searching for the Phillies boxscore.

"9-1, at Chicago, go Phils, whew," Callie said raising her index finger in the air. She took a sip from her coffee mug then rested the cup on the table and looked up at Mike, "What about Kacey, hon?"

"I said you might want to read her piece. Front page, above the fold."

"Why's that?" Callie said, scanning the first three paragraphs. Her affable demeanor vanished abruptly, a look of concern on her face growing more serious the further she read. "How did she get this? Did you know about this?"

"Is that a serious question?"

"Yes, it's a serious question..." Callie said, still reading the piece.

"You think she'd tell me anything before she told you?"

Callie flipped to page ten and finished reading the article, then lifted her head and stared at Mike.

"What?" Mike said, standing up on his way to the garbage can to clean off his plate.

"She didn't tell you?" Callie asked.

"Tell me what?"

"That she was writing this story?"

"C'mon, Cal. No, she didn't tell me anything," Mike said. Callie took another drink from her coffee and looked blankly at Mike. He fixed his belt then lifted his jacket off the back of his chair.

"Didn't you work on that bill?" he asked, leaning over to give Callie a kiss on her cheek. Callie said nothing.

"Now you have two reasons to call her. Be careful. It might get ugly in the bowels of power."

Callie acknowledged Mike's advice with a nod of her head, but sat quietly as she watched him walk out the front door.

SEVEN

"Cal, it's me. We're running a story in the morning about Senator Lank and I thought you might know something. I'll try your cell. Call me, girl. Love ya."

Callie listened to the message timestamped July 20, 8:34pm. She had seen Kacey's call on her cell phone a little later that evening, but chose not to answer it. At the time, she had been meeting with Senators Shulman, Gorman and Macklin, in Shulman's office, at the Russell Office building. A meeting not unlike others she had been to, but it was strangely a little more petty than usual and one she would not soon forget.

"Look, the way I see it, we can support the Summit bill as is, it's a solid bill. We don't need any of the earmarks you want to stick in there, Callie. I don't see why we have to muddy up the works with pork and destroy a perfectly good bill," Gorman had said.

Callie had not been in the mood for his pontificating. Senator Gorman had a habit of jumping on his high horse and forgetting that most of the people he was preaching to in Congress were all too familiar with his act. Callie's great dislike for Gorman grew over time for various reasons. He tried to strong-arm her on a bill in both 2008 and 2009 and rallied a group of ten senators to kill another bill that would have cost Callie thousands of dollars in bonus money until she stepped in and saved the legislation with some maneuvers of her own. He was a major TV whore and did all he could to grab soundbite opportunities. But the most compelling reason for her disdain had to do with Gorman taking a shot at Callie last year on Fox News. Without actually mentioning her by name, everyone on the Hill knew exactly who he was talking about.

"We get the point, Mike. Except all of us here know what you're really like so save your bullshit for C-Span," Callie had told him. "Bottom line, fellas, is we need this earmark in the bill and with all the pork that's in it now, another 200 million is not going to matter."

"If we do this, Callie, what can we expect in return?" Senator Macklin asked; getting straight to the point, as usual.

"You want more money? We already gave three-hundred thousand to your PAC. What more do you need?"

Senator Shulman seemed irritated and Callie knew he would be as soon as she mentioned the three-hundred thousand she'd given to Macklin. "I don't get it, Callie, I'm asking you for nickels and dimes and he's getting three-hundred thousand?"

Callie rolled her eyes as soon as she saw his lips move. "Charles, last year we gave your Political Action Committee a lot more than that so don't start..."

Shulman interrupted loudly, as if he could ever do it any other way. "That was last year, Ms. Wheeler."

Callie smirked when she heard the condescension in Shulman's voice and shook her head. "I told you, we're not going to start keeping score because I'm not willing to play things that way. If you have a complaint about our donations, call Barry and bitch to him. I don't recall any of you ever crying when we gave you envelopes of unreported cash. So do me a favor and slip this earmark in and stop your whining." Callie's disgust was apparent as she stood up and gathered her things. "There's an extra seventy-five thousand dollars for you on passage of the bill and only on passage of the bill. But if you screw me on this, guys, I will make sure you pay." With that, Callie had lifted her purse onto her shoulder and walked out the office door, secure in the knowledge that she did not make any new friends.

• • •

After that childish meeting from the night before, the last thing Callie wanted was to start her day this way. The clock in her office read 7:30 and she knew it would all implode after Kacey's piece got passed around the mythical water-cooler. Callie sat in her chair and replayed the message from Kacey two more times to see if she could detect anything in her words or her voice. She was keenly aware of the firestorm that was about to erupt and before she could finish the thought, her cell phone rang. Callie ignored the call then turned her chair around and stared out the window at the impressive D.C. skyline in front of her. Less than thirty seconds later, her office phone rang, but Callie let the call go to voicemail. Her cell rang again, but she disregarded it and stared straight ahead into the emerging morning sky. She swiveled her chair slightly to the left and thought for a moment about pouring herself a stiff drink, then abandoned the idea; it was too early in the day for her nervous system. The office phone rang one more time, less than a minute later, followed by another cell phone call. Callie turned back to the window without missing a beat, allowing the parade of calls to continue. She would respond to her phone messages only after she spoke with Kacey. Until then, everyone else would have to wait.

Callie peered at the clock on her wall which she kept five minutes fast, 7:41, then checked her computer clock which had just changed to 7:37. She picked up her office phone, hit a button then pressed speed-dial. Callie turned her chair back around to take in the view of the grey skies above the Nation's Capitol and listened to the phone ring four times before Kacey picked up.

"Helllooo," Kacey said, her tone blessed with lifelong morning grogginess.

"You still asleep?"

"No, not anymore."

"Sorry, I just got your message from yesterday."

Kacey was still in bed, her eyes closed and teetering on the border of dozing off. "You have time for lunch?"

Callie paused for a long moment. She was looking forward to meeting Mike, but at this point didn't think she had much of a choice. She needed to find out what, exactly, Kacey knew. "12:30 at Fridays?"

"See you then," Kacey said. "Good night."

"Night, Kace."

Callie swirled back around to hang up the phone, only to find Barry slouching in a turquoise armchair across from her desk. With everything that was happening, Callie forgot to close her office door and had no idea at what point Barry walked in and made himself at home.

"How long have you been here?"

"Your office or the building?" Barry asked.

"In my office."

"I just walked in and caught the tail end of your conversation," Barry said. "Was that Kacey?"

Callie nodded her head in agreement.

"What does she know?"

"I have no clue, but we're having lunch at 12:30."

Barry stood up and began to pace back and forth. Callie had worked with him long enough to know his nerves were probably shot and when that happened Barry couldn't sit still. Callie always joked that if he were a poker player, she would dry him up.

"We have to keep ourselves out of this," Barry said, sitting back down in the chair for a moment before he stood up again and renewed his pacing. "I don't think the Senators will talk," he said as if he was trying to convince himself of that fact more than establish it as a piece of information for Callie to know.

"Well, someone talked," Callie said, stopping Barry in his tracks.

Barry considered her words for a moment then shook his head as he thought out loud. "I can't see anyone in Lank's office saying anything. None of them know except..."

"Joel? No way." Callie cut him off mid-sentence. "He would never say a word."

Barry leaned over and placed his palms on Callie's desk. "How the hell did this happen, Callie?"

"Maybe you need to talk to Lank. Whatever this is, it had to come from someone close to him."

Barry lifted his hands off the desk and buttoned his jacket as he stood up. "I'll call him, but we need to make sure this goes away and fast."

"I was thinking about doing some damage control, but no one will be in yet," Callie said, nodding her head. "Plus I'd rather wait until we find out what she has."

"Do you trust her?" Barry asked.

"With my life."

Barry started to pace again, but said nothing for close to a minute. He stopped again in front of Callie and looked down at her.

"I think you need to talk to Lank," Callie said, looking her boss in the eye.

"I know these guys, Callie. Most of them won't do anything to incriminate themselves, but if more information comes out, they will stick it to us first, believe me."

Callie took a moment to think about what the consequences would be if one of the Senators talked. She stared at Barry with an all too serious look on her face. "What then?" she asked.

"I'm not sure we can afford to wait that long. We need to get out in front of this and take that option off the table for any of those cowards on Capitol Hill." Barry sat back down in the chair and relaxed a little, at least for the moment. "We might have to go into defense mode right away. "What about Mike?"

"What about him?"

"What did he have to say?"

Callie paused for what seemed like an eternity. "Nothing." What Callie and Mike talked about was none of Barry's business, but either way, it wasn't in her best interest to discuss it with Barry.

Barry stood and turned for the door. Callie followed behind him as if only to move the day forward and that would not start until he was gone from her office. "See what Kacey knows," Barry said. "We may have to handle it ourselves."

Callie looked curiously at Barry, not sure what he meant by that, or how he thought they could handle it themselves. He walked through the open doorway then doubled back with the express purpose of looking in her eyes when he delivered his next piece of advice.

"Callie, we need to close ranks on this and fast. Do not trust anyone." Barry started to leave then turned back to Callie once more.

"And I mean anyone."

Callie watched Barry walk down the hall, then scurried back to her desk, sat down and picked up her cell phone. She leaned back in her chair and dialed Mike's number.

"Hey, you," Mike said when he picked up.

"I think I'm going to need a raincheck on lunch, sweetie."

"Why's that?"

"I have to get together with Kacey...talk about this piece in the paper."

"You have any idea where it came from?" Mike asked.

Callie hesitated a moment before she answered, "Not as of yet, but that's why I have to dump you today." Callie stood up and sashayed over to the corner of her office, kicked off her white Ruthie Davis pumps and spread out on the couch.

"What about dinner? You want to go somewhere?" Mike asked.

Lying down, Callie closed her eyes, and enjoyed a momentary escape from the barrage of land-mines that awaited her. "I'm thinking maybe we could eat in...jacuzzi...your legs wrapped around me...falling asleep in your arms..."

"I guess eating in's not so bad," Mike said with a smile she could not see.

Callie laughed. "You guess not, huh?" She smiled, immersed in the excitement of their solitary secret. "You see Todd, today?"

"I did."

"Did you tell him about us?"

"I did."

"Did he say anything about it?"

"He did."

"Duh...why are you making me work so hard...what did he say?"

"He said you're really hot."

"He always says that. What did he say about us, the marriage thing?"

"He said you made a good decision."

"You made a good decision, as in you Mike, or that I made a good decision as in I, me, Callie?" Callie was engrossed in conversation. She paid no attention to the calls that continued to pound her office phone.

"As in you over there. He said you, Callie, made a good decision."

"Screw him. I mean, are all CIA guys assholes?"

"What do you mean all CIA guys?"

"Mike, you speak eight different languages, what do you think I mean?"

"Are you saying I'm an asshole?"

"I just asked a question..." Callie said.

"Oh, no, I don't care if you called me an asshole just so long as you marry me."

"Don't make me regret my good decision..."

"Ouch. That's cold, Cal."

Callie hung up the phone, stood up from the couch and slipped back into her heels, knowing that play-time was over. She walked to the window and recalled what Barry had said about having to handle it themselves. What was he referring to? What she did know from her own experience with him was when Barry got involved, things did not stay clean and simple for long and usually those who were in the way, did not stay in the way. What she had to do now, she thought, was make sure that anyone close to her did not get in the way.

EIGHT

The Capital Beltway, it could be argued, was the site of the worst congestion in the entire country. Mike Ferguson sat in it on his drive back from the Capitol following a frustrating meeting with Senator Reid McCombs. McCombs was President Conroy's closest ally in the Senate and it is assumed that when Conroy wants to get something off his chest, McCombs does the dirty work for him. The one great thing about being a field agent, Mike thought, was not having to deal with people like McCombs. Mike could never understand why legislators like McCombs, who claimed to have the Country's best interests at heart, constantly behaved as if that concept was the last thing they had on their mind.

"In my opinion, the money we are wasting with this new covert ops thing is shameful," McCombs had told Mike, who sat across from him in the Senator's office.

Mike had been through this drill plenty of times with numerous lawmakers over the past six months, however when it came to McCombs, Mike got the sense that he was acquiring some actual insight as to how the President felt on the matter. If anyone thought to press him on it, Mike would have to admit that he enjoyed playing possum with politicians a little more than he should have and this get together with McCombs would be no exception.

"What exactly is it that you object to, Senator?"

"All of it, actually," McCombs said with disdain in his voice.

"So you object to us pursuing the bad actors who get their rocks off terrorizing innocents all around the world?"

"Bad actors? According to who? You, Mr. Ferguson?"

"I am only one person and others are involved, but yes, I do get paid to make those type of decisions," Mike said.

"You do? Under what constitutional authority?"

"Excuse me, Senator?" Mike was quite familiar with this dance. It was the same one he had tangoed to with the various other politicians who considered the CIA a useless relic of the cold war.

"You heard me," McCombs said. The Senator reached to his right and picked up a conveniently accessible copy of the Constitution, then opened it up to a random page. "Please, Mr. Ferguson, point me in the right direction. I have my Constitution right here," he said as he shook the pamphlet in his hand.

"Senator, I have some critical work that needs my attention," Mike said, trying to remain respectful. "There are some nasty people looking to do severe damage to our country and it would be my preference that they didn't."

McCombs jumped to his feet with the Constitution still in his hand, and railed away at Mike. "Do you think I'm playing games with you? You don't think I'm asking you important questions? Are you not the Deputy Director of Covert Operations?" McCombs stepped out from behind his desk and walked towards Mike in a huff, but still remained far enough away to keep a safe distance between them, just in case. "I would like to know under what provision of the Constitution do you get your authority? Can you at least tell me that?"

Mike stayed calm and collected as he responded knowing it

was sure to piss off the Senator. "I believe it is Congress, sir."

"Bullshit. Don't play games with me, Mr. Ferguson. I am Congress," McCombs said in his blustery best. "As the Majority Leader of the Senate, I can bury your entire disgusting operation." McCombs was prone to grandstanding like this, which could occasionally be effective on ten-second soundbite TV, but not with anyone who knew he was talking out of his ass.

"I am pretty sure our authority comes from Congress."

"Not the Constitution? Is that what you're telling me?"

"Actually, Senator, our authority comes from the Executive Branch and we serve at the will of the President, sir, but of course you control the funding and can cut..."

"You're goddamn right we do," McCombs said, interrupting him loud enough that it brought the secretaries in his outer office to a standstill. "I promise you we will re-assess every dime we've spent on your criminal activity."

Mike had little time for Congressmen who put their careers in front of the safety of the country, but had even less patience for people who wanted to bury the Agency. Especially those who didn't have the guts to say so in public. McCombs and Conroy made a big deal in the press about their slashing of the Intelligence budgets when Conroy was in Congress and President Watkins controlled the White House. When something went wrong, like the Khobar Towers debacle, they were the first ones to blame the very agency they themselves had gutted. "Senator, if you would like to discuss policy issues, Director James would be more than happy to do so. As for me, I really need to get back to work and keep this country safe."

"You keep this country safe from the *bad actors*," McCombs said, using air quotes with his fingers when he mentioned the words 'bad actors'. "But who will keep the country safe from the likes of you?"

Mike raised up a bit in his chair and clenched his jaw, but that was all the emotion he would allow McCombs to see. "Senator, I was okay with you making me wait thirty-five minutes for this meeting. I was also okay when you questioned my authority and even with you calling me in here to say things that should be said to my boss. I get all that. But, I've got serious matters that need my attention including some really bad people trying to harm you, me, and everyone else in this country. So with all due respect, Senator, you are wasting my time and I'm about done with it."

McCombs was back in his seat behind the safety buffer of his desk about to say something when Mike stood up and startled him for a brief moment. The Senator gathered himself long enough to rip into Mike, one last time. "I do not speak for the President," McCombs said, an obvious lie to a trained body language specialist like Mike. "But you should know he is not happy. When budget talks come up, it will be he and I that cut your budget in a substantial way, and it will be a joy to do so. The world is different now. You and those in the CIA like you who fly around the world chasing ghosts that don't exist will have to find another way to get your nuts off."

Mike turned and headed for the exit without saying a word. He opened the door and was all ready to leave, but paused in the doorway. His gut told him to keep walking, but his head told him that just wouldn't cut it. McCombs gazed at Mike's large back as he stood silent for a moment. The Senator was obviously pleased with himself. He had delivered the President's message with a clear blow to the head. However, when compared to what else the President had in store for Mike and the Agency, it amounted to a small jab with plenty follow-ups to come. The smirk on the Senators' face evaporated quickly after Mike turned back around and closed the door behind him. Mike walked up to the desk that separated the two men and leaned over it, his nose inches from the lawmakers' face. "Senator, in my line of work, I can't afford to make mistakes. If I am right 99.9% of the time, I'm a failure and people die. Unlike you, being wrong at my job is not an option. So do what you want with my budget, I really don't care to argue about it," Mike said. "But know one thing. If something goes down, I will throw you under the bus without hesitation. On top of that, I will mention you specifically by name and that you claimed to be doing the President's bidding."

Senator McCombs jumped to his feet, but stayed safely behind the desk. "Go ahead and try that. I'll deny it publicly over and over again and then it's my word against yours. Who do you think they'll believe? A sitting US Senator or a CIA operative in charge of Covert Operations?"

Mike straightened up and pulled out a pen from his shirt pocket. He clicked down on it. "…And then it's my word against yours. Who do you think they'll believe? A sitting US Senator, or a CIA operative in charge of Covert Operations?" Mike watched McCombs slump in disbelief as he listened to his own voice being played right back at him through the speaker located in the middle of the pen.

Mike smiled and slipped the pen back in his shirt pocket. "Honestly?" Mike said with a smile. "I'm thinking they'll believe me. You have a good day, Senator."

• • •

As Mike pulled onto the George Washington Parkway, he was interrupted by the beeping of his cell phone. He'd missed a call from Akiva. He knew there would be no message, that wasn't Akiva's style.

Mike first met Akiva at an intelligence briefing in Langley soon after he had finished his time at 'The Farm' and was awaiting assignment, which he already knew would be somewhere in the Middle East. Akiva Solomon, an Israeli Mossad agent built like a brick house, was without question the smartest man Mike had ever met. He also happened to be the only person to ever kick Mike's ass in a fight. Akiva had challenged Mike to a sparring session soon after they were first introduced and proceeded to teach Mike a lesson in street fighting he would not soon forget.

"What the hell was that?" Mike asked Akiva, who hovered over him with an instant icepack in his left hand. Mike was sprawled on the ground unsure which had taken a worse beating, his ego or his body.

"*Lebatt b'tachat.*"

"To kick ass?" Mike said. "You mean an ass kicking?"

Akiva was surprised with his linguistic skills. "*Atah mayvin ivrit?*" (You understand Hebrew?)

"*Kayn, ani mayvin.*" (Yes, I understand.)

Akiva smiled at the young man who appeared to be a quick study. "How you know Hebrew?"

"I learned it from my sister who dated an Israeli guy. I was maybe ten or eleven...he taught me some, I studied the rest."

"You know many languages?" Akiva asked, as he handed Mike the icepack he'd been holding, then reached into his bag and pulled out another for himself and placed it on his right temple.

"I know a few, I guess."

"How many is a few?"

"Eight," Mike said.

"You know eight languages?"

"Yeah. It's not something I share with people because they think I'm a freak or something, but languages and dialects always came easy to me," Mike said resting the icepack on his left eye. "Dude, what was the stuff you were beating on me with?"

Akiva sat down on a stool near Mike's head. "What do you

mean 'stuff'?"

"Was that Ju-jitsu?"

Akiva smiled. "Ahh...no, no, Krav Maga."

Mike had never seen anything like it before. "Where'd you learn that?"

"Israeli Defense Forces, everyone in the army knows it."

Developed and refined by Imi Lichtenfeld, Krav Maga incorporated years of military training Lichtenfeld had acquired and combined them with the skills he learned as a boxer, wrestler and gymnast. Translated as contact combat, Krav Maga was adopted by the IDF in 1948 and Lictenfeld was its head instructor, teaching thousands of students not only quick strike self defense, but an aggressive offensive attack that rendered most opponents powerless within a few short moments. Mike Ferguson's introduction to the discipline was as eye-opening as it was painful.

Mike tried to sit up, but reconsidered when he felt his ribs attempting to separate from each other. Instead, he relaxed on the ground and continued to nurse his wounds. "Do they know it as well as you?"

Akiva laughed at the question. "No, I know it better." Akiva leaned over and held out his hand. Mike grabbed onto it and took advantage of his new friend's generosity. He sat up, but kept the icepack pressed firmly against his left eye. "Can you teach it to me?"

"It is different than your karate training," Akiva said.

"How so?"

Akiva moved his hands as he spoke "It is more hand-to-hand combat in street. Karate teach power in the punch, we teach less power. Quick strikes take opponent by surprise."

"I like that. Would you teach me?"

"You know Spanish?"

"I do," Mike said.

"Will you teach me?" Akiva asked. "You teach me Spanish, I teach you Krav Maga. We have deal?"

"*B'seder.*"

Akiva smiled hearing Mike agree in Hebrew. "*Mitzooyan*," Akiva said. (Excellent.)

They spent the next two weeks in intensive training before both men had to head out to new assignments. Akiva went back home to Israel and his work with the Mossad while Mike was sent to Libya to collect intelligence on a splinter cell operating freely inside that country and from there to his post in Saudi Arabia. Mike had eventually become proficient at Krav Maga, a tool which served him well on numerous occasions. The two spies had become fast friends and their relationship eventually became more personal than professional. Whenever possible, both men would negotiate their schedules to spend some time together, even if only for a day or two.

Mike had spoken to Akiva less than a month earlier, so it came as a bit of a surprise to hear anything from him so soon afterwards. He parked his car in the CIA parking lot, called his friend, then headed to his office.

"*Habbibi, mah shlomcha?*" (My friend, how is everything with you?)

"Mike, my friend, everything is good by me. How is by you?"

"Great."

"I sent you something. Check my outbox. You have to see, very important," Akiva said.

A great number of communications in the clandestine community were usually done through "dead drops." A dead drop is a form of contact between an intelligence agent and their case officer that does not require them to meet directly. Instead, the information would be left at a pre-assigned destination, or inside an object somewhere out in the public, such as a mailbox, tree stump or a sewer. Over the years, the two friends had devised a system where letters, both English and Hebrew, and numbers, were interchangeable in emails or word documents and the two men were the only ones who knew what the code meant. Moreover, to retain security, they often changed the system every few months, so what the number four represented one month, might be totally different the next. These messages sent from dummy accounts, were deleted every few weeks, and never sent directly to the other party. Instead, they were sent to a bogus address and because that email account was inactive, the email was left in the sent box of the person who sent the email. Mike or Akiva would then go into each other's dummy account, enter the password and find the intended message in the Sent box.

"Will do," Mike said as he unlocked his office door and headed straight for his desk.

"I have to go. Be careful, my good friend. Shalom," Akiva said.

"Shalom."

Mike sat down and logged into his secured CIA account. He proceeded to sign into Akiva's dummy account, entered the password, then checked the Sent box. He needed less than a minute to decode the message. He printed it out and placed it on his desk then leaned back in his chair, immersed in thought. A few moments later, he straightened up and searched for something else on his desk. Within a minute, he found what he was looking for. He studied it, thought about it for a moment, then put it back where he found it. Mike turned back to his computer, Googled something else, and after reading the results, printed the information and left it on his desk with the two previous pieces. He picked up one more report, read a few lines, stared at the print on the page then placed the memo next to the other three he had set to the side. He rechecked each transcript three or four times then sat in silence when he realized what he might be dealing with. Mike picked up his cell phone and called his partner.

"Todd, I think we got a problem."

NINE

Callie checked her watch before stepping out of her office building and onto the K Street sidewalk. She headed west towards 21st Street. Back when she first started at M&G, Callie used to enjoy strolling the downtown area on her way to a mid-day meeting or an early dinner reservation, but now she found it increasingly difficult to saunter the streets without bumping into someone she knew. For most people that wouldn't be a problem, but for the number one lobbyist in the nation's capitol, it put limits on availability that she didn't have. Callie soon hired a car service to drive her from place to place. She was through with encountering random acquaintances she barely recognized, and more often than not, spending the majority of their conversation trying to figure out how to end it.

But she was walking today. The TGI Fridays where she had arranged to meet Kacey was less than a five-minute walk from her office. The whirlwind morning showed no signs of slowing down and Callie thought it might not be a bad idea to step out and grab some fresh air. Her mind danced as she hung a left onto 21st street. Before she could turn the corner, Jenny Bledsoe, the chief of staff for Marcy Stillman, was rambling straight towards her. Bledsoe's boss, the newly elected freshman Senator from Oklahoma, defeated long time incumbent Harry Males in a hotly contested run-off race that came down to less than one-hundred thousand votes. More importantly, it deadlocked the Senate at a 50/50 split between Republicans and Democrats.

Callie knew Bledsoe from the time she spent working in Mike Gorman's press office. They had gone back and forth a few times regarding Gorman's irresponsible appearances in the media including what he had said about Callie on television a year or so ago. Callie wanted nothing to do with Jennie and she felt confident Bledsoe harbored the same disdain for her, that is, until she accepted her new position with Senator Stillman.

"Callie Wheeler, I've been trying to get a hold of you for the longest time."

Callie knew Bledsoe was lying, but she played her part. She looked forward to seeing where the conversation was going to end up. "I'm sorry, Jenny, I must have missed your messages," Callie said with a business-like attitude. "Been busy with the election season heating up…I'm sure you understand."

"Don't worry about it." Jenny Bledsoe stood barely five feet tall, with short black hair, sunk in eyes and a small stud on the side of her pierced nose. Her pale features and emaciated body looked similar to those of a drug addict in need of rehab. Callie always felt a little awkward towering over her the way she did, but was comforted by the feeling she got that the Senator's aide was actually afraid of her. Naturally, Callie tapped into that fear and enjoyed the power it brought, whether real or imagined.

"Callie, I wanted to see if we could set up a meeting, with me, you, and the Senator to introduce you to her and have you get to know her a little. She's a firecracker and I think you'd like her a lot."

Callie knew all about Stillman and wasn't going to bend over backwards to search her out though she was intrigued by what Bledsoe's new boss could potentially do for her. She viewed Stillman as a lightweight who came to Congress by bludgeoning her opponent with money. It comes in handy when you're the sole heir of the fortune from one of the wealthiest oil families in the state of Oklahoma. She thought about the possibilities and although Callie was careful which new members of Congress she dealt with, Bledsoe gave her an opening to explore and she could not let it pass without further inspection.

"Did the Senator actually mention that she wanted to meet with me or is this idea coming from you alone?" Callie asked, knowing Jenny would answer the way she thought Callie would want to hear.

"The Senator asked me who the most influential people in Washington were, and naturally, I mentioned your name. I told her that we had a very good relationship due to all our past experiences working together and stuff."

It came as quite the surprise to Callie to learn that they had "a very good relationship," primarily since they couldn't stand the sight of each other. She continued to play along even though she knew Jenny was full of crap. "I'll tell you what. Send me an email with three potential appointment times that work for Senator Stillman and I'll check them against my calendar and see if we can make it work. How's that sound?"

Jenny couldn't stomach the thought of being dictated to by Callie Wheeler and her response reflected that. "Callie, the Senator is very busy, as you know, so it might be hard to find one date not to mention three. Maybe you could send me three dates that work for you and..."

Callie had entertained her long enough. "Jenny, either send me the dates or pass on it, but don't start playing games with me.

I don't have the time see whose tits are bigger, okay?"

"I was just saying..."

"I know you were just saying, but I don't care," Callie said. The irritation in her voice signaled the end of the discussion. "If you want to meet with me that's what you'll have to do, if not, I'm not losing any sleep over it."

Bledsoe was visibly uncomfortable with Callie and having to beg someone she despised so intensely. "I'll see if we can find some time."

"You do that. I have to run, but it was nice catching up with you," Callie said, lying without blinking an eye. She saved the good-bye and ignored Bledsoe's response as she walked down 21st Street before crossing over Pennsylvania Avenue. Callie hesitated as she approached the restaurant, stopping for a brief moment then backtracking a few feet and turning left onto Pennsylvania. A few hundred yards before the Kaiser Permanente building, she reached into her purse and pulled out a small notebook and a pen. She tore out a piece of paper and hurriedly jotted down a note:

Mark,

Been awhile. I think we need to talk when

you have a few minutes.

My love to Karen,

Callie

She folded the piece of paper and slipped the notebook back into her purse. She stepped inside the Kaiser offices and approached the reception desk.

"Could you please give this note to Doctor Goldstein?" Callie asked, extending it to the nurse behind the counter.

"Doctor Goldstein won't be in until later this afternoon," the nurse said in a very pleasant tone as she took the note from Callie's hand. "Would you like me to put this in an envelope Miss...?"

"Wheeler, Callie Wheeler, and an envelope is not necessary,

ma'am."

The nurse smiled at Callie. "I will leave it in his mailbox then, if that's okay with you."

"That would be great," Callie said with a smile. "Thank you and have a wonderful rest of your day." Callie exited the building and hurried around the corner to meet Kacey.

As soon as Callie stepped into the restaurant, she spotted Kacey in a corner to the left of the bar. Kacey waved to her the moment they caught each other's eyes. Callie glided over to the table and the two women hugged as if they hadn't seen each other in years before taking their seats.

"You look amazing," Callie said. "Seems this promotion fits you well."

"I'm lovin' it."

Callie first met Kacey at Kirby Park, just off of Main Street in Kingston, when they were both toddlers. Once their mothers had seen how well they played together, they arranged their schedules to make sure they were at the park at the same time each day. As the two girls grew older, they became inseparable, spending virtually every free moment together. Kacey's first boyfriend in the highly competitive world of middle school dating came to her via Callie. She had introduced Kacey to Billy Markum at the Cherry Blossom Festival. Billy had a huge crush on Callie, calling her numerous times each day and peeping in her home on weekends. Callie convinced Billy that he stood a much better chance with Kacey, so, as most pre-pubescent boys do, he went for it. Their relationship lasted almost a week, which in sixth grade, is like a lifetime.

They had gone to separate elementary and middle schools, Callie in Kingston, Kacey across the bridge in Wilkes-Barre, until Kacey convinced her parents to move five miles away so the girls could attend the same high school together. It was at Valley

West where Callie looked after Kacey and they became the most popular girls in the class of '99. During their senior year, Callie refused to run for homecoming queen, because doing so meant she would have to run against Kacey, who had dreamed about winning the crown since the fifth grade. Not only did Callie refuse to run, but she garnered enough votes from friends to guarantee Kacey the victory. Kacey never forgot the gesture, one that Callie put almost no stock in. "It's what friends do," she said afterwards without giving it a second thought. They spent alternating weekends at each other's homes and would go on vacations with each other's families. Kacey's wavy auburn hair and soft facial features had always drawn people towards her, but as pretty as she was, she wasn't Callie. In all the time they'd spent together, Kacey never heard Callie utter a word about her own looks, but would make it a point to tell Kacey she was the prettiest girl in the room. Kacey knew better, but liked that Callie always went out of her way to make her feel special.

"Do you like this job better?" Callie asked, referring to Bob Kravitz finally promoting Kacey to the political section of the paper.

"I really do."

"It's too bad they didn't assign you to the social page," Callie said as she slowly lifted her right hand from under the table and raised it in front of her face, pretending to move her pony-tailed hair out of her eyes.

"The social page? That's newspaper hell. Why would you..." Kacey stopped mid-sentence when she noticed the ring in front of Callie's mouth. Her scream reverberated throughout the eatery. Rightfully assuming everyone had to be gawking at her, Kacey quickly covered her mouth and screamed into her hand, "Oh my god, Cal, when did this happen?"

"Two nights ago," Callie said. She raised her other hand in an attempt to settle Kacey down. "Now, before you get angry at me, we didn't tell a soul. My parents don't even know yet...you're the only person that knows."

Kacey grabbed Callie's hand and brought the ring closer for inspection. "How could you do this to me?" she said while she checked the stone for blemishes and coloration.

Callie laughed at her best friend, "It's all about you, is it?"

"Damn right," Kacey said, ogling the two-carat diamond.

"We just wanted to share something between ourselves. Please don't be upset with me," Callie begged for understanding from the only person she actually wanted it from.

"Okay, I'm going to forgive you this one time, but next time you'd better..."

"Next time?"

"You know what I mean. When you get this kind of big news...wow, this is so awesome." Kacey released Callie's hand and pulled a napkin from the dispenser on the table.

"Are you crying, Kace?"

Kacey wiped the tears from her eyes. "Yeah, so what? One of us has to." Kacey blew her nose gently into the napkin. "I'm just so happy for you."

"Aww, thank you," Callie said, releasing the band around her hair and letting the long brown strands fall just past her shoulders.

Kacey took a moment to gather herself. "How did he ask you?"

"Believe me, it wasn't all that romantic. We were arguing over my dad's rule, ya' know..."

"The Sleep In Your Own Room Rule?"

Callie nodded her head. She was comforted by the familiarity of her best friend. "Yup, that's the one. Anyway, he basically says why get married when we have everything we want now. You know the same old BS he's always saying. Then he acts like he's leaving and gets down on one knee, reaches under my pillow, pulls out a box and...that was kind of it."

"It's about time," Kacey said.

"I know, right?"

"When we gonna celebrate?"

"We were thinking next weekend at the beach, but I've got it rented out until September. Sort of sucks."

"We gotta do something..."

"We will, we're just not sure yet."

"I hope you'll call me and let me know," Kacey said with a mischievous smile.

"Ha-ha, very funny. What about you? Still seeing David?"

"Not anymore. I guess he didn't like that I asked him whose panties were under my bed."

"Ouch."

"Whatever, better now than later." Kacey glanced at her watch then took a sip of water from the glass in front of her.

"Cal, I have to get to the Hill for Lank's press conference."

Kacey's comment jolted Callie. "Lank's press conference?"

"Yeah, we heard about it around 11:30."

Callie, who had been a little uneasy broaching the subject, jumped on the opening and took the conversation where she wanted it to go in the first place. "About Lank. I don't know him all too well and I have no idea about this campaign money you wrote about."

"Don't know what it is Cal, but it feels to me like there's something bigger here."

Callie knew there was, but wanted to hear what Kacey thought about it before offering any opinion. "What makes you say that?"

"Not really sure. Instinct, I guess."

"Anything's possible, but keep in mind, this is D.C.," Callie said, leaving her comment vague on purpose.

"This one just feels different," Kacey said.

Callie pulled a carrot off Kacey's plate and took a bite. "How did you find all this out?"

"Yesterday I get this e-mail, from whom I have no idea, Senator Lank has been getting cash payments from a developer," Kacey said as she ate a spoonful of the chocolate dessert then tapped her mouth twice with a napkin. "Seems to me the Lank bill had more to do with Jonas Foster than it did the public good."

Callie hesitated for a moment acting surprised. "You mean the Lank-Gorman bill? What does that have to do with Jonas?"

"I'm not really sure." Kacey shook her head as she swallowed some water. "Cal, you really don't know anything about this?"

"I really don't."

"Off the record?" Kacey asked.

"Off the record."

Kacey took one last drink then stood up. "I have to run." Callie rose to kiss her on the cheek.

Kacey flung her purse onto her right shoulder then picked up her black leather bag that contained all her working notes, and turned to Callie. "If you knew something you'd tell me, right, Cal?"

"Kacey, we've been best friends longer than I can remember. Of course I'd tell you."

"I know you would. Thanks for meeting me so quickly...I'll call ya' later." Kacey started to leave the restaurant, but stepped back towards Callie. "Tell Mike I said he made a great decision."

Callie laughed. She remembered her conversation from earlier in the day. "I think I'll do that."

"Later, Cal-pie"

"Bye, Mer-maid"

Kacey blew her a kiss on her way out of the restaurant. Callie reached into her purse and nervously fumbled her Revlon Super Lustrous lipstick. She ran 'Cherries in the Snow' slowly across her lips, then did it once more. She pulled a napkin from the table dispenser and pressed her mouth twice against it, eventually dropping it on Kacey's dessert plate. Callie inched her chair closer and rested both her elbows on the table. She ran her hands through her soft brown hair, gathered it up and wrapped her flowered ponytail band around the back of it. Callie had never been in this position before and was unsure of how to handle it moving forward. For the first time since they had met twenty-seven years ago, Callie Wheeler had lied to her best friend.

TEN

August 3, 2011

Chairman Rice pounded his gavel once again as the murmurs in the hearing room only intensified the noise. "Quiet please!"

The day was still young, yet the worry on Rice's face belied his usual calm demeanor. His decision to have Callie testify looked to be a sound one at the time, but now Rice began to have doubts of his own. With the entire country watching the proceedings, the real problem at this point seemed to be that any backtrack would look like the Senate was running scared and afraid to hear what Callie had to say. Rice took a macro view of the situation and settled on the best course of action from his seat as Chairman. If Callie testified in front of them, Rice argued, at least they had a chance to respond or redirect, which was the main reason why her uninterrupted opening statement had become so problematic. In hindsight, giving this woman an open forum turned out to be a very bad idea, but now that she started, Congress could not cut her off without being accused of hypocrisy by stifling the one witness who could shed light on the very problem they had promised to fix. Instead, the entire dais was at her mercy and Rice understood that as well as anyone. "Ms. Wheeler, it is quite abnormal for this body to entertain an opening statement without a copy in advance for the entire committee."

Callie, confident as ever, knew she struck a nerve and put them on the defensive. Any hope the legislators entertained about Callie somehow letting them off the hook soon fell by the wayside. "Mr. Chairman, I'm not really too concerned about what is normal in the Senate."

"Well you should be!" Rice startled the entire room with his uncharacteristic outburst, the lone exception being the woman it was intended for. The information Callie knew regarding each and every member who was staring straight at her, made her extremely dangerous. She also recognized it granted her the leverage and the confidence to continue in the face of all the hostility directed her way.

"With all due respect, Senator, I'm testifying on my own volition and only because you said yourself that the country needed to understand what happened here. I am taking you at your word, even though I know with most of you up there, that's a losing proposition. I can give you all the information you're looking for and then some. The choice is yours."

Callie stared up at Chairman Rice undaunted. She'd made her proverbial bed and she came prepared to lie in it. Callie knew all she had done since taking the job at M&G and while she could not take it back, she felt the need to expose it and the behavior of the others who had infested the process. Just maybe, she thought, the American people would finally pay attention to what was happening in Washington and wrestle back control of their government from the massive culture of corruption. The only obstacle in their way were members of Congress, the most powerful of whom, were sitting in judgment before her.

Rice removed his bifocals and placed them on the desk in front of him. "Ms. Wheeler, I'm going to confer with my colleagues for a moment after which time I'll decide if your unauthorized opening statement will be allowed to continue."

Callie poured herself a glass of water, lifted it with her left hand and before bringing it to her lips, leaned into her attorney sitting to her right and whispered in his ear. "They can screw me all they want on this…I'm still going to say what I want to say." Callie moved away from Goodman, took a long drink, then placed the glass back on the table.

Callie's defiant behavior left Goodman feeling uneasy, but she'd also surprised him by the ease at which she handled herself. He turned to Callie and offered her the counsel he'd been paid to give. "I'm not sure if you're trying to get them pissed at you, but whether that was your intention or not, you've done a hell of a job," he said in a voice barely above a whisper.

"Do I look worried?" Callie said, still facing her attorney. Goodman looked at her for a moment and shook his head in agreement to her rhetorical question. Peeking over his right shoulder, he caught a glimpse of twelve huddled Senators surrounding the chairman, their arms moving nervously with a number of them talking at the same time. Looking back at his client, he smiled. He no longer wondered who seemed more uneasy.

"Callie, it doesn't matter. If they give you a chance to walk, then walk. At the very least you have to consider it."

Callie pushed her chair back and bent over slightly, reaching under the witness table to pull a compact from her purse. She understood the signal she was sending, not only to the Senators at the front of the room, but to a larger audience, both in the gallery and across the nation. Her calculated move was meant to agitate, which is exactly what it did. Callie checked her makeup, fluffed her hair and smiled, then purposely positioned the compact next to her, knowing what sort of effect it would have. She did not care.

"I'm not going to think about it, Miles. I need to do this and

I'll deal with the consequences later."

"But there are other ways…"

"No, this is the right thing to do," Callie said interrupting her lawyer. "I've ignored the right thing for too many years. It has to stop."

Chairman Rice returned to his chair and called the session back to order. "Ms. Wheeler, what you have done here is wrong and shows a total disregard for the integrity of this body. Nevertheless, I have decided to let you continue with your statement and even give you some latitude. It is my hope, however, that you'll take this opportunity to salvage whatever is left of your reputation. You can start by addressing this committee with the proper respect is deserves."

Callie's face conveyed her contempt for the Chairman and the rest of the members as she pulled her microphone closer. "Senator, please don't lecture me on the integrity of this body or how I should address you. Spare me the self-serving notions on the sanctity of this institution and the illusion of greatness that sits pompously before me," Callie said, then glared at Senator Shulman. "I know all too well about the integrity of this body and in all honesty, I believe I am showing each of you the exact respect you deserve."

There was a flurry of camera flashes and more talk from the gallery. Chairman Rice gaveled the room quiet. Callie took advantage of the silence before Rice could respond. "I arrived at M&G that first day, nervous, but excited at the prospect of working on Capitol Hill and hoping to effect this country for the better. Little did I know at the time, my life would take me in directions I never could have imagined and it all started the moment I sat down early that first morning…"

Monday, January 2, 2006—Six Years Earlier

"Ms. Wheeler, your schedule will be synced with the one I keep for you on my computer, every morning at 6:00 AM. To access it, just hold down the shift button, and press the letter S."

Callie was in her new office at 1900 K Street NW, sitting behind the second most expensive desk she had ever seen. Against the wall to her left, empty bookcases and an old metal filing cabinet surrounded an ugly cactus and a tall empty vase that stood in the corner. The beige paint on the walls gave the room a bland appearance, salvaged only by the large bay window behind her that unveiled a tenth floor view of the D.C. skyline. Sitting across from Callie and dressed in polyester grey pants and a Kmart twill brown top was Donna Walkin, her new secretary who at the moment, acted very much like Callie's boss as she went over all the pertinent information Callie needed to know.

"You have a meeting with Derek in less than five minutes and while you're with him, I will be setting you up with a copy machine passcode and a parking garage access key. I usually arrive here by 8:00 AM each day, and leave at 4:30. My lunch break is at 12. I don't do overtime, ever. If you need anything, I'll be at my desk arranging your direct deposit and all the different e-mail accounts and whatnot that you will need to have here."

Callie accessed her schedule by following her secretary's instructions. She took a moment to familiarize herself with the format, quickly scanning the information, then scribbled a note on her day planner. She lifted her head. "It says on this schedule that I have a meeting on Capitol Hill at 10:30. Who is that meeting with?"

Donna gave her an unwelcome smirk then stood up and walked to the door. "Mr. Gladstone will fill you in on all of that. Welcome again to the firm and I will be outside if you need me," Donna said in a matter of fact tone then closed the door behind her and left Callie alone to get used to her new surroundings. Callie studied the decor and wondered how anyone could spend their days in such a dreary depressing atmosphere. She wrote another note in her day planner reminding herself to ask Derek what changes she could make to her office in an attempt to produce a more livable work environment. Next, she pulled out two 5x7 pictures from her purse and placed one at each corner of her desk. The first was a picture of Mike holding an umbrella and kissing her on the cheek, the emerging sun in the background glistening off her wet hair. The second was a photo of her and Kacey locked arm in arm, taken on the day of her Law School graduation. Callie searched her computer for some sort of radio station that would have to suffice as background music until she could transfer her own music library onto iTunes. Before she could settle on a selection, Derek Gladstone knocked on her door and opened it without giving Callie a chance to react.

"Everything okay?"

"Perfect," Callie said with a smile. "There is one thing Mr. Gladsto...Derek."

"Fire away."

"My office?" Callie looked around for effect. "May I re-decorate it?"

"Any way you'd like. I, myself, am partial to red and white, but whatever makes you comfortable, have at it."

"Thank you, Derek," Callie said with a bright-eyed smile.

Derek motioned Callie to the conference table. Callie followed. He held out a chair and waited for her to sit, then sat down next to her.

"I brought you some reading materials, a sort of what-to-expect manual that you can read when you have a few minutes." Derek slid the folders towards her. "What I wanted to talk with you about now, though, were the kind of things that are not written down in the manual."

"Should I get some paper?"

"I'd prefer you didn't, Callie. What I'm about to tell you... well, we try not to write any of it down."

Callie shook her head, frustrated that she didn't pick up on that. "Which is why it's not written down in the manual," Callie said as she shook her head again, disappointed with her initial reaction.

"I don't have to tell you that we are an instrumental cog, if not the most instrumental cog, in how things get done in Washington." Derek straightened his tie then pressed down on his lapel. "What is critical, is that they like you. Get them to like you and you will own them."

"By them, I'm assuming you mean Congressmen."

"Actually, I am speaking about all of them. Congressmen, their staff, their janitors...but, yes, mostly Congressmen."

Callie nodded and crossed her legs, which Derek noticed and took a moment to enjoy.

"There will be some Congressmen who will try to bully you. They're not testing you, they're just assholes. You need to show them you won't be pushed around, but you also need to do that creatively so they don't know, that you know, they're assholes. You'll need the assholes, so be smart."

Callie kept listening.

Derek leaned his forearms on the table. "There will also be some Congressmen who will hit on you from the time you arrive until the time you leave and then hassle you after you've left. You'll need them too. Whatever urges you have to tell them to fuck off, don't. Always remember: you are in the people business."

"Never let them see me sweat?"

Derek smiled and bobbed his head. "Something like that," Derek said. "To be successful at this job, Callie, you have to find a way to get the members to believe they're telling you what to do. But the real secret to the job is getting the members to do what you want them to do."

Derek watched his pupil. She had been concentrating on his every word. "Is this making any sense?"

Callie nodded and Derek continued. "Most importantly, and never forget this: they all think they're the shit. Make them think you think they are...and you do whatever you need to do to get their votes."

Callie took special note of his last comment, but said nothing.

"We get paid an enormous amount of money from our clients to deliver results..." Derek's words faded as he searched for the correct way to phrase his next sentence. He knew Callie's reaction to what he was about to say would define how effective she was going to be at this job. He pushed back from the table and paused a moment. Glancing at his dark blue Valentino jacket, he wiped some imaginary dirt from his sleeve before getting to the point.

"Callie, the fact is, when you walk into a room, everyone stops to look."

Callie was not sure she liked where this was going, but again, kept quiet and retained eye contact with her new boss.

"We need you to use that to our advantage."

Callie had lived her entire life with the nuisance of her looks inserting itself into every situation. His words did not surprise her, they just left her feeling as if she had been there before. "What exactly are you asking me to do?"

"Look, Callie, you're a very bright girl. You have to know that women who look like you...well, they have a distinct advantage when it comes to dealing with men. In the same way that I know that I can get women to do what they do not necessarily want to do, simply because I look a certain way. I don't apologize for it, it's just a fact."

"I understand what you mean, Derek. I'm just not always comfortable thinking about myself in that way."

He jumped on her words before she had time to think about them. "You might as well get used to it, because quite honestly, there hasn't been a woman who looked like you on the Hill in I don't know how long. These bastards will be on you like white on rice," Derek said. "So basically you have two options. You can try and fend them off, complain about them and get nowhere, or you can use it to your advantage...our advantage and get done what we need to get done."

Derek's assessment left Callie feeling awkward. She repositioned herself in her seat. "Just tell me that my appearance wasn't the only reason I got this job."

"Callie, you have nothing to worry about. You were without question the most impressive candidate we had apply for the position and we'd have hired you if you looked like Alfred E. Newman. But, I'd be lying if I didn't tell you that you bring to the job certain assets that most others don't. We'd be fools not to capitalize on that."

Callie appeared to still be a little uneasy, although she wasn't about to quit her job over it. She crossed and uncrossed her legs, unconscious of her skirt that rode halfway up her thigh. Derek, once again, took advantage of the opportunity and stole a glance. "I can't say I'm all that comfortable with the idea, but I do understand it and appreciate your honesty."

"You'll be the talk of D.C. and not just Capitol Hill." Derek said trying to move the conversation in another direction. "In about an hour, you and I will make our way over there and I'll introduce you to some people who you'll need to know. Trust me, you'll understand everything we just spoke about before the day is out."

Derek stood up and headed for the door. "I'll send up some

brochures and you can pick out whatever furnishings you like. Try to keep the cost under fifty thousand, if possible."

Callie smiled and stood up, not sure she heard him correctly. "Fifty thousand dollars?"

"You need more?"

Callie chuckled. "Oh no, fifty thousand is plenty. Are you sure about that number?"

Derek opened the door, then turned around. "Compared to what you're about to do for this firm, fifty thousand is a bargain."

• • •

For someone with the charisma and personality of Derek Gladstone, the Capital Rotunda was the equivalent of a candy store to a child. On this particular visit however, he had come to the Capitol to introduce the newest member of his firm to the men and women who worked there each day. Callie followed Derek inside and could actually feel her heart skip a beat. She surveyed the circular lobby-type room and smiled with excitement as she viewed the eighteen tall Corinthian columns that surrounded the Rotunda. The columns supported a coffered dome whose glazed window, at its peak, flooded the entire space with natural light. The marble walls and twin marble staircases accented the structure and the corridors used to connect both houses of Congress. Callie stood behind Derek and scanned the many faces that until this moment she had only seen on television. Glancing over Derek's right shoulder, Callie observed Senator Wilbur Lank, a good old southern boy from Memphis, Tennessee. He walked towards Derek with a smile.

"How 'bout that. If it isn't my favorite D.C. lawyer. Haven't heard from you in a few weeks, buddy. How've ya' been?" Lank extended his hand to Derek.

"Great, Senator...and you?"

"Shot a 38 on the back nine yesterday. Still sort of jacked about that," Lank said as Derek shook his hand. "When you and I gonna' play again, Counselor?"

Derek had played enough rounds of golf with Lank to know that hell would have to freeze over before he shot a 38. "With you shooting that number, just about never," Derek played along with his fabrication.

"Hadn't took you for a coward there, counselor." Lank slapped Derek on the back. "I was hoping I could get you and your partner back on the links. How 'bout St. Andrews?" Lank was referring to the famous golf course in England that played host to the British Open every year.

"I'll talk to Barry. Maybe we can work something out before too long." Derek was prepared to entice one of the most influential leaders of the Senate with his new game changer. "I'm sure we can arrange an outing for you and a few of your colleagues."

"That'd be somethin' we'd be fixin' to do if the opportunity presented itself," Lank said.

Derek turned to Callie, who had been waiting patiently off to his right, and motioned for her to join them. "Callie Wheeler, meet Senator Wilbur Lank, one of the most powerful men in the Senate and all of Congress. I believe he's in his sixth term, isn't that right Senator?"

When Senator Lank finally noticed Callie he could not help but stare. "Soon to be a seventh if I don't screw things up too bad. Ms. Wheeler, is it?" Lank said, extending his hand.

Callie found it hard to stay calm standing face-to-face with one of the most influential people in America. She sensed her heart rate increase dramatically and felt a rush of adrenaline travel through her body just as it had during her playing days. Ever since she could remember, she aspired to work in politics and now to be standing in the halls of Congress sharing ideas with its members was almost too much for Callie to wrap her head around. She also knew she had only one chance to make a first impression. The importance of staying professional while she spoke to Lank would be critical although if the need arose, she knew she might have to be flirtatious as well. As Callie prepared to address Senator Lank, Derek's words from earlier in the day echoed in her head: "You do whatever you need to do to get their votes…"

"I have appreciated your work for a long time, Senator," Callie said, shaking his hand.

"The pleasure is most assuredly mine," Lank said. He covered her right hand with his left and let it rest there for what felt like an eternity.

"Senator, Ms. Wheeler is our newest associate and she'll be working with us on the Walker Investment Bill I mentioned to you last week."

"Ms. Wheeler, I'm assuming you're good at what you do if you're working for M&G, but you'll have to be one hell of a magician on that bill." Lank finally released Callie's hand, but could not stop staring at her body, something Callie quickly took notice of.

"May I ask how you're voting, Senator?" Callie asked.

"I am voting against it."

"Oh…" Callie said, feigning surprise, "is that right?"

"Probably not what you wanted to hear…"

Callie bobbed her head in agreement, "No, not what I wanted to hear…"

"It's a bad bill…just don't think I can support it."

Callie smiled as she looked into the Senator's eyes. After vacationing up and down her body, they had finally settled on her face. "And here I thought you were on the leading edge of progress, Senator. Obviously, I must have been mistaken."

Senator Lank seemed surprised by her candor and his body language gave it away. Not expecting that type of response from someone he'd just met, Lank reached into his jacket pocket, took out a comb and ran it through his greying hair a few times nervously. It was quite evident that Callie touched a nerve and she knew it.

"I'll have you know I am on the forefront of progress in the Senate…"

"That's what is so surprising--"

"Not at all, I just don't see the value of another tax break for wealthy citizens." Lank returned the comb inside his jacket.

Callie, wearing a bright red blouse and a blue pencil skirt that accentuated every curve on her body, flirtatiously crossed her left foot in front of her right one, which drew the attention of the Senator. "Maybe we need to better educate you and the other Senators on the brilliance of Walker," she said, as Derek stood off to the side and proudly watched Callie take the Senator head-on.

"And how do you suppose we do that, Miss Wheeler?"

"Senator, the Walker Bill will effect each one of the fifty states, including yours. I would think that visiting a few of those states would be something you and your colleagues might have an interest in doing."

"Quite honestly, Ma'am, we're quite busy here on the Hill, as I'm sure your boss must have told you--"

"It was one of the first things he told me," Callie said, assured that Derek never mentioned anything even remotely close to that.

"We really don't have time to go gallivanting from state to state for a bill that, quite honestly, has no chance of ever getting passed."

"I'm sorry to hear that, Senator…"

"Please, there's no need to apologize."

"It's really too bad, though. I had hoped to fly some Senators and their families out to Hawaii to see what Walker can do for a community, since they have already enacted the law on the state level."

As she spoke, Callie took note of the change in Lank's demeanor with one simple mention of an all-expenses-paid island vacation.

"Sadly, I see you've already made up your mind, and being that you are so very busy, I realize that maybe it was naive on my part to think you would be interested," Callie said, then extended her hand. "I'm sorry to have bothered you, Senator. I hope we can work together in the future."

Senator Lank ignored her outstretched arm. "Ms. Wheeler, I hope I didn't give you the impression that I was firm in my vote against Walker. I think maybe an educational excursion just might be worth the effort."

"Are you sure, Senator? If you're too busy, I can talk to Senator Lucas. He seems to be open to learning more about the Walker Bill." Callie had no idea if Lucas would be willing to hear about the legislation, but she and everyone else who followed politics was well aware that the two men did not like each other. If Callie wanted to get Lank's attention, mentioning Lucas by name would be the way to go about it.

Lank wrapped his arm around Callie's shoulders and gave her a gentle squeeze, which again seemed to have taken a little too long. "Ms. Wheeler, I think maybe you misunderstood me. I never said I was dead set against the bill. I said it didn't have a lot of support. But I'd like to get behind an educational effort on this and find out more about Walker and how it can help my constituents."

Derek, who had witnessed the entire exchange, smiled like a proud father who just witnessed his daughter's first prom date.

"Senator, I have always admired your open-mindedness along with your willingness to listen to new ideas. It's possible I was right about you after all," Callie smiled and innocently tugged at her blouse.

"Seems you've misjudged me, Ms. Wheeler. I've been in this body for more than thirty years. There's much you can learn from someone like me and a lot more you can learn about me," Lank said. "You don't last this long on the Hill without being fair and open-minded."

Lank smiled and began moving toward the senate chamber. "Derek, call me when you have St. Andrews set up and honey, let's get together later this week and see if we can't get this educational thing going," he said, pointing to Callie, as he continued to walk away. Passing Lank as if on cue, Senators Steven Branch and Hiram Dansby had Derek in their sights.

"Derek, I heard you were up here this morning. How goes it?" Senator Branch reached out his hand towards Derek, but at the last instant shuffled past him and turned his attention to Callie. "And who might you be? More importantly, why haven't we met?"

Derek jumped in before Callie had a chance to respond. Like everyone else who'd spent time on the Hill, Derek knew of Branch's reputation as a womanizer. "Senator Branch this is our new associate, Callie Wheeler. She'll be helping us out on the Walker Bill."

"Pleasure to meet you, Senator." Callie looked him in the eye, but didn't greet his hand with hers.

"What? No handshake? So, I'm guessing a hug would be out of the question?"

Senator Dansby, a two term Republican Senator from Alaska, saved Callie from the awkward moment by stepping towards her and introducing himself. "Ms. Wheeler, my name is Hiram Dansby."

"Good morning, Senator. Congratulations on your award," Callie said and extended her hand to meet his.

Dansby recently had been recognized by a local magazine in his home state for integrity in the public sector. Standing nearly six feet tall, Dansby owned a long face with a slightly squared off chin, yet was a captivating presence with a confident, but humble demeanor. "I was hoping it would remain a local story, but the Washington Times took care of that for me."

"It's still very impressive," Callie said with a smile.

Senator Branch, worried about being overshadowed by his colleague, stepped closer to Callie and steered the conversation back towards himself. "So tell me, this Walker Bill any good?"

"Very good. Have you decided which way you're going to vote?"

"No, not just yet, but I'm open to persuasion if I can be convinced that this bill would help my state."

"I would expect you to feel that way, Senator," Callie said, consciously stepping closer to Branch as she noticed him looking at her legs.

"Of course, it would also have to make good financial sense for the country." He worked his eyes towards her hips.

"Of course."

Branch gradually moved up to her chest, staring at it with no reservation. It was something Callie had grown used to, men who spent more time talking to her breasts than to her face.

"When would you like to get together to discuss the bill?" Callie asked, as she gently ran her hand through her hair.

"I have some time during lunch tomorrow, if you're available?" Branch could not stop looking at her, ever so gently shaking his head in the process, enamored with the alluring woman who toyed with his imagination. "I can give you as much time as you need."

"If you will excuse me for just one moment gentleman, I will check my schedule." Callie reached into her purse, pulled out her

Blackberry, and searched her calendar. "Would 12:30 work?"

Branch smiled wide, "12:30, would be perfect."

Callie turned to Senator Dansby. "Should I pencil you in as well, Senator?"

As soon as Callie finished her question, she knew she'd made a mistake. Branch grabbed the moment and stuck his nose where it didn't belong, "Hiram has a vote in committee at 12:30. Isn't that right Hiram?"

Derek, who had been standing off to her left monitoring the conversation, jumped in and offered his own opinion. "I think a one-on-one meeting would be best in this situation, Callie." Derek looked at her and signaled with his eyebrows, something she recognized instantly. "Why don't you meet with Senator Branch at 12:30 and if Senator Dansby would like to know more about the bill, you can discuss it with him at some point after that."

Callie knew she missed an opportunity to take advantage of Senator Branch's proposition. As much as Callie wanted to believe she was prepared for any situation, she understood the reality of a learning curve, regardless of how sure she was that she could get the job done. Although Callie had been dealing with people like Branch her entire life, internally she felt disappointed that she'd missed the obvious play he made for her. Callie made a mental note to be on the lookout for the overt ones, then quickly regrouped and regained her balance. "That works fine for me, Senator. If you would like to meet after you cast your vote, I'd be happy to go through the bill with you and point out all the advantages it has for Alaska," she said turning her attention to Dansby.

"I think I'll have some time after 1:30 tomorrow. We can meet in my office and go from there, if that works for you," Dansby said.

"Certainly…"

"But I have to say, I am inclined to vote against the bill."

"Fair enough, Senator. I appreciate the opportunity."

Senator Dansby checked his watch. "If you'll excuse me, I have to run to a meeting. Ms. Wheeler, I look forward to talking with you tomorrow."

"I have to run as well," Branch said. "I'm excited to hear more about this bill, Ms. Wheeler. I think you'll find it time well spent."

Branch brushed up against Callie as he attempted to catch Senator Dansby, who'd already started his trek through the concourse. Predictably, Branch whirled around and waved to her, totally ignoring Derek once again. Callie turned to Derek and spoke in a whispered tone. "That thing with Branch...I should have seen it coming...and about the Hawaii trip..."

"That was great..."

"I was afraid it was gonna be a problem..."

Derek smiled at Callie and pulled her off to the side. "A problem? No, you did exactly what you were supposed to do: get votes," Derek said. "Lank was hooked. It couldn't have gone any better..."

"Thank you, Derek." Callie felt a mixture of humility and renewed confidence.

"No, thank you. He's an enormous get. Enormous." Derek shook his head as he thought about the implications of attaching Lank to the Walker Bill, "And he'll bring others with him. As for Branch, he's just a jerk and there are plenty more exactly like him. If you play it right, you'll have them doing whatever you want them to do."

Callie remained unimpressed with Branch; he was like a teenager in a man's body. "They really let guys like that work here?"

"Guys like that are why we're still in business. I'm not sure how they get here, but once they get here, they want to stay here and they'll do just about anything to get re-elected. Understanding that is the key to all that we do."

ELEVEN

Monday, January 9, 2006

"I would say she's even more than I thought she'd be," Derek said as he dined with Barry at the Capitol Grille, one of Washington D.C.'s premiere steakhouses.

Barry picked up his glass of Stella Artois beer, kicked his head back and took a long sip as Derek continued. "She doesn't ever seem to get rattled. She kind of relishes the pressure, know what I mean?"

"I know what you mean," Barry said with an obvious detachment in his voice that had become all too familiar to Derek in recent days. Though these bouts of contempt that Barry showed were not new, they arrived with much more frequency than at any other time since the two had gone into business together.

The restaurant, located down the block from the Capitol on the corner of 6th Street and Pennsylvania Avenue, had established itself as one of the more prominent meeting spots for anyone who made their living on Capitol Hill. The food was prepared to perfection, the ambiance a mixture of comfort and exclusivity and the service, exceptional. Derek and Barry were alone in the Fabric Room, a private dining space inside the Grille decorated with red and green floral patterned wallpaper and two round tables that seated a maximum of twelve people. The two men were awaiting their after dinner guests and while the Grille was not known as an everyday hangout for the Washington elite, Derek and Barry each had their own reasons for dining there.

"Branch told me Callie was with him for less than twenty minutes before he was convinced to change his vote."

"What does that mean, convinced?" Barry asked.

Derek looked at Barry and smiled. Barry returned the smile with his now typical cold stare. The recent change in Barry's behavior irritated Derek much more than he let on. In this case it was just something else Derek would need to add to the mental list he kept of "things about Barry that piss me off."

"Why did she only spend twenty minutes with Branch?"

"She actually spent close to an hour with him. The more she flirted with him, the more he wanted to stay with her."

"And Dansby?"

"He's not sure he's going to change his vote, but he told me she gave him a lot to think about." Derek picked up a piece of grilled chicken with his fork and tucked it in his mouth then wiped his lips with a red cloth napkin that was on a plate to his right. He took a sip of water and checked his watch. "Manning, Shulman, Gorman, Laughlin, Westerbrook, Carter, Wilson, Macklin, King and Styles all said they were going to switch their votes. She turned ten percent of the Senate in less than a week. Very impressive."

"Do we have enough votes to get it through?"

"She has the exact count, but I think so."

"That's great," Barry said with a small hint of emotion, surprising Derek, who was happy to see any sign of life, no matter the size.

Barry moved closer and rested his elbows on the table. "There are bigger things to work on besides the Walker Bill," Barry said. "We need to take care of Albright and Snowden now and make sure they get the Shulman proposal out of committee."

The mention of their guests had both men looking uneasily at the open door of the private dining room. Barry stepped out to see if the Senators had arrived. Glancing in each direction, he undid the button on his sport coat and walked back inside the Fabric Room. He closed the door and turned his attention back to Derek. The time for Barry to make his move had come. "Oh, and one last thing," he said. "Let me do the talking with these guys."

The past few weeks with Barry had already taxed Derek's last nerve, but telling him how to behave with Congressmen he'd been dealing with for over a decade was just the sort of thing that had Derek rethinking their business relationship. "Any particular reason why you want to take the lead on this?"

"You're too easy with these two."

Derek could feel his entire body tense up at the accusation. "What does that mean?"

"You know exactly what that means. How's the family and kids bullshit. You think I give a fuck about their families? They can drop dead, for all I care." Barry's voice was filled with emotion, all of it directed at his partner. "What I want, no, what I need, is for these guys to deliver on Shulman's legislation. That's all I care about."

Derek's cell phone rang. He had no interest in answering it. He picked up the red napkin and dried his clammy hands, a direct result of the nervous energy he felt each time Barry questioned his abilities. Derek took a moment to dab his forehead of the small drops of sweat the conversation had produced. He clenched his teeth in obvious frustration and did his best not to make a scene. "I'm sick of arguing about this, Barry. You do the financials, I take care of the members. Period."

"I don't think so," Barry stared at Derek, uninterested in his division of responsibilities.

"What do you mean you don't think so?"

"I'm not sure how well we're doing on your side of the partnership."

"How well we're what?"

"You heard me and you're right, we're not going to argue about this anymore," Barry said, just as Senator Albright knocked on the door. Barry walked toward the table and sent Derek one last message before he turned to welcome their after dinner guest. "Now shut your ass up and let me handle this."

Wilson Albright III came from a long line of Washington diplomats, most recently his father Wilson II, who had been a seven-term Senator from Virginia and Chairman of the Senate Intelligence Committee for more than half his career on the Hill. Albright ran for his father's seat and won in a landslide on name recognition alone, almost a decade after the elder Albright announced his retirement.

Barry held the door open and Albright quickly walked inside. "Hope I'm not interrupting anything?"

Derek had not anticipated Barry's attack especially considering the week they'd just had. He had been incredibly pleased with Callie, who'd taken the Hill by storm and set the firm on the kind of trajectory it hadn't enjoyed since their golden days during the Bannon Administration. The roundhouse that Barry threw at him was unexpected, but as he sat at the table and listened to Barry exchange pleasantries with the young senator, he knew he should have seen it coming. It had become apparent since Conroy took the White House that Congressmen who had once been close to Derek were going elsewhere. At the same time, Barry became more distant and cold, while keeping Derek out of the loop on several important office decisions. Derek's initial response was to let it go, and chalk it up to office politics. However in recent weeks Derek had been much more protective of his territory, something that had turned their meetings, like the one they just had, into bitch-fests. He knew sooner or later something would have to be done including, if things continued to deteriorate as they were, taking back sole control of the firm he started and loved. As for the moment at hand, Derek chose to let Barry handle the situation. He sat back and kept his mouth shut.

"Senator, thanks for coming on such short notice," Barry said.

Albright acknowledged Barry with a quick nod in his direction. "I think David should be here any minute. Do you mind if I sit down?"

"Be my guest."

Barry extended his arm to a chair on his left and sat down across from the Senator. Within moments, Senator David Snowden, a tall heavy man from Texas with a huge neck and three crooked fingers all remnants from his playing days with the Dallas Cowboys, was escorted into the Fabric Room. He was welcomed by both Barry and Derek and took a seat next to Albright.

"Gentleman, I'd like to talk to you about the clean energy bill which we discussed last night. This legislation will open up a whole myriad of avenues for investment into the United States and I hope you understand how appreciative our client will be in return for your vote," Barry said.

Albright spoke first. "Barry, there are people in my state who would be very unhappy with me if I choose to vote in the affirmative on this bill."

Snowden followed. "I cannot see any way the bill, as you explained it to me yesterday, can be beneficial to my state. If I vote against the interests of my constituents, I'm going to have to explain that vote come election time." Snowden shook his head and took a drink from the glass of water in front of him.

"I understand your predicament, Senators, but my client will be very thankful."

The two legislators sat quietly for a few moments. In street parlance, this was better known as a shakedown and Albright, who had every intention of supporting the bill, took the time to make sure he played it just right. He could walk away and vote for the bill as he intended to do at the outset, or he could play the game and see what he could get out of it for himself. He chose the latter.

"How thankful?"

Barry turned to his right, opened his briefcase and pulled out an envelope. He lifted his head and looked at the two men sitting across from him, both of whom showed a great interest in the package he held in his hand. Barry had enough experience to know that he had reeled them in, but peeked inside the envelope anyway, just to make it seem as if he was unsure of its contents. Following Barry's charade, he placed the envelope on the table between himself and Senator Albright. The Senator picked it up and dropped his hands under the table, turned away slightly, then opened the lip on the envelope to check out the merchandise. Albright turned back around and fidgeted with the knot of his necktie.

"I think your client can count on my vote," Albright said as he stuffed the envelope in his jacket pocket. "However you'll still need to talk to the Committee Chairman."

Barry acknowledged the point with a bob of his head although the point was moot. "We're working on a plan to bring him along." Barry leaned forward from his seat in order to get a closer look into the eyes of his next target. "Can we count on your vote as well, Senator Snowden?"

Snowden appeared a little uncomfortable sitting at the table empty-handed. He lifted his glass and enjoyed a long drink, then slowly dried his mouth and cleared his throat. "I'm still not sure if this is such a good idea for the people of the commonwealth of Texas. I can think of plenty reasons why this bill won't work for us." Snowden went to great lengths to insure he pronounced each word slowly and carefully as if he was still contemplating what he planned to do. He took one last drink of water to bleed the moment and brushed his lips again with the napkin, before clearing his throat a second time. "Can you think of any reasons why it would work for us?"

Barry reached back into his briefcase and pulled out another envelope that looked like an exact replica of the one he had just given to Albright. "I can think of 75,000 reasons." Barry slid the envelope across the table. Snowden stared at it for a few moments, chuckled and slipped it into his overcoat that rested on the empty chair next to him. "I think your reasons to vote Yea, far outweigh your reasons to vote Nay," Barry said.

Albright stood up, cleaned off his suit and prepared to leave. Barry offered his hand once he was on his feet. Snowden and Derek stood up as well.

"I need to be getting back up the block for a late night caucus," Albright said. "But first I'd like to thank you for your interest in helping the 'Albright in '06' campaign. I hope you'll allow us to follow up with you in case you choose to make any additional contributions towards my re-election."

"Of course. Please be sure to add both of us to your mailing lists, electronic or otherwise. Yours too, Senator Snowden."

The four men exchanged pleasantries and handshakes as the Senators exited the restaurant. Derek walked back to the table, grabbed his winter coat and headed for the exit. He left no doubt as to his unhappiness. It was on full display.

"Where are you going?" Barry asked.

"We're done here," Derek said.

"You're leaving? We're not done."

"I've heard just about all I want to hear for one day."

"We have things to talk about," Barry said as he arrogantly sat back down in his chair.

"No, we're done...and one more thing..."

"I thought we were done..."

"Fuck you, Barry." Derek opened the door and turned back to Barry, his body halfway onto the sidewalk. "Remember who built this firm, who brought you in and who kept you here," Derek said with an anger he reserved for only his most hated of enemies. "I'm going to forget this ever happened." Derek stepped out the door to leave Barry all alone, just the way he liked it.

"You do that, Derek."

TWELVE

The beaches on the east coast of the United States were crowded spots during the spring and summer. While people flocked to them in droves during prime vacation seasons, there weren't many who enjoyed the ocean as the cold eastern winters pummeled the population. Callie Wheeler was the exception.

From time to time since she'd enrolled in law school, Callie and a number of her friends would spend a few weekends each year at her beach house located just off of 67th Street in Ocean City, Maryland. It was during her sophomore year in college that Callie had been willed the house from her Uncle Jeff, who, besides being her high school basketball coach, was a successful real estate investor until his untimely death in 2002. Having no children of his own, Uncle Jeff willed Callie, and both of her brothers, two beach houses, each to do with as they pleased.

Callie continued in her uncle's footsteps, using both homes as rental properties during the popular getaway periods. From March to October, she would garner rental fees anywhere between 2500 to 5000 dollars a week, depending on the time of year. With four bedrooms and more importantly a total of ten beds, homes like the ones Callie owned were in high demand. The scarcity of available accommodations in Ocean City during the summer months assured Callie a consistent stream of income year after year.

Callie, on the other hand, enjoyed the fresh chill of the winter air on the beach which is why at various times throughout the school year, Callie would spend time 'down the ocean' as it was known in the Baltimore-Washington corridor. She had set aside and looked forward to President's Day weekend 2006 as a romantic Ocean City rendezvous with Mike. What she did not count on was the lasting memory she would end up with from that visit.

"Why do you do this?" Mike asked, all bundled up in a Washington Redskins sweatshirt, his right hand running through his girlfriend's brown hair, his left one wrapped around a Heineken. He had attempted to get comfortable as he spread out in a lounge chair on the deck of the beach house, but gave up after Callie found a comfortable spot on top of him. She was dressed in a 'True Blue' UCLA Bruins National Championship sweatshirt, covered up by an electric blanket she used to bundle around herself and her man.

Callie lifted her head off Mike's chest. "Why do I do what?"

Mike looked into Callie's eyes, "Why do you come here in the winter?"

"Why not?" Callie asked.

"'Cuz, it doesn't make any sense?"

Callie folded her arms on his upper body and rested her chin on her hands. "I find it hard to believe that you, who sat on a frozen pond in Moscow for three days, are actually complaining about forty degree weather in February."

"I'm not complaining, I'm just asking why you do it when you don't have to," Mike said as he moved his right hand under Callie's blanket and gently caressed her back. "Sitting on ice in Moscow was part of my job description. It's not like I was in a good mood and said to all my friends, hey I got an idea, let's go sit on a pond and freeze our asses off."

Callie slapped Mike playfully on his stomach then rolled her body next to him and settled her head into his shoulder. "I like it here. It's become a winter rendezvous. You should feel lucky that you were even invited."

"Yeah, I feel real lucky…"

"Stop bellyaching," Callie said. "You know, the first time Kacey and I did this, we had a strict 'No Men' rule. Don't make me regret the change." Callie closed her eyes. She could hear Mike's heart beating steadily underneath her. She felt the breeze of the cold air skip across her back and listened closely as the water danced with a gentle wind that hurried across the Atlantic Ocean, a mere footsteps away from where they were cuddled.

Mike kissed Callie on her forehead as she slid her hand under his sweatshirt and caressed his chest. He stroked her hair in silence, while the sounds of the waves washed up against the shoreline. "Tell me what she was like, Mike?"

"What who was like?"

"Aubrey."

"My sister?"

"Yeah, tell me about her." Callie propped herself up on both knees, grabbed the blanket in her outstretched arms, and repositioned herself on top of Mike, this time settling on his left shoulder, her back pressed gently against his chest. Mike took one last swig of beer and placed the bottle on the deck below his chair. He wrapped both his arms around her, relaxing them on top of her stomach. Callie grabbed his fingers and intertwined her own with his.

"She must have been really special…"

After Mike's only sister, Aubrey, was born, their parents had tried for years to have another child. Four miscarriages later, Mike arrived. His mom was forty-three, his dad closing in on fifty. Mike was forever known in the family as the miracle baby. Two days before he turned six years old, his parents were driving home from a charity event. Their car was struck head on by a drunk driver. The driver, like Mike's father, was killed on impact. He had crossed the median line on Highway 17 in Phoenix and plowed into the Ferguson's 1979 Ford Mustang at close to ninety miles per hour. Mike's mom survived for two days before succumbing to internal bleeding and complications from numerous brain and head injuries. Aubrey was a seventeen-year-old Yale University freshman when the accident occurred. The following day, Aubrey pulled out of school and raised Mike as if he was her own.

"She sacrificed her interests for mine."

"But what was she like though?"

"Why do you want to know?"

"Because I want to know everything about you," Callie said as she caressed his arms.

"You already know everything about me," Mike said.

"Oh, really?" Callie turned over and rolled on top of Mike so she could look him in the eyes. "How many women have you had a relationship with?"

"That's not important."

"Of course it's important."

"Trust me, its not that big a deal," Mike said.

"Why won't you tell me about any other women?"

"Because it doesn't matter. I want to be with you and I'm with you."

Callie raised her eyebrows. "That's your answer?"

"Why's it matter who else I've been with?"

"See that's what I'm talking about. I know nothing about you." Callie rolled off of Mike and onto his shoulder once again. Mike pulled her towards him and rolled her back on top of his chest.

"You know everything about me," Mike said again.

"Pfft, I do not."

"Of course you do. What's my favorite color?"

Callie shook her head in protest, refusing to answer. "C'mon Cal, what's my favorite color." Again she refused and this time covered her mouth with her right hand. "Oh, so that's how you wanna' play," Mike said before he reached underneath her arms and tickled her. Laughing, but undeterred, Callie reinforced her stubbornness by covering her right hand with her left one until Mike's fingers made it impossible for her to withstand. "My favorite color?" Mike asked again as he continued to attack her vulnerabilities with his tickling fingers.

"Blue," Callie said blurting the answer out between her laughter. She was still on her back resting on his chest while she watched Mike wiggle his fingers above her just in case she thought she was home free. Callie raised her hands and grabbed his forearms, "No, stop...stop..." Callie said, as she settled down and turned back over, her chest now pressing up against his. "You don't play fair."

Mike ignored her complaint and continued making his point. "My favorite book?"

"Primal Fear, but the movie wasn't as good."

"Correct. Favorite song?" Mike asked as he ran his hands through her hair.

"Hotel California by the Eagles, but only the acoustic version on the Hell Freezes Over album."

"Yes. My favorite day in history?"

"The day you met me," Callie said with an innocent smile.

"Umm...not quite."

Callie reached up, grabbed his nose with her thumb and index finger and wouldn't let go. "The day the Diamondbacks won the world series."

"Correct...well, now that's my second favorite day."

"Good boy." Callie released Mike's nose then pulled herself up a little higher and kissed it.

"Who's my favorite singer?"

"Freddie Mercury...okay, I get the point, but I still don't know anything about any of your past relationships."

"What is there to know? I told you the longest relationship I ever had was with the CIA."

"Very funny. What about women?"

"Three months. Jaynie Bickford. She was boring and slept a lot, but a great cook, so I milked that for two months longer than I wanted to. You happy now?"

"No."

"Why not?"

Callie feigned shyness as she kissed Mike softly on the lips, "'Cuz you already told me about her."

Mike pushed Callie off of him, grabbed her hood and pulled it over her face. "You suck..."

"I didn't realize you were so sensitive?" Callie said as she uncovered her face and pushed the hood behind her head.

"Bite me."

"My pleasure." Callie pulled the electric blanket over their heads and bit Mike's bottom lip after she kissed him.

Mike ran his tongue along his newly indented lips, "Ya' know I'm starting to like it here..."

Callie's cell phone pierced the quiet, but she ignored it choosing instead to make out with her boyfriend. "You need to get that?" Mike asked between kisses.

"I'm good..."

The phone rang again, stopped, then rang a third and fourth time before Callie reached into her sweatshirt pocket and shut it off. She spent the rest of the evening making love to Mike. What started on the deck, continued in the den then moved to the master bedroom upstairs. It wasn't until the following morning that Kacey, who had made the ninety-minute drive down to Ocean City, used her key to enter the beach house. Once inside, she found Mike and Callie cuddled together on the couch watching the morning edition of SportsCenter on ESPN.

"I've been trying to reach you all night," Kacey said, standing next to the television.

"We were kind of busy," Callie said with a sly smile then hunkered into her boyfriend's shoulder.

Kacey turned to her right without saying anything and walked into the kitchen. She grabbed the first chair she saw and carried it with her into the den. She set it down directly in front of Callie, sat on it, then stared intently into her friends eyes. From the look on Kacey's face, it was obvious that something wasn't right. "Kacey, what's going on?"

"Derek's dead."

"What?"

"He had a heart attack in Vail."

"He just took a physical..."

"Last night on the slopes..."

"You sure about this?" Mike asked as he steadied Callie's shaking hands and held her tight.

"Has to be some mistake," Callie said, trying to restrain the tears that were forming in her eyes. "Who told you?"

"An aide in Senator Gorman's office."

"Maybe he's wrong?"

Kacey shook her head and said nothing as she fought back tears of her own. She stared at Mike and let her eyes confirm to him the information was correct. Mike nodded in response, an acknowledgement that he got the message.

"It can't be. He was given a clean bill of health three weeks ago."

"Barry put out a statement…"

"He did what?"

"This morning…"

Callie stood up on her wobbly legs and struggled walking to the foyer. She reached into her purse and turned on her blackberry as she simultaneously drew it out of her bag. Kacey shook her head and looked at Mike who shrugged his shoulders then motioned with his head for her to help Callie. The moment Callie's phone woke up, email notices confirmed her worst fears. She slowly crumbled to the floor and released a ravine of tears. Kacey slid down next to Callie and wrapped her arms around her best friend. The din of the television was the only sound that could be heard as Kacey pulled her close, allowing Callie's head to fall gently onto her chest.

THIRTEEN

Thursday July 21, 2011

"Barry, you have a call on line one," said the voice through the telephone intercom.

"Who is it, do you know?"

"He said he spoke to you last night, very late."

Barry was expecting the phone call as a follow up from a call he had received the previous day. Sitting behind his desk, Barry ejected a disk from the right side of his desktop computer. He rolled back his chair, opened up the center drawer and removed a CD case then slipped a DVD inside. "Please ask him to hold for a moment."

Barry picked up an eighteen-carat gold Cross pen from his desk and scribbled something down on the notepad to his left, then turned and lifted the telephone handset from its cradle. "Hello?" Barry said.

"Mr. Miller," said the voice on the other end said. "How are you?"

Barry recognized him instantly. The man on the phone spoke with a deep Middle Eastern accent and Barry took special note of how meticulous the man had been with his choice of words. He talked slowly, succinctly and with a purpose. "Are you prepared to do what we discussed?"

Barry took a deep breath before he answered. "I am."

"Good."

Barry knew him by only one name, Ibrahim. He'd never met him and knew almost nothing about him. But he knew he was a man of his word. Ibrahim had already sent Barry and the firm in excess of thirty-million dollars over the past two months. He seemed to be as well financed as any client M&G had ever done business with. Ibrahim rarely mentioned anything about himself, but when he did, he was extremely specific and very short. None of that mattered to Barry. As long as he kept getting paid, he didn't care who Ibrahim was, what he requested or what sort of agenda he advocated.

Barry Miller was something of an outcast growing up. Born in Baltimore the third son of four, he attended the Park School for all thirteen years of his childhood education. While at Park, Barry had failed to form any lasting relationships, but definitely acquired more than a few enemies. In a 2003 cover story in the New York Times Magazine published about the firm, four students in leadership positions during his time at the school all remembered him as someone who wanted to fit in and worked hard at it, but was never quite able to. Nevertheless, he knew how to maneuver within the system and had soon developed a reputation as someone who got things done, no matter the cost or collateral damage.

Barry learned how to exploit people to get what he wanted from teachers, students and anyone else who tried to take from him, what he'd felt was rightfully his. Following a successful senior year in which he fulfilled his duties as President of the Student Council, Barry attended the University of Maryland where he seemed to have found his calling. He became a campus leader by organizing protest rallies against the proliferation of nuclear weapons and trickle down economics. More importantly, he learned how to take control, as well as take full advantage of any situation. By his junior year, he was a weekly contributor to the Diamondback student newspaper at College Park, editorializing on anything from tax cuts to Donna Summer's latest album. He graduated Magna Cum Laude from Maryland and by his first year at Columbia University Law School, he'd already mastered how to manipulate any opportunity presented to him. The day after he graduated, Barry joined the prestigious New York Law firm of Holtzman, Walters and Berg.

Barry was working and enjoying his time at Holtzman for three years until a former Columbia classmate introduced him to Derek Gladstone. Derek had already opened his own practice in Washington D.C. and looked to expand his fledgling business. A year after he had met Barry, they were in business together and just as their venture started to show signs of growth, they hit the jackpot when Derek's former college roommate and football teammate became President of the United States. Barry didn't care much for Derek, but envied the access he was able to secure. Together, they had built the firm into an international brand, but even with all their success, Barry was still unhappy with the relationship. He had wanted his own lobbying firm and with Derek's tragic death, his dream had finally come true. Since then, Barry purged the firm of any lawyers or office staff loyal to Derek, with the lone exception being Callie Wheeler. As the one legitimate rainmaker at the firm, Barry had no choice but to keep her. People could call Barry a lot of things, but fool wasn't one of them.

"We will have everything you asked for by the end of the week," Barry told Ibrahim.

"Are you personally making sure of that?"

"I am. It will all be taken care of. The second phase will begin shortly thereafter," Barry leaned back in his chair. "But I should warn you, what you've asked for will carry a very high price tag."

"Money will never be an issue. Whatever you need, you tell me. I do not care if you keep it for yourself, I only need you to make it happen."

"I'm just preparing you…"

"We are well prepared. We've been working on this plan since 1993. I can assure you, we have thought it through until the very last detail. All you have to do is follow my instructions."

"I think I can do that," Barry said as he straightened up and pulled himself closer to his desk.

"Then, my friend, you will be a very rich man."

Barry listened for Ibrahim to hang up the phone before he set the one in his hand, back in its cradle. Barry leaned back in his chair again and rested his head on his clasped hands that were now behind his neck.

"I definitely think we can do that."

• • •

Kacey knew she had hit on something big the moment she set foot in room S-325 of the Capitol Building or as it was more commonly known, the Radio and TV gallery. Every news outlet had a camera in place as well as a reporter to accompany the cameraman for a live shot to be taped and used later on in the day. Kacey grabbed a spot in the back of the room and did her best to remain as inconspicuous as possible. No one in attendance actually knew if there was anything to her story, but the fact that Lank had called a hurried press conference, meant that someone had to be running scared. While she felt a little uncomfortable with her name being out there so prominently for the first time in her brief career, Kacey enjoyed the attention her story was getting. She resisted the urge to find Senator Lank and thank him for helping publicize her piece.

"Great job, Kacey," Bob Turner said as he walked over to Kacey who had positioned herself in the back left corner. Bob was the beat reporter for the Washington Times and had broken some big stories of his own over a respectable twenty-four year career. "I remember what it felt like the day I broke my first national story. To this day I still appreciate when my competition acknowledges my work. So here's to you Miss Mercer." Bob lifted the coffee he held in his hand and gestured towards Kacey. He raised the mug to his lips and enjoyed a long sip.

"Thanks, Bob," Kacey said. Turner bowed his head in acknowledgement and took off to find his usual seat in the second row. Kacey smiled at him until he moved on, then crouched down in search of her digital recorder that appeared to be hiding somewhere in the jungle that was her purse. As she rummaged through her belongings, Kacey noticed out of the corner of her eye, an expensive pair of black Louis Vuitton shoes planted less than five-feet from her. She clutched the three-inch recorder in her hand and stood up, only to find an almost famous face standing in front of her.

"Are you Kacey Mercer?"

"Who is it that wants to know?"

"I do."

Kacey looked all around her trying to see if she had missed something. "Okay, and who are you?"

"I'm sorry, I thought you would recognize me."

Kacey smiled at his arrogance. "Why is that?"

"I'm the Washington Bureau Chief for NBC News, Kirk Arthur? Does my name not sound familiar to you?"

"I gotta' be honest with you...Kurt did you say?"

"Kirk, Kirk Arthur."

"I gotta' be honest with you Kirk, I don't watch your channel all that much."

Surprised she had not recognized him, Kirk continued on with his resume' even though he obviously felt slighted that Kacey did not know who he was. "I'm sure you must have seen me on the NBC Nightly News."

"Sorry, don't watch it," Kacey said, unsure if she had seen him or not, but at this point, she couldn't help but enjoy the moment.

"I also do live shots on the Today show a few days a week. You've probably seen me there."

"Nope. Don't have much need for idiot TV."

"Idiot TV?" Kirk tried not to show his ire at Kacey's morning show description. "It is the highest rated show on morning television," he said, with more than his usual pompousness.

"I find it sort of lowest common denominator type of thing, like most morning shows on free TV."

Kirk grew more frustrated with each passing moment, "I see you're one of those cable news people. In that case, I also do guest spots on the Morning Joe on MSNBC. Perhaps you have seen me there?"

"I'm sorry, Kurt," Kacey said, messing up his name on purpose.

"Kirk," he corrected her with animosity in his voice.

"I'm sorry, Kirk. I didn't even know MSNBC had a morning show."

Kirk had heard enough and straightened his hair before he came after Kacey. "Well, if it means anything, I didn't recognize your name until this morning either."

"I'm not offended," Kacey said with a smile that referenced Kirk's own sense of self-importance.

Kirk straightened his tie and checked his lapels as he tried hard not to show the growing disdain he had worked up for the young reporter. "I have to tell you, I've seen many a reporter break a story one day and working on some obscure blog the next."

"And?"

"And it takes more than one lucky break to make it on this beat. Rest assured that if there is a story here, all these reporters will be out to get it."

"I'm sorry, Kurt, but what are you trying to tell me that I don't already know?" Kacey asked, again mistaking his name just for the fun of it.

"Kirk. It's Kirk. I believe I have at least earned the right to have my name said correctly."

Kacey bent down and pretended to look for something in her purse in an attempt to let Kirk know she was through with him. "Is there a point to this?"

"My point is, I'll be the lead anchor on NBC one day and you will, in all probability, be nothing but a footnote in Washington Politics."

Kacey stood back up and stared her bully straight in the eye. "Hey Kurt, please tell me you're not all like this?"

Kirk shuffled over to his cameraman and whispered something in his ear. Both men turned around to look at Kacey who waved at them with a huge grin on her face.

The sudden burst of noise coming from the front of the room drew Kacey's attention. Senator Lank entered the gallery and stepped up to the podium just as Kacey pulled a notebook from her bag. She readied her recorder then checked it again to make sure it was in working order. Lank surveyed the room and waited patiently until all the cameras were fixed on him before he began.

"Ladies and Gentleman. Thank you all for coming this morning. I am going to make a brief statement. The allegations leveled against me in this morning's Washington Post are absolutely one hundred percent false. I have never met, spoken to, or accepted any money from Jonas Foster and while I support the right of a free press, it is my hope, and the hope of the American people, that they would use that right responsibly, and not print baseless and fabricated accusations. I apologize that I cannot take any questions at this time. Thank you again for coming and god bless this great country."

Senator Lank left the microphone bank and hurried down the hall while the press shouted questions at him. Kacey, still planted in the back of the room, frantically wrote notes on the steno pad she used as a backup for her digital device. Scribbling, she failed to see the well-dressed professional looking man walking in her direction. Kacey was still writing on her notepad, when she finally noticed him standing directly in front of her.

"Ms. Mercer, I'm Joel Hughes, the Senator's Chief of Staff," he said. "I would appreciate, if the next time you have any questions about the Senator, you ask them of me." Joel reached into his jacket pocket and withdrew a business card which he handed to her.

"Nice to meet you, Joel," Kacey said. "I called the Senator's office for a comment all afternoon and evening yesterday, but sadly, no one returned any of my calls."

"I never received any messages," Joel said, trying to convince her he hadn't, even though he had.

Kacey turned back a few pages in her steno pad. "I called at 2:20, 3:35, 5:15 and 7:45. I left messages three times with someone named Alice and once on the office voicemail."

"Please understand, I am very busy and--"

"Which is it, Mr. Hughes? You never received any messages or you're very busy?"

"Both."

"Can I quote you?"

Joel knew he'd been caught and tried to make the best of the situation, "I would appreciate if this conversation remained off the record."

"I would appreciate if the Senator would return my calls. Have a good day, Mr. Hughes." Kacey said, then smiled, gathered her things and walked away.

FOURTEEN

At first glance, the brown building that sat on the corner of North Holliday and Saratoga Streets looked like any other empty office space in Baltimore. However, the band of people wrapped around the block who were waiting to go inside told a very different story. Men, women and children occupied the line that began in the middle of Holliday Street and continued almost a half-mile onto Saratoga Street. Most of the people who stood in the line were dressed in used clothes, their feet barely kept warm by worn out shoes. The majority of them looked like they hadn't showered or bathed in weeks. All any of them wanted was a warm meal and a place to sleep.

A group of four men walked out of the shelter and proceeded down Holiday Street. Three of the men were dressed in expensive suits. The other, a well-dressed man in his mid-forties, was Ken Farmer. Farmer did most of the talking as they turned the corner and walked down Saratoga, all the while, observing the people who were waiting on line.

"Gentleman, the fact is we don't have enough funds or beds to handle the demand. And it's getting worse. Truthfully, I'm afraid to see what this will be like in the winter," Farmer said. "We desperately need your help."

Mike Molosky, CEO of Antrell Paper, the largest paper supplier on the east coast, was the first to speak. "What do you think you will need to make it through the next six months?"

"Based on the current demand and growth rate, I would say at least two million dollars," Farmer said. "I was told your foundations had the resources."

Ishmael Watson, a tall sixty-one year old African-American man, served as the Executive Director of Feed the Families, a faith based organization that raised funds all across America, to help the poor. "We can't do all of it, but we can help you get through a few of those months."

"We can pick up at least two months," Molosky said.

All three of the men turned to the fourth and waited to hear what he had to say.

"We might have enough funds for a month, not sure about two," Andrew Press said. Press was the owner and CEO of Madison Electric. He had been brought to the meeting by Watson. "I would love to help with more, but at this point, I don't think we can."

Watson seemed genuinely interested in the fate of the shelter. "What is your next move if this facility can't accommodate your needs, Mr. Farmer?"

"Our next move would be to either trim the number of people we can help, or find another facility, because it seems that three floors are not going to be enough." Farmer said.

Molosky was impressed with all the programs Farmer had set up without any government assistance. "Mr. Farmer, thank you for what you're doing for the city and these people. You're offering them a service that is immeasurable."

"This city is lucky to have you, Ken," Press said.

"I appreciate your kind words. I can't thank you gentleman enough. I believe with those months committed, we should be able to get through the winter." Farmer shook the hands of each one of his donors before escorting them back inside.

FIFTEEN

Kacey Mercer's front-page story staggered Barry Miller. He'd spent the early dawn hours of his day fielding anxious calls from worried legislators who feared the worst was still to come. He advised Lank to get out in front of the situation and hold a press conference without taking any questions from the media. Barry needed to make certain that Senators kept a low profile and allowed the story to blow over without bringing any unwanted attention to themselves. Never one to stay out of the spotlight, Charles Shulman, had concerns of his own and stopped by M&G to voice them to Barry, who had anticipated his unannounced arrival.

Shulman paced the room nervously. "What concerns me is how much the Post knows."

"We know from the reporter that the only Senator they're looking at is Lank," Barry said. "You'll be okay."

There were more than a handful of representatives in the government that consistently ran to the nearest camera and irritated the public the minute a story broke. Shulman was the most prominent and obnoxious among them. When something important happened on Capitol Hill, television cameras always found him and he seemed more than happy to oblige them, unless the outlet in question was Fox News. Over the years, Shulman had learned to stay disciplined in his message and always reiterated the daily talking points he'd been given. He was notorious for always finding fault with anyone but himself or the Democratic Party.

Shulman bullied his opposition and used an all too willing media to advance his agenda. Throughout his career in Congress, people had routinely underestimated him and he thrived on pressing that advantage. By casting himself as an underdog, he seized every opportunity to pounce on his opponents naiveté. Most of all, he was vicious and played political hardball as well as anyone in the nation's capital. Shulman had to win at everything, no matter the cost. He knew Barry to be the same way. He trusted him as much as he trusted anyone in Washington.

"How do I know I'm not next?" Shulman asked. He stopped pacing and sat down in one of the two chairs across from Barry's desk.

"You don't, but tell me Senator, what options do you have at this point?" What Barry understood about Shulman that most others didn't, was his extreme insecurity and the fact that his bullying emanated more from fear than confidence.

Shulman sat in silence and thought about Barry's question. As much as he could be a pain in the ass, he was also extremely practical. More importantly, he lived in constant "cover your ass" mode and Barry had learned quickly how to manipulate that idiosyncrasy.

"Look Charlie, you'll have to trust me on this," Barry said.

"It's not you I'm worried about." Senator Shulman let the comment hang there while peering at Barry with a stern look on his face. Of all the people in Washington who made Schulman uncomfortable, Callie Wheeler was far and away the worst. After she established herself as a power-broker among the D.C. elite,

Shulman understood he needed to go through her if he wanted to get in the game. He disliked her personally, but respected her ability to adapt to any situation she was thrown into. Shulman couldn't decide if he admired her tenacity or hated her for it, but either way, he resolved to use her as much as he could, in order to get what he wanted.

"I wouldn't worry about that. We've got it all under control," Barry said.

Shulman stood up again and resumed his pacing. "We all have way too much to lose if you don't. You need to make sure this does not become a problem for us because if it does, we'll have to take matters into our own hands," Shulman said. "And that won't be pretty."

Barry knew the Senator was serious about his threat, but chose instead to let it go. "This will blow over in a few days. My advice is to lay low and don't say anything stupid in the press."

Senator Shulman appeared even more nervous than he'd been before. He sat down on the couch in the corner of the office and picked up the March 2010 issue of Washington Magazine that featured M&G on the cover. Ruffling through the pages, he landed on page 61 where the article on the firm began. Callie's picture was on the opposite page. Below the alluring full page image read the caption "The most powerful woman in Washington." Shulman stared at it for a few moments then stood up and threw the magazine back onto the coffee table in disgust.

"Barry, make sure this stays where it is and doesn't get out of hand. There will be a lot of very angry people if it does."

Barry stood and extended his hand on the hope that Shulman would leave. "We'll be fine."

Shulman shook Barry's hand. "We had better be."

Shulman turned and left the office without uttering another word. Barry locked the door behind him, walked back to his desk and reached underneath the middle drawer and pulled out a CD case. Written in small print on the bottom lefthand corner, were the letters S.Ins. Barry popped out the DVD, which had the capacity to store much more information than a regular CD, and pressed it into his computer. He clicked on a few items then began to type. Three minutes later Barry removed the disk, put it back in the CD case, then reattached it underneath the middle drawer.

Barry pulled out his cell phone and dialed a number. "We're going to need some help on the Wanda Act. Please make sure we have a chance to discuss it tomorrow before the day on the Hill begins. Thanks." Barry hung up the phone and began to pack up for the night. A knock on the door interrupted the stillness of the office.

"Who is it?"

"It's me, you got a minute?" Whitaker Jordan asked.

"Hold on, just a second," Barry trekked to the door and unlocked it. "Come on in."

Whitaker stepped inside. He was carrying a folder, a pen and a notepad in his hand. "I wanted to give you a rundown on where we are."

"I was wondering about that myself. How close are we?"

"We should have it all done by tomorrow evening," Whitaker said, then sat down and slipped the contents from his hand on top of the oak table to his left.

"Excellent."

"Anything else you need from me before I leave?"

"No, Whitaker, you're fine," Barry said. "Just let me know as soon as you're finished so I can alert the client."

"No problem. See you in the morning."

Whitaker stood up, gathered his things and left. Barry knew Ibrahim would be happy with the progress they had made in such a short time. In his head, Barry was already spending the millions of dollars he would be making on this deal, but reminded himself to settle down and be patient. He knew there were more pressing issues to worry about before he counted his money and the one problem that needed his immediate attention, above all else, was the most powerful woman in Washington.

SIXTEEN

"Some days, I think it depends on what I had for lunch. In the morning I could wear a size four and by eight o'clock, I could barely fit into a six."

Callie and Kacey were at Arundel Mills Mall, about a forty-five minute drive from Kacey's home in downtown D.C. Kacey was at work in the late afternoon when Callie called and mentioned she needed a therapy session and suggested Kacey come along. "Therapy" was their code word for shopping just as it had been in the sixth grade and as a rule, once one of them needed "therapy," the other was required to join, unless of course there was a valid excuse, such as their own death. Where they went was left up to the one who received the phone call and Kacey suggested Arundel Mills.

Callie held up a black sleeveless dress with ruffles running along the left side. "So what do you think? A four or a six?"

"I think a four would look great," Kacey said.

"Me too," Callie said as she pressed the dress against her body. "Thanks."

Kacey walked over to the mirror and toyed with her skirt.

"You'll never guess who called me today?"

Callie shook her head.

"Miss Tobin," Kacey said.

"You serious?"

"She saw my piece on the paper's website and said she had to call to tell me how proud she was." Leslie Tobin was a high school journalism teacher at Wyoming Valley West and it had been Miss Tobin who encouraged Kacey to major in journalism at Wilkes.

"That's so nice, Kace. What else did she say?"

"She asked about you."

"No, she didn't?"

"Yeah, she really did. I told her you were the most powerful woman in Washington."

"Oh my god, not that again."

"Relax, she said she already knew it." There were not many things that got under Callie's skin, but if there was one, the Washington Magazine piece would be it.

"HaHa, very funny. It was nice she called."

"It was great. I kept calling her Miss Tobin, can you believe that? Like, thank you, Miss Tobin...yes, Miss Tobin...what a loser."

"Yes, quite the loser with a front page story in the D.C. paper of record," Callie said. "And above the fold no less. You are such a loser."

Kacey smiled while she picked up a pink top and held it against her shoulders, looked in the mirror and hung it back on the rack. "You hear from anyone about the article?"

"Not really," Callie said. "Early on this morning there was a lot of chatter, but as the day moved along, people just went about their business." Callie could not believe she was lying to Kacey again, something she had never done during her entire life up until that afternoon, and now she had perpetrated it twice in eight hours.

"And Lank, did you guys hear from him?"

"I didn't, but I don't know about anyone else. I doubt it, we don't have all that much to do with him." In her head Callie started to keep a running count. She knew Lank spoke to Barry, which was lie number three and she had a whole lot to do with him, which brought the number to four.

"So what do you think happened?"

"Am I being interviewed, Kacey?" Callie snapped at Kacey unconsciously having grown tired of the conversation and her own dishonesty.

"C'mon Cal. I was just asking your opinion." The more she thought about it, the more bothered Kacey became by her accusation. "Why would you say that? I just wanted to know what you thought about it, no need for any hostility."

"Sorry, Kace, I didn't mean to bark at you. I really have no idea about all that stuff. I barely know Lank and to be honest, I've always thought he was a bit of a jerk."

"He does seem that way, doesn't he?"

Callie picked up a pair of red Marcy pumps and showed them to Kacey. "What about these with the dress?"

"Those are beautiful, Cal. You'll kill in them. How much?"

"$255.00"

"How much?"

"I'm not sure I like the suede, though…"

"Did you say 255?"

"Yeah, why?"

"Callie, that's more than my electric bill last month."

"These really are beautiful though," Callie said.

"Can you afford them?"

"I think I can splurge. It's been a long day," Callie said, then asked the salesperson for a size eight in red and black. She picked up a pair of grey pumps and stared at them for a moment, before putting them back down when the saleslady returned with her shoes. "As far as Lank, I don't know him well enough to say anything one way or the other." Callie held the red shoe in her hand while her head recognized lie number five.

"Bob Kravitz must be happy, huh?" Callie asked, trying desperately to move the attention off of her.

"He walked by and told me nice job, so I guess that's a good thing."

Callie rolled her eyes as she tried on the red shoes. "Duh, yeah it's a good thing." She stood up and walked around a few steps. Approaching the mirror, Callie stared at her feet. "How do they look?"

"They look good enough to go a few months without electricity."

Callie turned to the saleswoman and asked her for another pair in an eight and a half. "Eight and a half still?" Callie asked Kacey while the woman went to search for the size.

"What?" Kacey said, stunned by her question. "Uh...no, you're not."

"Uh, yes, I am."

"You can buy 'em, but I'm not gonna take 'em."

"I am going to buy them and you are going to take them," Callie said. "Look at these shoes on my feet and tell me you don't want a pair."

Kacey looked down then turned her head away. "I don't want a pair...who am I kidding...of course I do...but I can't let you buy them for me."

"There are only so many Payless shoes a girl can wear," Callie said, pointing to the worn out black heels on Kacey's feet. "I can afford to and I'm going to. Don't like it, too bad."

Kacey stopped trying to pretend. "Thank you, Cal-Pie..."

Callie purchased a pair of red and blue shoes for Kacey along with the red and black for herself. At the checkout counter, they both agreed to the saleswoman's request to be added to the DKNY e-mail list.

"Your names, please?"

"Callie Wheeler."

"How do you spell that?"

"C-A-L-L-I-E." Callie handed the woman behind the counter her business card with her e-mail address. "Use this address if you don't mind."

"Thank you, Ms. Wheeler." Turning to Kacey, the salesperson continued, "And your name?"

"Kacey Mercer. That's Kacey with a K."

"Thank you." Kacey pulled out her own business card from her purse while the woman behind the counter typed her name then lifted her head and looked at Kacey. "Your e-mail address?"

Kacey placed her card on the counter. "The Washington Post? Are you the one who wrote that piece this morning about the Congressman?"

Callie answered for her. "Yes, she is. Pretty cool, huh?"

"Very cool," the saleslady said. "Nice article, by the way."

"Thank you very much," Kacey said, then turned to Callie and opened her mouth wide, surprised by the recognition. "Cal, you wanna' run back to Jewelry Barn and grab those earrings?"

Callie took the four pairs of shoes from the saleslady, thanked her, then handed two bags to Kacey. "Lead the way, superstar..."

• • •

Mike sat up in bed. He was engrossed in the Vince Flynn novel, resting on his lap. Callie sat at the night table just inside the master bathroom and brushed her hair as she prepared to join her soon to be husband.

"So the lady says, "Are you the woman from the paper?" What are the odds that a cashier in Hanover is going to read the Washington Post and on top of that check the byeline?" Callie said as she smoothed Dove body cream along her arms.

"What are the odds that a woman in Maryland would be reading the Washington Post? Is that your question?" Mike asked.

"But know whose name is on a byline on the front page?"

"I'm not that shocked. It's a pretty big story for one, and two, she might be tuned into politics."

"It's possible, but I don't really see it," Callie said.

"Could it be that you're too close to the story to realize how big it is?"

Callie stood up and stopped in the bathroom doorway. "You really think it's that big a story?"

"That a Congressman might have taken bribes and illegal campaign contributions? Yeah, I think that would be a pretty big story."

Callie shut the light in the bathroom, walked to her bed and sat down, her hairbrush still in her hand. "Really?"

"Look at it this way, Cal. These guys pass the laws that limit the people, but not themselves? Are they above the law?"

Callie could not have been more uncomfortable with an issue and having stayed on it too long already, tried to steer the conversation someplace else. "How'd your meeting go with the sanctimonious prick?"

Mike closed the book, removed it from his lap and placed it on the nightstand. He turned his body to the side to face Callie then rested an elbow on his pillow, before easing his head into his open hand. "Made me wait for over a half hour as if his time is more valuable than mine. When he finally lowered himself to see me, he lit me up with all that where do you get your authority from, bullshit. Worst part is, I know Conroy told him to do it."

"How did you guys leave it?"

"I told him if he wanted to screw with our budget be my guest, but if anything goes down, I'm going to name names including his, speaking on the President's behalf."

"Good for him, he's such an asshole." Callie laid her brush down on the nightstand next to her side of the bed then nestled into Mike's shoulder. "Did you tell Biggs?"

"Tell him what?"

"About us," Callie said.

"I didn't tell him."

"We're finally getting married and you didn't tell him?"

Mike turned onto his back and reached for the book, opened it up and pretended to read it. "I'll get to it at some point."

Callie sat up, grabbed the book and threw it over her shoulder before picking up the hairbrush from the nightstand. "What am I going to do with you?" she said, playfully hitting him across the upper arms with her plastic weapon. Callie rolled on top of him and made herself comfortable on his chest before slapping him again with the brush.

"I might have to use some of those CIA torture techniques…"

Mike held onto her hips as Callie leaned in and kissed him softly on the lips. Sensing his moment, Mike attempted to kiss her back, but Callie pulled away.

"No, no, mister. I am in charge of this torture session. You don't get to kiss me."

"And what if I become a hostile prisoner?"

Callie bent over and pressed her body against his, holding his arms down with hers. "Ve chave vays of making you talk," she said in a terrible German accent then leaned in and kissed him again. In the blink of an eye, Mike grabbed Callie mid-kiss, flipped her over then pinned her to the bed.

"Not very intimidating, counselor." Mike said.

Callie, knowing she overplayed her hand, looked for a way out, "I love you, Mikey..."

Mike wasn't buying. "Nice try," he said. "Now let me show you how torture is supposed to feel." Mike softly ran his hands over Callie. She closed her eyes and lost herself in his touch.

SEVENTEEN

Some people drove cars to get from one place to another, others drove a car because they liked the ride or the way it made them feel when they sat in the driver's seat. Barry Miller drove his car, a 2011 Bentley Continental GT, so everyone in town would know he was the owner. It wasn't just a car, it was a fashion statement and the $190,000.00 price tag added to its panache.

For Barry, the last eighteen-plus hours had been total chaos. He received more than thirty phone calls from Senators and another sixty plus from Representatives in the House, all concerned about Kacey's article in the Post. Most of them had been the typical "I better cover myself" phone calls from Congressman who might have done something they were not sure about, but didn't want to get caught up in a scandal this close to the upcoming election season. There had been more than a handful however, who informed Barry in no uncertain terms that he needed to keep his house in order or things could get a whole lot worse.

As he sped up Route 270, Barry took one such call from Senator Mickey Bane, the chairman of the Senate Appropriations Committee, whose fiery rage left him unapologetic and in unbridled attack mode. The article had sent shock waves through every corridor of Capitol Hill and left its members, including Bane, on edge wondering what revelation would come next.

"I hope you understand what I am saying. If not, I will repeat it, Barry, so listen good."

"Senator..." Barry tried to calm him down, but Bane was just getting started. "This is some bad shit, this here piece on Lank. Did he do something with bribes and shit? Who the hell knows, but this shit is gonna stick on him something serious if we don't get it cleaned up."

"Senator, listen for a second."

"I'll tell ya' something else. There are a whole lot of us up here on the Hill who don't wanna' get anywhere near this, not with a..."

Barry rolled his eyes as he listened to the other end of the phone. "Senator," Barry said again talking over him, but getting nowhere.

Senator Bane kept barreling along. "Do you think this is the sort of shit any of us wanna' deal with right now? An election year around the corner? Fuck, no, and if this gets worse we are all fucked worse then a whore at a sex addicts convention..."

Barry raised his voice an octave attempting to quiet Bane for just a few seconds, but to no avail. "Senator...Senator..."

"Barry you need to take care of this. Tell me, how the hell did anyone even find out about Lank? If they found out about him they'll find out about others and who knows what shit will stick--"

Barry pulled the receiver away from his ear and screamed into the phone in a last ditch effort to get a word in. "Senator Bane, just stop and let me talk!" Barry said. "Calm down a second."

Bane's side of the phone line went silent while Barry tried to explain his position and at the same time bring some calm to an overly combustible situation. "All they have is a small story on Lank that they can't prove. There is nothing about you and there won't be if you keep quiet, which is exactly what I told Senator Shulman last night."

"Look here, Barry, I'll tell ya' what I'm worried about and what a whole lot of others up here are worried about too." Barry took Bane's relative calm as a good sign. The Senator continued in a much calmer, more logical tone. "That barracuda you got up here...she is one nasty piece of work and it seems to us that this here Ms. Wheeler, is our biggest concern. I think, or should I say we think, that you need to make sure she doesn't become a problem."

Barry had his fill of Congressmen telling him about Callie. "Senator, she will not be a problem. Callie Wheeler is slicker than all of us. Think for a second, Mickey. It's in her best interest to remain quiet."

Bane had cooled down to a much more rational level, but didn't share Barry's optimism. "This woman is a wild card, Barry. She's done a lot of bad shit up here..."

Barry interrupted again. "That's my point, Senator, think it through. Her hands are all over this stuff. She's the last person who's going to talk."

"You would think that, but you still have to make sure she stays quiet. I can tell you that there are a bunch of us up here who want to make sure she doesn't talk...if ya' know what I mean."

"Don't start talking crazy, Senator..."

"I'm not sayin' anyone would do somethin', I'm just sayin' that I'm hearin' things."

Barry tried again to assure Senator Bane that he had it all under control. "Senator, you can tell everyone, that I'm on top of it and I swear to you, that if you all stay quiet and just deny, deny, deny, this thing will be a non-issue. Stay under the radar and we'll be fine."

Bane hung up the phone without saying another word, which took Barry by surprise. Unlike his initial gut response to the fall-out from the story, he now had reason to be concerned with the reaction over on Capitol Hill. He knew this could go two ways, good or bad. But no matter which way it fell, Callie would have to be handled carefully and the sooner he took care of it, the better.

Friday July 22, 2011

Inside the Capitol building, Callie had finished her morn-ing business and stopped near the doorway to chat with an aide from Senator Rice's office when she was met from behind by Joel Hughes, who grabbed Callie's arm and led her outside onto the steps of the east side entrance. Once there, Callie ripped her arm away from Joel's hand and rubbed it in an effort to ease the pain of his grip. "What the hell is wrong with you, Joel?"

Joel moved closer to Callie, leaned in and spoke in a low force-ful tone, but loud enough for Callie to tell he was not happy. "If Lank goes down, I will make sure he takes you with him."

Callie continued to caress her arm then gave Joel a slight push away from her. "First of all, get out of my face," Callie said. After overcoming the shock of Joel's aggressiveness, she gathered herself and gave Joel another soft push. "Second, no one is going down."

"I'm not losing my job over this, Callie. I was just the delivery boy."

Callie liked Joel a lot and Joel liked Callie. They had become good friends, starting three years ago with their introduction on the first day he worked for Lank. He wanted to ask her out on numerous occasions, but knew she was living with someone and settled for being a friend she could count on. He ended up in a two-year relationship with an elementary school teacher from Laurel, Maryland, but had broken up with her after she cheated on him with a co-worker. Joel, a handsome thirty-two year old graduate of Michigan State University, had a naturally muscular frame even though he never worked out a day in his life. His almost perfect head of brown hair was well groomed and his light brown eyes conveyed a Boy Scout innocence that kept women guessing, but left their parents happy. He made it a point to try and get along with everyone, but understood there were times when his patience was finite. Joel also might have been the only person in Washington that could have gotten away with what he'd just done to Callie.

"Do you know how many Senators we paid off on the Lank bill alone?" Callie said. "You know how much money was involved?"

Joel had been uncomfortable with the entire set up. Lank had given him instructions to find Callie Wheeler, who had a package for him. He picked it up without knowing what was inside or asking any questions about its contents. By the third time around, he felt confident there was something shady going on. Though he never talked much about it with Callie, he knew enough to be quiet and keep it to himself.

He hesitated, but asked anyway. "How many Senators were there?"

"The less you know the better. Suffice it to say, you have plenty of company," Callie said. "In both Houses."

Joel wanted nothing to do with this story and remained silent as he paced back and forth on the steps. Callie knew Joel wasn't the type to fly off the handle or do something rash without thinking. After a few minutes of silent pacing, he trudged back towards Callie.

"This is bullshit, Callie, you have to fix this. Lank will bring everyone down with him. He's one vindictive son of a bitch."

"Joel, don't worry so much." Callie pulled out an envelope and slipped it to Joel. "This is for the 'Yes' vote on the Wanda Act. It should keep him quiet for a while."

Joel carefully took the envelope, looked around and stuffed it in his jacket pocket. "I still don't like this. You're going to need to make sure this thing is handled correctly or a boatload of people will be in deep shit. Including me."

"You're an innocent party in the whole thing. Just stay quiet."

Joel ran his hands through his hair. "I'm trusting you on this, Callie. Don't leave me flailing in the wind."

"I got your back, Joel," Callie said. "And make sure you tell Lank it all stops as soon as he opens his mouth to the press."

"Cal, take care of us." Joel turned and hustled back inside.

Callie, still on the steps of the Capitol building, was checking the messages on her Blackberry when Senator Shulman approached her, also from behind.

"Wanda Act is coming up for a vote next week," Shulman said in a whisper.

From the sound of his voice, she could tell who was stating the obvious in her ear. Turning around slowly, she found Shulman crowding her space and showing no signs of backing away.

"There are a lot of eyes on the Hill right now. Best you find a way to lock in my vote," Shulman said. "Regular amount."

Callie had no patience for him. It showed in her face and her body language. "I'm not sure we need your vote, Senator."

Senator Shulman moved as close as he could be to Callie without being inside of her clothes. He grabbed her elbow on the exact spot Joel did a few minutes earlier. "Trust me, Miss Wheeler, you need me on your side more than ever," Shulman said. "You make sure I get my regular amount and because you are such a bitch, add a little extra."

Shulman let go of her arm and backed away. He looked at her with deep menacing eyes, before finally walking inside. For the first time since she arrived on the Hill six-years-ago, Callie actually felt intimidated and concerned with the physical nature of her last two encounters. She tried her best to keep it together, rubbing her elbow as Shulman walked away from her.

"Asshole," she said to no one.

EIGHTEEN

"I don't know what they're going to do at quarterback, but as long as they beat the Cowgirls, I'll be happy," Walter said, referring to his beloved Redskins. Anyone who spent more than two minutes in the nation's capital quickly learned about the dominant religion among the population there. Its followers liked to be called Washington Redskins fans.

"It's Cow-boys, as in the Dallas Cowboys, or as you might know them, winners of five Super Bowl rings," Kacey said.

Walter and Kacey were walking the tray line together in the cafeteria of the Post. For Kacey, the opening of Redskins training camp signified the start of months of abuse at the hands of Walter and her fellow co-workers, most of whom fell under the Redskins spell, as she liked to call it. Every day of the week from September thru December, she heard about the team and what all the amateur coaches in the newsroom would do to fix it. To combat the onslaught, Kacey would turn the screws after a weekend win by the Cowboys with her famous 'Cowboy final score signs' which she posted all over the building. Kacey spent most Sundays in the fall praying to the football gods for a Dallas win. When the Cowboys failed to do so, the entire staff at the paper conveniently found her during the week to comment on her team's effort. Her only consolation rested in the knowledge that the Redskins lost a lot more than the Cowboys did.

"How could you live here and not root for the Redskins? It's almost like you should be treated as an illegal alien."

"You mean I should get free health care and free in-state college tuition?" Kacey said.

"Don't start," Walter said as he picked up a potato soup from the counter. They'd debated the topic of illegal immigration ad nauseam and anytime she could, Kacey worked to get under his skin with references her conservative father would be proud of. "Honestly, they should deport you," Walter said.

"So if you can't beat them, deport them? I guess that's one way to handle the Cowboys. Maybe it should be on the welcome sign at National Airport," Kacey said. "Welcome to Washington D.C., where we deport anyone who beats our sports teams." Kacey looked up towards the ceiling and began to count one finger at a time. "One, two, three, four…"

Walter watched her with curiosity before interrupting. "What's this about?"

"I'm just thinking a sec…Wizards, Redskins, Nationals, Crapitals…"

"Capitals, Washington Capitals. For the hundredth time."

"Yeah, whatever," Kacey said. "Either way, it's going to be an awfully long list of deportees."

"Haha, very funny." Walter paid for both their lunches and sat down at the table to his left. Kacey, holding a salad and a Diet Coke, sat across from him. "Forget the Cowgirls, tell me how the last couple of days have been since the story came out."

Marge Viviano, a tray in hand, shuffled past their table. "There you are," Margie said, then slid behind Kacey's chair and planted a big kiss on her cheek. "I'm so proud of you."

"Thanks, Margie."

Marge sat down next to Kacey, peeled off the top of the Dole fruit cup on her plate and pulled a spoon from her pocket. "Your story was the lead on NBC News last night," Marge said.

Kacey took a drink from her soda then spit it out when she heard NBC News, laughing as she reached for a napkin. "Did they have a spot with that Kirk Arthur guy?"

"They did."

"Did they mention us in their report?" Walter asked.

"No, they didn't, which pissed me off. He made it seem like it was their story. Anonymous-source situation."

"Who did? Kirk Arthur?" Kacey asked.

"Yeah."

"I knew he was going to do something like that."

Walter swallowed a spoonful of soup and turned his head towards Kacey. "How did you know?"

"Because he didn't like that I was busting his balls. I simply refused to acknowledge his celebrity status."

"No, you didn't?" Marge's eyes lit up.

Kacey laughed, "Oh, yes I did."

Marge was grinning ear-to-ear enjoying the gumption of her protégé, "Did you really not know who he was?"

"Who knows? I might have seen him a couple times on television, but he started in with all that 'Don't you know who I am?' crap," Kacey said. "He seemed really offended that I didn't know who he was."

"I could see him being that way," Walter said. "You shook 'em all up. Got to love that."

"You think so?" Kacey asked.

"Hell, yeah, you did. Nothing gets this town going more than a story about political corruption," Walter said. "The entire political establishment jumps in front of cameras and microphones to profess their innocence, all the while calling their handlers to keep their names out of the papers."

"Television guys, websites, print, they will all try and beat you on this story, Kacey," Marge said. "You better secure your source."

Kacey had no interest in sharing with anyone how she got the story except for Bob and Walter, who already knew. As much as she liked her, Kacey knew Margie well enough to know she wanted to jump on the by-line and grab the story as her own and Kacey wanted no part of that. More importantly, Kacey, herself, had no idea who her source was or if she would get any other information, but Margie didn't need to know any of that.

"Most definitely," Kacey glanced at Walter. He shot her a look back that said he liked her answer. "I have to make a call, guys, so I'll catch up with you in a bit." Kacey wanted Margie to think she was taking her advice.

"Good luck," Marge said.

Kacey left the cafeteria and hurried back to her desk. While she rifled through her notes, she replayed the recording of Lank's press conference from the day before. She reached into her purse and pulled out Joel Hughes' card. She had a few follow up questions that Lank never addressed at the podium. Before Kacey had a chance to dial, Walter was at her desk.

"Don't let anyone know you don't know who the source is. You played that right with Margie and that's how you have to play it with everyone else too."

"I realize that." Kacey shuffled through some loose papers on her desk, then glanced at her steno pad. She stopped the recorder and looked up at Walter. "What if the source went to another paper? Or television or a website?"

"I don't think they would," Walter said. "Whomever the

source is, had to see it in the paper, right? No one else got the story. No paper, no TV, no Internet. No nothing."

"Yeah, so?"

"Why go anywhere else now, if they got the desired effect from you already?"

Kacey stared at the card in her hand and thought about what Walter said. But why her? Why didn't the source go somewhere else. Maybe the New York Times had the story? Wouldn't it pick up more traction on the web?

"I know what you're doing, Kacey. Stop wondering if I'm right. Trust me on this. You gave the source exactly what they expected and then some. That source isn't going anywhere, and they're definitely not going on the Internet."

"And what if they do?"

"So they do and you broke a huge story, but unless you turn on your source, they aren't leaving you. Stay loyal."

Kacey was nervous. She tapped Joel's card on her desk."You think I should ask the source to deal with me alone?"

"You have their phone number?" Walter asked.

"No, all I have is an e-mail. I'm assuming I would just e-mail them back."

"I don't think you have to," Walter said. "You've been e-mailing back and forth until now?"

"Not at all. The e-mail I got told me not to respond. They will contact me if there is anything else they want to tell." Kacey dropped the card on top of her phone, picked up a pen and flipped over a few pages of her steno pad to the first empty page.

Walter thought about it for a moment. "No, you'll be fine. I've got to get back to work, but don't worry about this, it's your story."

Kacey picked up the phone and nodded to Walter as he walked back to his office. She checked the number on the card and dialed it. From behind her, Bob Kravitz slipped a note onto her desk where she could see it. Kacey read the information then lifted up her head to say something to Bob, but he had already disappeared. She read the note once again and shook her head in disbelief. Her legs suddenly felt heavy and her mouth dried up. The phone she dialed began to ring, but the only thing on her mind was talking to Bob.

Kacey let the answering machine pick up and quickly left a message. "Joel, it's Kacey Mercer from the Post. Please return my call before 5 pm today. Thank you." She hurriedly slammed the phone down, stood up and headed straight to Bob's office where she found him sitting behind his desk when she walked in.

"Who told you that?"

Kravitz leaned back in his chair. "A very reliable source. You should check it out."

"She told me herself that she didn't know anything about this."

Kravitz picked up a paper clip from his desk and unfolded it. He looked at Kacey, raised his right eyebrow, but said nothing. Kacey slumped in the chair to her right after witnessing Bob's gesture. She immediately understood what it meant. "Yes, I believe her...she wouldn't lie to me, Bob. We're like sisters."

Bob opened his desk drawer and used the mangled paper clip to fix the hinge on a bracket inside. "I'm not saying it's true, Kacey, I'm just saying you should check it out." He raised his head and looked her square in the eyes. "It's a very reliable source."

It couldn't be true, Kacey thought. She would never have lied to her, it was impossible. In all the years they had known each other, she never once thought Callie had been dishonest with her. Not even over guys. She knew about Henry Morris hitting on Callie, even though he had made out with Kacey the night before. Callie told her. She knew about Callie and Jack behind the old

Paramount Theatre back home, because Callie told her. It had to be bad information.

Kacey stared at an old coffee stain that had seeped itself deep into Bob's carpet while her mind played out the different scenarios she was wrestling with. She slowly picked her head up and for a moment caught a glimpse of her reflection emanating off one of the awards behind Bob's desk. She gazed at herself and chuckled at the sight of the new silver earrings dangling from her ears. She had purchased them the night before while shopping with Callie at Jewelry Barn in Arundel Mills. Kacey looked away from her reflection and replayed their conversation in her head. Callie had snapped at her, "Am I being interviewed, Kacey?" That had never happened before and she recalled how put off she had been by Callie's response. Kacey wondered if she would have given anyone else a pass like she gave Callie. She attributed it to the stress of her job. Now, she wasn't so sure.

"She looked me straight in the eye…I asked her point blank." Kacey straightened up in her chair as her face and body language took on a firmer posture.

The change in her demeanor did not go unnoticed by Bob who took her new resolve to mean something assured her his information might have some credibility. "All I am saying, Kacey, is you might wanna' look into it."

Kacey stood up and walked to the door. She reached for the doorknob, but before she turned it, spun back around to look at Bob, who'd stopped fidgeting with the broken section of his desk long enough to return his attention to Kacey.

"Who would you believe?" Kacey asked before she walked out of his office. She left the door wide open.

NINETEEN

Todd Goodwin walked down the hallway towards Mike's office a little preoccupied, texting. He seemed a tiny bit agitated, but continued to text at a frenetic pace without picking up his head to see where he was walking. Before long, he stood outside of Mike's office door.

"What the hell is with you and that thing? You text like a tenth grade girl," Mike waited for Todd to enter his office .

Todd raised his index finger. "I'll be just a minute."

"Doesn't anyone speak anymore?"

Todd finished his barrage of text messages and headed inside.

"Close the door."

Todd turned around to close the door just as his blackberry beeped, alerting him of an incoming text.

"You pull that thing out of your pocket and I will break your arm, then put two bullets in the middle of your phone."

"Not the phone. Beat the hell out of me all you want, but leave my phone alone."

Mike pointed to the armchair across from his desk, motioning for Todd to sit. Todd looked at Mike shuffle through some papers.

He reached into his pocket for his phone.

Mike, head down and searching for something in his pile of information, didn't miss a beat. "If you touch it, I break it."

Todd lifted up both his hands, palms facing Mike, signifying his backing away. "I'm good, partner. Just don't shoot it."

Mike took a piece of paper and stretched out to hand it to Todd. "Remember this?"

• • •

Todd and Mike had been working together at the CIA since Mike arrived in 1996. Todd was twenty-eight years old at the time, seven years older than Mike, and had joined the Agency two years before him. It was Todd who helped Mike get acquainted with the job and mentored him on some of the finer points of the intelligence service. Todd figured out early on that Mike was different than anyone else he'd worked with at Langley. Sharper, smarter and blessed with an innate feel for the job that could not be taught.

The two men had become close over the years and trusted each other with their lives. Mike and Todd were in the West Bank during the summer of 2001, collecting intel on a radical wing of Islamists who had made overtures about destroying American landmarks. Todd had dropped Mike off at the corner of King George Street and Jaffa Road in Jerusalem at 10 o'clock on a sunny Thursday morning. They had made plans to meet up again at the same spot at 2:00 pm after Mike's meeting had concluded. Mike had been following a lead he picked up a few nights earlier from a day laborer in Beit Jala. He spent the first three hours and forty minutes in Jerusalem that day, searching for a man he was supposed to have met, who it turned out, did not show. Todd called Mike and told him he would pick him up a few minutes early, which he did at 1:55 pm. Five minutes later, fifteen people, eight of whom were under the age of eighteen, were murdered when a homicide bomber blew himself up inside the Sbarro Pizza store at the corner of King George Street and Jaffa Road. Mike felt lucky to be alive. He owed his life to Todd and from that point on, Mike, who was a rising star at the Agency, did whatever he could to make sure Todd became a permanent member of his team.

• • •

Todd took the piece of paper from Mike's hand and gave it a long look. "What am I supposed to remember?"

"Look at the guy in the middle real close, look at his eyes. You remember him, the guy we busted a few years back?"

"Which guy?"

"The guy in the middle," Mike said. "What the hell was his name…Kahlid Farhzat?"

"The one with the bomb books in Baltimore?"

"Same one."

In June of 2003, Mike was called to the Green Acres apartment complex in Baltimore, after the landlord failed to collect overdue payments from a renter of one of his apartments. The landlord attempted to connect with the renter more than a dozen times with no response. Neighbors had not seen anyone use the apartment in over a month at which time the landlord decided to open it up himself. Upon entry, he immediately called the local police department who referred the case to the CIA due to the contents they'd found inside. The entire apartment was empty except for a large cache of gunpowder, C-4, ignition switches, timers and deodorant cans. The musty smell seemed to have been enhanced by the stuffy air from intense summer heat and no ventilation coming in or out. In addition to other bomb making materials, they came across books with titles such as "Blaster's Handbook," "The Chemistry of Powder and Explosives," "Improvised Radio Detonation Techniques" and "The Do-It-Yourself Gunpowder Cookbook." Mike and Todd traced the apartment to a man named Khalid Farzhat and found him a short time later at Big Daddy's Pool Hall in Glen Burnie, Maryland, late one night. Khalid denied the charges, claiming he had sub-rented the apartment to another man and then moved out to Catonsville, Maryland, a few miles away. While he was not allowed to sub-lease the apartment, the authorities could not hold him on the bomb charges since there was no proof that any of the materials in the apartment belonged to him. Both the FBI and the CIA did an extensive search for his fingerprints, but each effort came up empty.

After the arrest, Mike had done his homework on Khalid and what he found shook him up. There had been other questionable dealings in America with Khalid. In all, authorities suspected him of being the mastermind behind at least twelve incidents around the world where the combined deaths had totaled over 500 people. He seemed to have no affiliation with any known terror group, but was linked in some way, to all of them. His motivation appeared to be driven by ideology, although Mike never ruled out the possibility that money played a major role in his actions. He had heard nothing regarding Khalid since late 2004, until he got the message from Akiva.

"Did you know he's running a charity?" Mike said while he stared at his computer screen. "Something to do with homeless children or something like that."

"What?"

"Yup. Raising funds for the needy in Baltimore."

"How is that possible?" Todd put his hands on his pants to stifle the sound of the vibrating phone in his pocket.

"He has a new name. Ken Farmer." Mike said.

"You sure it's the same guy?"

Mike pulled out a picture from one of his files and held it up close to the one on his computer screen. Todd stood up and walked behind Mike's desk to get a closer look. Other than the mustache in the old photo, an exact match. "This is one bad dude," Mike said. "I think we better tell Biggs."

"Any chance this new thing is on the level?"

Mike stood up, looked at Todd and shook his head. He picked up the three files regarding Khalid that he'd put to the side along with the picture Todd had just returned to him. He started to laugh. "Any chance you're still dating the same girl from two weeks ago?"

"Did you have to go there?"

"Go where? You still dating her?"

"That ain't right, man..." Todd said as he followed Mike out of the office and closed the door behind him.

TWENTY

Monday July, 25, 2011

Summer days in the nation's capital are long and usually, for the political class, fairly uneventful. There is the occasional fight over tax cuts or programs that have outlived their usefulness, but for the most part, Washington summers were pretty boring. Until the summer of 2011.

Kacey Mercer's story grabbed the attention of everyone inside the Beltway. News organizations and bloggers were everywhere looking to find out more information, but Congress and their staffs closed ranks around Senator Lank and the usual reliable leaks coming out of D.C. were nowhere to be found. Taking Barry's advice, denials were issued from all camps. Without any credible evidence to the contrary, the story, got pushed to the background. Barry Miller felt like he dodged a bullet. Just in case things got any worse, he began to initiate his own form of damage control.

Callie was at her desk when Donna Walkin buzzed her telephone intercom. "Ms. Wheeler, Mr. Miller would like to see you in the conference room."

Callie had been on the phone when Donna interrupted her. "Can you please tell him I'll be there in two minutes? I'm just finishing up with Senator Macklin."

"Will do."

Callie returned to her conversation with the Illinois Republican. "Senator, I have a few different issues to discuss with you once the Wanda Act passes next week. Please let me know when it's a good time to come by your office so we can talk."

"I will instruct my staff to clear some time on my calendar whenever you decide to drop by. All I ask, is that you call a day or two in advance to give us time to work you into the schedule," Macklin said. "I do love the time we have to ourselves, Ms. Wheeler. You know, when it's just the two of us."

Callie rolled her eyes and tried hard not laugh out loud. "I do as well, Senator," Callie said, in a voice not much louder than a whisper.

"Please call me, Gerald. I think we have known each other long enough and umm…well enough to drop the formalities. I'm sure that would be okay with you, Callie."

Callie was not sure why Macklin chose this moment to ratchet up the charm after all the years they had worked together, but she decided she could play the game as well as he could. "Of course, Gerald."

"Then I shall see you in a few days, Callie." Macklin said. "I'll be counting the minutes."

"As will I, Senator," Callie said, a look of pure disdain on her face.

"Gerald," Macklin said.

"Surely."

Callie hung up the phone and felt like she needed a bath. She began to gather her things and make her way to the conference room. Before she left her office, she sent a text to Kacey asking if she had gotten her phone message from earlier in the day. As she walked down the hallway, her mind turned back to Macklin. She thought about the timing of his new informal approach. It confused her. Was he trying to catch her with her guard down? Did he think by flirting with her in that way, she would be more inclined to protect him should anything else come out? What sense would it make, she thought, since she would in all likelihood, be implicated in any story that implicated Macklin? Or was he trying to actually make a pass at her, which he had already done quite a few times over the years. She had no idea what his agenda was but knowing Macklin, she would find out soon enough.

The conference room was empty except for Barry who sat at a long, cherry table surrounded by thirty high-back chairs. Normally he'd be seated at the head of the table in front of the long projector screen that extended from the ceiling. It came as a bit of a surprise to Callie to find Barry facing the glass wall of the conference room with his back to the long window that showed off the D.C. skyline. He sat in the middle of the table, directly in front of the heavy glass double doors that Callie walked through, his laptop facing him. She assumed there would be others from the firm waiting for her as well, but as she sat down across from him, it was just her and Barry.

"Callie, I just got off the phone with Representative Singleton. He said you did an outstanding job on the Wanda Act."

"Thank you. I'll be sure to acknowledge the kind words he said to my boss, the next time I see him."

A small smile appeared on Barry's face, then disappeared. He pulled out four pieces of paper and placed them in front of Callie. "The first two sheets on your left were the votes in both Houses on the Wanda Act before we got involved, or should I say, before you got involved. The next two are the votes as they stand today."

Callie looked at the sheets to her left, then did the same to the ones on her right. She lifted her head and smiled. "I'd say we earned our money on this one."

"I'd have to agree," Barry said. "On top of all that, we will have saved over six-hundred-thousand dollars that we originally budgeted for this project."

Barry pulled out an envelope from his jacket pocket, opened it and removed a check made out to Callie Wheeler then set it down in front of her.

Callie rolled her chair closer to the table, leaned forward and looked at the check, but did not pick it up. "Three hundred thousand dollars?"

"Courtesy of Wanda Pharmaceuticals."

Callie had received bonus money before, but outside of one occasion, nothing this large in one check. "I don't know what to say...Thank you."

"No, thank you. We banked almost ten times that amount in fees from your work and they were more than happy to pay it. Consider it a reward for a job well done from all of us."

Part of Callie's job at M&G was to help Congressmen structure the language in particular bills in order to benefit her clients. The legislation would be written to sound universal in its scope as if it could apply to anyone, when in reality, it was only applicable to her client's situation. In Wanda Pharmaceuticals' case for example, the government would give tax breaks to any company in North Dakota with revenues over seven-hundred-million dollars a year, whose products help cure ailments and or diseases, and whose work force was over five thousand people. In theory, any company in North Dakota could take advantage of that tax break. In reality, only Wanda Pharmaceuticals qualified for it. In return for their support in helping them get the legislation passed, her clients would donate money to a Congressman's Political Action Committee (PAC) or their re-election campaign and it is all perfectly legal under Federal law. This is the system Washington politicians set up for themselves and those were the rules that

Congress played by. More importantly to Wanda Pharmaceuticals, no one in Washington did it any better than Callie Wheeler. The Wanda act would save the company hundreds of millions of dollars in the long run. It made the cost of doing business in Washington a bargain.

Callie picked up the check, looked at it then slid it into the envelope and placed it inside her day planner. She knew Barry too well and sensed something more was on the way. He would have normally dropped the check in her mailbox or just stopped by her office and left it for her. Callie gathered her hair, slipped it behind her right ear, crossed her legs and leaned back in her chair. She was waiting for Barry to show his hand.

"Callie, I wanted to talk to you about something and I know what you're going to say, but stay with me on this. We have more than enough votes for the Wanda Act to pass and you did a great job on it. The client is happy and you already know how I feel."

Callie acknowledged Barry's compliments with a nod of her head. "Thank you."

"What I want to do now is move you to start work on another bill. I've been going back and forth with the client on this, but he insists he wants you."

"And who would take up the Wanda Act through the President's signature?"

"We're going to let Rachel and Murray handle that."

"Really?" Callie knew Rachel Parks and Murray Green were rock solid in Barry's corner. Derek had been against hiring Rachel, but threw Barry a bone and regretted it from her first day. Murray was pulled from another K Street firm, by Barry, and given a huge signing bonus to come over to M&G. Callie had her own run-ins with Murray when he was at Kensington Partners, but as long as he left her alone and stayed away from her projects, she would not interfere with whatever he had going on. Barry knew she could have cared less for either of them, but with Wanda in the bag, he assumed she would be okay with it.

"Is that why you gave me the check? You wanted to drop these two on me and figured you would soften me up first before they destroyed my legislation?"

"Now wait a second. One, they're not going to destroy your legislation and..."

"You know what I mean."

"And two, it was not my intent to pay you off. But now, when I think of it, it's not such a bad idea."

Callie was not amused. "Yeah. Whatever."

"Listen, we have to protect each other, you and I. We know a lot of information no one else does and we need to watch each other's back."

"I get that, but what does this have to do with you pulling me off the Wanda Act?"

"I'm not really pulling you off. I need you're help with earmarks for a new client."

"Sure sounds like you're pulling me off," Callie said. She didn't believe a word that came out of Barry's mouth. Questions bounced around in her head. He knew never to talk about what they both knew. Why would he ever mention that? What's going on with Wanda? Why Murray and Rachel and not Whitaker? Something did not feel right, but Callie played along.

"I need you to work on getting roughly fifty million-dollars inserted into the Secondary Education Bill that Senator Oxford is sponsoring with Senator Buck."

"What's the money for?"

Barry reached for the laptop at his right side, turned it around and slid it towards Callie. Callie read the webpage then lifted her head.

"So this is for re-education of veterans?"

"Something like that. We need to get funding for a new program that teaches soldiers injured in battle, how to find employment and train for new careers."

Callie sat silently for a moment. Again something didn't add up, she thought, but now was not the time to say anything. "Isn't that covered by the veteran's administration?"

"Not nearly enough. This private organization will pick up the pieces," Barry said. "I know what you're thinking on this, but trust me, it's a good program."

Trust him? Callie was not sure that was a gamble worth taking, but she couldn't let Barry know that.

"They've given us a healthy budget to work with," Barry said. "Plus there's a one percent bonus in this for you."

Callie wasn't sure if he was actually trying to buy her off, or just enticing her to take the project and leave the Wanda act to Barry's lackeys. A half a million, no matter the motives, was still a half a million.

"An offer I can't refuse, huh?" Callie sat in silence for a moment while she considered the angles he might be working. No matter what she came up with, all roads still led back to the money.

"One percent? That's a half a million dollars, Barry. You sure about this?" Callie asked as she pushed Barry's laptop back towards him.

Barry smiled and reached for the computer. "Absolutely."

"Okay. I'll do it."

"Great," Barry said. He stood up and started to gather his computer and a few other items. "I'll set you up with all you need."

Callie listened, but kept silent.

"There is one thing, Callie," Barry said as he headed for the door.

Barry's last minute addition did not shock Callie at all. "The vote could come up as soon as next week so we have to move on this yesterday."

"No problem. I'm on it," Callie said as Barry opened the conference room doors and walked out. Callie sat in her chair for a few minutes thinking about what had just transpired. She had never been taken off of a bill until it was either dead or signed into law. It didn't surprise her, but she had to admit, it caught her a little off-guard. It was not something she was used to and now that it happened, she didn't like how it felt.

Callie walked to the corner of the room, opened up a bottle of Diet Coke and poured herself a drink. She continued towards the large window and took in the view of the Capitol, which she could never get enough of. Callie took a sip of her soda then folded her left arm under the elbow of her right one and stared out the window. Something didn't feel right about this, but she still couldn't put her finger on it.

"What are you up to you little shit?" she said quietly to an empty room then took another sip of her drink.

Looking through the glass wall behind her, Barry Miller enjoyed the view of Callie's backside encased in a tight grey skirt, then stepped away from the wall and dialed his cell phone. "All set," he said and walked back to his office.

TWENTY-ONE

Walter Bloom had been enamored with journalism ever since he first learned about it as a teenager. He would read the early morning dailys in his hometown of Brooklyn, New York then rush to pick up the afternoon editions on his way home from school. He had always spoken fondly of the time when a paper would produce different editions each day and still got upset at the thought of a world moving into the digital age. He was dragged kicking and screaming into the twenty-first century and while never a big fan of newspaper websites or e-mail, he now viewed them as a necessary evil. His desire for excellence in reporting fueled him to become the top reporter at the Washington Post, something he took pride in especially after turning down numerous opportunities to be a featured columnist at the paper. After the Lank story hit the public arena, he'd been approached by Bob Kravitz on two separate occasions to take the lead on it, but Walter vehemently refused. Instead, he told his boss he would help Kacey if the story became too big, but wanted her to receive all the credit.

Walter was carrying a folder in his right hand and an apple in his left when he arrived at Kacey's desk. Kacey was in her chair, eyes closed, and her earbuds replaying the last seventy-two hours worth of information she stored on her digital recorder. She was oblivious to Walter, who'd been in front of her for over a minute before she took notice of him.

"Oh, Walter," she said, a bit startled when she recognized him hovering over her. "I'm sorry, I didn't see you there." Kacey took the earbuds out of her ears and stopped the recorder. "What's up?"

"May I?" Walter asked, pointing to the chair on the side of Kacey's cubicle.

Kacey bobbed her head. "Of course."

Walter sat down and placed the folder on top of her desk. Inside of the file that he had marked 'Lank' in red ink, were a large number of clippings and notes about the Senator, which he'd accumulated over many years.

"Don't look at that yet," he said. Kacey pulled her hand back from the top of the folder as if it were on fire.

"What is it?"

"I'll get to that in a minute, but leave it there and don't look yet."

"Why? What's in it?"

"I said, don't worry about that. It's nothing extraordinary, just something I think you should be aware of."

Kacey leaned back in her chair. "Okay...if you don't want me to look at it, what do you want?"

"I had a few questions about this Lank story. You got a minute?"

"Sure, go ahead."

Walter pulled out his notes and referenced them before addressing Kacey. "So the bill in question was Lank-Gorman, correct?"

"Correct, but known more as just the Lank Bill," Kacey said.

"If I'm not mistaken that was an eminent domain bill, disguised as an Appropriations Bill that they basically passed in secret right before the Memorial Day break, what, about five years back?"

Kacey nodded her head. "A little more than that, 2006, Yes."

"Tell me what you know about eminent domain."

"You mean the bill?"

"No, I mean the whole concept of eminent domain."

Kacey reached for her steno pad and flipped it back a few pages. She searched her notes, then turned back a few more pages until she settled on the information she was looking for.

"Should I read you from the notes I have here?"

"Yeah, let's see what you've got."

"Eminent domain is an action of the State to seize a citizen's private property, or seize a citizen's rights in property with due monetary compensation, but without the owner's consent. The property is taken either for government use or is delegated to third parties who will devote it to public or civic use or, in some cases, economic development." Kacey looked up at Walter. "That is the dictionary definition."

"Okay, good, but what does it mean in regular people terms?"

"It means the government can take a person's land and do with it what it wants, if it feels it is in the public interest."

"How does the government get that power?"

Kacey sorted through her notes again, flipping back and forth through the pages looking for the answer to Walter's question. "Got it," she said. "The Fifth Amendment of the Constitution. But eminent domain was limited by the Takings clause in the Fifth Amendment in 1791, that said, and I quote, "Nor shall private property be taken for public use, without just compensation." All that means is if the government wants to take land they have to pay for it. Public use, however has been redefined."

"How so?"

"Governments used to take over land or property because it had become beaten down, impoverished. Basically what they called blight. However, in 2005 the Supreme Court ruled in the Kelo v the City of New London case that New London, Connecticut could take non-blighted private property by eminent domain and then transfer it for a dollar a year to a private developer, solely for the purpose of increasing municipal revenues. Basically, the goal was increased tax-revenue for the state."

"Exactly. So what was the purpose of Lank-Gorman? I don't get it. Couldn't Congress impose eminent domain on impoverished areas whenever it wanted?"

"Well, yes and no. In truth, the courts ruled that the States had that right," Kacey said. "What the Lank-Gorman Bill did was give the Federal Government, in this case, Congress, the power to designate any area it wants, anywhere, as vital to the government's interest be it impoverished, or not."

"So the bill threw out the words 'blight' or 'impoverished' and just said they could do whatever they wanted, to whatever land they wanted, so long as the owner was compensated?"

"Pretty much," Kacey said.

"And who decides what is just compensation?"

Kacey put her notes down and looked at Walter. "Congress."

Walter shook his head and dropped his own set of notes on Kacey's desk. "Does that sound right to you?"

"Of course not," Kacey said. "Basically what it means is the Federal Government can take your home and land, pay you what they think it's worth, and that's that."

"The States have no say?"

"You got that right. Lank-Gorman gave Congress the power to override the States."

"What does Jonas Foster have to do with all of this and what's his connection to Lank?"

"I'm working on that. I think I might have something, but I haven't gotten confirmation on it."

Walter's face seemed to lose some of its life. He scrunched his mouth towards his nose and shook his head again in obvious frustration. "How did this happen?"

"Don't look at me, I was working in the City section in 2006."

"And Conroy signed it into law?"

"Sure did. Memorial Day 2006."

"How did a guy like Conroy sign a bill like that? Did anyone know?"

"They called it an appropriations bill, not an eminent domain bill, so no one figured it was anything special, I guess," Kacey said. "As a matter of fact there was barely any press on it, as far as I can tell. On top of that, this eminent domain stuff was hidden away deep inside the bill, like page 1,621 or thereabouts."

"The Constitutional issues, States rights, free market, I don't understand how it flew under the radar."

Kacey was staggered by Walter's sudden concern for States rights and the free market. For as long as she had known him, he always associated with the far left of the political spectrum on most issues, something that gnawed at her ever since they had gotten to know each other better. It got to the point where they had borderline riots when the two of them talked politics. "Excuse me? States rights?" Kacey said. "What is that about, Walt?"

Walter shook his head, again. "I know...I'm scaring myself." Walter stood up and stared at Kacey. The toothpick he took out of his shirt pocket and put in his mouth accentuated the confused look on his face.

"I know what that means," Kacey said. "What's really bothering you?"

"Been on this beat a long time. This one here smells awful."

Kacey's phone disturbed their meeting. The ringtone was reserved for one person only. Kacey let it continue to ring.

"Want to get that?" Walter asked, after noticing Callie's picture pop up.

"No. I'm okay. Let's get back to Lank a minute. What are you thinking?"

Walter reached for the folder he'd handed her earlier and opened it up. Inside were various press clippings of Senators Gorman and Lank. "Look at these."

Kacey read the first few articles and lifted her head, glaring at him with a curious look. She scanned a few more, closed the folder and stood up. "Here." Kacey handed it back to him.

"No, you keep it and give it back to me when this story is over."

"What do you mean when the story is over?"

"I've known Lank over thirty years and Gorman more than twenty. There is just no way that they are smart enough to be sponsoring this bill, as you can probably see from their press clippings. They're just not that bright," Walter said. "There's got to be more to this story, Kacey. A whole lot more."

TWENTY-TWO

Charlie Palmer's Steak House was located across the street from the Capitol building, at the intersection of Louisiana Avenue and First Street. The restaurant had long been considered one of the more upscale eateries in the Constitution Avenue district. Like other venues near the House and Senate, it had played host to many of America's power brokers, in both the regular and private dining rooms. As the mid-summer day turned into night, Callie sat in the private dining room with Senators Macklin, Bane and McCombs. She was hard at work attempting to insert Barry's ear-marks into the legislation.

"So basically what you need us to do is hide the fifty-million in the Secondary Education Bill," Senator Bane said.

"How you insert it, I don't care. I just need you to get it done," Callie said. "And we need it done in the morning."

"We can wait to get it in right before the vote," Macklin said. "But getting it by the President is another matter."

"I'll handle the President," Senator McCombs said. "We'll be fine."

Callie opened her briefcase and removed three large envelopes then handed one to each man. "Gentlemen, on behalf of my client, please accept these donations to your re-election campaign. I think you will find what you are looking for inside."

Callie looked at each of them as they checked out the contents of their envelopes. Senator McCombs smiled. "Thank you, Ms. Wheeler."

"Yes, Ms. Wheeler. On behalf of the Bane for Senate in 2012 committee, I thank you," Bane said.

Macklin checked inside his envelope, sifted through the contents with his fingertips, then not so innocently brushed his hand across Callie's and kept it close, his pinky finger resting on hers. She looked down at his hand and feigned a smile, then gently moved her hand away from his.

"Thank you, Callie. I do appreciate your contributions to my campaign," Macklin said. "It is because of great patriots like yourself, that government runs as well as it does. Please tell your clients I am much appreciative of their generosity."

"Do we need to do anymore to insure the bill passes?" Callie asked. "I'm trying to get a sense of what kind of votes we have. Barry handed this to me earlier today and I had no idea how quickly this was going to come up in the House."

"I think we have the votes in the Senate," Macklin said.

"I'm not sure I'm ready to bring this up for a vote yet," Senator McCombs said. As the Senate Majority leader, he was responsible for setting the agenda and the schedule for the Senate. "There's talk that the House is preparing to vote on it by the end of the week, but I'm still not sure what I'm going to do."

Callie could sense McCombs trying to shake her down for something extra. She'd been through this with him a few times before when he would attempt to strong arm her. But ever since Conroy had been elected President, McCombs had become incorrigible. He liked to let everyone know who was in charge of the Senate and he wasn't about to let Callie Wheeler or anyone else dictate to him when things should get done. Callie knew his ego needed to constantly be fed, which is why for the last twelve months, she'd worked hard to find creative ways to deal with him.

"Senator, I understand you want to wait this out, but I'm fairly certain we'll have the votes to get this through, if not by the end of next week then very soon after. I am also quite confident that my client would be incredibly thankful for you going out of your way to squeeze this in," Callie said.

McCombs had waited all evening for this opportunity and once she gave him the opening, he took full advantage of it. He stood up from his seat, walked towards Callie and whispered in her ear. "May I see you a moment, please, in private?"

"If you'll excuse me, I'll be right back." Callie stood up and headed to the corner of the private dining room where she huddled with Senator McCombs. He wasted no time getting to the point. "How appreciative do you think they would be?"

Callie reached into her skirt pocket and pulled out a small notecard. "They mentioned something to me about a five-hundred dollar a plate fundraiser they were interested in hosting for Congressional leadership. If you would like, I could speak to them about penciling you in next March."

McCombs slow played his hand by taking a few moments before he responded. "I was hoping we could work something out sooner than that?"

"What did you have in mind?"

"We could use some postage money for the campaign..." McCombs let the comment hang in the air, waiting for Callie to react.

Ever the professional, Callie ignored her own frustration with Mcombs and played along. "How much postage do you need, Senator?"

Callie had done this before with others in both Houses and

knew they liked to get their postage sponsored in nice round numbers.

"About one-hundred thousand."

When someone like McCombs wanted postage from Callie, it meant he wanted money and Callie knew the drill. She would ask her client to sponsor postage for McCombs' re-election committee and they would send him a check for whatever amount he wanted. McCombs would then buy a few dollars worth of postage, and pocket the rest of the money. It was an old scam run by Congressmen for decades and McCombs was no different than the rest. He would ultimately report the number as postage costs in his Senate filings and no one would know any different.

"I'll see what I can do, Senator."

"Get back to me on this right quick. The Senate schedule fills up in a heartbeat. Wouldn't want this bill being backlogged, if you know what I mean."

"I'll take it up with my client first thing in the morning and get back to you by noon."

McCombs hurried back to his seat where Bane and Macklin munched on some chocolate mousse. Callie, who followed McCombs back to the table, had enough of the congressional theater and decided it was time to call it a night.

"Let anyone who's on the fence understand my client's prepared to do what it takes to get this passed." Callie picked up her things and headed for the door. "Gentleman, as always, it is a pleasure doing business with you. Please keep me posted."

Callie walked out of the restaurant while the three men continued their conversation over dessert. She stepped out onto First Street and turned left down the alleyway to the Colonial parking garage where she had parked her car. Callie entered through the door on the first floor and began the trek up the stairs, but unlike all the other times she used this parking facility, she did not hear the loud noise of the door closing behind her. The heavy metal doors made a distinct sound when they closed which caused them to echo through the drab, concrete walled stairwell. Callie took a peek behind to quell her curiosity and caught a glimpse of someone looking up at her. She considered the possibility that others were in search of their vehicles, but changed her mind when she heard garbled whispers and the shuffling of feet that were quickly climbing the stairs.

Callie raced to the third floor door and flung it open, rushing towards her Mercedes which she had parked a few spots from the door. She turned off her alarm as she approached the car and leaped inside, gently closing the driver side door shut. She lied down across the front seats, lifted her head and peered through the passenger side window. Two large Middle Eastern men opened the garage door, stepped onto the third floor and looked around. Callie slid down to the floor and closed her eyes. She did her best to appear lifeless, though her hands betrayed her when they began to tremble. Her heart beat so loudly inside her chest she feared it would give her away.

The two men scanned the area but failed to locate her. Callie heard them speaking in Arabic. They ambled past a few cars, including hers, looked around, conversed a little more then headed back into the stairwell. Callie looked out her window just in time to see them exit through the door. She stayed down a few minutes longer before getting up to start her car. Her hands were still shaking. She stabbed them at the ignition, missing more than once. She grabbed her right hand with her left, pulled it forward towards the steering wheel and eventually slid the key in its place.

Callie pulled out of the spot then drove slowly around each corner looking to see if the men were still in pursuit. On her way to the cashier, she negotiated every turn, her eyes darting back and forth searching for her pursuers. Her heart rate increased at such a rapid pace, she could feel it beat inside her throat. At the toll-booth, she paid her fee and pulled out of the garage. Survival impulses ran through her nerves. Turning right onto Louisiana Avenue, she saw the same two men walking past the restaurant. One spoke into his cell phone, the other looked to be motioning to someone inside the steak house. Callie hurried past the restaurant, raced down the block and started on the twenty-five minute ride to her home.

Callie had never experienced anything like that before. She was a mess driving to the house she shared with Mike on the corner of Delaware Avenue and Taylor Street in Chevy Chase. She called him, but it went straight to voicemail. She tried to reach Kacey at home, but there was no answer, then tried her cell and received the same response. Panicked, Callie called Mike two more times as she drove, but he didn't pick up until she had already turned left onto Chevy Chase Parkway, less than five minutes from her home. She was barely able to speak, her body still shaking from the incident.

"Mike, Mike. Please be outside when I get home, please Mike…"

Mike had never heard her like this. "Callie, what's wrong?"

"Be outside, Mike, please be outside…"

"What happened, Callie?"

Callie hung up the phone. Mike raced outside onto the wraparound porch and stood there waiting for her. He reached behind his back and checked his Ruger, then returned the firearm to his pants and waited anxiously for Callie to arrive. He saw Callie pull up in front of the house in a panic. Their home, which they purchased together two years earlier, was the first one on a street with no outlet. It was also the largest home on a block that turned unusually dark in the evenings exactly how Mike liked it. Mike ran off the porch to meet her. Callie, who had always parked in the driveway, pulled up in front of the house. She hurriedly jumped out of the car and into Mike's arms. She left the door of her Mercedes open. The motor was still running.

Mike held her. He stroked her hair, softly kissing the top of her head as she rested on his shoulder.

"What happened? Why are you shaking? Cal? What happened?"

She said nothing. Callie tried hard to calm down in the safety of Mike's embrace. Mike assumed he would find out what happened soon enough and chose to comfort his fiancé instead.

"Shhh...you're okay...I've got you now, Cal. You're home."

Callie tried to talk, but couldn't say much. She was still shaking. Instinctively, Mike's eyes scanned the pitch black night looking around for anything suspicious. He had his left hand around Callie. His right was waiting to pounce on the Ruger. He took one last look at darkness, then wrapped both his arms around her and led her into their home. Mike stepped back outside a moment later, his pistol firmly in his hand and ran to her car to shut it off and retrieve her belongings. He did another scan of the immediate area then went back inside the house locking the door behind him.

Three hundred yards away in the dark, two different light-skinned men, sat in a car parked down the block from Callie's home. One of the men pulled out his cell phone, dialed, and waited for an answer.

"She's home," he said. "He's with her."

The man listened to the voice on the phone, then hung up.

"Well?"

"Not tonight. Another time."

The two men drove down Taylor Street with their lights off. They stared at Callie's home as they cruised by.

Inside the house, Callie, a little calmer, held a gin and tonic in her hand and tried to relax on the sofa. Mike strode into the room and sat down next to her.

"You've never seen these men before?"

"Never. Not once."

"You're sure?"

Callie was annoyed with his question. "Mike, faces and names are my job. Believe me, I've never seen them."

"They came out of the blue, just like that?"

Callie raised the glass to her lips and took a sip from her drink. "I have no clue what they wanted or why they were after me, but I have no doubt that it was me they were after."

Mike wrapped his arm around Callie and held her close. He kissed her on the head in an attempt to pacify her. "The best thing to do now is to be aware of your surroundings. I know you think they were after you, and it's possible they were, but you can't be certain."

Callie pushed herself away from Mike and glared at him with a look of disbelief that exposed her instant anger. "You don't believe me?"

"I believe you, Cal," Mike said. "Just in my business..."

Callie could feel the blood race to her head. She was furious with Mike for questioning her account of the events. "I was the only one around. Who else could it have been?"

"There could be a lot of reasons why they were there..."

"They followed me up the stairs, came out on my floor, looked around, didn't find me, then left and you think there are a lot of reasons they did that?"

"All I'm saying is it's possible you weren't..."

"Fuck you, Mike," Callie wasn't in the mood. She stood up and took her drink with her as she started to walk away.

"Where you going?"

"Anywhere but here."

"Callie…I didn't mean anything…c'mon, Cal."

Callie slammed their bedroom door shut, leaving Mike sitting on the couch wondering exactly what had just happened.

TWENTY-THREE

Callie nudged the microphone slightly away from her. She watched as Miles Goodman poured her a glass of water. Callie lifted the cup slowly to her lips and took a long drink. Callie found great strength in knowing that the entire chamber was waiting for her next move. She milked the moments of silence, dabbing her mouth with a napkin and straightening her blouse. Callie wanted to send a message to each Senator on the dais that in fact she was the one in charge of the hearing and not the other way around. Miles Goodman awkwardly fidgeted with his tie while he waited for Callie to continue with her statement. All eyes in the Senate continued to focus on her.

"I had no idea why I was being followed. More importantly and much more bothersome to me, was the question that kept gnawing at me. Why did Barry ask me to add the earmark to the Oxford Secondary Education Bill when he just as easily could have done it himself? I actually should have figured it out when he offered me the half-million dollar bonus, but I was intrigued by all that money. I know all of you know what I'm talking about," Callie said. "How could I pass that up?"

Callie's words drew the attention of all the Senators on the committee and it appeared obvious to anyone who had been watching them that they were still uncomfortable with her testimony. Most of the legislators on the dais would have left the room if this was a regular day at COLA. However, with the entire country focused in on this event, anyone leaving the hearing was in danger of appearing irresponsible and weak. Worst of all, it would leave a lasting impression on the viewing public's mind, that Congress surrendered to the woman in front of them who seemingly had no fear. Callie was undeterred.

"What I soon came to realize was that the money I was given to get the earmark through was nowhere near enough. It was child's play compared to what was to follow."

Senator Lank, having listened to the ongoing assault long enough, interrupted the proceedings quite loudly.

"Mr. Chairman, how much longer will this woman be allowed to continue?"

Chairman Rice leaned over to hear Senator Shulman, who had covered his microphone and whispered in Rice's ear. "I warned you about her, Les, you should have stopped her when you had the chance. This is not good."

"So what do you think?" Rice asked him, his hand covering his own microphone.

"I think the best we can do is let her finish and then go after her hard in direct questioning," Shulman said. As much as he wanted to shut her up, it was no longer about keeping her quiet as it was about discrediting her and all that she had to say. Callie had taken control of the hearing and any move to silence her now would be a public relations nightmare for Congress. They had no choice but to wait for her conclusion.

"Is there much more of this Ms. Wheeler?" Chairman Rice asked.

Callie was defiant. She did not hesitate in her response, which she knew would keep them on edge.

"Mr. Chairman, I am not even close to being finished but if you like, I would be more than happy to focus my remarks only on what I know about the Senators who sit on this Committee," Callie said. "The problem is, none of us have that kind of time."

The hearing room exploded with cameras flashing and a loud grumbling that rose from the gallery. The Senators continued to look helpless. Callie's confidence did nothing to change that impression. While the members on the dais sat uncomfortably and wondered amongst themselves how much worse things were going to get, Callie smiled and looked to the shocked Chairman for direction.

"Mr. Chairman, when would you like me to continue?"

Wednesday, July 27, 2011

"Mike, I need you to drive me to the gym."

Callie was standing over Mike's sleeping body dressed in tight black shorts, a white tank top and wearing a pair of white Nike running shoes.

"I need your help. Come on. Get up. You need to drive me to the gym."

Mike, having spent the night in the guest room, rubbed his eyes and turned to face the clock hanging on the wall across from his bed. "It's 5:30 in the morning, go yourself."

Following the events of the previous evening, Callie preferred an escort. "I'm not going by myself after last night. You have to drive me there."

"Are you serious, Cal?"

Callie folded her arms and waited.

"What?" Mike barely opened one eye and closed it again.

"I'm not going out there alone…"

"Nothing's gonna happen to you, Callie. Just go yourself."

"You really expect me to go by myself?"

Mike could sense the frustration in her voice, but he ignored it and rolled over away from her. "You're gonna be fine. Just go. I'll call you later."

"You still don't believe me, do you?"

Mike sighed as he rolled back over. "I believe you, it's just that no one's gonna…"

"Ya' know what, Mike? Go fuck yourself."

Callie grabbed a water bottle she'd left on the antique table near the bed and headed out the guest room door. "And don't bother calling me."

She stormed across the hall and down the stairs then slammed the front door on her way out. Her eyes were buzzing all around her as she scanned the area from the front porch. She could feel her pulse racing. Callie checked her immediate surroundings for any signs of life, then did the same thing two more times before she rechecked all over again. She briefly considered going back inside and skipping her workout, but she refused to let fear get the best of her. Searching the street, yards and sidewalks one more time, she sprinted the forty feet to her vehicle and without fastening her seatbelt, started the car and immediately began pulling away. From the guest bedroom window, Mike watched as Callie safely made a left onto Delaware Avenue. No one was following her.

Callie was on her way to Crunch gym on Wisconsin Avenue in downtown D.C. Since finding the gym in 2009, Callie and Kacey had worked out there together each Wednesday and Friday morning. One day they would go through an intensive treadmill workout, the other a sixty-minute stationary bike class called the 'Long Ride'. Callie became concerned when she hadn't heard from Kacey since Sunday afternoon and that conversation lasted less than a minute. She didn't think too much of it until the silence carried on into a third day. Now, she was hoping that before they were finished at the gym, she could get some clarity as to what exactly was going on.

The treadmills at Crunch spread out along a balcony overlooking the free weights section below, directly across from the cycling area, which was always full at this time of the day. In the midst of a few dozen treadmills, Callie worked out on her favorite machine directly in front of a group of TV's, some showing Fox News, while others were tuned into CNN. As she usually did when she was warming up, Callie was reading the morning edition of the Washington Times when Kacey stepped onto the treadmill to her left and began to work-out without any acknowledgment that her best friend was standing right next to her.

"Hey you." Callie nodded her head in Kacey's direction. She could not recall the last time they had gone a day or more without speaking to each other. Callie was unsure how to approach her and for the first time that she could remember, there was an icy awkwardness between them. It was real and palpable. She thought for a moment about ignoring the issue entirely, but reasoned that if she wanted to find out what was happening, the easiest way to handle the situation, was to approach it head on.

Kacey did not acknowledge Callie's greeting. With her iPod attached to her bicep and earbuds in her ears, Kacey turned to Callie and gave her a cold half-smile, but said nothing.

"Kacey..." Callie flipped the newspaper to the floor and tried to talk to Kacey as she continued her mild jog, but Kacey was still pretending not to hear anything. Kacey, in the midst of her own warm-up, increased the tempo of her treadmill, then continued to ignore her best friend.

"Kacey..." Callie spoke a little louder this time. It made no impact as Kacey looked straight ahead as if nothing was happening around her. Unbeknownst to Callie, Kacey had not turned on her ipod and heard all three attempts by Callie to draw her attention. She chose to ignore her even though she wasn't sure that was the best thing to do.

Just like Callie, Kacey was in unfamiliar territory and unsure how to handle it. Callie had been her idol, her sister and her confidante. She was everything Kacey wanted to be and more. Picking up the pace on her treadmill, Kacey thought about all the years they'd spent together. People constantly asked what their secret was. How had they been able to keep their friendship so close? Kacey kept a virtual list in her head for those kind of questions, rattling Callie's attributes off like a list of state capitals. Smart, confident, fearless, intelligent, funny, tough, incredibly sexy and drop dead gorgeous. But more than anything else, she would always say, Callie was honest. It was the one trait she revered most about Callie. Now, that trait had disappeared and Kacey felt lost without her. The last few nights were filled with tossing, turning and long blocks of time lying on her back, her arm resting on her forehead worried about the future. She felt empty and distant without the comfort of her confidante, but Callie had destroyed her sense of trust and shattered the innocence of their youth. Things would never be the same between them and Callie's dishonesty was the sole reason for that.

Kacey raised the incline on her machine and snuck a peek at Callie running next to her, obviously troubled and confused. Callie caught notice of the glance and tried once more to grab her attention.

"Kacey...Kacey..." Callie said, each time louder than the last.

Kacey fought back the urge to answer.

Callie pressed the stop button on her machine, slowed her pace to a walk, then a minute or so later, stepped off the treadmill and stood directly in front of Kacey.

"Kacey."

Kacey took her earbuds out. She acted surprised to see Callie standing in front of her. She had given serious thought to skipping her workout that morning. She couldn't shake the sense of betrayal and disappointment that had washed over her, but decided to come to Crunch anyway. Like Callie, she had no idea what to do or how to handle her own confusion. She knew they had to talk but it wasn't a conversation she looked forward to having.

"Kacey, what's going on?"

"What do you mean?"

"I've been calling you, texting you, I left messages at your house, your office…you couldn't call me back?"

Kacey jogged a bit longer then turned off the treadmill. She stepped down so she would be face-to-face with Callie. Her mind was flooded with memories. They may have argued for a few minutes over one thing or another, but they never fought. There was rarely a night where she did not look forward to seeing or talking to Callie the next day and she knew Callie felt the same way. Kacey felt special being Callie's friend. She wasn't like the other girls who would get in a clique and forget about everyone else. She was loyal to a fault and Kacey could always count on her. Friday night football games, Callie was there, saving a seat for her at the stadium off of Pierce Street. Summer time at Tioga Park, she would always include her in whatever games she and the other kids were playing, even when Kacey would show up late. When Callie went off to college in California, they spoke numerous times each day without fail. Kacey was keenly aware that she had no other relationship in her life as honest or as real as the one she had with Callie.

This was dark, new territory for both of them. Kacey felt betrayed and needed to tell Callie how much she'd hurt her. She told herself if there was ever a time to be just like Callie, this was it. For the last three days, she had debated exactly what to say to her and how to say it. She'd played the conversation in her head more than a thousand times, but of course, thinking it turned out to be a whole lot easier than giving it a voice.

"I can't believe you lied to me."

"When did I lie to you?" Callie said, lying again.

"Stop it, Cal."

"Kacey..."

"Don't," Kacey said, cutting her off before she said anything else. "I can't believe you, Callie, I love you more than my own flesh and blood. You mean the world to me..."

Now it was Callie's turn to interrupt. "You mean everything to me too, you're my best friend and always have been." Callie seemed encouraged by the moment. Maybe the situation might not turn out to be as bad as she'd previously thought. She was wrong.

Kacey shaken, but not unglued, held it together. "How could you do this to me? We never lied to each other. Ever."

"Let me explain."

"An explanation of why you lied to me? Are you really going there?"

"It's not what you think..."

"It's not what I think? Please tell me you didn't just say that..."

"That's not what I mean," Callie said.

"Excuse me?"

"Kace, you know more about me than anyone else on this planet..."

"I thought I did..."

"You do."

"I do now, that's for sure."

Callie wanted to tell her what was going on, but could not bring herself to do it. No matter what she said at this moment,

Kacey was not going to hear it.

Instead, she introduced her to the Callie she thought Kacey should have met a long time ago. "Kacey, let me assure you that what I did was what I should have done. I am entrusted with millions of dollars every single day. I am. Me. Not you or anyone else in this City. Me. Not everyone can do what I do and I'm damn good at it. This country, the United States? The things that happen here? They happen because of me. Make no mistake, it is because of me. I get laws passed. I change people's lives and I do it to help those who have no access. I am their access Kacey. Me. And I won't apologize for being good at my job, not to you, not to anyone. Forgive me if you got your feelings hurt. Grow up. This is what it's like to play in big girl world in D.C. Either get in or get the hell out of the way."

Kacey was brushed back by what she was hearing. Never, in all the time she had thought about this conversation, did she expect it to go this way. In her head, Callie apologized and said something contrite, maybe deferential, but she never expected this. She couldn't have even imagined it.

"Who are you? I don't even know you anymore. What happened to the girl I knew that was humble...modest? The one everybody wanted to be around?"

"Big girl world, honey. I guess that girl grew up. Follow her lead," Callie said. Her voice held a coldness Kacey had never heard in it before. Callie's body language had changed. Her chin was higher. Her shoulders wider. Any traces of the vulnerability and contrition that she had begun this conversation with had vanished in the blink of an eye. The woman standing in front of Kacey was someone she did not recognize. Kacey knew at that moment she'd lost the best friend she would ever have.

She picked up the towel and took a few deep breaths to gather her thoughts. She pretended to dry herself off. Kacey laid the towel back onto the treadmill then informed the woman standing across from her that she might be a bit more advanced in the culture of Washington than Callie had given her credit for.

"Listen to me, and listen good, Callie. I'm sitting on a story for two days now that points to you as the go-between for Lank and Jonas Foster. I haven't been able to bring myself to run it, but we have a very reliable source that puts you as the facilitator to millions of dollars funneled into the Lank campaign. I couldn't get corroboration to go to print with it, but thanks to this introduction to 'big girl world,' I think I just did."

Callie's heart sank into the pit of her stomach. Kacey's words left her unable to speak. She stood in front of Kacey dumbfounded by what she had just heard. Kacey was far from finished.

"There's some bad stuff that went on with this Lank thing and I didn't want to believe it." Kacey picked up her towel again and wiped her forehead with it. "But as bad as that stuff was, it wasn't the worst thing. You want to know the worst part of all this, Callie?"

Callie's feet felt like they were buried in cement, her tongue glued to the roof of her mouth. She couldn't move nor could she believe what was happening in front of her. Kacey was on a roll and took the rhetorical question she'd just asked and ran her best friend over with it.

"You looked me straight in the eye and lied to me. You told me you knew nothing about Lank and I believed you," Kacey said. "The last few days I've wondered how you could do that to me... your sister...your best friend. But now that you've lectured me on the greatness of you, I have no need to wonder anymore."

Callie didn't say a word. She stood there in silence knowing that anything she could say would not matter. The damage had been done.

"I still can't believe, standing in front of you right now, that you lied to me so effortlessly. In a million years, I'd have bet against it," Kacey said. "Just so you know, we're going to be running the story in tomorrow's paper. If you care to comment, you can reach me at my office. If not, I could care less. I am sure you will have plenty of chances to answer after it hits the streets."

Kacey snorted as she walked past.

"Seems to me big girl world's gonna get a whole lot messier...I can't even look at you anymore. You disgust me." Kacey picked up her water bottle, draped the towel over her shoulder and jogged towards the staircase. On her way to the first floor, she froze halfway down the steps then turned around and hurried back towards Callie who was still standing in the same place Kacey left her. "I am so disappointed in you," she said softly, then left.

Callie tried to make some sense out of what had happened. She was bent over, hands on her knees as she struggled to organize her thoughts. The reality of her actions had come back to haunt her. Callie slumped to the floor. Her entire body went limp. She leaned back against the treadmill and dropped her weary head in her hands.

Once in the locker room, Kacey found an empty bathroom stall and cried.

TWENTY-FOUR

"She's convinced they were coming after her," Mike told Todd, standing behind him in line at Starbucks.

"Who does she think sent them?"

"She has no idea."

Both men stood in silence as they listened to the two women in front of them argue over who would pay for the lattes they had just purchased. The blonde wanted the brunette to pay, the brunette wanted the blonde to pay. Mike pulled out a ten-dollar bill from his pocket, reached around the two woman and slid the money on the counter. "On me, ladies," Mike said.

The blonde-haired woman turned around and looked at Mike. "Thank you sir, but we can pay for this ourselves."

"Then do it already, because the fifteen people behind you could give a shit whose turn it is to pay," Todd said. The blonde shot him a nasty look. "We'll pay when we're good and ready."

"Please ma'am let me pay for you," Mike said. "My treat."

The brunette smiled and brushed up against Mike's side. "Thank you, Honey. My name is Veronica."

"His name is Taken," Todd said. The two women scowled at

Todd, who stepped towards the counter as he pushed by.

"Nice to meet you, Veronica," Mike said. "And you are?"

"Sam, short for Samantha," the blonde said.

"Nice to meet you Sam and Veronica. If you will excuse us, we're running a bit late. Please enjoy your drinks on me," Mike said.

"Aren't you sweet? Thank you. I look forward to seeing you again," the blonde woman said. "Of course, next time I hope you're alone." Both women shot Todd nasty looks on their way out the door. Mike smiled and waved, then turned his attention to the young girl behind the counter. "Two black coffees. No sugar, please."

"What do you think? Is there anything to this?" Todd asked.

"I think there may be something to it, but why? And who? That's the only thing I can't figure out."

"Did she say what they looked like?"

"Nope, too dark in the garage. Couldn't get a good look. Middle Eastern maybe."

"Strange," Todd said.

"Hope it's not something she's imagining," Mike said. "I'd never seen her like that. Shaking, barely able to speak. She was legitimately afraid. Real strange."

The teenager behind the counter brought the men their coffees. Mike looked at Todd who turned his pockets inside-out in a dramatic way. Mike sent Todd a look that let him know he thought Todd was full of it and knew he had stashed money elsewhere. Mike handed the girl behind the counter a twenty-dollar bill.

"What are you really thinking though?" Todd picked up the coffees the girl had left for them.

"Don't know yet. I want to believe her, but I just ..." Mike stopped mid-sentence to take his coffee from Todd. "I really don't know."

"Thank you," Mike said. The girl handed him his change and the two men walked towards the exit. "Maybe it's a stress thing?"

Todd held the door open for Mike. "Maybe," Todd said. "By the way, thanks for the coffee."

"Why thank me? You paid for it."

"I paid for it?"

"Hell, yeah. The last three weeks at the range I've taken about ten of those twenty-dollar bills off of you," Mike said. "Come to think of it, you've paid for coffee every day this past month." Todd opened the door and sat behind the wheel of his Ford Expedition. Mike sat in the passenger seat and buckled up.

"Want to try your luck again?" Todd said.

"I thought you'd never ask."

"You want to shoot at Langley or the SAR?" Todd asked, using the common place name for the Small Arms Range.

"Doesn't matter to me, Dude, your money is my money no matter where we shoot."

"You're not concerned I'm gonna beat you?" Todd asked as he pulled out of the parking lot.

"Am I allowed to shoot with either hand?"

"Either hand."

"Nope, not concerned at all."

"I hate your ass, you know that?"

"I know that, but you still paid for the coffee...again."

"Shut up and leave me alone. I gotta' concentrate on the road."

"Uh-huh."

● ● ●

Pebble Beach Golf Course, located in Pebble Beach, California, is generally considered one of the finest golf courses in the world. For a golfer, the manicured greens, long finely trimmed fairways combined with weather that looked like it was hijacked off of a postcard, there could be nothing better. Regardless of their skill level, Pebble Beach gave most of the people who played it, an experience they would not soon forget.

Barry Miller and the seven Senators who came with him to the west coast, were enjoying their few days of "recreational exploration," better known as an IRS deduction they all planned on using next April. As part of a two day excursion that Barry organized from time to time, the eight men were scheduled to play eighteen holes of golf on both days before flying back to Washington. Barry referred to excursions like these as oiling the tin man. Others would call it something else ranging from bribery to payoffs, but to Barry, it was a way to reward his friends for helping out M&G's clients.

At the ninth hole, Senator Gorman had parked his golf cart behind the others that were already empty. Barry sat in the seat next to him while Senators Shulman and Bane pulled up directly behind them and hurried to join the other four who had already begun to play. Senator Gorman and Barry were in no rush.

"Charles, you guys go ahead and start, we'll be there in a minute or two," Senator Gorman said to Schulman as he marched by.

Gorman squeezed a Nike golf glove onto his right hand then turned to Barry. "We need to keep this close to the vest. The way I see it, if we do this right, we'll make out like bandits."

Barry kept his eyes focused on the six other legislators in front of him. "As I told you before, patience is the key. We need to help the chips fall exactly where we want them to."

Gorman worked the matching glove onto his left hand. "What will we accomplish by playing it that way? Instead of, say, being more proactive?"

"First of all, we are being proactive, we are just doing it in a more surreptitious way. When this sorts itself out, it will be a major windfall for all of us financially...on top of what we've already made in this venture. The ability to call our own shots on this without some figurehead possibly screwing things up, will be the best part. It's what we've been waiting for these past five years."

Gorman put his head down and wrapped his hands around the steering wheel of the golf cart. "What about the Wheeler girl?"

Barry dismissed the question with a wave of his hand. "She knows nothing about any of this other stuff and she never will if we all stay quiet. As for her being neutralized, she's a non-issue."

Senator Gorman seemed surprised by Barry's comment, but appeared more interested in covering his own ass than worrying about anyone else's. "What do you mean a non-issue? Doesn't she know too much?"

"You mean knew too much. Past tense."

"What did you say?" Gorman snapped his head up and looked at Barry.

Barry kept looking straight ahead. "I said, she knew too much. As in, she had to be terminated because she knew too much."

"You fired her?" Gorman asked, a shocked look dominating his face.

Barry turned his head and looked Gorman in the eye. "Who said anything about firing her?"

The Senator sat in silence for a moment. "You told me she was irreplaceable. The best you'd ever seen?"

"She was, but as the saying goes, graveyards are full of irreplaceable men. And women."

"You guys gonna play or schmooze? What's it gonna be?" Senator Schulman called behind to Barry and Gorman.

Barry held up his index finger, "Give us another minute." He turned back to Gorman. "Bottom line: She's become a huge liability for what we need to do moving forward."

"So, what do you plan to do about it?" Gorman sensed he might be treading on territory he wanted nothing to do with. Nevertheless, he understood that Callie was extremely dangerous and if it came down to him or her, it would have to be her.

Barry pulled out his own FootJoy golf gloves and slipped them on his hands as he spoke. "The amount of information she knows is staggering. I've played this out in my head hundreds of times, and the way I see it, we have two options to consider at this point. One will have no residual effects and the other, well...."

"Or we could just cut her in and that would take care of all our problems as far as she's concerned," the Senator said, hoping to steer the conversation someplace other than where it was heading.

The look Barry shot at Gorman was one he would not soon forget and never wanted to see again. "Are you out of your fucking mind?"

"What? What's so wrong with sitting her down and letting her know what's up?"

Barry leaned in close to Gorman and whispered through his clenched teeth. "First of all, use your head. She's engaged to one of the best, if not the best, spy this country has. Not a good mix for what we're doing. Second, I can't actually stand the sight of her..."

"Really? 'Cuz I could look at her all day...and all night," Gorman said.

"You know what I mean. I've already put a plan in place to deal with her as clean as possible. In all honesty, the woman makes my skin crawl. There's something about her that I can't put my finger on. I just hate being around her. Bottom line, the less I have to do with her, the better."

Barry stepped out of the cart and rested his shoe on top of the seat he'd been sitting on. He bent over and took both ends of his untied golf shoe, tied it, then sat back down inside the cart.

"Mike, you have to understand that this girl is a major rain-maker and I am filthy rich, basically, because of her. The real issue, as I see it, is what will hurt me, and us, more. If she stays with the firm, I'm afraid…no, I know, she will cost us much more than she brings in long term." Barry thought about what he just said. "Much more. If we brought her in on this, she would hold us up for millions…I'm talking tens of millions…and she has the goods and the balls to do it."

Barry again leaned in close. This time their faces were barely an inch from each other. "I did not invest five plus years of my life setting this up, so that I'd have to share it with her. That's my money, it's *our* money, and there is no fucking way I am giving any of it to her. Once the process with her plays out, you'll see that this move was the right one. I'd prefer we keep this from ending like last time."

"Right. We need to do better than last time," Gorman said as if his brain suddenly kicked in and reminded him of something he should have already known. A wry smile came to his face as both men stepped out of the golf cart. "I hope I don't ever get on your bad side."

"Me too," Barry said, only half-joking. "The Lank story hitting the papers screwed us big time and now we have to make sure we cover our tracks. Getting out of it unscathed with no residual effects and at the same time, taking her down would be the ulti-mate. Somehow we have to make her inconsequential."

"And what about Jonas Foster?"

"Foster will do whatever I tell him, trust me," Barry said.

"Trust you? Now that's scary…"

Barry grabbed his golf bag from the back of the cart and start-ed shuffling towards the ninth hole to join the others. "You are playing Pebble Beach today…"

"That I am, my friend."

Barry and Gorman joined the rest of the group and couldn't help ribbing the Senators who had yet to finish their tee shots. "You old farts ever going to move off of here?" Gorman asked.

Senator Lank, who was about to tee off, turned to Gorman and gave it right back. "Slow and steady beats fast and sloppy every time. Your wife confirmed that for me last night, Mike." The group laughed then watched Lank tee off, only to see his shot go awry and find a soft spot in the trees.

"You're all over the place, Senator. Your wife confirmed that for me last night," Gorman said as the group erupted with laughter again. Lank turned around and tipped his hat to Gorman. "Touché."

Lank started down the fairway to retrieve his ball. The rest of the group stayed back and waited for Barry to tee-off. Barry turned his back to the group and whispered in Gorman ear. "Lank and his committee are on board with Foster, we have that all taken care of. This other stuff I just told you, we keep to ourselves until we have to get the others involved. You hear me?"

"I hear you," Gorman said. He noticed a look on Barry's face that suggested he should not only hear Barry, but listen to him as well.

TWENTY-FIVE

Callie arrived at work more than an hour later than usual. On most days, she could be found in her office by 7:45 in the morning, but following her confrontation with Kacey, her day took a while to get started. After Kacey had left her, Callie sat in front of the treadmill for close to thirty minutes and wondered if their relationship had suffered the sort of damage that was beyond repair. She jumped back on the treadmill, but five minutes later, stepped off. Her mind was all over the place. She could no longer focus on her workout. She left the gym and drove back home only to find an empty house with Mike having already left for the day. Following a long shower, Callie tried to shake off the malaise. She took her time getting dressed and slowly made her way into the office.

If anything positive came out of the early morning conflict, it may have been the fact that it made Callie forget all about the events at Charlie Palmer's the night before. She was at her desk when her cell phone rang and disturbed the relative calm she was trying to cultivate. No number lit up the display. Somewhere in her subconscious, she hoped it was Kacey. She answered the phone.

"This is Callie."

Silence.

"Hello?...Hello? Kacey, is that you?" The thought of losing Kacey weighed much heavier on her than she could have imagined. She believed their relationship would be able to handle any sort of adversity. Was it possible she miscalculated? Could it be this phone call from Kacey was proof the mental gymnastics she put herself through since the morning dust-up at the gym had been an overreaction? Maybe their friendship could withstand anything, after all?

Or maybe it wasn't Kacey.

Callie pulled the phone away from her ear, looked at it, then brought it back again. "Okay, one last time then I hang..."

On the line, a deep voice interrupted her. Callie tried to place the accent. "Last night we miss you. This will not happen second time."

Callie's body began to shake. All thoughts of Kacey, of anything, evaporated in an instant. Callie's real issues hit her with a sudden slap in the face and now she had to deal with the most urgent one in her life. And it was on the phone.

"Who are you? How did you get this number?"

"Next time you won't be so lucky," the voice said, before hanging up.

Callie heard the line go dead. She could not stop her body from shaking, this time much worse than the night before. Callie hung up the phone, tried to press the number one on her speed dial, but found it impossible to keep her hands stable long enough to hit the correct button. She slowed herself down and tried again. She dropped the phone on the floor. Callie took a deep breath and bent over to pick it up. The quivering of her hands shocked her as she looked down and noticed them reaching for her phone. She squeezed her right hand with her left one, but the trembling seemed to only be getting worse. Callie fell to her knees and grabbed the phone with both hands, hit speed dial and pressed the number one. The call was going through, but not quick enough for Callie. "Come on, come on, Mike. Answer the phone, Mike." The second ring made her more uptight when he failed to answer. "Pick up the phone! Mike, c'mon…please, pick up." Callie considered hanging up then redialing, but let it ring one last time.

"Hey, Cal."

She was still on her knees in her office and barely spoke above a whisper. Her voice cracked. She spoke so fast she was difficult to understand.

"They got my cell number. I told you. I told you. They just called me. You know who called me? You know who? They did, they called me, Mike, they called me." Callie's nerves were splintered into a thousand pieces, her body shaking with no end in sight. "I told you they were after me. Now you believe me, Mike? Now do you believe me?"

"Who did? Who called you?"

"Who called me? Who called me?" Callie's body continued to shake furiously, her hands hardly able to hold the phone in place. "I can't believe it. They called me. Those guys from last night. How'd they get my number, Mike? Why me? Why are they calling me? What do they want? Why are they calling me?"

"Callie, calm down, take a deep breath…"

"What? Calm down? How can I calm down…?"

"Tell me what they said…"

Callie's hands continued to tremble out of control. She tried inhaling and breathing out in a slow steady fashion, but it was all for naught. "They said I won't be so lucky next time. What do they mean, I won't be so lucky? Next time? When's next time?"

Mike looked out the window while he spoke with Callie. There were a lot of questions that he kept to himself. What's this about? Could she really have been a target? Of whom? If her imagination hadn't run away from her, Callie could be in serious danger. A wave of thoughts ran through his head, none of them good. What he had to do now was keep Callie safe until they could figure out exactly what was going on.

"Callie, I'm coming right over. Stay in your office. Talk to no one." Mike grabbed his keys and ran to his car. "Lock the doors, stay low and do not answer your phones until I get there. Most of all, no one enters your office and I mean no one. I'm on my way."

Callie rushed to the office door and locked it. She hurried past the conference table and headed to the corner of the room where she had a mini-bar installed a few months after she'd arrived at the firm. No matter how hard she tried, Callie could not control the incessant trembling of her hands as she attempted to pour herself some scotch. On her first attempt, she missed the glass entirely. The Johnny Walker Black Label ended up all over the counter top while a small sample fell onto the carpet. The thick smell of the alcohol permeated the office air, which only increased Callie's desire for a drink. She tried again to pour the liquor. She missed most of the glass. Callie sat down on a chair at the head of the conference table and stared at the top of her hands. They were still shaking. She took a deep breath and tried one more time to pour a drink. Unlike before, she used her left hand to steady her right, and finally poured the glass of whiskey. She made her way back to her desk, but instead walked over to the window. She slowly lifted the glass to her quivering lips and took a drink, still working hard to keep her hands steady.

Callie's phone pierced the quiet. She rattled the ice in her glass, startled. Callie looked at the phone, but did not move to pick it up, just as Mike had instructed her. She glanced at the caller id, which read "Joel Hughes." Callie let the call go to voicemail.

• • •

A handful of reporters, Kacey Mercer among them, were gathered in the Radio and Television Gallery of the Senate building. Earlier in the morning, a national press release spread the word that a handful of Senators had scheduled a press conference with the express purpose of addressing the allegations that were leveled against Senator Lank, by the Washington Post. Six different television cameras surrounded Senators Macklin and King who stood in front of a bank of microphones. They were flanked by eight other Senators behind them. The number of networks in attendance served as a testament to the fact that Kacey's story was still very much alive, not only in Washington, but across the country.

"Ladies and gentleman, thank you very much for coming today, especially on such short notice," Senator Macklin began. "I will make a few remarks and then open up the floor to some questions, but I must advise you, there is important business being voted on today in less than fifteen minutes, so while we will try to answer all of your questions, we do need to be brief. As always, we appreciate your cooperation on this."

"The attack on Senator Lank in the Washington Post and the subsequent reporting done by every news outlet that covers the Hill, was vicious and as the lack of evidence has now shown, full of untruths. However, as erroneous and irresponsible as it may have been, we understand that there is a perception out there that Congress has been derelict in its oversight of itself. In order to combat this perception and to guard against anything like this ever happening again, we have formed a watchdog group in the Senate, most of whom are standing behind us," Macklin said, pointing to the lawmakers who stood against the wall.

Senator Macklin stepped away from the microphone allowing Senator King to take his place. "We formed this group to stop the money grubbing practice of earmarks that is plaguing Congress today," King said. "We have heard the undertones from the press and the public. In order to combat the belief that business is somehow awry on Capitol Hill, this group of dedicated Senators have taken it upon themselves to combat the earmark problems inserted in every bill that comes up for a vote on the Senate floor. We will work diligently with each member of our body and are confident that with the full cooperation from our colleagues in the House, we will rid the entire Congress of a practice, which for far too long, has infested our unparalleled system of government. What we believe is most important following the unsubstantiated allegations against Senator Lank is to clean up the halls of Congress so that we can get on with the people's work. That is why we stand unified today as a group and willing to fight the special interests head on. Thank you. Now if you have any questions…"

Kirk Arthur, of NBC News, stood front and center with his hand raised. Senator Macklin, back at the microphone, acknowledged him with a nod.

"Senator Macklin, what are your thoughts or do you have any comment on the recent allegations regarding Senator Lank accepting illegal contributions from Jonas Foster in exchange for help on the eminent domain bill?"

"I have known Senator Lank for more than twenty years and the allegations against him are reckless and uninformed to say the least. He is an unquestioned leader of this body and as honest a Senator as we have in Washington," Macklin said.

Senator King leaned into the microphone the moment Macklin finished his answer. "May I add that Senator Lank has no equal when it comes to integrity and public service. I am confident that when this is all said and done, he will be exonerated and his name and reputation will be restored."

Tara Michael of CBS News also stood in the front row, just a few yards away from Kirk Arthur. Their rivalry and hatred for each other was legendary on media blogs, and in newsrooms all across America. It was commonplace to watch them jump on any opportunity to discredit each other. In Washington, there was a protocol in dealing with their personal war that quickly became the usual practice at these events. When one asked a question, the other would be called on next, which is exactly what took place. "Senator King, why are you and your colleagues taking this stance now?"

"Because, Tara, we need to rid this great body of the slimy practice of back room dealing, and secret handshakes, so we can tackle the real problems that face the people of this great nation. To that end, the Ethics committee will be holding hearings on this very issue within the next ten days."

Macklin moved closer to the microphones and started talking before King had concluded. "Furthermore, the less we have to deal with the underbelly of Washington, the better we can serve our constituents."

Kirk Arthur screamed out a follow-up before anyone else could get a question in. "The underbelly of Washington?"

"The special interests groups and the lobbyists that do their dirty work. As a unit, the Senators in front of you have pledged to clean up the halls of Congress and you can hold us to that pledge until we do just that," Macklin said. "Ladies and gentleman, we have a vote to get to. Thank you for coming and god bless America."

· · ·

Mike and Callie sat on the right side of the steps on the Lincoln Memorial. Callie leaned on his shoulder, Mike's arm wrapped around her.

Mike had shown up at M&G within minutes of hanging up the phone. He banged on Callie's door, which caused some people at the firm to check outside their offices to see what the commotion was all about. Mike's reaction confirmed the reality of the threat. The incident at the garage had, at least to Mike, taken on a whole new meaning. Callie opened the door and pulled him in.

"Now you believe, me?"

"I believe you. Forgive me?" Mike hugged her tight. He pulled back and kissed her on the lips.

"Take me away from here?"

"Absolutely."

They chose one of their favorite spots and while it was full of tourists taking pictures and strolling in the plaza area, it was private enough for them to spend some time alone.

"I missed you last night," Callie said.

"I missed you too. I'm not suited for the guest room," Mike said. Callie had taken Mike's bedding and threw it in the hallway after she retired for the evening. Mike knew it was hopeless to negotiate with her, so he bit the bullet and spent the night downstairs in one of their three guest rooms.

She leaned into Mike and rested her hand on his chest. "I have to talk to Kacey."

"About this?"

Callie thought about how to answer him. She had only told him a small portion of what happened at the gym, but the part she did tell him, had been all about Lank. Mike had known that Lank and Callie had done business together and that Callie had done business with Jonas Foster, but he had no idea to what extent she was involved. Callie had told Mike on the way over to the Lincoln Memorial that Kacey had a story that would paint a picture of her that was extremely unflattering. She never told him any information about what she had done. She wanted to keep it that way.

"No, I don't want her to run the story without a comment

from me," Callie lied.

Mike was not concerned about the newspaper as much as he was about protecting Callie. If Kacey had a story that involved her, he was sure they would work it out. He never wanted Callie to know too much about his work and he felt he needed to return that courtesy to his fiancé. Whatever Callie had going on was none of his business. If she wanted him to know, she would have told him. All he knew was he wanted to be with her. Mike turned Callie's face towards his and gave her a tender kiss.

"What was that for?"

Mike kissed her again. "No reason."

Callie looked at Mike, kissed his cheek, then settled in on his shoulder.

"We're going to find out who's behind this," Mike said. "The whole thing doesn't make much sense."

Mike and Callie sat in silence, lost in each others company. No matter what stress she encountered each day, she always felt safe with him and loved the peace and calming influence he brought to her life. She admired how composed he was at all times and the fact that he never got too worked up when things went against him, or too excited when they fell in his favor. Callie loved the fact that he was not afraid to let her know how he felt about her and at times he didn't have to say anything at all. Maybe it was the way he looked at her when he thought she wasn't paying attention or an innocent caress he gave her when he figured she was asleep. She just knew and that was enough for her.

"Thanks for taking me here."

"I won't let anything happen to you."

They sat in silence for a few minutes more as they watched the tourists flock to the monument.

"I know you won't."

TWENTY-SIX

Kacey could feel a cloud hanging over her entire morning. The reality that her life had changed began to hit her after she left the Capitol, following the Senate Press Conference. She took a stroll to 'Aatish on the Hill', an Indian cuisine restaurant located between 6th and 7th Street on Pennsylvania Avenue. She thought for a moment about the possibility that maybe this whole episode with Callie was a good thing in some weird way. Kacey entertained the idea of living her life without Callie in it and part of her felt fresh, new, freeing. But a deeper part was still searching for ways to fix the relationship, if that was even a possibility at this point. Ultimately, she thought, the next move would have to come from Callie.

The restaurant was sprinkled with a few tourists, but mostly filled with Congressman and staffers who wanted a break from the cafeterias in the Capitol buildings. Kacey stepped inside and, as always, took notice of the pink drapes at the front of the restaurant and the Indian themed decor in the back. The bottom of both side walls were covered with ash-paneled wood and on top of them, three foot high mirrors ran across the length of the eatery. Stand-

ing on the buffet line, Kacey could almost taste the lamb and on-
ions whose enticing scent spread throughout the restaurant. Her
thoughts of gluttony were quickly interrupted by a familiar voice
whispering in her ear from behind.

"Great to see you again, Ms. Mercer."

Kacey turned around, and smiled reluctantly when she recognized Joel Hughes. "Hello, Mr. Hughes."

"Call me Joel."

"Hello, Joel. My name is Kacey. How are you?"

Joel smiled and played along. "Doing well, and you?"

Kacey walked down the line, poured some soup, then grabbed
an apple. Joel, right behind her, poured the same soup but skipped
the fruit. "Not my best day, but I'm hanging in there," Kacey said.

Joel picked up a kabob and a fountain drink then followed
Kacey to the cashier. Kacey reached into her purse to pay for her
food, but Joel had already beat her to it.

"Please, let me get that." He handed the cashier a twenty dollar bill before Kacey could object. "For both of us."

Kacey smiled at Joel and waited for him next to the cashier,
unsure if she stood there out of plain etiquette or because she actually wanted to.

"Thank you," Kacey said to him while he waited for his
change. "Would you like to commiserate with me?"

"It would be my pleasure," Joel said with a smile on his face.

He stretched out his arm and let Kacey to lead the way to
their table. Kacey took him through the middle of the restaurant
before settling on a small empty table against the wall in the back.
As he followed behind her, Joel's eyes could not help but stare at
the way her backside filled out her red mini skirt. Joel held his
tray of food in his hand while he pulled the chair out for Kacey,
who acknowledged his action with a smile. "A gentleman. I forgot
there were still some of you out there."

He placed his tray on the table. "We are hard to find, but we're still here," Joel said.

"My lucky day then, huh?"

Joel sat in the seat across from Kacey. "My thoughts exactly. How about that?"

Kacey chuckled and flirted back. "How about that, indeed."

A look of confusion spread across Kacey's face and she began to scan her tray. She quickly scoured the floor before her eyes returned to the table obviously in search of something. Her look soon changed to one of frustration when she realized she had no spoon for her soup. Joel, not missing a beat, picked up on it right away. "If you'll excuse me for just a second," Joel said.

Kacey's eyes followed him as he stood up and quickly strode over to a man he seemed very familiar with. The owner of the establishment had been standing near the front window of the restaurant and greeted Joel with a huge smile and a gentle pat on the back. Joel drew closer and whispered something in his ear. The owner nodded and vacated his post for less than thirty seconds, returning with a soup-spoon that he handed to his old friend. Joel hurried back to the table where Kacey had been patiently waiting and watching him, dually impressed with his chivalry and unique style.

"Thank you, Joel. That was very sweet," Kacey said as she waited for him to sit down before starting in on her soup.

Joel opened a napkin and placed it over his suit pants. "So, what are we commiserating?"

"The loss of my best friend."

"I'm sorry to hear that." Joel bowed his head.

Kacey took notice of the change in his demeanor. She covered her face with her right hand, embarrassed when she realized what she must have sounded like.

"Oh no, I'm sorry. She didn't die," Kacey said with a smile.

"She just lied to me."

Joel giggled at the misunderstanding. "Doesn't sound like much of a friend."

For the first time since they had sat down, there was a moment of awkward silence as they continued to eat. Kacey thought about how much information she actually wanted to tell this man she barely knew, before she threw him a morsel to help the moment pass.

"Actually, we'd been best friends since before we were in kindergarten." Kacey slid her spoon through her soup, staring at it as she thought about Callie and how much she missed her already. "It just hurts."

Joel wasted no time picking up the pieces for her. "Maybe it's time you found a new friend."

Kacey looked in Joel's soft brown eyes and smiled. "Maybe it is."

• • •

Ken Farmer sat in his beaten down office on North Holiday Street. Beneath the darkened windows, the room bordered on empty with the exception of two old wood chairs that were situated across from a 1970's metal desk which he sat behind as he talked on the phone. The only light in the workspace spread from a dim bulb which protruded from a lamp with no shade.

"I do not care what you say, this needs to be done and it needs to be done right now!"

Ken's patience was running thin. He shook his head and listened to the other voice on the line. He wanted no part of whatever that person had to say.

"We have no choice. I do not ask you for a lot, but this I must insist on."

Beads of sweat formed on Ken's forehead. The veins in his neck popped to the surface. He shook his head in anger again and exploded on the caller. "We need to act soon or this will cost us dearly. You already know how I feel."

Ken slammed the phone back into its cradle, stood up and began pacing the room as he cursed under his breath. The news he received had not been what he expected to hear and his tolerance for ineptitude had run its course. Either the caller took care of it or he would have to do it himself. That was something no one wanted to see come to pass for all the wrong reasons. He grabbed a clay paperweight from his desk and threw it against the wall, smashing it into little pieces that scattered all around the dimly lit room.

• • •

Joel held the restaurant door open for Kacey and followed her out onto Pennsylvania Avenue. When they first met on the Hill just over a week ago, the circumstances under which they had been introduced to each other did not leave much room for socializing. Now that she saw Joel in the light of day, Kacey was more than a little interested to find out what else he had to offer. She looked closely at the smooth structure of his face and the way his eyebrows thinned out the closer they got to the middle of his forehead. She noticed the small scar on the bottom of his chin and wondered how it got there. She found the air of confidence that he gave off refreshing, but not at all arrogant. Maybe, Kacey thought, it was indeed time for a new friend.

"Thank you for lunch, you almost cheered me up." Kacey gave him an opportunity to take the bait.

"My pleasure and thank you for the beautiful company," Joel said. "You walking my way?"

Kacey blushed at his compliment. "I believe I am."

"Would you mind very much, if I walked with you?"

"I'd like that," Kacey said, not ready for her lunch break to end. They walked down Pennsylvania Avenue in silence for a few moments, before Joel took the lead.

"How long have you been at the Post?"

"I interned at the paper while in college which eventually turned into a job. After five years there, I got assigned to Congress in January. Not the most exciting beat...although your boss changed that quite a bit."

"Ah, my boss."

"Do I detect a problem?" Kacey asked, turning her head to look at him.

"No problem. He's just, well, my boss."

"That clears it up for me," Kacey laughed and playfully bumped into him as they slowly continued up Pennsylvania.

"I don't really feel comfortable talking about him."

"Is that because it's me or..."

"Oh no, not at all. Please forgive me. I wasn't even thinking about you being a reporter," Joel said as he pulled a leaf from a nearby bush. "Now I really would rather not talk about him." He laughed uncomfortably, not sure if she would think his joke was funny.

"Not a problem." Kacey said. They continued in silence for another minute, Joel peeking at Kacey as they walked while she stole her own look at him. "I wasn't asking as a reporter or anything like that, I was more interested in you. I hope that's okay."

"That's fine and I like that you're interested, because I was thinking about when it would be a good time to ask you on another date."

Kacey smiled and look at Joel mischievously. "Another date? Did we have a first one that I missed?"

"I sure hope not. I just spent seven dollars on you."

"A man and his money are soon parted."

"I believe it's a fool and his money are soon parted," Joel said.

Kacey laughed. "Is that right?"

"Ah, jokes on me, huh?"

Kacey nodded her head and smiled as she bumped into him again hoping to send him the signal it was clear to approach.

Joel picked up on her trailing words and seized the opportunity to get a date out of her. "Where I grew up, if a girl made a guy the butt of her joke, she was obligated to ask that guy out on a date."

"You're not really going to try that 'where I come from stuff' on me, are you, slick?"

"Did you just call me, Slick?" Joel asked.

"I sure did."

"When was the last time someone used the word, 'slick'? 1985?"

"Nicely played."

Before they knew it, they had reached the steps of the Russell Senate Building. "This is my stop," Joel said as he gently touched Kacey's arm. "About that second date, would you want to catch a movie with me sometime?" Joel asked.

"Yeah, I'd like that." Kacey checked her watch and looked at Joel. "I'm sorry Joel, but I do have to be going." Kacey smiled at him as she started to walk away. "Thank you for commiserating with me."

"Can I call you later to set up a night that works for both of us?" Joel asked, hoping that she heard him.

"Sure, but I really have get back to work," Kacey walked away from the Capitol building backwards, still facing Joel. Her day had somehow turned out a lot better than she had been prepared for.

Joel was on the steps of the Capitol building before he realized he forgot something. "Kacey, I don't have your number!" he said, loud enough for everyone down the block to hear.

Kacy continued to walk backwards with a huge smile on her face then yelled back at him. "You should. I left it with your office about two dozen times."

Joel shook his head and smiled as he stared at Kacey. She turned her back to him and walked away.

TWENTY-SEVEN

"We're confident he's up to no good." Mike said. He was sitting across from Director Ted Biggs in the Director's office. Todd sat in the chair next to him. They had made the decision to approach Biggs after debating the issue for the past day and a half. Biggs leaned back in his chair and played with the Bic pen he was holding in his hand, clicking the top over and over again. "I have two questions. One, what makes you so positive that he is up to no good and two, are you sure this is our jurisdiction?"

"As opposed to who? The FBI?" Todd asked as he picked his head up from the notes he'd been taking.

"Or Secret Service? D.O.J?" Biggs added.

"The way we see it, sir, his past actions as an enemy combatant on foreign soil make him within our jurisdiction," Mike said. "Our assets overseas are convinced something is going down, but they're not exactly sure as of yet what that something is."

Mike was all too familiar with knowing something was going down, but not being able to connect the dots. Early in that summer he spent in the West Bank in 2001, he'd heard through different channels that a group of radical Islamists were planning something big and all signs pointed to a major city in the United States. Mike shared his thoughts with his case officer, Ted Biggs, Todd, and two other members of his team that he trusted. He was assured that his information would be passed on to the proper authorities and that the FBI would be made aware of threats to targets in the United States.

President Bannon had made great strides in breaking down the walls of secrecy between the intelligence services and eventually signed an Executive Order which required the intelligence agencies to communicate with each other. It was not an easy process after the fiscal destruction of the military and intelligence services by his predecessor, President Geoff Watkins, the former Democratic Governor of New York. Watkins bragged incessantly to anyone who would listen, how under his leadership, he had gotten the country back to fiscal soundness. He made sure to inform the entire world at every opportunity that it was him and only him, who should be given credit for leaving his successor, Bannon, with a budget surplus.

What Bannon found when he got to the White House however, was that the alleged surplus had only been made possible by the gutting of both the Armed Services and the Intelligence apparatus of the United States. Bannon did his best to stay professional in public, but those inside the government often heard him ask, "What is the use of being able to run the hundred-meter dash, if you've cut off both your legs?" To Bannon, that analogy was the best way to describe the decimated military budget that he would need to rebuild.

Ted Biggs had told Mike about the numerous people above him who were hell-bent on keeping intelligence information within the Agency. As they became engulfed in the bitter fight for new budget money, every defense and clandestine agency felt that the need to share credit and information with any other department seemed counterproductive. Due to the slashing of finances, the limited field assets around the world had left the country blind and by the time Mike's information got passed on to the FBI, it was too late.

September 11, 2001. Mike was in the Gaza Strip when he heard the news just before three o'clock in the afternoon. Akiva had called and told him to get to a television. Within minutes, the streets of Gaza were flooded with people who were celebrating the deaths of thousands of his fellow citizens. Mike did all he could to contain his anger. He debated whether to blow his cover and wipe out a bushel of them or head to his safe house in Jerusalem where he could find a quiet place to mourn for his countrymen.

He opted to find his way back to Jerusalem. He couldn't stand being around people who thought and acted in such a barbaric way. Mike watched the news services in horror when he saw the second plane fly into the World Trade Center in real time. He was immediately overcome with a profound sense of failure and an overwhelming feeling of responsibility over the incident. That sense of failure soon turned to rage as he witnessed people leap to their death from one hundred floors above the ground. For the second time in his career, he had passed on valuable and viable information to his handlers, and the Country failed to take the necessary precautions. His disdain for the political class had no limits, but he would need to channel it towards something productive, which he did.

In the aftermath of the tragedy, the Agency was reshuffled. While it should have rid its Intelligence services of the same type of political hacks that were responsible for the failure of September 11, it had done just the opposite. Congress had moved to put in place more bureaucracy through unqualified political appointees, having ignored the professional assessment of a desperate need for consistent directional leadership. Instead, they exchanged ineptitude for more ineptitude. In their infinite wisdom, the ruling classes in Washington selected journeymen politicians who were put in place by the party in power, for the sole purpose of keeping that party in power.

National security be damned.

Mike had never gotten over the feeling that he let his Country down. At the same time, he became hardened by the political process and watched it destroy the lives of so many of his colleagues and fellow citizens. As he flew up the Agency ladder, he had no tolerance for anyone he did 'not grow up with' in the Agency and had zero faith in the political appointees who headed the CIA.

"I'm a bit wary, if this is FBI territory," Biggs said.

"Let us see what we can find out, and we'll get back to you on it," Todd said.

Biggs stood up from his chair and walked around his desk towards a filing cabinet, where he pulled out a few files and laid them on top of a pile of papers. "Guys, I'm not going through another colonoscopy with the President and some worthless politicians. If this is strictly domestic, we pass it on."

"I understand," Mike said.

The two men stood up and left the office. They headed down the hall in silence and waited until they were out of earshot from Biggs or anyone else.

"There is no chance I'm letting the FBI screw this up," Todd said.

"This guy's up to no good and his kind of no good, is usually a world-wide kind of no good," Mike said. "We can't let those guys get this."

"We won't," Todd said.

• • •

Callie was in the lobby of the Hart Senate Office Building on her way to a meeting with Senator Macklin. She had called two days earlier and had been told the Senator rearranged his schedule in order to meet with her in his office at three o'clock. Standing in front of the South elevator, she was greeted by Senator Dansby, who'd noticed her out of the corner of his eye.

"Ms. Wheeler."

Callie turned and smiled when she saw him. Over the years, she had grown to like him very much, but appeared uncomfortable around him, partially because his vote was unable to be purchased. He was just a nice guy who worked on Capitol Hill for all the right reasons.

"Life treating you okay, Ms. Wheeler?"

"I've had a bit of a rough day, but maybe that will change when I meet with Senator Macklin in a few minutes."

Senator Dansby laughed. "Your logic escapes me. That's never been my experience, but let's keep that between us."

Callie smiled as if to let him know she agreed with him. "Deal," she said. Callie leaned over and pushed the 'up' button of the elevator. "How are things in Alaska?"

"I just came back from there actually. Kind of miss it sometimes, know what I mean?"

Callie contemplated what Dansby said. Within the context of the day's events, she understood it a lot more than he thought she might. "I come from a small town myself, and there are some days, I wish I had never left."

"Like today, I take it?"

"Something like that," Callie said with a bittersweet smile. "Any particular reason you were home or just a visit?" Callie looked up. The elevator had stopped on the ninth floor.

"Actually I went to have a frank discussion with my family about my running for another term."

"Seriously?"

"Very," Dansby said. "Things here have changed over the last few years and I'm not sure if I want to be a part of it anymore."

Callie knew exactly what he meant and felt embarrassed standing in front of him, having this conversation. She never really knew if he understood the extent to which he was right, or exactly how much she had to do with the changing of the culture, but the one thing she knew she did not want see was a man like that leaving Congress.

"Senator, I think your leaving would be a big mistake."

Dansby looked at Callie, surprised by her response. They had never had too much to do with each other, but he'd been told on many occasions that if he wanted anything, she was the person who could make it happen. She'd pleasantly surprised him. It was as if she knew something that others did not. He liked that.

"Thank you, Ms. Wheeler. I appreciate your opinion."

The elevator announced its arrival with a loud ping.

"My pleasure, Senator. I do hope you decide to run again. If you will excuse me, though, my chariot has arrived."

"Surely. Thank you and please send regards to Mr. Ferguson. He's a good man and a great asset to our Nation."

"Yes, he is," she said. "Have a wonderful rest of your day, Senator." Callie stepped into the south elevator and exited on the third floor. She took her time strolling to the end of the hall until she found herself in front of Senator Macklin's office. His Chief of Staff greeted her as soon as she walked through the door.

"Hello, Callie," he said, a tinge of disgust in his voice. "The Senator said you could wait inside. He will be with you shortly."

"Thank you, Brian." Callie said then sauntered inside Macklin's office which was littered with plaques and pictures of the Senator's long career in politics. One such award caught Callie's eye. Inscribed in gold on top of a black background, the marble plaque read:

"To Senator Gerard Macklin, Man of the Year, for his unflinching code of ethics, his clear vision for a god fearing America, and his honest and forthright leadership for our Country." Presented by Citizens for an Honest America 2011.

Callie couldn't help but snicker. Senator Macklin hurried into his office and reached out his hand.

"Callie, how are you?"

She gave Macklin her hand, but when she tried to retrieve it, he pulled her towards him and grabbed her ass with his other hand.

"Excuse me, Senator." Callie pushed him off of her and took a few steps back. "I stopped by to make sure we have all we need on the Oxford Secondary Education Bill, including all the earmarks and the rest. Just as we discussed the other night."

"Well, Callie," Macklin said, as he walked to his desk and sat down, "I thought we had the votes, but it seems some Senators want..."

Callie interrupted him. "You guys want to shake me down?... Again?"

Macklin leaned back in his chair and smiled at her. "'Shakedown' is such an awful phrase. I think they just want to be more... convinced, shall we say."

"Convince them with this." Callie took the large manilla folder she held in her hand and dropped it directly in front of the Senator. Macklin still had a big smile on his face when he looked up at Callie.

"What do we have here, sweetheart?" Macklin, confident he had made his point, prepared for his surprise when he picked up the folder. He opened it and found pictures of various Senators, including himself, in compromising positions with numerous different women. Not the sort of surprise he expected.

A confused Macklin looked up from the pictures in his hand. "What the fuck is this?"

Callie had a big smile on her face as she answered him. "Let's just call it earmark insurance." She motioned towards the pictures he was still holding in his hand. "We need that earmark."

Macklin stared at her in a daze. "Where did you get these, Ms. Wheeler?"

"I don't think that information is important right now. What is important is that you understand there are a lot more where they came from." Callie smiled confidently and prepared to go. "I trust I can count on your...", Callie looked at the plaque on the wall as she said her words. "Honest and forthright leadership."

Senator Macklin sat speechless. He attempted to play hardball with Callie and lost. Callie opened the door and stepped out to leave, but stopped and turned back to Macklin.

"Don't you ever touch me again you piece of shit."

She bounced out of Macklin's office and left the door wide open. Macklin sat helpless, holding the pictures in his hand and more convinced than ever that Callie Wheeler had to be stopped before she did any more damage to him or anyone else in Congress.

TWENTY-EIGHT

Callie left Macklin's office hopeful she had taken care of his obnoxious behavior once and for all. Following a short cab ride back to M&G, Callie gathered a few items from her desk, then, after some serious internal debate, made the decision to go talk to Kacey instead of putting it off for another day. If Kacey was going to run the story, it would be advantageous to do what she could to have some influence on it or with any luck, get her to delay it as long as possible.

When she exited the building onto K Street, Callie had no idea what she was going to tell her now ex-best friend. She headed east down K and turned left onto 17th. Callie chose to take a less populated route than risk bumping into someone she did not want to see. Her mind raced in a hundred different directions. As usual, the questions she volleyed back and forth in her head made her oblivious to anyone or anything around her. Would Kacey be there? Would she talk to her? How angry would she still be?

At L Street, Callie turned right. She never recognized the construction barriers in her way nor did she hear the catcalls from the workers who stopped what they were doing just to stare and bark at her.

Kacey had to hold the story, she thought.

Callie drifted back to a time when they hadn't a care in the world besides what each other would wear the next day. She thought about the sleepovers, up all night doing their hair and trying on each other's clothes. She thought of the sweet smell of the chocolate chip cookies they baked at 3:30 in the morning. As she continued down L Street, she laughed thinking about the time she covered for Kacey when Pop showed up at Callie's home, but she'd snuck off to be with Jeff Crow.

The more she thought about it, the more confident she was she could persuade Kacey to kill the story altogether. Callie strolled another two blocks and made a left onto 15th. She entered the offices of the Washington Post and said hello to the security guard at the door, who recognized her right away.

"Hi Cliff, how've you been?" Callie waved at the older African American man who was closing in on sixty.

"Been doing great. How about them Nationals though? Terrible huh?"

"I like the new pitcher. What's his name again?"

"Strasburg?" Clifford said with pride as if he were his own child.

"Yeah, that's it, but he's gotta get to pitching again, don't ya' think?"

"My boy's been hurt. When he comes back we gonna stick it to y'all."

Callie signed in. "You know you ain't gonna beat my Phillies, Cliffy."

Cliff waved a slow arm. "Why you like them crumb bums."

"Who do you want me to root for?"

"The Dee Cee Nats, you live here now, hon. Give up on them Wilkes Borough teams," Cliff said sounding out the letters D C loud and deliberate for emphasis and, of course, mispronouncing her hometown as he always did.

Callie laughed. "Peey Aaay born and bred, Cliff, gotta' stick with my peeps." Callie imitated Cliff saying the letter P A just as loud and just as deliberate.

"You going to see Ms. Mercer?"

"I am, kind sir."

"Yup, she should be up there. You seen her story yet?"

Callie nodded her head as she leaned on the security guard table. "I did."

"We're awful proud of her, stickin' it to them crooks up there. I love it."

"I love it, too."

He handed her a visitors badge with the date and time written on it. "You know where you goin' right, Callie?"

"I'm good, gorgeous," she said.

Callie smiled and waved good-bye then took the elevator upstairs. She stepped out and cautiously approached Kacey's cubicle only to find it empty. Callie stepped towards the desk and picked up a picture of her and Kacey on the boardwalk in Ocean City. She stared at it momentarily and ran her hand across the glass. She was still holding the frame when Walter Bloom spotted her and waved hello. Callie waved back, feeling a little out of place.

"Hi, Callie. How's your boss?"

"Coming back from LA tonight. You doing okay, Walter?"

"I'm good, thanks for asking. How's the boyfriend?"

Callie lifted her hand and showed off her new diamond ring. "Fiancé."

Walter latched onto her outstretched hand and pulled it closer to get a better look. "Your man treats you well. What is that... two-carats?"

"How'd you know?" Callie asked, surprised at his expertise.

Walter pointed to his eye and curled up the side of his mouth like a 1950's Hollywood detective. "I could tell ya' doll, but then I'd have to whack ya'…"

"Kacey told you, didn't she?"

"I never give up my sources. Occupational hazard," he said, letting go of her hand. "Kacey went to the vending machine to grab a bite for dinner. She'll be right back."

"Thanks, Walter. Great seeing you again."

Walter gave her half a wave and wandered away. Callie sat down in Kacey's chair just like she'd always done. She looked around the desk and found another picture of the two of them that Kacey still displayed, which Callie took as a good sign.

Out of the corner of her eye, she saw notes with the name 'Callie?' written in various places. Callie leaned over slightly to try to make out what she had written when Kacey approached from behind and saw Callie sitting at her desk. Kacey stood there quietly, startling Callie, who jumped in her seat.

"Find anything you like?" Kacey's voice was as cold as an Alaskan morning. Callie picked up on it right away, just as Kacey had wanted her to.

Callie stood up and awkwardly moved off to the side. For the first time ever in Kacey's company, Callie was unsure of herself. She felt the perspiration trickle down her back. The sweat on her palms left her uneasy and insecure. Callie readjusted her purse strap onto her shoulder and took note of Kacey's cold hard stare.

"Can we talk?" she asked.

Kacey brushed by her and sat down.

"I'm not sure we have much to talk about."

"You said if I wanted to comment on the record, I should be in touch with you."

Kacey turned to face her. "I'm listening," she said albeit not too enthusiastically. "But I'm not going to entertain any excuses, so if that's why you're here, save us both the trouble and take your boney ass somewhere else."

It was up to Callie to make it right. Kacey's resolve surprised her, but she was even more surprised by her own feelings of inadequacy and embarrassment. She tried to look Kacey in the eye, but Kacey had already turned back towards her desk.

Kacey opened a package of ranch dressing and poured it over her salad. "You know, Callie, I thought that the next time I'd see you I would melt and lose the deep feelings of betrayal that you caused, but just the opposite has occurred and I realize now, I no longer want anything to do with you."

"Is there someplace here we can go?" Callie asked, knowing she had very little room for error. "In private?"

Kacey pushed her salad away. She motioned for Callie to follow her towards the stairwell. She opened the door and walked down a flight of stairs, then sat down on the fifth step from the bottom. Callie attempted to sit down next to her, as she had always done in the past, but Kacey moved towards the middle of the step making it impossible for her to do that. Callie proceeded to the bottom of the stairwell and faced Kacey, her uneasiness still very apparent. Callie knew this would be difficult, but she seemed unprepared for the feelings of detachment she was experiencing and the distance she felt from her best friend. At no time in her life could she ever remember feeling more alone than she did at this moment.

"Kacey, we can't go on like this."

Kacey stared at Callie, but said nothing.

"I'm sorry I lied..." Callie said as she struggled to find the right words. "I need you in my life, Kace."

Kacey was unmoved by her opening plea. "How could you look me straight in the eye and lie to me? For all I know, you've been doing it our entire lives."

Kacey knew better than that. She wanted to get under Callie's skin.

"That's not fair, Kacey and you know it."

"What's not fair? You lying to me?"

"No, you know what I'm talking about. I've never lied to you…"

"You never what?"

"Well, I…I just…"

"Exactly." Kacey said shaking her head.

Callie had no idea what to say. She had promised herself on the way over that she would keep her composure and be honest with Kacey. More importantly, she wanted to clear the air. She wanted her friend back.

"What do you know about Jonas Foster and Lank?" Kacey asked.

Callie played with her bracelet, stalling for time. Her hesitation was not a good thing.

"I can't tell you now, but trust me…"

Kacy interrupted her, raising her voice a bit. "Trust you? You're kidding, right?"

"No, I'm not kidding. Kacey, the story you have is nothing," Callie said.

Kacey was visibly upset, but not enough to end the conversation. "Go on."

"I'll tell you everything when the time is right. I can promise you that what you have now is nothing. Lank is small potatoes."

Kacey's upper lip hardened. Callie knew she didn't buy it.

"Stop playing games with me. You're just trying to save your own ass," Kacey said.

"Kacey, please don't print the story."

"Can you give me a comment on the record?"

"I'm sorry, Kacey. I can't."

Kacey stood up and started to climb the stairs, then turned around.

"Fuck you, Callie. Don't call me, text me, nothing. I am so done with you, you are such a conniving bitch...trying to get me to...oh, I am so done with you."

Kacey walked up the stairs.

"Someone is trying to kill me!" Callie said.

Kacey stopped in her tracks and turned around, an actual look of concern on her face. "What?"

"I don't know who or why, but someone is after me."

Kacey wanted to believe her, but was skeptical. "Why would someone want to kill you?"

"I don't know, but I'm telling the truth."

"Of course, you are."

"Kacey, you don't want to believe me that's fine. Just hold the story." Callie had started to walk up the steps towards Kacey. "Write this story and someone will steal the real one out from under you."

Kacey had heard enough. She turned and walked back upstairs. "Good luck, Callie," Kacey said with her back towards her. She opened the stairwell door and left Callie all alone. Callie slumped on the bottom step and dropped her face in her hands wondering how much worse things could possibly get.

• • •

Mike, dressed in shorts and an Arizona Cardinals tee-shirt, sat on the backyard deck, relaxing on a beach lounger and milking a Bud Light. He had brought home a new group of field reports to catch up on some work, but couldn't get past the first few. It was the kind of summer night that made you want to live slowly. Callie had warned him he'd be on his own for dinner; she'd be home late.

Mike treated himself to barbecued steak and when he'd finished, took the time to appreciate the beautiful Mid-Atlantic evening. Callie entered the house through the front door and dropped her Marc Jacobs black shoulder bag near the closet. She tiptoed to the kitchen and quietly slid open the sliding door then stepped onto the deck. Mike seemed preoccupied with his reading. Callie bent down behind him and slipped her hands through his collar and began to caress his chest. Mike leaned back and closed his eyes as she kissed the top of his head.

"How was your day?"

Mike put down the paper and gently ran his fingers along her arms. "I don't even know where to start," he said.

Callie stood up and walked around in front of him. She hiked up her skirt and straddled Mike, giving him a long passionate kiss.

"I needed that," Callie said before she kissed him again.

Mike placed his hands on Callie's exposed thighs as she sat up. "Any other incidents, Cal?"

Callie stared into Mike's eyes, leaned over and kissed Mike on the lips again, then sat up. "No, no more incidents and you'll also be happy to know that Neil was always somewhere around me," Callie said referring to the private security detail Mike placed on her. She outlined Mike's face with her index finger then tapped him on the nose. "Tell him I said thank you, but he doesn't have to do that anymore."

Mike tensed up just a bit, enough for Callie to take notice. "Until we find out what's going on, you need protection, so forget about that. You have no choice."

Callie stood up, swung her leg back over Mike and stepped away from him. "I'm not going to live my life in fear."

"Cal, right now you have no choice."

She walked to the edge of the deck, turned around to face him, and leaned back onto its top rail. "Or I could carry a gun?"

Mike, beer still in hand, stood up and ambled towards Callie. "Or we can just give you trained protection, like Neil."

Callie wrapped her arms around Mike's neck. He touched the small of her back. "Do me a favor and let me protect you the way I know how...and don't tell me it's not that serious when we both know the last twenty-four hours has been as serious as it gets."

"But Mike..."

"But nothing. This is what I do. Let me do it. Okay?"

"You win." Callie swayed to make-believe music in her head. She started to sing softly..."You are the love of my life, and I'm so glad you found me, you are the love of my life, baby put your arms around me..." She continued to sing as she gazed into Mike's eyes..."You are my love, the love of my life..."

Callie kissed Mike then rested her head on his shoulder, which for a brief moment in time, helped her forget what could have possibly been the worst day of her life.

TWENTY-NINE

Thursday July 28, 2011

For the most part, three o'clock in the morning looks the same in most cities around the United States. Streets were void of traffic. Every sound echos for blocks and the only thing you hear is the electricity dinging inside the street lamps when you stood beneath them. There were those rare occasions when a person, or a group of people, made it a point to work late into the night, but rarely did a company call its ownership meetings for that time of the morning.

Jonas Foster Development was not your typical company.

Barry sat at the head of the conference table. With him were Senators Shulman, Gorman, Macklin, King, Lank, Bane and McCombs. Seated to Barry's right was Jonas Foster. Foster was the CEO Hollywood would have chosen to play the part. Blessed with a full head of black hair that was slowly being invaded by a sprinkling of grey, his well defined cheek bones and sturdy chin gave him a look of self-assuredness. Combined with his newly manicured fingernails, he projected to the world a man who understood what it took to present a powerful image of leadership. Earlier in April, the Wall Street Journal called Jonas Foster Development, 'the most aggressive, dominant and financially stable Development company in America.'

Behind Barry was a large projector screen. Per Barry's mandate, the offices of M&G closed at 8:30. The rest of the building was to close by nine o'clock. Outside of a Security Guard on the first floor, the only people at 1900 K Street were in the room with him.

"Gentleman, thank you all for coming," Barry started. "The purpose of this meeting tonight is to update you on the progress of Jonas Foster Development and our plans moving forward."

He clicked the remote in his hands. The room went dark as a screen popped out of the ceiling and rolled down behind him. Soon thereafter, images appeared on the screen. Barry motioned towards Jonas Foster, who stood up and took the remote from his outstretched hand.

Jonas reached into his pocket and pulled out a small red notebook with a green elastic band around it. On the cover, the letters JFD were displayed prominently in permanent black marker. Jonas opened the book, leafed through it, then pulled a pen from his jacket pocket and wrote something down inside the notebook. He placed the notebook on the table in front of him and turned his attention to the big screen behind his back.

"Hello again, everyone and welcome. Thanks to your help, Jonas Foster Development is now the fastest-growing developer of real estate in the United States and the world." Jonas clicked on the remote and changed the slide.

"We currently have multiple revenue stream projects in the following cities as you can see on the board in front of you: Miami, Orlando, Boca Raton, Memphis, Pittsburgh, Buffalo, Detroit, Cleveland, Seattle, Madison, Los Angeles, Denver, Atlanta, Salt Lake, Houston, San Diego, St. Louis, Manhattan, Las Vegas, Reno, Albany, Philadelphia, Nashville, Chicago and of course right here in Washington, D.C."

Jonas paused for a moment to let the Senators comprehend the extent of the company's holdings before he continued. "Profits from the malls, condos and other properties currently rented from fiscal year 2010 were estimated at 674 million dollars. Based on our agreement, that means everyone in this room will receive in excess of 27 million dollars each, with the rest of the profit being used for discretionary projects and working capital."

The group of Senators around the table clapped and smiled. Jonas picked up the red notebook and consulted it again before discussing the following information.

"More importantly, when the current fiscal year closes, you can expect at least a ten to twenty percent increase in revenues. With Barry's plan and all your help inserting the language in the Lank bill, in the last five years, we've been able to purchase over six thousand properties at close to forty percent below market value and another eleven thousand below fifty percent." Jonas surveyed the room and continued addressing the small crowd from his prepared statements and the slides on the screen. While he did, he thought about all that had happened since Barry had approached him with an idea a little less than eight years ago.

Jonas Foster had been a popular man on the University of Maryland Campus. During his first two years of college, he spent most of his time at any party he could find and earned a reputation as someone who could hold his liquor with the best of them. More importantly, at least to him, was his success with the ladies. He left Maryland at the start of his junior year, although no one knew exactly why.

He never returned to his education and instead embarked on a career in the real estate business back home in Texas. He struggled early on, but made a few substantial deals that gave him a nice flow of steady income while he built his company. By late 2004, Jonas Foster was back in his hometown of Dallas and had established himself as a businessman with a stellar reputation for honesty, integrity and good character. He had taken advantage of the real estate boom of the nineties and had a nice portfolio that earned him a few hundred thousand dollars a year in income. But it would be on a vacation in Las Vegas that he met an old acquaintance from college, Barry Miller, when things started to really happen for Jonas Foster.

He started Jonas Foster Development in November of that year after Barry had convinced Jonas that he could help him expand his business holdings. In return, Barry insisted on a few conditions in order for their relationship to work. By January of 2008 Jonas Foster Development, or JFD as it was known in Texas, had turned a small stake into an emerging empire.

"The good news is we are only just getting started," Jonas told the eight men at the table. Jonas handed the red notebook back to Barry and as he had done each time they all met, excused himself for the evening and left Barry and the Senators to talk alone. Barry shut off the projector and turned the lights back on. He paced the front of the room then wandered over to the beverage area in the corner and poured himself a glass of vodka without offering anything to anyone else. Drink in hand, he slowly walked back to the head of the table.

"All of you have played a huge role in the success of Jonas Foster. During the past eighteen months, we have begun to expand beyond our borders. We will update you with our progress overseas before years end. Does anyone have any issues they need to discuss before we adjourn?"

Senator Lank stood up, straightened his tie then cleared his throat. The past ten days had been tumultuous for him, but he seemed very happy with the support he'd received from his colleagues on Capitol Hill. His constituents led a massive letter writing campaign to the Post accusing them of fabricating the story without any hard evidence. While he still heard his name too much in the press, the trip to Pebble Beach served as a great stress reliever and now he focused his concern towards what to do moving forward.

"How protected are we regarding the media?"

"Senator Lank, and this goes for everyone else too," Barry said. "There is no possible way the media can ever get wind of this information or your involvement in Jonas Foster, unless someone in this room talks. We are it. We are the only ones who know about any of this, so it is in your personal and collective best interests to keep quiet." Barry took a sip of Smirnoff then ran his finger across his lips. "I believe you all have 27 million reasons to do just that."

Barry brought the glass to his lips again and finished the vodka with one last swig. "The Board of Directors that I picked for this venture have no idea of your involvement with the company and will receive a totally separate accounting of our finances. We need to close ranks on this and make sure no one, and I mean no one, in this room says a word. I'm talking no leaks, none. Because believe me if one of us goes down, we will all go down. I don't think there is any doubt about that, is there gentleman?"

Barry sat down in his chair and rested his elbows on the table. "Most important, if they ask about Senator Lank: deny and keep denying. Outside of the people in this room, no one has any idea that you have a stake in this company. No one..."

Senator King interrupted Barry mid-sentence. "I think we can all agree that no one needs to be talking. What I can't figure out is how did they find out about Senator Lank and Jonas?"

Barry hesitated before he answered. The question bothered him too. "That I don't know. But remember, we are dealing in cash. The story they have is about money with no trace. It was never deposited anywhere. That is why it's imperative we forget this meeting ever took place. We are the only ones who know about this and as long as everyone stays quiet, you will all be able to deny and it will go away. Last thing on this and it's important. Keep in mind they have no smoking gun; the Lank money was never accounted for. Deny, deny, deny."

Barry raised the screen behind him into the ceiling. "As always, the money you receive will be washed so many times, it will look transparent. Furthermore, it will all be sent to the Cayman accounts we set up two years ago. Same withdrawal rules apply."

Senator Macklin, still reeling from his visit with Callie earlier in the day, was obviously on edge when he stood up to speak. "What about your associate?"

Barry took a few moments before he responded. "Just play ball with her for the time being. We have begun to take care of her on two different fronts. We are not talking weeks or months, gentlemen, we are talking about days here, if not hours. At some point we may need you all to be ready to pounce, so do as I say and in short order we will no longer have to worry about Callie Wheeler. All I ask is that you be careful with her because she knows too much for her own good. But very soon, that won't matter."

Barry looked around the room. "If no one has anything else, this meeting is adjourned."

· · ·

Barry was the last person to leave M&G following the meeting. He was happy with the outcome and for the first time in nearly two weeks, started to feel like his life had begun to fall back into place. On the phone, he could hear Ibrahim through the hands free-device in his car as Barry made his way home for a short night's sleep.

"What is your estimate, Mr. Miller?"

"We will need eleven million dollars now, another ten in about a week. That should be enough for the immediate future."

"That will be fine. I take it everything is set for the Oxford Secondary Education Bill as we discussed?"

"Yes, Ibrahim. No problem there. Everything is moving forward as planned."

"Are you prepared on your end?"

"We have everything in place. All we need from you is the go ahead," Barry said.

"I will let you know as soon as we are ready." Ibrahim hung up the phone leaving Barry with a loud dial tone over his bluetooth device.

Barry pressed a button on the dashboard, which disconnected his end of the call. "You are this close, Barry…" he said to himself with a very large grin smeared across his face.

THIRTY

Callie sat at the kitchen table frantically searching through the pages of the day's edition of the Washington Post. She was still wearing the pink cut-off Tom Brady jersey she slept in, too focused on what might lie ahead to worry about who saw her step on the lawn to retrieve the paper in just her underwear and top. She had spent a wonderful evening alone with Mike, but tossed and turned for most of the night. She woke up at 4:10 in the morning tortured by her concern about how damaging Kacey's piece in the paper would be. Callie thought about telling Mike the entire story, but they were so engrossed in each other, she figured it could wait until after she assessed the devastation from the article.

Mike, dressed in a blue Armani suit and a gold tie, held his jacket in his hand as he entered the kitchen and witnessed Callie searching each page in desperation. He placed his coat on the back of one of the chairs, walked over to Callie and kissed her on the top of her head.

"You were up early."

"Uh-huh"

"What's that about?"

"Nothing," Callie said.

Mike strode towards the counter. He poured a cup of coffee. "What the hell are you doing?"

Callie barely heard him. She continued to search the paper. "What the hell am I doing about what?"

"Callie…"

She kept flipping the pages, back and forth in each section.

"Callie…look at me," Mike said.

Callie picked up her head.

"What are you doing?" Mike poured his coffee, but assumed it wasn't worth it to ask her if she wanted a cup.

"I'm looking for something."

Mike walked to the table and sat down next to her. "What are you looking for?"

"It's not here. She didn't write it."

"What's not there?"

"Kacey. She didn't write about Lank." Callie sat dumbfounded as she turned to her fiancé.

"Isn't that a good thing?"

"Yeah, I think so."

Callie realized she had dodged the bullet. At least for today. Feeling much better despite a lousy night's sleep, she handed the paper to Mike and got more comfortable in her chair. "What? No coffee for me?"

Mike waved her off to study the sports section.

"Oh, Mike. Remember, tomorrow night we are at the Kennedy Center for the President's birthday party."

Callie reached across the table for her daily planner. She pulled it towards her, opened it up and removed the raised lettered invitation.

"What time does that start?"

"Private dinner at six, program at eight, reception afterwards,"

Callie said. She closed her planner and ran her fingers across the raised black lettering.

Mike picked his head up from the Post, looked at his beautiful wife-to-be and took a drink from his coffee mug. "Remind me again why we have to go to this thing?"

"Umm…because he's your boss?"

"Oh, right."

The ring from the house phone interrupted their conversation. Callie stood up from her chair to answer it. As she moved across the kitchen, Mike couldn't help but stare at her creamy long legs. He smiled as he admired her perfect structure and took a long sip of his coffee without losing sight of her finely trimmed physique. Callie picked up the phone with her right hand, shifting the invitation still in her left one.

"Hello?"

No response from the other line.

"Hello?"

Callie was about to hang up the phone when she dropped the invitation on the floor. At the exact moment she bent down to pick it up, a bullet pierced through the bay window in the front of the house. The bullet impaled itself into the wooden support next to the sliding doors, directly behind where Callie stood just a moment before.

"Callie! Stay down!"

"Mike!"

"Stay down!"

Mike, his gun already drawn from the holster on the back of his belt, rushed over to Callie and moved her behind him and against the kitchen wall. He used his body to shield her as he crouched over and quickly rushed her to the corner of the den away from the sight-lines of the bay window and the sliding glass doors that lead to the deck. He looked around, still protecting her and motioned her behind the couch. "Callie, go over there and don't move. I'm serious. Stay."

Within seconds another bullet, this time coming from the back of the house, shattered the sliding doors. It was followed by a rally of five more shots that exploded inside the house, but missed their intended targets each time. Mike surveyed the situation and checked on Callie's safety once more, while he contemplated his next move.

"Stay behind there, Callie. Don't do anything stupid. Stay there."

Mike, now looking to go on the offensive, remained out of the line of fire as another round of bullets came flying through what was left of the glass doors. Pressing his back against the wall, he caught the shooter's reflection in a picture frame across from what used to be the sliding doors. Callie had insisted on hanging the picture of Mike and Akiva in the living room instead of Mike's study where he wanted it to be. Mike checked the glass protecting the photo and caught a glimpse of the shooter, who had made his way onto the deck, only steps away from entering the house. Mike stepped in front of the shattered glass and lodged two bullets dead center in the shooters forehead from less than ten yards away.

Not knowing if there were any more snipers around, Mike turned over the kitchen table and took cover behind it. From a distance, the sound of police sirens rang out and he knew that within moments they would be at his front door.

"What the hell?" Law enforcement was already in transit. That didn't make sense. He turned around and saw Callie curled up behind the couch, the kitchen phone still in her hand.

"9-1-1."

Mike looked out at the shattered bay window and saw the police approaching the house with their guns drawn. He told Callie to stay where she was before greeting the officers at the door.

• • •

Ken Farmer's home was the exact opposite of his workplace. His house screamed opulence with thick Persian rugs on the hardwood and fine furniture in every corner. The sink basins in each room were outlined in gold including golden knobs for hot and cold water. The kitchen refrigerator was the size of a small European automobile. Mahogany spiral staircases were the only steps available to enter each of the four floors above the basement, but just in case, there were two elevators on each level.

Farmer sat at his breakfast table eating in front of a fifty-two inch Hi-Definition television, a cook and a wait staff at his beck and call. WBAL Channel 11, the local NBC station in Baltimore, was broadcasting on the screen, but his attention had been distracted by the morning paper. He wore the bathrobe of a prince and his manicured feet were covered with slippers made of sheep skin. His cell phone rang a few times before Ken muted the television and answered the call.

"Is it done?"

Ken was not pleased. He began to pace the room, his anger gathering.

"I do not care! I told you this needs to be done!"

Small beads of sweat ran down his face. He grabbed a napkin from the kitchen table and wiped off the perspiration. He was surprised by the information that was being fed to him.

"Someone else? What do you mean there was someone else?"

Ken listened attentively to the person on the other line as his mood changed from anger to confusion.

"How can this happen?" His face was turning red again. "Makes no difference!" He shook his head. "This should have been done already. Nothing has changed. This has to be taken care of immediately. Do not fail me again!"

Ken hung up the phone then dialed another number. After a few rings, he spoke in Arabic. "Things have gotten messy. We have a problem."

• • •

Mike and Callie sat next to each other holding hands on the couch. Callie had spent five frightening minutes hiding behind the same couch she currently sat on, which was situated in the corner of the den just off the kitchen. She looked down at the enormous amount of shattered glass spread out in all directions around the room, the remnants of the incident covering a newly varnished wood floor. Two uniformed policemen stood at the doorway standing guard and another two in uniform could be seen through the broken bay window, patrolling the wraparound porch outside. The early morning sound of bullet-fire woke up the entire neighborhood, who were all congregating on the sidewalk in front of the house and along Delaware Street. A dead body was curled up on the deck out back, surrounded by pools of blood from the two bullet holes in his forehead, each one less than a millimeter away from the other. Two District police officers stood in the back of the house, assigned to guard the body until the medical examiner arrived.

Adam Edelman and Jay Jaffe were both veteran detectives in the D.C. Police Department, having close to fifty years experience between them. Mike had called Adam after the uniformed police officers had arrived at his door. He'd worked with Adam on a number of cases over the course of the last decade and Mike trusted him as much as anyone else he could think of in the department.

The two detectives sat on kitchen chairs they had dragged into the den and placed them across from the couch. Jay held a pen in his left hand and a notebook in his right, while Adam did most of the talking. Todd Goodwin showed up just after the detectives had arrived and made himself comfortable leaning against the wall behind the two detectives. Callie had changed into a pair of pink sweat pants and a white tee-shirt before the house got too crowded with law enforcement. Mike, still in his suit pants and a white shirt, was surprised at how well Callie had kept her composure during the entire incident, a far cry from her reaction to the event a few nights before.

"Ms. Wheeler, you said they started coming after you a few days ago?"

"Yes, sir, that's correct." Callie fiddled with the drawstring on her sweats.

Adam took a moment to think. "I'm a little confused." Callie and Mike looked at each other, also confused.

"About what?" Mike asked.

Adam hesitated before answering. "Well, the guy shoots one shot at Ms. Wheeler from the front of the house…"

"Correct," Mike said.

"Then a minute or two later, as you tell it, he is in the back and tries again?"

"Exactly," Mike said. "What seems to be the problem?"

"To tell you the truth, something here doesn't make a whole lot of sense," Adam said. "Why would he go to the back and switch weapons, if he only fired one shot from the front of the house?"

Now Mike was the one who seemed confused. "What do you mean switched weapons?"

"We found two different caliber bullets in your home." Detective Jaffe, who had been taking notes, offered up information Mike had no way of knowing until now.

Mike looked at Callie then Todd. "Two shooters?"

Detective Edelman thought about it some more, but said

nothing.

"They sent two shooters to shoot Callie?" Mike asked.

Adam stood up and walked to what used to be the sliding glass doors, peeked outside on the deck at the murdered shooter, then came back inside. He hesitated, as if he was trying to work something out in his head, before he looked up at Mike. Adam reached into his jacket pocket with his gloved hand and pulled out something as he spoke.

"Here's the other thing I don't get," Adam said. "The perp in your backyard? He has no identification, no car keys, brand new shoes, brand new gloves on his hands, nothing to identify himself with…"

"So," Mike said. "That doesn't seem unusual."

Detective Edelman handed Mike a picture from his jacket pocket. "All he had on him, Agent Ferguson, was this picture of you."

Mike stared at the picture, then glanced up at Todd.

"What in the world…?"

THIRTY-ONE

Callie sat at the witness table with Miles Goodman at her side. The day had turned out to be a battle of wills. The legislators were very familiar with Callie and the last thing they wanted was to have her testify for an extended period. Callie complicated things even further with her insistence on making an opening statement that had amped the tension in the room to combustible levels. As the question and answer period began, the Senators took their shots at her, but Callie refused to be bullied.

All three major networks had interrupted their daily programming to bring the drama to the public live in real time to satisfy the overwhelming demand. With Senators being told by their aides that the entire country was now tuned in, the pontificating from the podium intensified. They knew their constituents were paying attention.

The longer the testimony went, the more confrontational it became. Every prominent nightly news anchor and cable television host had arrived on the Hill to get their own bird's eye view. The hearing was filled with a standing room only crowd, but due to the demand, a row of people in the gallery were removed from their seats to make room for the group from CBS News. Through it all, Callie remained undaunted.

Chairman Rice had been patient and allotted Callie plenty of leeway in her comments, but he had his limits and Callie had passed them long ago.

"Ms. Wheeler, what we would like, is that you focus your attention only on issues pertaining to the purpose of this hearing, which is, the role that lobbyists like yourself have played in the governmental process and how that influence has corrupted our system in such a drastic way, that we need to address its very existence." Chairman Rice continued, as if he were a High School principal scolding a student in his office. "That, Ms. Wheeler, is the only reason why you are here."

Callie leaned in to confer with her attorney. He covered her microphone and whispered in her ear.

"Look, I think this has gone on long enough. You've made your point. In all honesty I think these guys are going to do everything they can to go after you and make your life completely unlivable," Goodman said.

Callie listened intently then turned to Goodman, his hand still covering her microphone, and whispered her response.

"I don't care. I need to get my life back and salvage some sort of reputation when this is all over with. They have gotten away with their bullshit long enough. As long as I have a chance to let them know exactly how I feel and on top of that, let the country know what is really going on up here, I'm going to do it."

Her attorney leaned back over and whispered to her. "Just know that they will come after you hard and when they come after you, they will get you."

"Not if I get them first."

Miles Goodman looked at Callie curiously. She knew exactly what she was doing. He slowly took his right hand off of her microphone and with his left hand, reached under the table and gave Callie's thigh a gentle squeeze of approval. Callie nodded her head slightly so that her attorney knew she understood the message he tried to convey.

"Mr. Chairman, I find it truly astounding that after everything that has happened, all the reports in the media, all the casualties from my entire sordid career in Washington, this body still fails to address any substantive issues that point to the actual culprits in this government and our political process."

Senator Macklin, consulted with the two aides sitting behind him and began to speak.

"Ms. Wheeler you can't possibly understand the massive responsibility we have on our shoulders as we attempt to rid this institution of vermin like yourself and save the very political process you pretend to care about." Macklin, his arrogance on full display, continued his attack. "Unlike you, we were elected to our positions by our constituents."

Callie knew she had total control of the hearing which was just how she wanted it. The Senators in front of her were reeling like a boxer who had been bloodied for half the fight, but understood there was still a long way to go. She had given her opening statement because she wanted to put the entire room on the defensive. Now that she had them there, she had no intention of letting them get away.

"Senator Macklin," Callie said, "you do not need to remind me about your positions."

Senator Macklin looked her in the eyes and recognized he'd just been given fair warning and a charitable stay of execution, at least for the time being. He could not even count the ways he hated the woman sitting before him at the witness table.

Chairman Rice looked at Senator Macklin to see if he was planning to respond. Macklin leaned back in his chair and shook his head.

Wilbur Lank made himself as invisible as possible sitting behind his makeshift desk on the podium. He understood his role in the process, now unfolding before the country, and offered minimal input once the hearing had gotten underway. His attitude changed as soon as he saw the commotion in the front row and the presence of Natalie Quinton, the lead anchor for CBS News. Her attendance would carry a little more weight with the public. Lank figured the time had come to rehabilitate himself in front of a national television audience.

"Mr. Chairman, may I be recognized?"

"The gentleman from Tennessee is recognized for two-minutes," Rice said.

"Ms. Wheeler, I was against your appearing before this committee today. I find your lack of ethics and integrity appalling, to say the least, but after hearing what you've had to say, I believe we've exposed you for the morally bankrupt ingrate that you are. I believe now that we've shined the light on you, you will soon need to scurry back into your darkened corner like the rest of the cockroaches on the planet. Our opportunity has arrived to finally put a nail in the coffin of the parasitic special interests groups that you and your kind represent." Lank tried to stare Callie down, but she just smiled and shook her head.

Callie was as confident as ever.

She looked over Lank's shoulder and locked eyes with Joel Hughes, who took his index finger and scratched his nose, signaling to Callie she was free to say what she wanted to the Senator. Joel would not interfere.

"Just so I understand, am I going to be lectured on ethics by you, Senator Lank?" Callie looked Lank straight in the eye and her demeanor let him and everyone else know that she wasn't planning on going anywhere, until she finished saying what she had come there to say. "I do not believe you're qualified."

The hearing room was overcome by another outburst of camera flashes and noise. Chairman Rice slammed his gavel down bringing the room to a standstill.

Senator Shulman finally reached his boiling point.

"Excuse me!" Shulman's voice exploded from his chest.

Callie knew him like a fly knew garbage. His loudness had two purposes. The first had been to show off for an ever increasing audience. The second, to embarrass and intimidate her. She smirked at him and winked as if to wish him luck on both fronts.

"Who do you think you are? We have invited you here to get to the bottom of this issue, not to sit here and be insulted by the likes of a no good hustler like yourself." Schulman, who earned the moniker from the media as the greatest camera whore in the Senate, took full advantage of the situation and barreled on at his whiney best.

"You, Ms. Wheeler, and I don't want to blame just you, but you are the major reason why the political dialogue in this country is at an all-time low. In the history of this republic, we have never witnessed acrimony to the extent we have heard it these last few years and it is solely because of your divisive actions. Through your underhanded activities, the political conversation in America is infested with poison. I, for one, am appalled by it. It flies in the face of every principle I know to be true."

"And which principle would that be, Senator?" Callie laughed. She moved closer to the microphone. "If you need to blame me for the disgusting political discourse in this country, give it your best shot, if you think that all the people watching will buy it. But stop your whining about the political discourse in Washington being the worst in our country's history. Aaron Burr shot Alexander Hamilton to death over political discourse in 1804, so spare me, Senator, and grab a history book."

Callie leaned back in her chair and caught a quick glimpse of Joel who sat in awe of her behind Lank. He gestured to her with a simple bow of his head and broke out the smallest smile in support of Callie's commentary. Callie lifted her index finger then touched the side of her nose to let him know she appreciated his support.

Friday, July 29, 2011

Kacey had taken Joel up on his movie suggestion. They'd gone to see 'Crazy, Stupid, Love,' just released across the country that afternoon. Joel held the door open for Kacey as they left the Galleria on Wisconsin Avenue in Northwest D.C. She walked through the door and waited for him outside.

"I'm so impressed. A chick flick?"

Joel looked at Kacey and smiled. "Whatever it takes."

"Did you like the movie?"

"It was okay,"

"Just okay? You mean you're not like the guy in the film all about the conquest and sleeping with as many women as you can?"

"Ha. Hardly," Joel said. Kacey bumped up against him as they shared a laugh together.

"You seem like you're in a better mood," Joel said.

"Honestly, I'm still pretty upset about all of it, but I promised myself I would focus on you tonight and not Callie."

Joel stopped abruptly as soon as he heard her name. Kacey, not realizing that he had stopped walking, kept moving forward a few steps before she noticed Joel was no longer moving next to her. Kacey turned around and looked at Joel who stood in the same place where she'd left him.

"What?"

Joel did not answer her right away. Instead, he wondered what the odds were, although he could actually see the two of them being friends.

"Did you say, Callie?"

"Callie Wheeler. We grew up together," Kacey said. "Do you know her?"

Joel seemed unsure of what to say. "She's the friend?"

The two of them kept moving in silence for a few moments before Kacey stopped abruptly.

"Oh my god, Lank," Kacey whispered. "So it is true."

This time it was Joel who shuffled back towards Kacey and stood looking at her with his eyebrows raised and his arms bent, palms up.

"How do you know her?" Kacey asked.

"She's a lobbyist, I'm a Senator's chief of staff. Sort of comes with the job."

They continued walking in silence. Kacey debated whether it was smart to ask more about the situation that started all of this and wondered to what extent he'd been involved in the Lank story. Now that she had put two and two together, would it muddle her chances with him, a guy who she could really like?

"Can I ask you something?"

"On the record or off?" Joel asked.

Kacey hesitated before she answered his question. She didn't want to blow the potential she had begun to envision with him, but she also knew that she had a job to do.

"I don't know."

"Fair enough."

Kacey thought about how she was going to ask her next question, trying to walk the line between reporter and date, without upsetting Joel.

"I got a tip that Callie was the go between for Lank and Jonas Foster. I'm thinking she would have had to go through you at some point. Am I wrong about that?"

Now, it was Joel who hesitated.

"Kacey, I really like you a lot, so please understand what I am about to say has nothing to do with you and how I feel about you." They continued walking. "As much as I hate Lank, and I really do hate him, I am also a professional and my job, as it is set up, is to make the Senator look good at all times. I guess you should know this about me now before we move any further along, but loyalty trumps everything, even relationships." Joel braced himself for her response, but she said nothing. "Even with no one around, I can't betray a core value of mine, no matter the cost."

Kacey wrapped her arm around his and held it tight, pulling him close so he'd know how she felt. She had finally found someone who believed in the same things she did and she wanted to be sure he knew she approved, even if it worked against her.

But, she also had a job to do and her instincts took over. She gave it one more shot. "So is that a yes or a no?"

"Kacey, forgive me here, but I don't think I can talk about this."

"Fair enough," Kacey said.

Kacey and Joel walked in silence for what seemed like a lifetime. Their date, which had been a friendly one, now turned out to be something very different, something more. She hoped Joel felt the same way.

"You okay?" Joel asked.

Kacey smiled. "Couldn't be better."

He tried to direct the conversation away from Lank and back to Callie. "I do really like Callie," he said. "She's a good friend."

"The best," Kacey said. "That's what hurts so much. It's like she's a different person."

Joel wasn't sure what to say. He wanted to bring the discussion back to the two of them, but he also didn't want Callie to hang over the rest of their evening either. As they continued down

Wisconsin Avenue, Joel took notice of a man across the street, selling roses on the corner.

"Excuse me for one second please."

Joel crossed the street, walked up to the vendor and bought one red rose for three dollars. Kacey smiled as she saw him reach the man with the flowers. Joel crossed back over to Kacey's side of the street and and handed her the rose.

"I'm sorry, I couldn't be more forthcoming with you, I hope this will make up for it."

Kacey accepted the flower and kissed him on the cheek. Joel gently placed his hands on her upper arms, pulled her close and kissed her softly on the lips.

"That was nice..." Kacey said. She slipped her arm back inside of his and they both continued their stroll down Wisconsin Avenue.

"Everyone always gravitated towards her, but she always took care of me," Kacey said, breaking the silence.

"Sounds to me like you miss her."

"In the worst way," Kacey said. "But, you know what? She's not that person anymore."

They walked in silence a little longer.

"I'll get over it," Kacey said.

"You sure?"

She tightened her grip around Joel's arm and looked at him with sad eyes, but said nothing.

THIRTY-TWO

"I knew there was a reason I hated these things," Mike whispered in Callie's ear.

Mike and Callie were at a private reception following President Conroy's birthday party at the Kennedy Center. Mike looked handsome in a Bill Bass tuxedo with a white cummerbund. Callie looked breathtaking in a one shoulder, full-length sheath gown, with a bow in the back. They had sat through too many phony, tedious speeches by friends of the President and the many dignitaries who had flown in from around the world for the event. The Royal Philharmonic of London performed classic Beatles songs in honor of the President's favorite band and in conjunction with The Prime Minister of England's gift to President Conroy, a signed photograph of the Beatles last picture ever taken together. Comedian and Hollywood celebrity Jake Choice hi-lighted a long list of actors who were in attendance, and headlined the event as the Master of Ceremonies.

Following the big public spectacle, the President hosted an invitation only reception for a few hundred people, two of whom, were Callie and Mike. Mike hated political events mainly because of the phoniness he refused to partake in, unlike the Congressmen and hand grabbers in the room. Mike and Callie were talking in the corner when Ted Biggs came by to chat.

"Callie, you look as beautiful as ever." Biggs leaned in and kissed Callie on the cheek. "Do you mind if I steal your date away for a few minutes? There are a few people I wanted him to meet."

"Of course, just make sure you return him to me."

"Don't I always?" Biggs winked at her and began to walk away.

Mike touched Callie's hand, smiled at her, and followed his boss across the room. He left Callie standing alone in the corner and in no mood to mingle with anyone. At every side were Senators and Congressmen who turned her stomach. Macklin, King, Bane and Shulman were among the many others that left Callie feeling a little uncomfortable with all she had been through the last few days. Within moments after Mike had left her side, Senator Macklin noticed Callie from across the room and made his way over.

"Ms. Wheeler," Macklin said. "That was quite the stunt you pulled in my office the other day."

"Oh, is that right?"

"I would say so, yes."

Callie could see his jaw tense up and knew him well enough to know he wasn't there to talk about her dress. "I don't know who you think you are, but you're treading on very dangerous ground sweetheart and if I were you, I'd make sure to lose all that stuff you got…and I'd be sure to forget we ever had that conversation in my office."

"Well, lucky you're not me then, huh?"

Macklin's eyes grew wider, his teeth seemed to clench even tighter and both his hands had balled up into fists. Callie watched as he grew extremely agitated and it became clear to her that he was going to take full advantage of a public situation with Mike nowhere in sight. Macklin got dangerously close to Callie, infringing on her space to the point where she tried to move back, but had no place to go. Macklin had made himself comfortable less than twelve inches away from her.

"Excuse me, Senator. Please back away."

Macklin drew even closer. "Here's my warning to you and listen real good you cunning little bitch," Macklin said, pointing his finger inches from her face. "Do not fuck with me. You think you can intimidate me? Are you out of your fucking mind? I will destroy you. Don't you ever try shit like that again, do you understand me?"

Senator Macklin stared Callie down, then slowly stepped away. Callie stood her ground and returned his look, but said nothing. Internally, she worked hard to keep herself together. She refused to give him the satisfaction of knowing he'd shaken her up. Mike, who was huddled across the room with a few people from the Agency, caught the tail end of the incident, excused himself, then quickly made his way towards Callie. Macklin marched away after his message was delivered loud and clear. Callie was once again scared for her safety and her nerves were completely shot. She took a sip from her glass of wine in a failed attempt to calm down.

"You okay?" Mike asked.

Callie was still trying to regain her composure. She nodded her head without saying a word.

"What was that about with Macklin?"

Callie's hands began to shake as she took another drink of wine from her glass, then placed it down on the table to her right. "You mind taking a walk with me?"

"Sure." Mike put down his cocktail next to Callie's and held out his arm. They left the room and headed outside to the Roof Terrace West of the Kennedy Center. Mike held the door open for

Callie who kept moving once she was on the terrace and left Mike trailing behind her. "Callie, hold on a sec."

Callie ignored him. Several other couples had stepped onto the terrace for air. Callie whisked past Senator Branch, who had tried to get her attention. She hurried past Senator Stevens who waved at her, but she ignored him as well and kept on walking. She kept the pace up until she reached the edge of the terrace overlooking the Potomac River beneath her. Washington and Virginia were across the waterway.

"Callie, what's wrong? What happened in there?"

Callie said nothing and looked straight ahead.

"Is it the shooter?"

Callie stood quietly, caressing her necklace with her index finger and staring out at the water.

"What's the problem? The congressman? Me? Talk to me, Cal."

Mike had never seen her like this and, at first, assumed she was still out of sorts because of the shooting from the day before. She had said very little for most of the evening and Mike could feel a definite distance between them. Was it something he said? Did he do something he shouldn't have? Or could it be she was still in a state of shock with all that swirled around her?

He stepped behind Callie and wrapped his arms around her, gently kissing the back of her neck. She stood there limp, not moving a muscle. The silence continued for a few minutes more. Mike attempted to comfort her, but he knew something was not right.

Callie had debated it for weeks in her head. She felt like the walls were closing in on her and knew that her window of opportunity would soon close. It was best if he heard it from her and no one else. She was sure they would be able to survive it, but she had thought her relationship with Kacey would survive it too.

The time was now and whatever happened, she would have to deal with the consequences. The one thing she was sure of, was once the conversation started, there would be no turning back.

"Mike, there's something I need to tell you…"

She turned to face him and rested her hands on his chest.

Mike was just happy to know that there was something to talk about. "Tell me, Cal," he said. "We'll handle it together."

She hesitated. "I'm not so sure." She lifted her hands off of Mike and slowly turned back towards the river. Mike began to sense something different about his fiancé. He moved to her right so that he could stand next to her. They shared a long moment of silence as Callie got all of her thoughts together.

"Remember when I was lobbying Senator Lank about his bill a few years back…"

Mike nodded. He sensed it was his turn to stay quiet.

"That stuff in Kacey's article about him and Foster?" Callie asked, still gazing across the Potomac. "All that is true…but that's nothing."

Mike looked out towards the river. "What do you mean it's nothing?"

"I mean it's nothing, as in, minuscule in the larger scheme of things. I did some bad things, Mike. Really bad."

Callie turned her head and watched for Mike's reaction.

Mike stared straight ahead. "Why are you telling me this?"

Callie looked down at the black water below. She was afraid to make eye contact. "Before we get married, you need to know… you took an oath to protect this country…to uphold its laws…"

Callie tried to hold herself together, but struggled mightily while she fidgeted with the bracelet he had given her for their third anniversary together. Mike never moved. He continued to lean on the railing and look across the river into Virginia. What he couldn't do, for the first time since they'd met, was look at his girlfriend.

"I can't even begin to count how many laws I've broken."

He tried to wrap his head around what Callie was telling him. He attempted to convince himself what she told him was untrue. He couldn't imagine that Callie would knowingly break the law. Regardless of how he felt about Congress or politicians, there was never any excuse to purposely commit a crime, no matter the scenario, so long as your life was not in danger. Mike fought his instincts and turned around to look Callie straight in the eye.

"How long has this been going on?"

Callie looked away and turned back towards the Potomac.

"I've been here six years...I can't remember a day, I didn't break the law."

Mike never turned back around to join her and rested his back against the railing. His emotions were in a free fall and he needed to be sure of the ramifications of what she was telling him before he reacted. Like drivers passing a traffic accident, bystanders on the terrace could not take their eyes off of them. Some moved in to get a little closer, but were too far way to make out the conversation.

"How bad, Callie?"

"Trust me, Mike...you don't even want to know."

Callie's bracelet fell on to the floor. She waited for Mike to pick it up and hand it to her, but he never moved. The look on Mike's face did not go unnoticed by the small group of onlookers who had been following the couple's body language.

"Why didn't you tell me about this before?"

"I didn't know how."

"What the fuck do you mean you didn't know how?"

"What am I supposed to say? 'Hi, hon, I just spent millions of dollars buying votes in Congress?'"

"What am I supposed to do, Callie?" Mike said, his frustration evident in his words.

"We handle it together."

Mike turned to face her. "What?"

"You said that. You said we'd handle it together."

"That was before I knew you were going to prison!" Mike's voice raised to a level she had only heard a few times in all the years she'd been with him, the last of which was the day before when they were attempting to dodge bullets in their kitchen. Every head on the terrace turned in reaction to his outburst. They pretended to look away.

"Callie, I work for the C.I.A."

"I know, Mike…"

Mike turned to Callie who began to cry and continued staring at the river.

"Look at me."

Callie tried, but she couldn't face him. Callie knew she had disappointed him, but more than that, she had never heard his voice so stern and demanding. For the first time since they'd been together, she was afraid to look at him or even continue the conversation she now regretted ever having started.

"Look at me!"

Callie turned towards Mike, tears rolling down her face.

"I cannot provide you with protection anymore. I can't be associated with this at all. I'll pick up my things as soon…"

"You'll pick up your things?…Mike, we can work this out, you said so…"

"We can't work this out! Don't you understand? I can't have anything to do with you! I can't marry you!"

Mike walked away and left Callie in tears, her third anniversary bracelet crumpled on the floor beneath her feet.

THIRTY-THREE

After Mike had left Callie to fend for herself at the Kennedy Center, she stayed for awhile on the terrace thinking about where should would spend the night. Without Mike at home, she was too afraid to stay there by herself. The sliding glass doors, which had been destroyed by sniper bullets the day before, were replaced by long wooden boards, making it look from the outside, like the remnants of a five-alarm fire. The possibility of men with guns waiting for her to come home left her with minimal options.

Callie leaned over the railing, reached into her small purse and took out her cell phone. She dialed Robyn's number, the only person she felt she could still trust.

"Hey, Robyn, what are you up to?"

Callie could tell from the moment she answered the call, that something was different about her. "Hey, Callie."

Callie heard Kenny yelling in the background, but struggled to make out what he was saying. "I was wondering if maybe you guys had an extra bed for tonight, being all the construction that has to be done at our house..."

Before Callie could finish her sentence, Robyn interrupted

her. "I don't think that would be a good idea, Callie."

"What?"

"I just think you should try and find someplace else to stay."

"What's going on, Robyn?"

"Nothing, it's just not a good idea."

Callie seemed surprised Robyn had turned her down so quickly. She knew she would have to find other arrangements, but before she did, she wanted to understand what exactly Robyn had in mind.

"Okay, I get it, for some reason you don't want me around, but can I at least get the courtesy as to why?"

Callie could hear Robyn and Kenny talking in the background, but again, could not make out anything they were saying.

"Robyn?...Hello?"

Robyn was still talking to Kenny when she pulled her attention back to the phone. "Callie, I...we don't think it's a good idea to have you sleep here. Why don't you and Mike just go to a hotel?"

Callie was too upset at Robyn's cold shoulder to tell her anything about her relationship and instead pressed on for more detail.

"Are you serious about this?"

"Yes, Callie, we are. It's not a good idea to have you here right now. I think you guys should go to a hotel and..."

"There is no you guys, Robyn, it's just me and all I need is a few hours sleep then I'll be out of..."

Robyn paid no attention to the last part of what Callie said and focused solely on what came before it. "What do you mean there is no you guys?"

Callie had little interest in sharing her personal life with Robyn, at least until she had a better grasp of it herself, but thought if Robyn knew she would be the only one sleeping over, she might reconsider.

"We had a fight…"

"You broke up?"

"I think so…"

Callie could hear Robyn tell Kenny that she had broken up with Mike, but that didn't seem to make her situation any clearer.

"Do you have a room for a few hours?"

Callie could hear Robyn and Kenny arguing in the background, which as best as she could decipher it, was not going to lead to the answer she was looking for.

"I'm sorry, Callie, you should really look elsewhere."

"What the hell is going on, Robyn? All I'm asking for is one night, not even one night, just five hours…"

"Callie, no."

"Can you at least tell me why you…"

"I don't want to get shot and neither does Kenny."

With that, the conversation came to a screeching halt. Callie understood she was now living with a target on her back and Robyn made it clear there'd be no need to discuss it any further. More importantly, Callie had received a crash course on who she could count on in her life and who she could not.

"I understand," Callie said.

Robyn hung up without saying good-bye.

Callie placed her next call to the D.C. Police department and requested two uniformed officers to meet her at her home. Her plan was to get some things together, after which she would settle on a place to spend the rest of her weekend.

Callie ordered a sedan service back to her house in Chevy Chase, where waiting for her when she arrived, were the two policemen she had asked for. She unlocked the door and walked inside with one officer escorting her, while the other stood guard at the front of her home. She inspected the new window that had been installed earlier in the day then rushed upstairs to her bedroom to gather a few days worth of clothes. Callie opened her walk-in and was immediately struck by the emptiness on Mike's side of the closet. Any ideas she might have had that things were not as bad as she imagined, quickly vanished at the sight of his possessions being totally cleaned out. As she pulled a few skirts off their hangers, she caught sight of something small, but distinctive, sitting on the shoe shelves to the right of her clothes. She stepped closer, crouched down and found a blue box with a note taped to the bottom of it.

"Please place the ring in this box and leave it on the top of your dresser. I'll be back in the morning to pick it up."

Callie's entire body went limp. Her arms and legs felt prickly, almost numb. She sunk to the floor and stared at the ring she had so patiently waited for. Callie rotated the ring back and forth at the base of her finger then extended her arm. She raised her hand in front of her face to get one last look at the gorgeous diamond that was affixed there. A deep sense of sadness and loss fell over her as she slowly slid the ring off her finger. She struggled trying to comprehend her new reality of 'me', Callie, against the old familiarity of 'us', Mike and Callie. Callie held the ring in her hand, stared at it and carefully set it down inside the box. She gazed at it one last time before she pushed the top closed. Callie got to her feet and felt nauseous. She stepped out of the closet and placed the ring on top of her dresser. She left no message.

Callie packed enough clothes to last her until the middle of the next week, brought her bags downstairs then thanked the officers for being there for her. Each man grabbed a suitcase and followed her to the car in the driveway where she popped the trunk and the two men put her luggage in the Mercedes.

Callie surveyed the area to make sure there were no suspicious people following her, just as the officers had done before they allowed her to walk out of the house. She opened the car door and sat inside, then started the car without having any idea where she was going. When she reached Connecticut Avenue, Callie thought about going to one of the beach houses in Ocean City, but remembered that both of them had been rented through Labor Day. For a brief moment, Callie considered driving home to Wilkes-Barre, then thought better of it. Whoever was after her, she thought, would move on to finding friends and family once they realized she would not be coming home.

Callie decided to drive up to Baltimore, which was far enough away from D.C. to get out of town, but close enough to be back at work on Monday morning without too much effort. She had settled on a small hotel called the Cross Keys Inn off of Falls Road in the Northwest Section of the city. It was quiet and tucked away, and so long as she told no one where she was going, Callie felt she would be safe from harm.

Monday, August 1, 2011

Callie spent most of the next twenty-seven hours in her hotel room then left for work just after 5:30 in the morning, hoping to beat the traffic into Washington. She arrived in her office by 7:00, turned on her computer then checked her messages by 7:10. For the first time since she came to work at M&G, her office voicemail was empty.

Callie leaned back in her chair and thought about the fact that she had not received a single phone call on her cell during her entire stay in Baltimore. She could not remember that ever happening to her before.

She was alone.

No one to talk to.

No one to share with.

Callie sat behind her desk wrestling with the depressing fact that all she had left was her work. She thought about her new, seemingly empty life and how she got there. Over the last number of years, Callie had only made time for three things, Mike, Kacey and her job though not necessarily in that order. Every other relationship she had outside of work, had essentially been put on the back burner. Good friends from college or law school like Robyn were relegated to occasional acquaintances that met only for sparse weekend get togethers. As far as her two older brothers were concerned, she was a successful ghost who only showed up at their parent's home on holidays once or twice a year, if at all.

Within minutes, she was introduced to her new life as Barry stormed into her office without knocking.

"Callie, I have to run to the Hill for some urgent business. I'm going to be making the pitch to Exxon Mobil tomorrow to see if we can get their account. Can you put together the standard package for them?"

"Will do."

Barry was at the door heading out, then said without turning around. "Leave it on my desk. I'll pick it up later tonight."

Callie had been through this drill with Barry plenty of times. "No problem."

Barry walked out of her office, stopped, then turned around and headed back inside. He had not been used to Callie answering him in short sentences without wanting to know more. Moreover, she failed to ask who might be assisting him with the presentation, a job he usually reserved for her. Barry actually was looking forward to her asking those kind of questions so he could inform her she wasn't needed, but Callie seemed too far away. All of this left Barry wondering if maybe the plan he had set in motion to neutralize her would be easier than he thought.

"You okay?"

"I'll be fine."

She had no intention of sharing anything with Barry or anyone else at the firm.

He closed the door upon exiting and left Callie alone with her work, the only friend she had left.

• • •

The soup kitchen on Holiday Street in Baltimore fed hundreds of people each day. There were a few large families that stopped in for dinner every night, but for the most part, there was usually a mixture of middle-aged men and women of all races. In the afternoons, lunch was less crowded, with the large majority of people who came in for the twelve o'clock meal, being elderly. Breakfast time however, the line for food ran out the door of the auditorium and extended around the corner.

Ken Farmer, along with a few volunteers, stood behind the tray line in the dining hall and served breakfast to an estimated three hundred people each morning. Most of the patrons were in need of a long shower and a bar of soap, but Ken served whoever was interested some hot cereal and a cup of orange juice. A man dressed in a Baltimore Orioles hat, beaten up work boots, a torn plaid shirt and ripped blue jeans stopped in front of Ken and looked him in the eye. Ken took a moment to focus then acknowledged him and served the man some oatmeal.

Ken turned to the female volunteer standing behind him and motioned for her to take his place. He followed the man in the Orioles hat to a long cafeteria table in the back of the room. A smattering of people were spread out along the benches, working on what could be their only meal of the day. The man shuffled to the end of the table, placed his tray on top of it, then sat down. Ken stared at the man until he seemed comfortable then took a seat across from him. The man in the hat reached inside his shirt and handed a large manilla envelope to Ken. Ken looked inside the envelope, then looked back at the man, then back inside the envelope after which he took a moment to think, but said nothing.

Ken pulled out his cell phone and sent a text message then looked at the man again and gestured with his head. The man in the Orioles hat stood up and walked away without turning back. Ken watched him leave, hardly noticing the slight limp from his right leg, and all but ignoring the untouched breakfast he left on the table.

Ken went upstairs to his third floor office. He reached inside the envelope and pulled out two large stacks of money with Bank of America paper clasps around each one of them. He slipped his hand back in the envelope and took out a small gold key and a passport. He opened up the passport and looked at a picture of himself staring back at him with the name Perry Walters written next to it.

He reached into the envelope one last time and pulled out a small red notebook with a green elastic band around it. On the cover written in black permanent marker, were the initials JFD.

• • •

"So what you're telling me is you have enough evidence to know that Farmer's got something going on?" Director Biggs sat at the head of the conference table with his brown bag lunch. Mike and Todd were seated to his left.

"I wouldn't say we have enough evidence, but I would say that what he's doing in Baltimore is total bullshit," Mike said. "On top of that, his M.O. is not to work much domestically. So this is definitely our jurisdiction."

Todd pushed a stack of reports in front of Biggs, who unwrapped his egg salad sandwich before reaching for the information. He took a few bites of his lunch as he read the first two reports in the stack and finished his meal in silence while he looked over the rest. He slid them back in front of Todd.

"But we don't know exactly what it is that he's up to," Biggs said, not sure if he was asking a question or making a statement.

Todd looked at Mike, then at Biggs. "No we don't, but that doesn't make him innocent."

"And it doesn't make him guilty, either," Biggs said, taking a drink from his can of pineapple juice.

"Ted, I'm telling you that he would never have shown his face out in public just like that. There is something going down and from his chosen location, my guess is, it's tied to the east coast somehow...and more likely a D.C. thing," Mike said.

"You know this? Or are you just playing a hunch?"

"It's just a hunch, but a good one," Todd said.

"So we should go to the FBI..." Biggs said.

"No, we shouldn't," Todd said.

"I'm not doing this again. If it's domestic it's FBI's..."

"Give us a week. If we don't have anything solid in a week, we'll give it to the FBI," Mike said. He looked at Todd for confirmation.

Biggs reached into his bag and pulled out a Fig Newton. He thought about the proposal Mike just offered. The look on his face told them he wasn't buying in.

"I'll tell you something else," Mike said. "I didn't tell the police this, but I'm feeling pretty good about knowing who is trying to kill me."

Biggs sat up straight in his chair now that Mike got his attention. "You think that's Farmer?"

"Either him or someone working with him."

"And why would he do that?"

Mike gave Ted a long look without saying a word. Todd, feeling like a third wheel, interrupted their private moment. "Someone mind telling me what's going on?"

Biggs took a minute to add it all up and looked at Mike again then gave him a nod. "You sure?"

"Definitely," Mike said.

Biggs stood up and made his way towards the door. "You have your week," Biggs said. "But just make sure you have enough evidence. I don't need the President and his hacks up my ass because you played a shitty hunch."

Biggs left the door open as he exited the room, leaving Todd and Mike by themselves. "You mind telling me what just happened?"

"Don't worry about it."

"Bullshit," Todd said.

"Dude, let it go. We kept if from the FBI which is what you wanted, wasn't it?"

"Yeah, it was, but what was that ab..."

"Drop it, Todd."

Todd knew that look, took Mike's advice and changed the subject back to what they were talking about before Biggs came into the room.

"So you're not going to marry her?"

"Marry her? I want to kill her."

"Back of the line, bud."

Mike stood up. "Tell me about it." He grabbed his things and headed for the exit. "What was she thinking?" Mike shook his head and looked at Todd who was still in his seat. "You think I did the right thing?"

Todd shrugged his shoulders. "I think so, yeah. What do you think?"

"I have no idea..." Mike said as he walked out the door.

THIRTY-FOUR

Callie stepped into Barry's office as she had done hundreds of times before. Regardless of how many times she had been there, she could never get enough of the lavishness he surrounded himself with. She breathed it in as she glided through the first room, which consisted of a small conference table and a big screen television on the wall, then cruised into the main area where Barry spent most of his time. His high-back chair was nestled behind a massive desk imported from Italy and surrounded by six rare paintings laid out behind it. Among the artwork were two paintings he bought at auction from Sotherby's, the work of the great Russian painter, Nicholas Roerich. Callie shook her head as she looked to the right of the desk and saw the set of luxurious white couches he'd moved into his space after Derek had passed away, something she found too creepy for even Barry. She refused to sit there whenever she visited his office. On the wall to the left, he'd hung a Sony Television which he kept set to CNBC all day with the stock report crawling across it. In her hand, Callie had the information packet for the next day's Exxon Mobil presentation, which she had come by his office to drop off as he had asked her to.

Callie stepped up to the left side of Barry's desk to put down the packet when out of the corner of her eye she noticed a CD case on the floor below his chair. The case had the letters 'S.INS.' written on the bottom left corner and two sided tape attached underneath it. Callie glanced around the office to make sure she was alone, then sat down in Barry's chair and felt under the middle drawer, which had a sticky residue to it. Callie was sure she knew what the letters INS on the disc cover meant, but while she had an idea, she could not be positive what the letter S in front of it stood for. Callie thought for a moment then hurried to Barry's office door and locked it.

Callie rushed back to Barry's desk and sat down. She picked the disk up off the floor and slid it into Barry's computer. No matter what she had thought about Barry before, nothing prepared Callie for what was staring back at her on the screen. She ejected the disk from the drive, put it back in its cover and placed it into the Exxon Packet that she had just left for him on his desk. Callie left Barry's office with the packet, and locked the door behind her. She hurried down the hallway, made a right turn, then a left, and hustled down the long hallway until she reached her office. Once inside, Callie locked the door and ran to her desk. She inserted the disk into her computer and copied all the files then removed Barry's disk and grabbed an empty DVD from her desk drawer. She slipped the new disk into her computer, copied all the information from Barry's disk onto it, then popped it out before erasing the information from her desktop. Callie picked up the disk and walked over to the mini-bar. She opened the small refrigerator that she'd installed underneath it and pulled out a key that was hidden inside a fake Coke can. She continued over to the right side of the room and pulled back a large framed picture of her and Mike that exposed a small safe door she had built inside the wall. Callie manipulated the combination dial and opened the safe. Inside, she'd kept one-hundred-thousand dollars in cash, some jewelry, a few manilla envelopes and a metal lockbox.

She pulled out the lockbox and balanced it on top of a chair nearby, then opened it with the key she'd taken from the fake soda can. She lifted up the top of the lockbox, dropped the copied disk inside of it, then closed the metal container and placed it back in the safe. After locking it, she put the key in her desk drawer then slid Barry's original disk back into the Exxon Packet and headed back to his office, locking the door behind her when she left.

She hurried down the hallways until she reached Barry's office door, which she noticed had been unlocked and left slightly open, definitely not the way she left it. Hesitant to go inside, Callie did so anyway. She conducted a thorough search of his entire space, her recent experiences helping to enhance her newly found paranoia. The office was empty. She locked the door, scurried to the desk and sat down in his chair. She placed her hand under the drawer and taped the disk where it must have been before it fell on the floor. As always, Callie tried to be logical about the entire episode. If she were mistaken, it would be Barry's problem to sort out. On the chance that it fell again, as it must have done before she saw it on the floor, he would think it was nothing out of the ordinary and get more tape to secure the disk for the next time. Callie carefully placed the Exxon Mobil packet on his desk where he could see it, before rushing out of his office. Once outside, she was nervously trying to lock the door when she felt a hand touch her on the shoulder.

"Callie."

Callie slowly turned around. Looking down at her was Murray Green, the man who took her place on the Walker Bill. "Barry sent me here to get a package that was supposed to be on his desk," Murray said, as cold and impersonal as he could be. "You have it?"

Callie exhaled and fiddled with the lock she now worked to open again. "I just dropped it off."

Callie walked back into Barry's office with Murray following behind her. She stepped behind the desk, snuck a peek at the empty floor below, then picked up the packet and handed it to Murray with a smile.

"There you go," Callie said.

"Thank you."

Callie sauntered out of the room and left Murray there to lock up. As far as she knew, she was the only one who owned a key to Barry's office, until she saw the open door on her return. Murray could close it up if he wanted to, but she wouldn't spend another minute worrying about it.

Back inside her office, Callie pulled the key out from her desk drawer and opened the lockbox. She removed her copy of the disk and in big letters, wrote the name Martina McBride on it. Callie slipped the disk along with the cash from the safe, into her shoulder bag. She closed everything up, grabbed her laptop from the floor behind her desk, and pulled together the rest of her things. She turned off the lights and locked her office door.

Callie only had two issues on her mind as she stepped into her car. Where was she going to sleep that night and more importantly, what else was on the rest of the disk in her bag?

• • •

Mike drove his Expedition SUV along Connecticut Avenue and as much as he'd made an effort to concentrate on the road, he couldn't keep his mind off of Callie. That wasn't all that unusual for him, but he never thought of her as his ex-fiancé before. He had spent the last three days beating himself up over how he could have missed the signs. He was a CIA agent. Yet somehow he missed the fact that the woman he'd been living with for the past six years continuously broke the law and to top it off, he had no idea. He played out every scenario he could think of in an effort to make the relationship work, but each time it came back to the same thing.

In his heart, he found it hard to justify Callie usurping the laws of the country for her own financial gain. It contradicted everything he stood for and more than that, she knew years ago when they first got serious with each other, exactly what he did for a living. Even after all the scenarios he conjured up in his head, Mike wasn't sure what had bothered him more: the fact that he was no longer with Callie or the fact that he still wanted to be.

Mike turned left onto Route 29 on his way into D.C., when his phone rang and disrupted his train of thought.

"Hello?"

"Mike?"

Mike recognized the voice on the other line. "Hi, Kacey."

"Is it true?"

Mike took a long time to answer her question, which needed no clarification. He knew exactly what she meant, but what he didn't know, was how she found out about it.

"Yes."

Kacey sighed. He wondered if she'd sighed out of frustration or exasperation. Either way, it was obvious she still cared about Callie as much as he did.

"What's happened to her?" Kacey asked.

"I have no clue..."

Mike's brevity convinced Kacey he was torn and recognized in his voice the same sense of helplessness, if not loneliness, that she had experienced herself. She listened on the phone as the silence between them became almost therapeutic for the thirty seconds it lasted.

"You okay?"

"Yeah, I'll be fine," Mike said.

"If you need anything or just want to talk, I'm here."

Mike thought about how much this whole thing would change his life. His every day had been about life with Callie. Now, he had to adjust to a new reality that he still had trouble believing.

"Thanks, Kacey. Hey, can I ask you something?"

"Sure."

"How did you find out?"

"About you and Callie?"

"Yeah…"

"Robyn told me. Seems Callie called her looking for a place to stay on Saturday night."

Mike had thought about what she would do after he had left the Kennedy Center and felt awful about the predicament he'd left her in, but saw no other way around it. He figured she'd be too smart to stay at the house, but after that, he had no clue where she would go. Robyn's seemed like a logical place to start.

"Did she stay there?"

"No."

"She didn't?"

Kacey knew this would not sit well with Mike, but she mentioned it anyway. "Robyn said she didn't want to get herself shot…"

"Did she really?"

"She did."

Mike couldn't believe Robyn would do that to Callie.

"Kenny?"

Kacey's hesitation told him all he needed to know. "She's just too afraid of him at this point…"

"What an asshole," Mike said.

"Truly."

"Kacey, I have to run. I appreciate you calling."

"Please keep me posted. I still care about her...and you, very much."

"I know you do," Mike said, as he hung up the phone.

Kacey looked up and glared at Joel Hughes, who'd been standing next to her desk.

"What the hell is going on?" Kacey said.

"Maybe you should call her?"

"She has my number," Kacey said, all the concern she had shown for Callie a few moments ago, was still not enough to quell her anger.

• • •

Callie left the office after taking careful steps to make sure she wasn't being followed. Besides the bags in her trunk, she was now carrying one hundred thousand dollars, her Macbook Pro and a disk named Martina McBride, that she was never supposed to know existed. Her best bet, she thought, was to head to New York Avenue and find a room at one of the Motels along the strip. She had reasoned that anyone looking for her would search a Hilton or someplace like the Watergate. As she saw it, she would be safer at a motel that rents by the hour.

She pulled into the Days Inn located a mile or so off of Maryland Route 295, better known as the Baltimore-Washington Parkway. She paid the desk clerk $85.99 in cash for one night's rent for a room with a double bed, a safe, and free WiFi, then took the keys to room 137.

After getting herself situated, she closed the drapes and sat by the desk between the television and the window. The rest of the room was exactly how she imagined it would be. The drab gold wallpaper hadn't been updated in at least two decades. The musty air was dense and laced with a tinge of ammonia that fought to mask the smell of old cigarette smoke. A cheap piece of art hung above the tan wooden headboard and a Gideon Bible was on the dresser next to the pay-per-view advertisement card.

Before she finished settling in, Callie opened up her computer, turned it on, then reached into her computer bag and took out the disk she had made that afternoon. Callie looked at the first few items on the disk, then scrolled down a bit and studied the information, after which she scrolled down some more. She raised her right hand to her mouth as she studied the contents on her screen, then stood up and paced the room not sure if what she just saw was real. Callie sat down on the bed, slid her hands underneath her thighs and thought out loud.

"This is incredible. You have to think this through Callie. Use your head." She stood up and walked back to the computer, leaned over and read it again. She scrolled down some more and realized that with each passing line of detail, she uncovered things that were more toxic than the items before it. She paced the room again.

"You have to take notes...and make a copy of this....no, two copies, you have to make two, maybe three, yeah three copies." She spoke as if she was giving orders to an assistant.

She bent over and checked her bag. She only had two blank discs. "Two's good, it will have to be two."

She took out a pen and paper and sat back down by the desk, as anxious as she had been in a long time. Staring at her computer screen, Callie paused a moment to catch her breath. Her mind was racing at warp speed. She knew what she had in her possession was as explosive and dangerous as anything that had ever been discovered in political Washington.

Realizing the need to be thorough and methodical, Callie decided it would be best to get comfortable before she settled in for the long evening ahead. She stood up from the chair and walked to the middle of the room then slid her heels off her feet. She unzipped her skirt and helped it fall on the bed then unbuttoned and removed her blouse, opened her suitcase and pulled out a pair of jeans and a white tee-shirt. She pulled her jeans up along her legs, buttoned them, then slipped her top over her head. Callie wrapped a band around the tips of her fingers and gathered her hair into a pony tail. Feeling a little more at ease, she sat down at the computer and scrolled up to the top, this time taking meticulous notes as she read. Slowly, she went through each item, deciphering what was important to write down and what was not, every few minutes shaking her head at the sheer magnitude of what filled her computer screen. Callie continued to scroll down and read the information, then finally stopped cold and sat in astonishment at the nerve of it all.

"What in the world?" Callie had trouble believing what she was reading. It only got worse. "Oh my god."

She wrote down some more notes on the legal pad she had with her, this time in a much quicker fashion as if she had to make sure she got it all in before it was taken away from her. She read, then wrote, then read again until she stopped for a moment and started to connect the dots.

Callie kept reading and writing then sat back in her chair and tried again to understand everything her laptop was showing her. The more she read, the more she understood that what she had been looking at was never meant to be seen by anyone but Barry. Now that she had it in her custody, it could not only destroy him and most of the leadership in Congress, but it would destroy the careers of a huge number of members in the House and the Senate. More than anything else, it could certainly end the Presidency of Alan Conroy.

Callie stood up from the desk and made sure her door was secure. She bounced over to her purse and pulled out her cell phone, began to dial, then stopped and disconnected. Sitting on the bed, she slid her phone into her pocket and picked up the motel room phone, started to dial then stopped and put it down.

"No, not this way," she said out-loud. "Be smart, Callie, be smart."

Callie walked back to her computer, thought about it for a few seconds and began to type an e-mail.

THIRTY-FIVE

"I'm telling you, habibi, this information I give you is solid. How you say, rock solid."

Mike was on a secure line talking to Akiva who had sent him an urgent message to call "immediately, if not sooner," as Akiva liked to say.

It was just over a week ago that Akiva had been linked to an episode in Iran. On the twenty-third of July, he was rumored to have been involved in the death of a nuclear scientist, the third such one to die a mysterious death. The death of the scientist was met with a great uproar from the rest of the world, who claimed all three were victims of Mossad plots and a part of Israel's continued spread of terrorism across the globe. President Conroy sent his sympathies to the Iranians, a public pronouncement that burned Mike to no end and gave him another reason to despise the President.

The world's dismay, however, did not move Akiva. He never discussed what he'd been up to or if he and the Mossad were carrying out any or all of these pinpoint assassinations. But Mike knew exactly how he felt. If it came down to the survival of his Country

and the Jewish people, versus the proliferation of a nuclear program from an outlaw regime that threatened Israel's very existence, he would choose his survival over theirs.

"Are you sure about this, Akiva?"

"I am double-sure, my friend. The man he approached was our
asset, who by the way, is an exact replica of Moizy Ginsburg. May
he rest in peace."

Mike smiled at the reference. Ginsburg was a close friend of
Akiva's, who had scared Mike half-to-death on the day they first
met in Jerusalem. Akiva and Mike had been enjoying a drink
together in Mike's safe house when they were interrupted by a
pounding on the door along with loud screaming in Arabic that
Mike did not hear, but Akiva did. With lightening speed, Mike
turned around and was about to squeeze the trigger of his Baretta
when Akiva laughed and stopped him from killing one of his best
friends.

"He said, open the door you American gentile so we can make
Hamotzii on the bread," Akiva said, referencing the blessing Jews
prayed before they ate bread.

"What? What is Hamotzii?" Mike appeared confused by a
word he thought was Arabic until he learned later that is was a
Hebrew word he had not heard before.

Mike kept his gun pointed at the doorway, until Akiva walked
over and lowered it.

"Relax, Mike, he's harmless...unless you piss him off." Akiva
went to open the door. "Don't piss him off."

Moshe Ginsburg, or Moizy, as he was known to his friends,
was a tall lanky Israeli paratrooper recruited by Akiva to join the
special forces. When Akiva opened the door, Mike saw a man
who looked identical to the hundreds of men he had met in Gaza.
Ginsburg had a very dark complexion, jet black hair and a mus-

tache surrounded by five days of beard growth. Very much like your average Palestinian male.

"Moizy, this is Mike."

"Shalom. I've seen you in Nablus a few times. I actually thought of killing you," Moizy said.

"If it makes you feel any better, I was just about to kill you too."

"You think you would have shot me?"

"No, I don't think. I know."

Akiva looked at Ginsburg and shook his head. "You would be dead."

Less than a year after their meeting Ginsburg had been killed in an operation that saved an Israeli soldier from a kidnapping, which while successful, exchanged the soldier's life for Ginsburg's, who wouldn't have had it any other way.

Mike double checked the information with Akiva. "We'll set it up with our guy. The sooner the better."

"Okay, we will use your asset as the seller," Akiva said.

"I am sending you his name by email. It's written in number, letter, number, hebrew letter, format, you figure it out and confirm," Mike said.

"Got it. I'll be in touch."

"Hey Akiva?"

"Yeah?"

"Thanks."

He waited for Akiva's e-mail to confirm that Billy Davis would be the asset they would use as the seller. As he read the e-mail, Todd walked in unannounced.

"You texted me?"

"Uh-huh," Mike said while he sent a coded email back, acknowledging the information.

"What's up?" Todd asked.

"I think we got our boy."

"What do you mean?"

"Seems like Kahlid is trying to buy enriched uranium," Mike said as he shuffled through some papers on his desk.

"This again?"

"This again, but this time it's no joke, they mean business."

"What are they looking for?" Todd asked.

"Enough for a small weapon. Portable...would kill a few hundred thousand people...minimum." Mike found what he was searching for and slipped the paper into a yellow envelope to his right.

"And you say Ken Farmer's trying to buy it?"

"Yeah, same guy, Khalid. Actually, not him exactly, but one of his boys."

Todd thought for a few moments before he spoke again. "You sure about this?"

"Hundred Percent," Mike said.

"How did you find out?"

"Akiva told me. Khalid's guy asked one of his assets."

"No shit."

"No shit," Mike said.

Todd hesitated again before he spoke. "Did we set up a meeting?"

"Happens in about six hours. In Moscow. How much says Kahlid is there?"

Todd smiled. "Hundred bucks."

"You're on," Mike said. "We finally got this prick. He's been dickin' us around for over a decade. It's time to shut him down for good."

• • •

Barry had spent the entire day working up a strategy to deal with Callie. He stood in the back of the private dining room at the Capital Grille, huddled in the corner with Senator Gorman. Barry had been eating his appetizer when he got a phone call and had to pull himself away to talk with no one else around.

He hung up the phone and motioned for Senator Gorman to join him in the back, where Jonas Foster became the topic of conversation.

"We have to handle it now," Barry said.

"Handle what? Foster?"

"Exactly."

"What does that entail?" Gorman asked.

"We pay him fifty million dollars to leave," Barry said.

"We do what?"

Barry looked at his phone and read a text message. "It's the deal we made."

"What was the deal, if you don't mind my asking?"

"We agreed that he would serve the company as its President and CEO until the time came for me to give him money to leave." Barry responded to the text then slipped the phone in his pocket.

"Why did he agree to it?"

"He actually didn't have much of a choice. He got messed up in some nasty deals back in Texas and needed some money," Barry said. "I had known him at College Park and we met again in Vegas while he was having some difficulty. Let's just say I made him an offer he couldn't refuse."

"I'm sure you did." Gorman said, before he laughed. "So he agreed to it, just like that?"

"Pretty much. I gave him fifty-million dollars of start up cash and told him when it was time, he would leave with a golden parachute." Barry motioned a waiter over towards him. He took his vodka rocks off the tray, then handed him a twenty-dollar bill.

"Keep the change."

"What's the problem then?"

"They can't do anything if he's still in control," Barry said, taking a sip of his drink. "And I have no interest in giving up fifty million dollars."

"So we get rid of him now," Gorman said.

"We have to be smart, but we also need to do it soon."

Barry walked back over to the table where he joined Senators Macklin, Bane and King. Senator Gorman soon followed.

"Okay, fellas, here is how it's going to go down," Barry said, drink in hand. "Tomorrow you hold a press conference announcing that you will not be passing the Oxford Secondary Education Bill, because of the earmarks that were inserted at the last minute."

"I thought we had the votes to pass that?" Bane asked.

"We did, yesterday. We don't, today." Macklin said.

"Correct," Barry said.

"What about the girl, Barry?" King asked.

"Name her as the lobbyist. As soon as you guys go public, I will let the media know she no longer works at our firm, but only after you drop the bombshell."

"What do we do about everything she knows?" Bane asked.

Macklin jumped in before anyone else could answer, too excited at the opportunity to destroy Callie's life. "We take care of that ourselves at the press conference."

"Correct," Barry said. "Remember, everything she has paid anyone has always been in cash. Very hard to prove."

"Does she have any evidence at your office?" King asked.

"Doesn't matter. She won't have access and we're running out of time. We have to cut her loose now."

"She can still attack us in public and connect our names to hers," Gorman said.

"She can," Barry said, "but she'll have to survive that long."

• • •

Callie was in her motel room thinking about her next move and munching on a granola bar. She grabbed the bucket from the bathroom counter and headed out to the ice machine on the second floor. Callie stepped outside of her room and again paid very close attention to her surroundings. She made a quick right and followed the signs on the wall, then walked up one flight of stairs and followed the arrow down a long corridor before coming to a corner. Callie turned the corner, checked to see if she'd been followed, then continued to the vending area.

Seeing no one, Callie walked to the ice machine and filled her bucket. Not wanting to be outside in the open for too long, Callie hurried back to her room and rushed around the corner, walking straight into the arms of a very large man she had never seen before. Callie began to tremble and stared at him with trepidation for what seemed like forever. The man stared back intensely. It took Callie several moments to notice the two small children walking behind the man who'd been holding her.

"You okay, miss?"

"I'm so sorry," Callie said over her shoulder as she rambled down the hallway. She hurried down the stairs and made a beeline towards her room. Callie struggled as she tried to pull the key out of her jeans pocket then fumbled with it once she realized it didn't fit into the key hole. Trying desperately to keep it together, she tried the key another time and once again it didn't fit. Sweat dripped from Callie's forehead while ice chips fell from the bucket that she'd pressed between her forearm and her body. Callie's cheeks were flushed from fear. Her hands shook profusely, something she had unfortunately gotten used to over the past three weeks. She tried the key one more time. She jiggled it back and forth and in her desperation, looked up at the door and noticed the number, 139. Her room was 137.

Callie hurriedly fit the key into the correct lock. She slammed the door shut behind her, locked it, then bent over at the waist and leaned her body against the back of the door. She placed the bucket on the floor and rested her hands on her knees trying to grab hold of her heart rate. Once she calmed down, Callie grabbed the phone and dialed a number. It rang a few times before someone answered it.

"I need to talk to you," Callie said. "It's urgent."

Callie listened to the voice on the other line.

"Yes, I'm fine. We just need to talk." She was trying to catch her breath.

Callie interrupted. "No, no, we can't meet there, it has to be somewhere else."

She listened for a minute then answered.

"Okay, ten o'clock tomorrow. I'll be there," Callie said. "And as always, keep this between us."

Callie hung up the phone, walked to the ice bucket and dropped three cubes in a glass. She poured a Diet Coke, turned on the TV and picked up her cell phone.

"Hi, this is Mike. Leave a message."

"Hi, Mike. Kind of hoping we could talk. You can call me. Miss you."

THIRTY-SIX

Ken Farmer sat across from a tall blonde woman at the Turandot Restaurant in Moscow. They had just arrived at the cafe when Ken's phone rang and interrupted his cordial conversation with the lady he purchased for the evening.

"Yes..."

Ken seemed surprised by what he had heard. "You know this to be true?"

"Yes, one-hundred percent," the voice on the line told him.

"Then we need to make sure they get the message," Ken said.

"Okay."

Dial tone.

Ken closed his eyes as he rubbed his forehead with his right hand.

"Everything okay?"

"It will be soon," Ken said. "Just a little change in plans."

Ken opened his phone and began to text. While he exchanged text messages over the next two minutes, his mood changed from frustration, to anger, to calm, and back to frustration again. His strategies were being turned upside down with each exchange.

"You sure everything is okay?"

"Things will be much better in about thirty minutes." Ken reached across the table and grabbed the blonde's hand. "Why don't we get back to our meal, then we can go back to the hotel for dessert."

• • •

Meridian Park was located between 15th and 16th Streets and surrounded by Euclid Avenue and W Street. The people in the Capitol Heights section of Washington knew it as Malcom X Park. The highlight of the park and its most unique feature is a thirteen-basin cascading fountain that settles into a larger pool of water at the bottom of it. On weekends and various evenings in the summer, the park was busy with neighborhood events and tourists from all over the country. Most of them came to see the famous drum circles late on Sunday afternoons, but on a sunny Tuesday morning in early August, the park was quiet and serene with only a handful of people milling around.

Callie stood on top of a rock-structured terrace overlooking the cascading waterfall where she had arranged to meet Jonas Foster. She had called him the night before from her motel room and arrived a few minutes early for their ten o'clock get together. Callie wished good morning to a middle-aged woman who was walking her dog and an elderly couple who had come to the park for their daily exercise. Callie took notice of the older man slowing down and staring at her, and again as he turned his head back to catch another look once he had already passed. She winked and waved at the smiling old man, who'd pulled his arm behind his back and made the okay sign with his fingers, out of view of his wife, who was walking next to him. Callie chuckled at the gesture then checked her watch and surveyed her surroundings a few times, while she waited for Jonas. She felt exposed standing in a public place all by herself. She didn't care. There was no other choice.

As the sun lit up the morning sky, Callie recognized a tall athletic figure walking towards her. Stepping out from amidst the trees to her left, Jonas Foster walked confidently up to the terrace, arriving at ten o'clock sharp. He leaned in and kissed her on the cheek. She hugged him and kissed him back.

"Been awhile, Callie. How are you?"

"I've had better days."

"Sorry to hear that." Jonas gave her the once over with his eyes, stopping to admire her legs, as he'd always done each time they met.

"You might want to reserve judgement on that until we finish talking," Callie said. "My lousy day might have some company."

Jonas finally made his way back up to her eyes and looked at her curiously. "And what makes you say that?"

Callie leaned over the railing and studied the waterfall for a minute before answering his question. She thought for hours about how to approach the conversation she needed to have with him, and be sure to do it without Jonas blowing her off as 'talking nonsense'. Her experience with Jonas in the past had always been cordial and very friendly, but she knew his allegiances lied with Barry. It would not be easy to get him to understand the kind of trouble he was in. Callie took some time to pull her thoughts together, then tried the avenue that seemed most logical.

"Jonas, can you tell me what the deal is with you and Barry?" Callie turned and rested her elbow on the rail so she could see his face when he answered her.

"Barry does some lobbying for my company on the Hill and gets paid very..." Jonas gave her the standard response he gave anyone else as if she was some reporter from the newspaper. Callie, however, was having none of it and interrupted him before he could finish his response.

"C'mon, Jonas, that's not what I'm talking about." She folded her arms and looked at Jonas.

"I'm not sure what you mean," he said. As usual, he was very handsomely dressed in a neatly pressed white shirt, navy blue pants which looked sewn onto his body and a blue-striped tie. Each cufflink bore the initials 'JF' and was encased in gold. Callie's inquiry left Jonas feeling a little uneasy. Small beads of sweat began to form on his forehead. Something Callie took notice of right away.

"Jonas, I don't have time for any bullshit. Tell me about JFD."

Uncomfortable with the trajectory of the conversation, Jonas turned around and looked out over the waterfall, his eyes now away from hers. "I'm not sure what..."

Callie interrupted him again. "No games, Jonas. What's up with your company."

"Callie, hon, I have an appointment with some contractors in a few minutes and I have to get my things together. I'm not really sure what you want from me."

"I know they fronted you the money," Callie said. "And I know you're not the millionaire you pretend to be."

His body froze as he heard the words come out of her mouth, almost as if they were in slow motion. He tried to move, but his arms tingled like they knew the jig was up. "Want to take a walk with me?"

Callie trusted Jonas, though she didn't have any trust in his relationship with Barry. She hesitated at the suggestion, thinking about the possibility that he might have called Barry after they spoke the previous night, even though she told him not to. She also knew him well enough to know from looking at his face, that he was harmless, especially since she saw more pain in his eyes than anger. She took him up on his offer.

"Sure."

Jonas and Callie strolled in silence along the sidewalk leading from the terrace. He'd always feared that one day this information would somehow leak out though he thought it would find its way into the media, but he ignored the possibility and kept up the facade…until now.

"Barry set me up with fifty million dollars to front a company for him," Jonas said, his hands in his pockets. "In return, he'd send me off with roughly the same amount when he had a team in place to take the company over from me. It's supposed to look like I'm selling it to his people whenever he tells me he's ready."

"And what happens to you after you sell the company?"

"I ride off in the sunset with fifty-plus million, never to be heard from again."

"And you were willing to live with that arrangement?" Callie asked looking at the leaves on the ground in front of her as the two of them kept walking.

"Who wouldn't be?" Jonas seemed surprised by her question.

"Did he tell you when the transition from you to them would take place?" Callie slowly built her case brick by brick so he could clearly see the dangers he faced.

"No, he just said when the time came, he would let me know, pay me my money and say good-bye."

They walked a few more feet in silence, before Callie spoke up.

"Jonas, that's never going to happen."

Jonas stopped abruptly and stared at Callie. "Why do you say that?"

Callie opened up her purse and pulled out the disk.

"What's that?"

"This is information that came into my possession. It's a copy of a disk that no one was ever supposed to see." Callie held it in front of her face, but not too close to Jonas in case he had any ideas. "It belongs to Barry."

"But you saw it..."

"I saw it." Callie slid the disk back inside her purse.

Jonas extended his arm suggesting they continue their stroll. "And what does that disk have to do with me?"

"That fifty million dollars you were supposed to get?" Callie asked rhetorically as she nodded her head and started back on the trail.

"Yeah?"

"It's never going to happen."

Jonas paused for a few seconds and thought about what she said. "No chance, Callie."

"I'm telling you, Jonas, it's never going to happen."

"What do you mean?" Jonas looked at her while his hands, desperately looking for something to do, started to play with the bottom of his tie.

"I mean, you'll be dead long before you ever see any of that money."

"Get the fuck outta' here, Callie. Who told you that?"

Callie stopped in front of a bench along the walkway. "Mind if we sit?"

Jonas extended his hand towards the bench. Callie sat down, crossed her legs and clasped her fingers in front of her knee, then sat up straight. Jonas sat down next to her.

"When I first started with Barry, I was fresh out of college and looking to be somebody," Callie said staring out at the beautiful tree lined path they had just came from. "I'd been a bit wary of him from the get-go and sort of worked closely with his partner, Derek, did you know him?"

Jonas shook his head and let out an awkward sigh. "Yeah, I knew him. He wasn't too friendly to me though. I think he felt Barry'd been cooking something and I landed smack in the middle of it."

Callie turned to Jonas."Derek told you that?"

"No, but I could tell. Barry, he hated the guy and told me never to discuss anything of substance with him. Ever. I mean, Callie, he really hated him." The serious look on his face told Callie all she needed to know about Derek and Barry, though it hardly qualified as a news flash.

"That sounds about right," Callie said then smirked in disgust before she continued. "After Derek died, I had to work a lot closer with Barry and he told me if I paid attention, I would be the most powerful woman in Washington." Callie slid her hands under her thighs and felt the embarrassment wash over her as she retold her brief history to him. "I mean, who wouldn't want that when you're in your early twenties, right?"

Callie sneezed quietly. Jonas smiled and couldn't help himself from injecting a lighthearted comment into their conversation. "Bless you. Funny how the elegant are able to sneeze without anyone else knowing it happened."

"Thank you," Callie smiled as she pulled out a tissue from her purse, gently wiped her nose, then returned the conversation to where it needed to go. "One of the first lessons he taught me: always have insurance."

"Insurance?"

Callie gave her head a nod and continued. "Always make sure you have something to use as blackmail. He called it, 'whatever insurance'. This disk in my purse is Senatorial Insurance."

Jonas seemed more confused than he had been a moment ago. "What does that have to do with me?"

Callie uncrossed her legs and, bent at the knee, crossed her legs at her ankles then settled her hands on her lap. "One of the notes on there, is what to do after you're dead."

Jonas took a long time to let her words sink in. He stood up and nervously paced in front of the bench. Callie stayed in her seat. He stopped in front of her and put both hands in his pockets.

"What else is on there?"

Callie paused for a short time before she answered.

"Everything."

"Everything? That's not good is it?"

"Not for you, it isn't." Callie stood up and waited for Jonas. He was too preoccupied to realize Callie had begun to walk back towards the fountains. "Come, Jonas."

The two of them strolled together in silence.

"So what now?" Jonas asked.

"That depends how far you're willing to go."

Jonas stopped and gently grabbed Callie's forearm. "We're talking about my life here. Do you have a plan?"

Callie could sense the desperation in his voice. She wrapped her right arm around his left one and resumed walking. "I do, but I have to get some ducks in a row first. As soon as that's done, be prepared, because it won't be pretty," Callie said.

They reached the parking lot on 15th Street and headed towards Callie's Mercedes.

"I'm trusting you here, Callie. Don't screw me on this." As the reality of the situation became clearer, Callie sent him a look of genuine concern.

Callie opened the door of her car and turned back to Jonas. "Have I ever screwed you on anything we've done together?"

"No, you haven't. Can't say the same about your boss, though."

"I'm not my boss," Callie said in her most defiant tone.

"I know." Jonas took a few steps towards Callie and gave her a hug.

Callie looked into his eyes for a short moment. She needed to know she could really count on him. "From here on out, Jonas, we have to stick together. Please give me your word."

"You have my word," he said.

"Good. Stay close to your phone and be prepared to act. I have a feeling when this one goes down it will go down quick."

"Will do. You be careful."

Callie got in her car and waved leaving Jonas standing alone in the parking lot as she drove by.

• • •

The last week at the Washington Post had been a mixture of both good and bad. The original congratulations the paper received for breaking the Lank story, had given Kacey a quick shot of notoriety, but as the days passed and no follow up stories could be corroborated, Kacey's sudden fame became sprinkled with skepticism about the story from inside the newsroom and out. Bob Kravitz had stuck by her side as did Walter Bloom, but even Marge, her mentor, began to doubt if the story had any traction. The lawmakers on Capitol Hill had done an outstanding job deflecting all the accusations about Lank by constantly staying on the offensive, even as newspeople from all around the country attempted to work the story. By Monday evening, every outlet had given up on it and went off to follow the next item in the news cycle. Kacey, Walter and Bob, however, stuck by the original report and its source. They ignored the negativity and followed their reporter's instincts, continuing to believe there was something bigger there.

"He's funny and smart and very charming," Kacey said. "And he's easy to look at, if you know what I mean."

"I'll have to take your word for it because that's not something I can make heads or tails out of." Walter and Kacey were in the break room searching for coffee. Kacey's new boyfriend, was the topic of their conversation.

"And he works for Lank," Walter said.

"But he hates him."

"So he tells you…"

Bob Kravitz stuck one foot into the coffee room and interrupted their chat. "Kacey, can I see you in my office?"

"Everything okay, Bob?" Walter asked as he poured milk into his cup.

As quickly as he showed up, he was gone.

"What do you think it is?"

"I have no idea," Walter said.

Kacey hurried down the hallway to Bob's office. Was he also giving up on the story? Did he have a reprimand from his bosses he'd been waiting to give her? A suspension?

Kacey found him sitting behind his desk. She sat down in the armchair across from him prepared to hear the worst, though she couldn't blame him for being upset. He had stuck his neck out for her on the story and it was dying a slow painful death with no life preserver. The loss of the paper's credibility would be catastrophic for both Kacey and Bob, not to mention the entire newsroom.

Bob searched his computer for something, too focused on the task to look at Kacey. A minute later, the printer behind his desk sprung to life.

"You wanted a lead on the Lank story?" Bob asked her. "I got this e-mail late last night."

Bob turned around, picked up the paper from his printer, then handed it to Kacey. She read the printout she was holding in her hand with nervous excitement.

"This is the same address I got the Lank story from."

Kacey looked down and read it again. "I think I have what you're looking for-please reply if you would like to meet."

No signature, no phone number, just one sentence.

"What do you think?" she asked her editor.

"I think if this is real, it's a big F-you to everyone who's been pissing on us the last couple days," Bob said. "Seems like a no brainer to me. Set it up."

• • •

"She just left me a small message," Mike said after he'd finished his last rep and sat up on the workout bench. The clatter of weights reverberated around the gym. Todd walked out from behind the bench after serving as Mike's spotter. "Nothing else?"

"Nope, just a call me type thing." Mike pulled off the sweat soaked tee-shirt he'd been wearing and pulled a grey US Army one out of his gym bag.

"Did you call her back?"

Mike stood up from the bench, took off his workout gloves and shot Todd a menacing stare.

"Why you mad at me? You know you want to call her."

"It's not a matter of want." Mike threw his gloves inside his bag then picked it up off the floor. "You coming?"

Todd let the comment go while he searched his own bag for his cell phone, which he had put in the side pocket, before they went to the gym.

"Oh damn, I almost forgot to tell you," Todd said.

"Tell me what?"

"Our boy, Kahlid, never showed."

Mike was floored by the information. "What?" Hell of a time to tell me, Mike thought. "Not possible."

"Not only is it possible, but it happened, or should I say, it didn't happen," Todd zipped up his satchel and flung it onto his shoulder. "They were all set to take him down and no one showed up."

"How could that be? It was a done deal," Mike said with a look of confusion on his face.

"Evidently not."

Mike took a moment to think this through. "How'd you find out?"

"I spoke with Billy Davis in Moscow a couple of hours ago," Todd said. "I know this might be a bad time to bring it up, but I believe you owe me some of my money."

An upset and confused Mike reached into his bag and pulled out a wad of cash. He counted off five twenty-dollar bills and handed them to Todd.

"About time I won something."

Mike thought about what could possibly have gone wrong. It had all been so meticulously planned. Maybe Akiva would be able to fill him in, but first he'd have to break the news to Biggs, which he knew would not be pleasant.

THIRTY-SEVEN

All the seats in the Radio and TV Gallery of the Senate Building were occupied within ten minutes. The standing room only crowd of news media and observers, waited with anticipation for the urgent press conference called by the newly formed Senatorial Watchdog Committee. Most hastily put together shows like this one were sparsely attended, however with barely an hour of advanced notice the media was out in full force after the Committee members themselves called each network news division and told them that their first event would have explosive information. They also made the unique request of asking them to carry it live. The three major networks chose not to interrupt their regularly scheduled programming, but did send news crews, all of which had already arrived and were sitting in the front row. The cable news stations along with the regular coverage offered by C-Span, carried the event in real time and without interruption as suggested.

Senators Macklin and King were at the podium preparing to address the media. Behind them stood the other eight Senators who sat on the Committee. A palpable air of excitement shimmied through the attendees in the hope that the Committee's anticipated revelations, would live up to the hype. After CNN returned from a commercial break, Macklin received the signal to begin. With a huge grin on his face, he stepped up to the podium and gave the assembled crowd what they were waiting for.

"Thank you everyone for coming on such short notice. Recently, a group of Senators stood before you, the American people, and promised to do whatever it took to rid the Senate of the insidious special interest influences that have plagued this body."

Macklin stepped away and Senator King took his place.

"Today, it gives us great pleasure to announce that we have defeated the Oxford Secondary Education Bill by an overwhelming majority."

Senator Shulman, needing to get his face on camera, insisted beforehand he be at the forefront. Macklin acquiesced. Shulman stepped up to the bank of microphones.

"The Oxford Bill was a good idea, but the massive amount of earmarks that were attached made it impossible for us to pass. Special interests tried to skip the Committee process and slipped in over fifty-million dollars worth of pork barrel spending."

Shulman stepped back and Macklin continued.

"The overwhelming majority of those earmarks were placed through various means, by Ms. Callie Wheeler, a lobbyist who works at..."

Senator Shulman stepped towards Macklin in a staged interruption and whispered something in his ear, after which Macklin continued. "My apologies, Ms. Wheeler was formerly employed at the law office of Miller & Gladstone. We have been informed that she is no longer employed at the firm."

As soon as the words left his mouth, the media in attendance began to shout questions at Macklin. He turned around and looked at the other Committee members then broke out a sly grin. The battle had already been won.

• • •

Across town at the offices of the Washington Post, Walter had been watching the press conference on television when he heard Macklin mention Callie's name. The first time Kacey informed him about the Lank story, his gut told him there was something bigger going on. The dog and pony show he was now witnessing on Capitol Hill, confirmed it. He ran back towards Kacey's desk to bring the media circus to her attention. Bob Kravitz had chosen to send Marge to the Hill to cover it and let Kacey work on the e-mail lead he had received the night before. Just in case anything came out of the kabuki theater on Capitol Hill, he covered himself by sending a good reporter there although he'd been skeptical about the entire thing. Kacey was on the phone when Walter got to her desk.

"C'mon hon. Shit's about to hit the fan. Come with me."

Kacey covered the mouth-piece and whispered to Walter. "I need a few minutes."

Walter grabbed the phone from her hand and hung it up. Kacey watched as he slammed it into its base.

"What are you doing?"

"They're throwing your girl under the bus."

"What?"

Walter grabbed Kacey's hand and pulled her out of her chair. They hustled down the aisle towards the television, where the entire newsroom was now watching the press conference live. Kacey heard Callie's name being thrown all over the place. Callie was being fed to the wolves with no one around to defend her. Kacey lifted her right hand and covered her open mouth.

"Oh my god, Cal."

• • •

Back on the Hill, Macklin was in his element. The entire

room was at his disposal. The time for payback had come. He had delivered on the threat he made to Callie at the Kennedy Center, just as he promised he would. She had played hardball with the wrong guy and Macklin and his friends made sure she was neutralized in the most public way possible. Barry's plan had been executed to perfection and in so doing, left no room for doubt as to where responsibility fell. Callie Wheeler was their target and they didn't miss. Senator Macklin peered at the front row and saw Tara Michael from CBS News, who'd been jumping out of her seat like a third-grader with the correct answer to a math problem. He motioned for her question.

"Senator Macklin, what do we know about Caler...Callie Wheeler?"

Macklin took his time and milked the moment for all it was worth. "Tara, Miss Wheeler is a master manipulator who specializes in manufacturing blackmail through various means. Photoshop, fraudulent bank statements, financial shenanigans and the like."

Not to be outdone, Senator Shulman, who despised Callie and hated the fact that he could not intimidate her like he could everyone else, added his own two-cents.

"She has used these illicit practices to strong-arm earmarks through Congress for her own financial gain, all done without the knowledge of her superiors."

• • •

Kacey had finally received the confirmation she needed that the story she had broken was indeed a whole lot bigger than she thought. More importantly, she was now convinced that Callie was right about all of it and had told her the truth that day in the stairwell. Kacey watched the Senators publicly lynch her best friend with each subsequent question and answer, while on the television screen in front of her, CNN rolled a ticker with Macklin's quote:

"…Miss Wheeler is a master manipulator who specializes in manufacturing blackmail…"

"Oh, Callie."

Walter leaned in to Kacey and whispered in her ear. "I'd bet you my last dollar they're full of shit. I know this group. There's not an honest bone among 'em."

Kacey looked at Walter. A tear rolled down her cheek.

"Call her, Kacey. You're all she has."

• • •

Not to be outdone, Senator King used his own time in front of the press to stick it to the woman he hated more than anyone else he'd ever met in Washington. The worst part from King's perspective was that as much as he tried, he could never push her around at any point in his career. Now he was about to do a lot more than that.

"We anticipate she will use her normal tactics to come after us. We, in the Senate, have all been through this before. The only question for all of you, is how many of her lies will you believe?" He stopped on purpose to heighten the dramatic effect of what he'd just said, then concluded the press conference. "If you will excuse us, we do have important Senate business to take care of working on behalf of the America people. Thank you all for coming and god bless America."

The Senators left the podium to a chorus of questions and camera flashes, all of which they chose to ignore.

• • •

Callie left Meridian Park and drove directly to her office on

K Street. She knew that with the information she had, she needed to get a few things in order before she could make her move. On the drive over, she'd made the decision that once she got upstairs, she would copy all the files she deemed necessary, clean out her safe then head back to the Days Inn and stay there until she put everything in motion.

She rushed through the rotating doors of the building into a small foyer that spilled into a bigger lobby. She smiled and waved hello to the two security guards, who did not wave back, something Callie noticed immediately since it had never happened before. As Callie made her way to the elevator, the larger of the two men stepped out in front of her. The other guard, upon seeing her entry into the building, picked up the phone to make a call.

"Hi, Cedric," Callie said to the same security guard she'd spoken to every day since his arrival three years ago.

Cedric stood in her way. She stopped suddenly and looked up at his enormous six foot five three hundred sixty pound frame. "I'm sorry, Ms. Wheeler, you can't go past here."

"Excuse me?"

"Ms. Wheeler, you can't go past here," he said uncomfortably.

Callie tried to move past as she spoke. "Cedric, I need to get to my office…and what's with the Ms. Wheeler stuff?"

Cedric shuffled his feet as he positioned his body in front of hers, not allowing her to pass. "Mr. Miller said we should not let you upstairs."

Callie had been caught totally off guard, which rarely happened to her when it came to Barry. This time, however, she never saw it coming.

"Mr. Miller said what?" Callie asked not really wanting to hear the answer.

"I'm sorry, Callie."

Callie's body had lost all its energy. Her shoulders slumped as she slid her purse down to the palm of her right hand. She lost her equilibrium for a moment. It weakened her knees and left her head with a momentary bout of dizziness that seemed to have knocked her back a step or two.

The magnitude of what was happening to her would be clarified in an instant when the elevator doors opened and Barry stepped out into the lobby. He walked to his right, stopped at the security guard desk and peered at Callie. The sight of him reinvigorated her spirit. The look she gave Barry was one Callie reserved for the likes of Macklin, Shulman, and the rest of the legislators who picked at her like leeches. Barry had earned it and she was going to make sure he knew this would not go unpunished.

"Callie, your services are no longer needed," Barry said.

Callie thought about all the times she had bailed him out and overlooked his vicious actions, behavior that not only affected her, but everyone at the firm. She let the moment sink in so she could vividly remember what it felt like. One day she would get the chance to turn the tables on Barry and when that time came, it would be this memory that she would draw upon.

"We will have your things packed up and sent to you later today." Barry stood with his arms folded, Whitaker Jordan standing by his side.

"Pack my things? The hell with that. I'm going upstairs to clean out my office myself..." Cedric stepped in front of Callie as she attempted to push past him. Barry pounced on her before she finished her words.

"Your office? No, you no longer have an office. I believe you mean Whitaker's office." Jordan smiled at the mention of his name.

Callie had already begun to do what she did best, adapt to the situation. She had the advantage of knowing what he did not know and Callie began to plan her next move now that the situation on the ground had changed.

What she needed Barry to believe was that she'd turned help-less and angry, which she did, but at the same time, she under-stood that thanks to Barry's ego and vindictiveness, Callie was about to bring down the entire United States Government, in-cluding Barry's old friend, President Conroy. She also figured that the smart play was to make Barry believe he'd gotten the best of her. No better time than the present.

"You asshole. How many bullets have I taken for this firm? How much money have I made you, you greedy bastard? What about loyalty?"

Barry showed no emotion as she went off on him. Callie was well aware if she put on a show for Barry, everyone in Washington would hear about it and rejoice at her downfall. Though she knew she was in a bad spot, she also had to prepare for what was to come next. She would figure out the rest later.

"Callie, you have to leave now," Barry stepped towards her, but stayed safely behind his massive security guard.

Callie stared at Barry, who broke out in a snarky smile, as Jor-dan, standing behind him, waved her good-bye.

"So that's it, huh? Everything I did for you, it comes down to this? I can't even clean out my office?"

"Jordan's office."

"Fuck you, Barry." Callie's face displayed the feeling of dis-gust she had for him and all his lackeys on the Hill. Barry, on the other hand, showed no emotion.

"Class move, Callie. Cedric, get her out of here...now!"

"I'm sorry, Callie, you have to go." Cedric said as he escorted her to the door, but not through it. "Bye, Callie...I'm really sorry."

Callie said nothing as she looked into his eyes. She ambled through the rotating doors onto K Street, with no job to go to, no home to sleep in and no friends to lean on.

THIRTY-EIGHT

Callie stood on the sidewalk at the corner of K Street and 19th, assessing what just happened and how it would effect the plan she'd already begun to put together in her head. More than anything else, the episode inside the lobby assured her that time was running out. Whatever her next move would be, it would have to be done quickly and as clandestinely as possible. Callie looked back inside and saw Barry in the lobby staring at her with a menacing look she had only seen directed at others. She looked at him long enough to make eye contact, then quickly turned away convinced that the enemy peering at her through the window was as dangerous and manipulative as anyone she'd ever come across.

She made her way to the corner in an attempt to regroup and try to understand how she got herself into this position. For the first time in three days, Callie's cell phone came alive, but her thoughts were focused on survival. The more she thought about the incident with Barry, the further confused she became. Still, the phone in her purse continued to beg for attention. It wasn't until Callie considered calling Jonas again that she heard her phone and hurriedly picked it up without checking the caller ID.

"This is Callie."

"You okay, Cal?" Kacey said, after a dash of silence.

"Kacey?"

"I saw what they were doing to you on TV and I had to call."

"What they were doing to me on TV?"

"You don't know?"

"Don't know what?" Callie asked as she backed away from the corner and scurried down K Street looking for a private spot on a street full of pedestrians. "What are you talking about?"

"Oh my god, you really don't know."

Callie leaned against the side of the building next door. "Kacey, what is..."

Kacey interrupted her. "Meet me at my place in twenty minutes."

"What?"

"Just meet me at my place, but don't turn on the radio or watch TV..."

"But Kacey..."

"But nothing. Leave now and come here as soon as you can."

Callie already started down the block in search of her car. "I can be there in twenty minutes."

"Okay, I'll meet you there, but don't listen or watch anything until you get there. Deal?"

"Deal." Callie hung up the phone and turned to her right. Before she had taken a step towards the parking garage, she lifted her head and recognized the two men who had followed her at Charlie Palmer's Restaurant, walking together in her direction. She hid her face behind her bag and hurried across the street. Callie stepped in front of a cab waiting at the light near the E*trade offices and slammed both her hands on the hood of the taxi.

"Dupont Circle!"

The driver motioned for Callie to get in. She slipped into the back seat of the cab and lifted her head just in time to see Barry yell and bang on the glass of his office building as he attempted to get the men's attention. Barry raised his hands in frustration while he watched her car pull away.

The drive over to Kacey's apartment should have taken five minutes to cover the few short blocks, but due to Washington traffic, Callie needed every one of the twenty minutes to get there. When she arrived at the Archstone Dupont Circle Apartments, she took the elevator to the eighth floor and walked down the floral patterned hallway to apartment 819. She knocked on the door and waited for Kacey to answer.

Kacey was in the kitchen cleaning up when she heard the knock. "Coming." She ran to the door, took a deep breath, then opened it. Callie was on the other side, unclear of why she had been summoned, but glad Kacey reached out to her. The two old friends stood and stared at each other for a long moment before Callie stepped inside and slinked into Kacey's open arms.

"I missed you," Callie said.

"I missed you, too." Kacey stroked Callie's hair as a tear streamed down her face, one she did not want Callie to see. Following the long embrace, Callie walked to the sofa in the den and sat down. Kacey sat on the love-seat next to her.

"What in the world is going on?" Callie asked.

"The Oxford Secondary Education Bill didn't pass."

Callie sat back and shook her head. "Macklin." She thought for a minute. "How did you know that?"

Kacey, not really sure how to approach this, hesitated before she answered.

"They said on TV…it didn't pass…"

Callie moved forward to the edge of the couch, her legs together, forearms resting on her knees. "On TV? You mean C-Span?"

Kacey fumbled with a pillow then pressed it against her stomach. "No, national. All the cable networks televised it live... Fox...CNN...MSNBC..."

"Huh? Televised what live? The vote?...I don't understand." Callie was more confused than she had been before she sat down.

"Cal, there's more..." Kacey's words drifted off.

"There's more..."

Kacey once again hesitated before she continued, but Callie cut her off.

"What Kace?"

"They said it didn't pass because of you."

Callie pulled back and sat straight up. "Because of me? They said that on TV?"

Kacey spoke very carefully. Not wanting to jump too many steps ahead, Kacey took her time explaining everything to Callie. "Macklin, Shulman, Bane, King...they said you stuck in all these earmarks without your boss's approval...you blackmail and threaten Senators, make up stuff about them. It was bad, Cal. Really bad."

Callie jumped on the comment right away. "It's not true, Kacey. I mean, I did place earmarks for clients, but that's my job... they said I did that on my own? That's total crap...it all came from Barry...he knew about everything."

Kacey was still treading lightly. "What about the blackmail?"

Callie leaned back into the large comfortable pillows of the tan couch and took her time answering the question. Kacey was trying to get to the bottom of it all, not so much for her news story, which she seemed unconcerned with at the moment, but for her friend. She desperately wanted to be there for her, but needed to understand to what extent she was involved and how it would affect the two of them in the future.

Kacey stood up and broke the awkward silence. "Cal, you

need something to drink?"

"Water, please?" Callie thought about what to say and how to say it. She had lived such a manipulative life for so long, she almost forgot how to just say things without worrying about the consequences.

"Sure." Kacey grabbed a large glass from the cupboard and filled it up with water from the water dispenser she kept next to the refrigerator. "You sure you don't want anything stronger?" she asked as she turned around, cup in hand.

"I'm sure. My head needs to be clear..."

Kacey walked back to the couch and handed Callie the drink, then placed two coasters on the coffee table in front of them.

"Blackmail?" Kacey asked as she sat back down on the love-seat.

"I did what I had to do..." Callie took a sip of water then placed the glass on the coaster in front of her.

Callie saw the look of disappointment in Kacey's eyes. She moved even closer to the edge of the couch.

"But I never manufactured any information, that's just not true..." Callie said, eyes wide open. "I didn't need to invent anything on these guys. What they did encompassed way more than I could've ever cooked up..."

Kacey listened intently, but said nothing.

"I'm not proud of it, Kacey, but I did my job and I did it the best I knew how."

Kacey took a long drink from her glass.

"Why, Cal?"

Callie leaned back into the couch and ran her left hand through her hair. She thought about the tailspin that her life had fallen into during the past few weeks and though it did not take her by surprise, the rapid pace with which it spiraled out of control left her unprepared for everything that followed. She paused for a minute before answering the question unsure how well it would be received.

"It was my job. Derek mentored me on how to make it all work, but Barry, he taught me how the game was really played. After Derek passed, I knew since I wasn't a part of 'his guys', I would have to play it the way Barry wanted me to if I wanted to keep my job." Callie lifted two fingers on each hand and made air quotes when she mentioned the words "his guys."

"After awhile, it became more than a game for me. I liked the power and the access...I liked being able to get things done the way I wanted them done...and I can't lie, I really, really, loved the money..." Callie picked up the water and took a long drink. She found it hard to look Kacey in the eye when discussing her behavior, but she knew if she wanted to fix their fractured relationship, coming clean was all she had left.

Callie swirled the water in the glass, turning her hand slightly in a circular motion then glared at the spinning water when she spoke. "It wasn't just about money for me, at least not all the time. I was a player in Washington...no, I was *the* player in Washington and I learned how to get whatever I wanted...and I liked that...I liked it a lot. I learned how to use information to my advantage no matter who I hurt in the process. I got to know who I could manipulate on the Hill and who I couldn't. Lucky for me, there were way more of the former, than there were of the latter."

Callie closed her eyes and took a long sip of water, knowing that she was about to tell Kacey what she had wanted to tell her for the last year or more. "One day it just got to a point where I couldn't live with myself anymore. I could barely get out of bed to start my day and there were times..."

She stopped short and raised her thumb and index finger to her eyes then slowly wiped each one of them simultaneously. Now it was Kacey who was confused, not really sure if this is what she expected to hear. Even so, she was glad to see that Callie was some-one she began to recognize.

"I don't understand..." Kacey said, her voice trailing off again.

Callie placed her hand on the empty part of the couch and patted it gently. "Come sit by me."

Kacey stood up and took three steps towards the sofa. Before she had a chance to sit down, Callie grabbed her right hand and held it as Kacey lowered herself onto the couch. Callie did not let go.

"Kacey, I was the one who sent you the e-mail about Lank," Callie said, gazing into Kacey's eyes.

Kacey sat speechless and took a minute to comprehend what she had just been told. "What? Why would you do that?" Kacey intertwined her fingers with Callie's. "Didn't you know I could have implicated you?"

"Of course, I did. Maybe, somewhere, I even wanted you to."

"I can't believe this. I have so many questions for you, but the only important one for right now I guess is why?"

"Because nothing in my life was real anymore. Nothing was honest. Not my relationship with you, not my relationship with Mike...it was all so fake...I was one person at work and then someone totally different at home. It became so incredibly painful to live that kind of lie day after day, night after night. Then one morning, I walked past the mirror we have in the den, you know which one I'm talking about?"

Kacey nodded her head in agreement. "The long one."

"Yeah, that's the one...I caught a glimpse of myself and stared for the longest time...I remember like it was yesterday...I was so ugly."

"What?" Kacey could not believe what she had just heard.

"No, that's not what I mean...I mean I couldn't look myself in the eye, because I was too ugly to look at. I couldn't tell if I was

Callie from the Hill or Callie from Kingston. I couldn't tell the difference between who I had become and who I used to be…and I just couldn't do it anymore…most days I didn't even know why I woke up in the morning."

Kacey sat next to Callie trying to process it all.

"So you sent the e-mails to Bob?"

Callie bowed her head. The two women sat in silence. The only sounds that were audible came from the noisy street eight floors below and the faint hum of Kacey's laptop on the dining room table twenty feet away. Callie wiped away a tear from her cheek then broke the quiet and looked Kacey straight in the eyes.

"Whose life are you living when you don't even know who you are anymore?"

Kacey squeezed Callie's hand. She started to understand that everything that had happened between them was done with a purpose, as if Callie needed some penance with her own self-inflicted exile.

"Why did you send the e-mail to me, of all people?"

"Because I love you and I wanted to see you do well."

"But I was doing well."

"You were doing really well. But I couldn't trust anyone else with this. There was no one else who would do this the right way. Most of them would chase it for a day or two then move on to the next big thing. I knew you wouldn't do that, especially if you were going to be mad at me…"

"So you expected me to be mad at you?"

"Honestly, I thought you'd be upset, but I didn't think it would turn out the way it did. Once it got to the point where you were angry like you were, the only thing I could do was let it play out."

"Oh, Cal."

Callie smiled as she held on tighter to Kacey's hand then

closed her eyes and pressed the back of it against her cheek and held it there. A few moments later, Callie released Kacey's hand and straightened up feeling like a thousand pound weight had been lifted off her shoulders.

"So if you know about Bob's e-mails, then you know I have information for you."

"I wrote you a response this morning."

Callie stood up and motioned for Kacey to do the same. "Okay, we don't have a lot of time...actually less than I thought we had when I wrote you the e-mail."

"What do you want me to do?"

Callie handed Kacey her car keys. "First, I need you to go to 1900 and pick up my car that's parked in my spot. They cut off my access card so twenty dollars should cover it." Callie rushed to her purse. She pulled out a twenty-dollar bill from her wallet, then handed it to Kacey.

"Give me your keys and I'll drop you off on K Street. You drive to your office, and we'll meet there in an hour. Please ask Bob and Walter to come." Kacey stood up, reached into her pocketbook and flipped her keys to Callie. "We have to leave now Kace, I'll fill you in on the way."

The two women rushed out of the apartment, but stopped on the steps when Callie pulled out her phone.

"What's wrong, Cal?"

"Give me a second. I need to make one call," Callie said, then threw the keys in her hand to Kacey. "I'll meet you in the car." Callie pressed the number, dialed it, then listened as it went straight to voice mail.

"Hi, this is Mike. Leave a message."

"Mike, honey, please listen to this whole message. You need to look into a guy called Ibrahim Hakef. There is something really bad going on and he's right in the middle of it. Be careful. He's a bad man…I love you, Mike."

Callie hung up the phone and made her way to the elevator to catch up to Kacey.

THIRTY-NINE

Barry was back in his office and sitting behind his desk while Senator Gorman had made himself comfortable on the couches to Barry's right. They were in the midst of a conference call with Ibrahim and Ken Farmer, who was minutes from landing at Suburban Airport in Laurel, Maryland. Farmer, on his way back to America on-board a private jet that flew him to and from the former Soviet Union, liked Suburban due to its proximity to D.C. and the simple private runways, away from the busy traffic of Dulles, National or Thurgood Marshall BWI.

Although unable to complete what he had flown to Russia to do, Ken believed they were one step closer to their desired outcome, one they had been planning meticulously for the past decade and a half. Even though Ibrahim had been convinced that the CIA was a step behind, he understood time was of the essence and his voice betrayed his usual steadiness when he spoke to the other three men.

"This needs to happen now. We have very little time."

"What happened in Moscow?" Gorman asked.

"Our plans got a little sidetracked, but we were able to keep operational security. We eliminated the problem," Ken said.

"So what do we do now?" Gorman asked.

Ken exhaled loudly, annoyed.

"We have a backup plan in place."

"And that's it?" Gorman asked.

"That is all you need to know," Ibrahim said.

"Now wait one second, here. I'm just as much a part of this as you guys are..."

"Shut up!" Ken screamed into the phone. "You handle your part and we'll handle ours."

Gorman did not believe he had overstepped his bounds, but he got the message anyway. He sat back and allowed the other three men to handle the rest of the conversation.

"As I was saying, we are running out of time. Mr. Miller, you need to take control of this company. You need to get rid of Jonas Foster. The sooner, the better."

"We need a few days to handle Jonas, it's not something that can happen overnight."

"You have until the weekend and if he will not go away, make him," Ibrahim said.

"Trust me, I have no intention of keeping him around," Barry said. "When he's gone, he'll be gone."

"He had better be," Ibrahim said. "I do need to know, Khalid, why has it taken so long to handle Mike Ferguson."

"We're working on it," Ken said.

"I don't want to hear that anymore." The tension was evident in Ibrahim's voice. "You requested the job and yet we are still where we were two weeks ago."

"He belongs to me," Ken said. "You know that."

"He already knows too much. After twelve years of careful planning, we are almost ready. We cannot afford to wait any longer. Make Mike Ferguson go away."

"I'll take care of it."

"You'd better…"

• • •

Mike stood across from the desk of Ted Biggs. He had arrived two minutes earlier while Ted was finishing up a meeting with his secretary in order to update him on the status of the Ken Farmer investigation. Over the course of the last fifteen years, Mike had become Biggs's go-to guy. Their relationship had been sealed years before by numerous covert actions Mike had undertaken on behalf of the Agency, with and without the knowledge of the Executive Branch. Even then, after the White House was informed, there were still events they'd never take credit for. Following his experience in Canada, Mike had been dispatched by Biggs to take out numerous enemy targets in Rome, Libya, Afghanistan, Zurich, Hamburg, Lebanon and the Gaza Strip. But it was his mission in Cairo that, unbeknownst to him until years later, put him in Khalid's crosshairs.

Mike was on assignment in Lebanon when Biggs had passed on information about a Hezbolah leader who had been seen in London boarding a plane headed for Egypt. Mustafa Saalem was notorious for supplying Islamic Radicals with money, access and weaponry which had led to the deaths of hundreds across the globe and in particular, Israel and Europe. He'd been a staple on the United States most-wanted list for his part in the bombing of the USS Cole, an American ship that was attacked while refueling in Yemen in October of 2000. The CIA had been after Saleem for years, when they finally caught a break in the winter of 2004. Two CIA operatives, who were stationed in England, had arrived in London from an information-gathering trip in Buenos Aries, when they spotted Saalem at a gate in Heathrow Airport, waiting to board a flight bound for Cairo. Mike was told to follow Saalem from the time he landed until he had a chance to eliminate him.

Saalem was met at the airport by Abdul Fahrzat, who proceeded to drive him to the Fairmont Heliopolis Hotel, located on Uruba Street b, not too far from the airport. Mike followed them into the parking garage and as Saalem stepped out of his car, fired two shots into the back of his head, making his body limp in an instant. Abdul dove back into the car and began to pull out when Mike plugged him through the driver's side window, exploding one shot into his brain and another in his ear. The back of the car swerved into a foundation column and sent Abdul flying out the front window and onto the cement, his face almost unrecognizable, when he was finally found more than an hour later. Mike slipped out of the hotel and made his way to Gaza, then from Gaza to his safe house in Jerusalem, before returning to Lebanon the next day. Abdul Fahrzat, the driver of the car, was the younger brother of Khalid, or as Mike knew him now, Ken Farmer.

"They definitely have their sights on a small nuclear device," Mike said pacing the floor as Biggs sat behind his desk.

"I hope that's all they want. Have you confirmed this?"

Mike continued to pace. He pulled out his black notebook and rifled through the pages. "We know from the Israelis that they had approached them about buying HEU, which is why we set up the sting operation that should have taken place yesterday."

Biggs jotted down the information he'd been given. "Do we know any more?"

"Akiva thinks they'll try and move on the HEU in the Ukraine."

"Do we know if they have the weapon?"

"As of right now, we're pretty sure they don't, but once they get the Highly Enriched Uranium, it will just be a matter of time. We can't let that happen. We've alerted all our assets in Europe and everyone has confirmed. The only one we can't get a hold of is Davis."

Director Biggs raised his eyebrow at Mike. "Why do you think you're gonna hear from Davis?" He dropped his pen and sat back in his chair.

Mike stopped pacing after he detected a change in Biggs' tone. "I sent him in last night for the drop and figured he'd contact me today to see how we're going to proceed."

Biggs stood up.

"I don't think you'll be hearing from him, Mike."

"Why's that?"

"Because he was shot dead last night."

Mike was speechless. He slumped down in a chair to his right and stared at Biggs before putting his head down for a moment to contemplate the loss of not only a great asset, but a good friend.

Less than ten seconds later, Mike lifted his head when he realized the unthinkable had just happened.

• • •

The same group of Senators from earlier in the day were back in the Radio and TV Gallery for another press conference. Unlike the morning event, there were only a handful of reporters in the room, much smaller than before.

Senator Macklin stood at the podium and looked over the sparse crowd. "Ladies and gentleman, thank you very much for coming. In light of the revelations our task force uncovered and shared with you earlier today, Chairman Rice of the Committee on Lobbying Affairs, will be holding hearings on the lobbying trade, starting tomorrow. Before you ask, no, we do not expect Callie Wheeler to participate."

Chairman Rice, who'd been standing with the seven Senators

that were part of the Watchdog Group, walked to the podium unexpectedly and startled Senator Macklin.

"I would hope she will agree to testify," Rice said, leaning in to the microphone. "I do not want to force her to."

Kirk Arthur, the only reporter in the room from the television side, shouted out a question before Rice could finish his words.

"So if she agrees to it, you would want her to testify?"

Senator Macklin took the question and ran with it. "The Committee feels we don't really need her tes..."

Chairman Rice interrupted him, obviously upset with Macklin for answering out of turn. "Of course, we would want her to testify. We believe her testimony is crucial if we truly want to clean up the Senate."

Shulman and the others on the Committee, were clearly unhappy, but they knew that Rice had the final say on the matter. Rice had insisted all day that he wanted to hear her testimony, regardless of what the others felt about it. Macklin's efforts to stop that from happening were futile, but he continued to try anyway.

"We're going to see if we really need her to testify at this point. Odds are she will plead the fifth and it would be an exercise in futility."

The Chairman shot a nasty look at Senator Macklin, then refuted his last comment.

"At the very least and in the interest of fairness, we would like to give Miss Wheeler the opportunity to address the allegations leveled against her from this podium a few hours ago. That will be all I have to say on this matter and we hope she will have a chance to join us first thing Wednesday morning."

With that, Rice walked away from the microphone and left the others behind to deal with the media in attendance.

FORTY

Founded in 1877, The Washington Post had to date, been responsible for breaking many of the biggest political stories in the history of the United States, including the takedown of a sitting President in 1973. Callie knew what she had in her bag could be the lynchpin to the greatest political scandal in American history.

She was seated in the conference room at the headquarters of the newspaper, looking at Bob Kravitz and Walter Bloom who sat directly across from her. Kacey Mercer sat in the chair next to Callie. In front of her on the conference table was a glass, a pitcher of water and a notepad, which she occasionally referred to as she shared with them the information she had uncovered. But more than anything else, Callie looked like a different person. The way she sat in her chair was different. Her body seemed more alive, her posture brimming with confidence, and even the pitch of her voice was more enthusiastic. Less defensive. Less combative. Happier.

"So the bottom line? What these Senators did was pass the Lank Bill which among other things, allowed for the Federal government to take land whenever and wherever it wanted, States be damned, then rigged the process in order for Jonas Foster Development to get all the contracts." Callie sat back in her chair and waited for them to grasp the hubris of Barry and his group.

"Unbelievable," Bob said.

Kacey, who had heard this all before, couldn't help herself and chimed in. "You haven't even heard the best part."

Callie looked at Kacey and nodded her head. "Once Foster got the contracts they went nuts buying properties," Callie said. "I remember the Lank Bill. I worked ten-to-fifteen hours a day, at the behest of Barry, to make sure we got the earmarks through. There were a ton of them...almost three hundred if I remember correctly."

"And this Eminent Domain law was one of them?" Walter asked.

"Exactly. Kacey, in a fantastic job of reporting," Callie smiled and looked over at her best friend, then smiled at Bob Kravitz who nodded and returned her smile, "uncovered the provision that allowed this to occur. It just so happened to be an earmark I had inserted on page 1622 of the bill, that was called 'Blight and Eminent Domain'."

"Did you read the provision?" Walter asked as he chewed on the white plastic cover of a medium point Bic pen.

"I actually did not. I usually wrote most of them for the majority of Congressmen, but these few, Barry had sent over to me a day before the vote was scheduled to take place and asked that Lank and Shulman take the lead on them. I believe Shulman was the sponsor who added that law to the bill at the last minute."

"Tell them the best part," Kacey said again.

"The Senators who sponsored the Lank Bill? They are all clandestine owners of Jonas Foster Development and have been sharing in the profits for the last two years."

• • •

Mike stormed out of Biggs's office and ran to his computer, where he began a frantic search. He felt like he'd been punched in the solar plexus, finding it hard to breath, unable to shake the feeling that he had been betrayed. His eyes were enflamed, his jaw tightened up in a controlled rage. None of it made sense, but when he started to add it up, he found it hard to draw any other conclusion. Just missing Ibrahim at the Khobar Towers in '96? Being picked up five minutes before the Sbarro bombing in 2001 and now the aborted takedown of Khalid and his men in Russia? How could he have missed it? He looked through his old computer files, but did not find what he was searching for. Mike sifted through old folders in his desk drawer, but still found nothing, then rambled to the file cabinet to his left and searched through every file inside of it, but came up empty. He sat back in his chair upset with himself for missing all the signs, even after Akiva had warned him years ago.

In a coded e-mail that only Mike and Akiva could decipher, his friend from the Mossad had warned him of a possible mole in the CIA. Mike had always heard rumors of Islamic Jihadists who were planted in America and received high-level clearance, but he told his friend they had found no evidence of any kind to substantiate the claim. Mike assured his confidante that Mossad was planting a crisis in America's intelligence apparatus when there wasn't any. Akiva swore to Mike that Mossad had come across information in Tunisia they concluded to be ninety percent reliable, but Mike and subsequently Todd and Ted Biggs, blew it off as Israeli imagination and paranoia. Now he wondered if he should have paid more attention to his friends advice.

Mike ran a finger print check on the classified CIA database. What the computer shot back ripped him to the core.

"Holy Shit," he said out loud to no one.

• • •

Bob and Walter were astounded by Callie's revelation.

"What did you say?" Bob wanted to hear it again, unsure if what he'd just heard, had been what he just heard.

Kacey jumped on it in a heartbeat. "She said that the Senators who sponsored the Lank Bill were owners of Jonas Foster Development and have been taking money out of company profits for the last two years!"

Bob shook his head in amazement. "Do you have any hard evidence of this? And I mean rock solid hard evidence, Callie?"

Callie pulled out the original disk that she had copied from Barry's office computer and placed it on the table in front of them.

"Martina McBide?" Walter read the disk and asked the question they all wanted an answer to.

Callie laughed and shook her head. "Don't mind that. It was just something to throw off any scent in case I lost it. But on here is everything I just told you and a whole lot more, including this entire scheme being done with the blessing and complete knowledge of one Alan Conroy." Callie leaned back in her chair and let her words sink in.

"Conroy? He's in on this?"

"I can't say for sure, Walter, but they definitely made payments to him early on," Callie said.

Bob Kravitz, ever the reporter, needed to make sure accusations of this level had merit. "And how do you know Barry didn't just add his name in there?"

"Two reasons. First, why would he do that if this disk was meant for his eyes only? Makes no sense. Second, and more importantly, it has the amount and the accounts all the monies were sent to, which you will see, traces back to Alan Conroy. I'm thinking it was look-away money since they had no revenue stream of any kind at the time."

"Or it could have been a payoff for signing the bill," Kacey said, looking at Walter and Bob.

"That too," Callie said.

The two men looked at each other amazed at the magnitude of the story they were sitting on. "This is unbelievable. Do you know what this will do?"

"Nuclear is the only word that comes to mind," Callie said with a reluctant smile.

"And then some," Bob shook his head in disbelief.

"And it's all on here?" Walter asked as he picked up the disk.

Callie quickly leaned forward and ripped the disk out of his hand and placed it back on the table in front of her. "Yes it is... all of it."

"Can I ask you a question?" Walter asked Callie.

"Go ahead."

"Is this the reason you sent the e-mails?"

Callie answered his question with no hesitation at all. "No, I sent the e-mail because I knew about a lot of the criminal activity taking place in Congress. I broke a lot of laws myself, but I had plenty of help doing it. It wasn't right and had to stop regardless of what would happen to me."

"Falling on the sword?" Bob said.

"Something like that, yeah."

Callie looked down and stared at the reflection she saw in the cherry oak table. For the first time in she didn't know how long, she wasn't repulsed by what stared back at her. She ran her hand across the tabletop and traced her reflection with her index finger then broke out in a little smile. Callie stretched out her hand, picked up the disk and waved it.

"On this disk is a copy of everything you need. It records who got paid what, when, how and by whom. The information will also show that Barry Miller was the one behind all the payoffs to Congress. The only thing I ask is that Kacey gets the byline on the story."

"And Walter Bloom," Kacey said looking at him with a wide smile on her face before a knock on the conference room door disrupted the meeting.

"And Walter Bloom," Callie said with a smile. She could hear the vibration of her cell phone from her purse, but let it go. "That will be Jonas…"

Kacey stood up and answered the door, smiling as she welcomed Jonas Foster into the room. "Thank you for coming, Mr. Foster."

"My pleasure. Thank you for having me."

Jonas sat down on the other side of Callie, the only person he actually recognized around the conference table.

"I asked Jonas to join us," Callie said. "What we would like you to do Bob, is in tomorrow's paper, mention that Jonas Foster Development is close to a deal with a businessman in Texas to sell him a majority stake in JFD. I'm pretty sure that'll rattle some cages a bit."

Bob filled up his glass from a small bottle of Coke in front of him, and took a drink. He looked at Callie and as much as he wanted to help her with this, there were some things he felt he could not do. "We've never run a story that we knew wasn't true."

Walter was quick to interject. "We can run it in the 'About Washington' column as a rumor. Maybe we can get a quote from Jonas."

Everyone in the room centered their attention on the man to Callie's right. "Absolutely," Jonas said.

Bob thought about it for a few moments, took another drink, then stood up. "Okay, but we run it with a quote. No quote, no blurb."

"I'll give you the quote," Jonas repeated.

Callie's phone vibrated again, but she ignored it. "Please sit on this story for a few more days. There is still one issue I have to take care of. After that's done, I'll give you the disk."

"We'll sit on it, but you have to promise us no one else gets the story."

"No one else, I promise," Callie said. "One last thing. There is a copy of the disk in my safe deposit box at First Union. Mike and Kacey have all my information…just in case something happens to me."

• • •

Mike pulled out his phone and dialed, "Pick up the phone, Cal."

He heard the phone ring a few times and sighed when it went to voicemail. "Hi, this is Callie. I'm not here right now. Please leave me a message and I'll call you back. Bye."

Mike hung up the phone without saying a word. His mind raced in all sorts of directions as he drove on the Capital Beltway, otherwise known as Route 495. He thought about Callie and her safety, Akiva, Biggs and Davis. His brain began to decipher some ideas about what to do with the new information he had just uncovered, when out of nowhere, an SUV squeezed his Expedition into the guard-rail. Mike fought hard to regain control of his car. He turned his head and saw Ken Farmer leaning out of the back window with a gun pointed directly at him.

He swerved his Expedition into the SUV sending the shots Ken fired, into the windshield and front window on the passenger side. He struggled for his gun as Farmer's car rammed into him again. Farmer pinched two more shots through the back seat window, and another punctured the front door. Mike turned his truck back at Farmer's and watched it bounce into the middle lane, barely missing a Ford mini-van. He finally jarred his gun from its confinement and waited to fire back at his pursuer. The SUV slammed back into Mike's truck, once again pinning him against the rail, but this time keeping him there. Ken's next shot ricocheted off the interior roof of the Expedition and pierced Mike's left shoulder. Mike screamed and fired one shot into the head of the driver, whirling Farmer's SUV out of control. Farmer tried to jump into the front seat to regain control of the car as it banged off of a Toyota Camry and swerved into a Dodge pick-up. Mike, trying desperately to handle his own vehicle, pumped another shot into the neck of Farmer, who couldn't keep the SUV from spinning out of control. Farmer's vehicle jumped in front of Mike's, then flipped over the guard rail onto the other side of 495, when an eighteen wheeler smashed into it and dragged the SUV down the highway before coming to a stop in a flash of fire and sparks.

Mike pulled his truck to the side of the road and dialed 911, anonymously calling in the accident he just witnessed. As soon as the call was finished, he drove off in his beaten up Expedition. He was on his way to Walter Reed Medical Center to take care of a bullet that was lodged in his shoulder blade.

FORTY-ONE

The hearing had drawn out past 7:30 in the evening. Callie had reiterated numerous times throughout the day that she would not return to testify and after a trying, introspective ten-plus hours, her testimony neared its completion. She'd spent the entire day under attack from the Senators in front of her and had not only survived, but now more than ever felt secure in her decision not to plead the Fifth. The question and answer period was brutal. Senators pontificated on her lack of ethics and moral standing, but never took any responsibility for their own indiscretions. Callie remained calm under the pressure and was masterful in her approach answering the same questions over and over again. Her answers were concise, poignant and honest. Nearing the end of her ordeal, Callie addressed the dais one final time, as confident at the end, as she was when she began.

"Mr. Chairman, thank you for allowing me to have my say. I believe the next few months will be very trying in Washington. This body has been entrusted by the people, to work for the people..."

Senator Shulman, as he had deliberately done the entire day, interrupted Callie once again. "I don't believe we need you to tell us why we are here, Ms. Wheeler."

Callie had entertained these people long enough. She had done her civic duty, some would even say her repentance. She wanted to go home and begin the process of piecing back together her once enchanted life which she had shattered beyond recognition. For the first time since she'd been hired at M&G, Callie felt as if she had something to look forward to, even though she had no idea what that something was. As she listened to Shulman snap at her, she thought about the fallout that would result from her testimony. She knew the country would also need to heal. Hearing Shulman's voice yet again, convinced her the hearing needed to be put to bed. Callie had indeed saved her best for last and let loose one final haymaker that she had been waiting to throw all day.

"I'm sorry you feel that way, Senator. Seated behind me is Kacey Mercer who tomorrow morning will be running a story on the front page of the Washington Post outlining, with documentation, the criminal behavior of the members of this Committee and a host of others in Congress and elsewhere."

From the gallery, Callie heard the various sounds of surprise and shock that overwhelmed the room. As TV cameras drew their closeups on her face, they witnessed the steely determination that had been her calling card throughout her career on Capitol Hill. Kacey, sitting behind her, caught a glimpse of Joel Hughes, seated in his usual chair behind Senator Lank. She touched the tip of her nose with her index finger and knew from his response, she had finally found her soft spot to fall and a place to call home.

Callie pulled the microphone closer and subtly slipped her hair behind her left ear. "I came to Washington to fight for the people with no voice and I let them down. For that, I offer my sincerest apologies and will spend the rest of my life working to make it up to them." Callie issued a look of disgust deeper than any she had displayed the entire day. "You, however, have failed the people of the United States and for that, you should be ashamed of yourselves."

She stood up without being excused by Chairman Rice, bent over and whispered something in Goodman's ear, then gathered her things. Looking to the back of the room, she caught a glimpse of Mike sitting in the right corner, decorated by bruises on the left side of his face and his left arm nesting in a sling. She smiled and winked at him. Chairman Rice banged his gavel three times.

"Ms. Wheeler, where are you going? We have not finished yet..."

Callie ignored Rice and turned to Kacey, Walter and Miles Goodman and they began to head out of the hearing room. Television cameramen jumped to follow them out while the C-Span camera stayed glued to the Senators on the dais, who sat in stunned silence. The giant mass of people in the corridor immediately surrounded Callie who was bombarded by reporters screaming questions at her from every direction. Kirk Arthur of NBC News, placed himself directly in front of Callie leaving her no room to walk as the mob of people that had encircled her, closed in tighter.

"Callie, what do you think your responsibility is in this whole thing?" Arthur asked.

Callie shook her head at the question. "Were you inside?"

"Yes, I was."

"All day?"

"All day," he said gleefully then moved his hand held NBC microphone as close as he could to Callie's mouth.

"Did you listen to my testimony?"

"Every word of it."

"Then how could you ask such a stupid question?"

Kirk was not prepared for that. Kacey, who had been standing behind Callie, waved at Kirk then whispered something to Walter. Callie pushed past.

She ignored most of the other questions that were being shouted at her, except for the one she heard from Natalie Quinton, the anchor for the CBS Evening News, which caught her attention. "Ms. Wheeler, would you agree with the statements made today by the Senators inside the hearing room, that you and other lobbyists, are the reason Washington is so dysfunctional?"

Callie stopped and searched out Quinton who had elbowed her way to Callie's left. Callie took a few steps towards her and peered through the first two rows of people, before making eye contact with the famous television personality.

"Was that you who asked the question?"

"Yes, it was," Quinton said. She leaned in closer to hear Callie. The cameraman with Quinton nudged the first two rows out of the way and found a place over Callie's left shoulder where both women could fit in the frame.

"Tell me," Callie said, "did I ever put a gun to the head of any member of Congress?"

"I don't know, did you?" Quinton asked in the style she had become known for. The crowd around them, which had grown bigger, laughed at the anchorwoman's response.

"Would you like to have an adult conversation, or should we wait until you get all your smarmy comments out of the way?"

Quinton acknowledged Callie's question with an embarrassed nod of her head, after which Callie's raised her eyebrows in response.

"No, I would think you did not," Quinton said.

Callie knew she would be on every news broadcast in America and wanted to let it be known the citizens of the United States deserved better. "No one forced any of them to take the money or go on any trips. They did that of their own volition. Blaming me for their greed and criminal behavior, is like blaming the hooker for sleeping with the husband. All they had to do was say no and people like me, would be out of a job. It's called integrity."

Miles Goodman grabbed her arm and shuffled her through the crowd as the cameras followed.

"They're all rotten...way to go Callie," a voice from the back of the room screamed out.

Kirk Arthur, who had pushed his way back in front of Callie, followed up the comment with a question of his own. "What about that Callie, are they all rotten?"

Callie continued to plod her way through the deluge of people when she spotted Senator Dansby walking in the opposite direction, trying to move around the crowd. He smiled at her and lifted two of his fingers to his right temple then gave her a quick salute. Callie acknowledged him with a smile and a nod of her head. "No, they're not all rotten." Callie's eyes followed Dansby until she lost him in the flood of people. Goodman took her by the hand again and pushed through the massive crowd that was blocking the exit.

"No more questions." Goodman said, then pulled his client out the front door.

• • •

Dusk had begun to settle on the nation's capital, the sweltering summer day evolving into a humid August night. Callie parked her Mercedes on R Street around the corner from the Dupont Circle Apartments. Kacey waited by the trunk for Callie to meet her there. Callie took her time lifting herself from the car, the weight of the days events having stolen some energy from her. Once at the trunk, she opened it and removed the black bag she had brought to the hearing. The women began to walk the few blocks up R Street towards Kacey's home.

"Do you like him?"

"I think I do. Yeah. Kind of a lot," Kacey admitted.

"He's a great guy, one of my favorites..."

Kacey gripped her purse tighter. "Okay, so if you knew him and you knew me..."

"He was living with someone, Kace, c'mon." Callie leaned in with her right shoulder and nudged Kacey off the straight line she'd been walking.

Kacey laughed and gained her equilibrium back, "Okay, I'll let you slide."

"Gee, thanks."

"Saw Mike in the back. You see him? I think he stayed the whole day," Kacey said.

Callie nodded her head.

"Did ya' get a chance to talk to him?"

Callie switched her bag to her left hand. "I didn't, no. He looked kind of beat up, huh?"

"He was there though, that's a start," Kacey said, nodding her head.

"I guess so."

A black Chevrolet Suburban screeched around 18th Street and headed in the girls direction. Callie took notice of a man leaning out the passenger side window, grabbed Kacey, then pulled her down behind a FedEx truck an instant before she heard two shots erupt out of a gun from the man's hand. Callie pulled Kacey up from the pavement and ran in a snake like fashion up R Street, ducking around cars and hiding behind cans as they made their way up the block. Callie heard another shot which careened off a mailbox just when she'd pointed to an alley across the street and started to make a run for it. Two men jumped out of the car and chased the girls on foot. Callie ran in a zig zag pattern to keep the men from getting off any clean shots while Kacey followed her lead.

At the end of the alley, a blue Pontiac pulled up and the driver waved for them to jump in. The two men who were in pursuit, were less than a hundred yards behind them, but chose to hold their fire, Callie noticed. The men stopped running and watched. Callie recognized Todd in the driver's seat. She jumped into the back seat of the car and held the door for Kacey. Callie reached for her hand and pulled Kacey in as Todd quickly sped away.

"Thanks, Todd," Callie said, short of breath and wheezing between each word, "You're... a...lifesaver."

"Lucky I got here when I did."

"You could... say that... again."

"What the ...hell was that," Kacey asked, looking at Callie who had settled in behind Todd's seat.

"Don't really know, but I'm pretty sure it was meant for me."

Todd joined in the conversation and added his own two cents. "That's why we have a twenty-four hour detail on you, Callie."

Callie was confused by Todd's comment. She hadn't had a detail in over a week.

"Your regular guy, Neil, is out of town, so they sent me over instead...don't worry, I'll take good care of you."

Kacey and Callie shared a long, confused, look. "Who assigns the detail?" Callie asked.

"Mike does."

"Mike sent you over?" Callie asked, trying to secure as much information as she could.

"He figured you'd be at Kacey's."

Callie looked at her friend and bounced her eyes in Todd's direction.

"Where are we headed?" Callie asked.

"Actually, I thought I'd take you back to my place. Best way I can protect you."

Callie looked at Kacey again. She carefully pulled out her cell phone and began texting someone from beyond Todd's sight line while Kacey engaged him in conversation.

"Cool with us. Where'd Neil go, he was here last night?" Kacey asked, thinking if he lied about Neil, he probably didn't know where he was anyway. As good a time as any to run with a lie of her own.

"He got called out on special assignment. It happens."

"Ha," Kacey faked a semi-laugh as she started to flirt. "I'm sure it does in your line of work."

"All the time."

Kacey kept Todd busy as Callie finished texting. Callie shook her head at Kacey indicating she'd yet to receive a response to her text.

"How's your sister, Todd?" Callie asked slipping her phone under her thigh as she tried to make conversation.

"Doing good. She was just here for a visit. She had to leave a few days ago though."

"It would be nice to see her again."

"Maybe next time."

"Yeah, maybe."

They drove for another ten minutes, mostly making small talk with some very awkward silences mixed in. Todd had chosen to bypass the beltway and drove down 16th Street instead, turning right onto Route 29, Colesville Road. Todd's house was located a few miles away, in the White Oak section of Silver Spring. He continued down Colesville, crossed over four corners at University Boulevard then made a left onto Burnt Mills Drive, before taking another left onto Childs Avenue. Todd pulled the car into the driveway of his home then turned off the engine. The colonial style house was tucked away in a quiet neighborhood consisting mainly of government workers and upper middle-class families. Callie and Kacey held hands in the back seat, unsure of what was in store for them, but knowing something wasn't right. Todd held the car door open. Callie stepped out first, Kacey following right behind.

"Chivalry is not dead. Thank you, Todd." Callie forced a nervous smile as she passed him.

"Sorry, ladies. I'm having some work done on the foyer. Gonna have to go 'round back." The dark of the night had begun to settle in with a soft misty drizzle spraying down from the sky. Todd walked behind the women as they negotiated the construction debris that was scattered all over the lawn. Large support beams and slabs of wood filled the walkway towards the back and the once pristine yard had been overtaken by empty bags of concrete mix and remnants of beige aluminum siding. The three of them worked their way around to the rear of the house. Callie held on tight to Kacey's arm as the moon lit up the darkened yard and directed them to the deck behind the home. Todd stood behind the women while they climbed the steps then unlocked the door as the two women watched his every move. He extended his right arm towards the open entranceway, his smile now all but gone.

Kacey and Callie entered the house first, Todd filing in afterwards then locking the door behind them. Callie coughed in response to the dusty smell of construction that filled the air. Sawdust covered the bare floors and flimsy metal frames lined the long narrow area having already been prepared for the drywall crew. She peeked above her head and noticed the empty metal brackets that had been laid out in place for the drop ceiling that had yet to be installed. Numerous lamps spread out in random areas on the floor replaced the exposed lighting.

Callie planned to continue with the small talk until she figured out what to do next. "I haven't been here in forever, Todd. You did a great job with the place."

Callie turned around and came face to face with a Glock 17

pistol that Todd had pointed straight at Kacey.

"Where's Jonas?"

Kacey's eyes widened as she glanced at the gun, then Todd, then back at the gun again. "What?"

"Don't fuck with me, Kacey, where is he?" Todd waved the gun from left to right and kept it pointed at Kacey's forehead.

"How should I know?" Kacey asked hoping he wouldn't pick up on her lie.

" 'Cuz your paper ran that shit about him this morning."

"What shit? I have no idea what you're talking about," Kacey said, her left arm clasped around Callie's right one.

Todd wiped his mouth with his free hand then quickly fired a shot right past Kacey's head.

"You know something now?" Todd heard the girls scream at the release of the bullet from its chamber. "And think hard because next time I won't miss."

"Okay, okay. He said he had to go to Texas for the day."

Todd fired another shot that whizzed past Callie's ear. "I'm not gonna ask you again. Where the fuck is Jonas?"

Callie, trying to hide her nervousness, knew exactly where Jonas was, since she had set him up at the Cross Keys Inn in Baltimore. "Why do you care where Jonas is? What does he have to do with you?"

"Ah, Callie Wheeler, the master manipulator." Todd smiled and continued to wave his gun back and forth. "Who played who this time?"

"What the hell are you talking about?" Kacey asked, not sure what was happening.

"I'm talking about her," Todd said pointing the gun at Callie. "She's been doing our dirty work for years. Let me be the first to offer my gratitude from the Brotherhood of Martyrs." Todd feigned a bow in her direction.

Callie thought about how she wanted to play this. She debated if she should keep pretending that she had no idea what was going on, or let him know that she knew his secret. She chose, like she usually did, to get straight to the point.

"Do you want me to call you Todd or will Ibrahim do?"

Kacey whipped her head around and looked at Callie. "What the…"

"After you tell me where Jonas is, it won't matter what you call me." Todd said, getting more impatient as the seconds ticked away.

"You know what I couldn't figure out?" Callie asked. "What you were gonna do with all the properties once you killed Jonas."

Todd pointed the gun at Callie. "JFD owns more than thirty thousand pieces of property around the country. That's a lot of revenue to sustain a war don't you think?"

"A war?" Callie asked.

"Makes for some great bases of operation. Now we have all we need to destroy you from the inside. Unlimited revenue, storage facilities, major traffic areas for our martyrs to do Allah's work… "

"So that's what this was all about?" Callie said as she put all the pieces together.

Todd smiled and tapped his temple with the gun in his hand. "Smart…" Todd pulled the Glock down and pointed it at Callie. "Enough with the bullshit, where's Jonas?"

"I have no idea." Callie said.

"Okay, have it your way. I'm done playing with you. I'll find him myself." Todd aimed the gun at Callie's forehead. "I liked you, Callie. Maybe in another time or another place we could have been something, you and me. You've served us well, but I have no more use for you."

Just before he could pull the trigger, a bullet smashed through the small window behind him and pierced the back of his head.

Todd fell to the floor like a sack of potatoes.

A moment later, Kacey opened the door for Mike, who walked in and glared at Callie.

"I got your text."

Her legs wobbled under her as she looked at Mike then held onto Kacey before falling to the carpet. Kacey leaned over and reached out her hand. Callie, sprawled out on the floor flat on her back, ignored it, her body laying no less than twenty feet away from Todd's lifeless one. His brains were splattered all over the wall.

"Thanks for not getting here ten seconds later," she said, only half-joking, in an attempt to lighten the mood. Her eyes alternated between being closed and staring at the ceiling above her. She caught a glimpse of Mike's arm in a sling. "What happened to you?"

"Fender bender."

"Is that right?" Callie said, closing her eyes and resting her left arm across her forehead.

"Well there might have been a bullet or two mixed in." Mike walked over to Callie and offered his hand. "Here," he said. Callie opened her eyes and latched onto his hand as he lifted her off the ground.

"Thank you."

"My pleasure." They stood and looked at each other in awkward silence for a long moment, until Callie lowered her head in a concerted effort to avoid any eye contact.

"That was a tough thing you did today," Mike said.

"I appreciate that." Callie kicked around the sawdust on the floor with her shoe. "Were you there the entire time?"

"Most of it," Mike said fixing the sling on his shoulder.

Callie hesitated for a moment unsure how to say what she wanted to tell him. "So you heard me talk about you...us?"

Mike nodded his head, but Callie still refused to make eye contact. "I did."

Callie paused and slowly lifted her head. "I meant what I said…about it all being my fault…"

Mike shook his head. "It wasn't all your fault…"

Callie finally looked him in the eyes. "But what I did was…"

Mike gave her words a dismissive wave with his right hand. "No reason to rehash it. It's over now…"

Callie dropped her head and intertwined her fingers as she brought her hands together. She desperately wanted to let him know how she felt, but the embarrassment she carried for the demise of their relationship, far outweighed her desire to ask if he was still interested in her.

For his part, Mike had struggled with their break-up from the moment he walked out of the Kennedy Center. After hearing Callie's testimony, he realized she was still the only woman he wanted to spend his life with. He needed to repair the damage he had caused, but now that the time had come, he was too proud to tell her how he really felt.

Kacey, who had been listening to their conversation from a few feet away, had no such reservations. She walked over to Callie and wrapped her right arm around Callie's left one. "So, are either one of you gonna get to the point?" She poked Callie ribs with her elbow.

Mike looked at her with a tilted grin on his face, "What point?"

Kacey raised her eyebrow. "Really?"

As uncomfortable as a fifth-grade boy asking a girl out on his first date, Mike nervously toyed with the sling on his left hand, barely looking Callie in the face. "Would you like to go to dinner sometime, maybe catch a movie?"

Callie recognized his discomfort and smiled at him trying to put his mind at ease. "That would be nice."

Mike smiled then looked at Kacey and gave his head a nod.

"How about a ride home?" Kacey asked, returning his smile with one of her own.

"I just need to make a call first." Mike pulled his cell phone out of his pants pocket and dialed a number. "Ted, I think you're gonna need to sit down for this…"

FORTY-TWO

When the article was published the next day in the Washington Post, it received prominent, above the fold, front-page headline treatment and soon thereafter was picked up by every major newspaper in the nation. The Washington Post website, under Kacey and Walter's bylines, ran companion stories along with the originals about the entire scandal, including a long piece about Ibrahim Hakef and Jonas Foster Development. During the first twenty-four hours after the story broke, the Post allowed the public to view their site for free, accumulating 6.2 million hits during that time frame and picked up close to 400,000 new subscribers. Kacey Mercer had become an instant celebrity. She was bombarded with requests for interviews from all three network and cable morning shows, along with each channel's nightly news program. Walter accompanied her at every appearance, but went out of his way to credit Kacey with the story, whether he was asked about it or not.

Over the next several weeks, Kacey wrote comprehensive articles in specific detail about Barry Miller and the many Congressmen who were caught up in the largest political scandal in

American history. The Senate, in its arrogant best, attempted to delay any proceedings regarding its members, until after the 2012 elections. Senator McCombs, the Senate Majority Leader, ignored the outcries of an impassioned public and refused to put the issue on the Senate calendar. It wasn't until two Senators, Albright from Virginia and Branch of Missouri, resigned instead of standing trial, that the balance of power tipped to the Republicans. Soon thereafter, new Majority Leader Hiram Dansby, vowed to make "cleaning up Congress" his top priority. He tabled all current legislation that was up for debate and scheduled nineteen trials consecutively, all under the threat of expulsion from the Senate. He made it clear from the outset that the usual slap on the wrist called censure, would not be an option for anyone who was involved with Barry Miller.

Most of the Senators in question, fearing the bad publicity that might negatively affect any future criminal jury pool, followed Branch and Albright and resigned in disgrace. Senator Shulman, however, protested his innocence at every turn, including a near fisticuffs with Bob O'Brian on Fox News. Callie watched from a distance while Shulman claimed she was the sole reason the country faced a constitutional crisis. After he continued to slander her in public forums, Callie released through Kacey, a tape of Shulman threatening her and demanding more payoff money than any other Senator, due to the power he wielded in Washington. Despite the mounting evidence against him, Shulman still refused to resign and was eventually expelled from the Senate on a 78-1 vote.

McCombs fared no better. After his removal as Majority Leader, he tried to paint himself as a victim and made a public appeal of his innocence on Craig Mattison's show on MSNBC. He claimed he was the main focus of a right wing smear campaign. Mattison jumped on the accusation and vehemently defended McCombs and other liberal Senators, until Jonas Foster testified at

McCombs' Senate hearing about his ownership stake in JFD and he too was expelled from the Senate by an 89-3 vote.

In all, twenty-one Senators were removed or resigned from their seats in addition to another forty-seven members of the House of Representatives. All seven of the Senators who were paid by Barry from the profits of Jonas Foster Development, stood criminal trial or took a plea deal on a combined one hundred and six counts, ranging from bribing public officials and falsifying tax returns, to racketeering and extortion. Shulman, Gorman, Macklin, King, Lank, Bane and McCombs all went to federal prison due to Callie Wheeler's cooperation with investigators. Shulman and McCombs were sentenced to seven years each, Macklin received six and Lank, Bane and King three apiece.

Following the revelations about Todd Goodwin, the CIA was derided and ridiculed in the press and lambasted by Congress. A protracted and painful investigation revealed information about Todd that was not only damaging to the intelligence services, but other federal agencies as well. Todd applied for and received a student visa in 1987 at seventeen years old, then with the help of computer hackers at Cal-Berkley, was able to delete his name from the system and created a fabricated new life for himself in America, complete with a birth certificate and social security number. Todd, or Ibrahim, was born in Algeria in 1970, the son of the famous hijacker, Mohammed Shamidi Hakef. Hakef was one of the planners of the 1972 Munich Olympic massacre and had escaped reprisal from the Israelis until 1984 when, on vacation in Monte Carlo with his family, he was shot in the back of the head three times while Ibrahim sat right next to him. Soon thereafter, The Brotherhood of Martyrs inducted Ibrahim into the terror organization and he had been chosen by its leader, Sheik Ahmed Nassar, to infiltrate the intelligence agency of the United States. His light skin tone and perfect American accent were enough to convince the terrorist group that it could be done and he was the man to do it. By 1992, due to his expertise in Arabic culture and the ability to speak six different languages, he started working as a field agent for the CIA. His first assignment from the Sheik consisted of recruiting and coordinating the bombing of the World Trade Center in 1993. He took the lead on the project and upon its failure, had been asked to return to Saudi Arabia, which he refused to do. Instead, he shared with Nassar, his plan to bring down the United States of America. The plan was in its embryonic stages and growing slowly, until he met up with a new recruit, who Ibrahim could tell from the moment he met him, was going to be someone special at the CIA.

Todd knew from Mike's relationship with Ted Biggs that getting close to Mike would be the quickest way to access classified information the Agency had on the Brotherhood and other terrorist groups. The plot almost came to a screeching halt when Mike found Ibrahim's safe-house location in Canada. Had he not been hungry, Todd would never have gone to dinner and surely would have been found in the apartment by Mike. His connection to Jonas Foster Development came when Nassar informed him of a Senator who had ties to a Muslim charity that had been funneling money to Hezbollah. Todd's phone introduction to Gorman, by the Sheik, led to his relationship with Barry Miller. He knew as soon as they spoke, that Miller would do whatever Todd wanted just as long as he paid Barry large sums of money. Ibrahim explained his plan to Barry, but never told him the reason he needed to get rid of Jonas, only that he would need to be gone. Gorman for his part in the scandal, received a life-sentence for treason against the United States and consorting with an enemy combatant.

Barry Miller was unaware that Callie had a copy of his disk in her possession, but was still concerned when he turned on the

TV in his office and saw Callie's all day testimony before Congress. He contemplated leaving town for a few days until the furor died down, yet it wasn't until he read Kacey's column in the Post the next morning, that he realized some of the information she had printed, could only have come from the disk he hid under his middle desk drawer. He attempted to flee the Country on a flight bound for Tangiers, but a slew of FBI agents stopped him in front of the Delta Airlines counter at Reagan National Airport. His name had been placed on the "No Fly List" thanks to a call from Callie to Ted Biggs at the CIA, educating him on what she believed Barry would try to do. Barry was taken into custody and immediately offered to make a deal with investigators until they informed him he would not be necessary, since Callie had given them far more than they needed. He decided against a plea agreement and acted as his own counsel during his trial. His first motion was to request in writing a trial within thirty days as any defendant is so granted by the sixth amendment of the constitution. He based his strategy on being the first one to tell his story, well before any Congressmen had a chance to tell theirs. Callie testified on behalf of the state and withstood all of Barry's accusations, the most prolific of which, inferred that she was the actual brains behind the entire scheme and he marched to her orders. The jury didn't buy it and the judged sentenced him to twenty years in prison.

Following the shooting at Todd's house, Mike spent the next few weeks beating himself up over the betrayal. He had a hard time dealing with the fact that a member of his group and his best friend at the Agency, had been the mole Akiva warned him about. He considered resigning from his position and leaving the CIA altogether, but former director Sam Miller talked him out of it with help from Ted Biggs. Biggs, however, did not survive the scandal and was unceremoniously let go, a move that Mike resented, but understood. Mike agreed to stay on, but only on the condition that he be allowed to dismantle his current team and assemble a new one from a pool of recruits that he would train.

Callie and Mike took it slow. They dated only once a week for the first month, then slowly increased the frequency, before he moved back into their home three months later. Callie cooperated with federal investigators in exchange for a lighter sentence which would be determined after all the other trials had been concluded. In the interim, she became the prime target of former democratic operatives who were bombarding the network's daily morning shows and Sunday programs. They ran constant stories in newspapers and on blogs across the country about her activities on the Hill, attempting to paint Callie as a power hungry, money obsessed lobbyist who was only in the game for her own prestige. The problem for the networks was that she readily admitted to all of that, so their stories had the opposite effect on the public's perception of her. America fell in love with Callie. She had gone from being the most despised person in America, to being one of the most beloved. Her testimony and the information she gave the government was the key to the successful prosecution or resignation of sixty-eight members of Congress, Barry Miller and six of his associates including Whitaker Jordan. The judge presiding over her case, gave her five years probation in lieu of jail time, and thanked her for the great service she had performed for her country.

Judge Susan Browne acknowledged at Callie's sentencing hearing that Callie had indeed contributed to the culture of corruption pervasive in Washington and in fact played a huge role in it. On the other hand, she also recognized Callie's cooperation with law enforcement and her consenting to testify at every trial in which her presence had been requested. More importantly, Judge Browne had been cognizant of Callie's refusal to hide behind the

Fifth Amendment, which was her right, and Callie's willingness to set the record straight at the expense of her own freedom and reputation, for the sake of her country.

Callie had become a world-wide celebrity overnight, but chose instead to keep to herself once all the trials had concluded. The country begged for more of her. In all, eleven different networks were after her with plenty of interesting proposals ranging from her own talk show to hosting the Miss Universe beauty pageant. Callie had enough money to last her ten lifetimes and felt no rush to return to the public eye. She enjoyed taking the time to slowly get to know Mike again and they both grew closer as a couple to Kacey and her boyfriend, Joel Hughes. Callie swore off politics. She told Mike there was only one politician she would ever consider working for and he was the only one who could change her mind.

That is exactly what he did when he became the forty-eighth President of the United States and needed her help in the worst way...

The End

Acknowledgments

Thank you to Paula Katz, Adam Edelman, Matt Walter, Michelle Schwartz and Jack Daniel for all your help and honesty in the production of this book. You guys are the best.

Thank you to Elliot King whose friendship, guidance and expertise was invaluable even if I chose to ignore some of it, much to his chagrin.

Thank you to Timmy Reed for his demanding and pinpoint editing skills and his unlimited patience with me and all my questions.

Thank you to Kelly Quane for her beautiful design and overwhelming patience with me and my constant badgering. Kelly, you are very talented and a joy to work with.

Thank you to Kevin Atticks and the rest of the staff at Apprentice House for taking a chance on a novice and working overtime to bring this manuscript to life.

And finally, thank you to My Creator who gave me life and has blessed me with far more than I deserve.

Apprentice House is the country's only campus-based, student-staffed book publishing company. Directed by professors and industry professionals, it is a nonprofit activity of the Communication Department at Loyola University Maryland.

Using state-of-the-art technology and an experiential learning model of education, Apprentice House publishes books in untraditional ways. This dual responsibility as publishers and educators creates an unprecedented collaborative environment among faculty and students, while teaching tomorrow's editors, designers, and marketers.

Outside of class, progress on book projects is carried forth by the AH Book Publishing Club, a co-curricular campus organization supported by Loyola University Maryland's Office of Student Activities.

Eclectic and provocative, Apprentice House titles intend to entertain as well as spark dialogue on a variety of topics. Financial contributions to sustain the press's work are welcomed. Contributions are tax deductible to the fullest extent allowed by the IRS.

To learn more about Apprentice House books or to obtain submission guidelines, please visit www.apprenticehouse.com.

Apprentice House
Communication Department
Loyola University Maryland
4501 N. Charles Street
Baltimore, MD 21210
Ph: 410-617-5265 • Fax: 410-617-2198
info@apprenticehouse.com • www.apprenticehouse.com